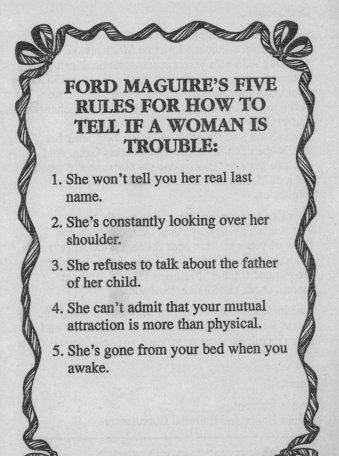

FORD MAGUIRE'S FIVE RULES FOR HOW TO TELL IF A WOMAN IS TROUBLE:

1. She won't tell you her real last name.

2. She's constantly looking over her shoulder.

3. She refuses to talk about the father of her child.

4. She can't admit that your mutual attraction is more than physical.

5. She's gone from your bed when you awake.

Dear Reader,

Welcome once again to a month of excitingly romantic reading from Silhouette Intimate Moments. We have all sorts of goodies for you, including the final installment of one miniseries and the first book of another. That final installment is *MacDougall's Darling,* the story of the last of The Men of Midnight, Emilie Richards's latest trilogy. The promised first installment is Alicia Scott's *At the Midnight Hour,* beginning her family-themed miniseries, The Guiness Gang. And don't forget *The Cowboy and the Cossack,* the second book of Merline Lovelace's Code Name: Danger miniseries.

There's another special treat this month, too: *The Bachelor Party,* by Paula Detmer Riggs. For those of you who have been following the Always a Bridesmaid! continuity series from line to line, here is the awaited Intimate Moments chapter. And next month, check out Silhouette Shadows!

Finish off the month with new books by Jo Leigh and Ingrid Weaver. And then come back next month and every month for more romance, Intimate Moments style.

Enjoy!

Yours,

Leslie Wainger
Senior Editor and Editorial Coordinator

Please address questions and book requests to:
Silhouette Reader Service
U.S.: 3010 Walden Ave., P.O. Box 1325, Buffalo, NY 14269
Canadian: P.O. Box 609, Fort Erie, Ont. L2A 5X3

Paula Detmer Riggs

The Bachelor Party

Silhouette®
INTIMATE™MOMENTS®

Published by Silhouette Books

America's Publisher of Contemporary Romance

To Leslie, who understood.
To my friends at PTN, who kept me sane.
And
to Wendy and Matt, who met tragedy with
courage and grace.
I love you all.

 SILHOUETTE BOOKS

ISBN 0-373-07656-8

THE BACHELOR PARTY

Printed in U.S.A.

CAST OF CHARACTERS

The Women:

Hannah Farley: Blue-blooded bad girl.

Emma Wynn: Once burned, twice shy.

Sophie Reynolds: Single mom with secrets.

Lucy Maguire: Not left at the altar for long.

Katie Jones: Always a bridesmaid....

The Men:

Matthew Granger: Stranger in a small town.

Michael Flint: Mr. Wrong has never been so right.

Ford Maguire: Lucy's lawman brother falls for shady lady?

Max Ryder: Mystery man appears in the nick of time.

Luke Cassidy: Single dad makes impassioned plea.

Why is Ford so suspicious of Sophie? Will she ever trust him with the truth? What's got Ford growling when his sister, Lucy, announces her engagement?

The Always a Bridesmaid! series continues each month in a different Silhouette line. Look for the flash next month in Shadows.

Books by Paula Detmer Riggs

Silhouette Intimate Moments

Beautiful Dreamer #183
Fantasy Man #226
Suspicious Minds #250
Desperate Measures #283
Full Circle #303
Tender Offer #314
A Lasting Promise #344
Silent Impact #398
Forgotten Dream #364
Paroled! #440
Firebrand #481
Once Upon a Wedding #524
No Easy Way Out #548
A High Price To Pay #627
The Bachelor Party #656

Silhouette Desire

Rough Passage #633
A Man of Honor #744
Murdock's Family #898

Silhouette Books

Silhouette Summer Sizzlers 1992
"Night of the Dark Moon"

*Always a Bridesmaid!

PAULA DETMER RIGGS

discovers material for her writing in her varied life experiences. During her first five years of marriage to a naval officer, she lived in nineteen different locations on the West Coast, gaining familiarity with places as diverse as San Diego and Seattle. While working at a historical site in San Diego she wrote, directed and narrated fashion shows and became fascinated with the early history of California.

She writes romances because "I think we all need an escape from the high-tech pressures that face us every day, and I believe in happy endings. Isn't that why we keep trying, in spite of all the roadblocks and disappointments along the way?"

Prologue

For the moment they were safe.

Sophie Reynolds sank down on the bed and cradled her daughter, Jessamine, close to her breast. Exhausted and scared, she waited for the sound of retreating footsteps to fade before allowing herself to relax.

Clover Rooming House wasn't as plush as the house on the Columbia that she'd planned to fill with children someday, but the third-floor room she'd just rented was large and airy and very clean, with creamy walls and starched lace curtains covering the dormer windows and plenty of room for the crib she would need to buy. Best of all, the first week's rent hadn't completely depleted her meager funds.

Katie Jones, the woman who'd rented it to her with a cheery smile and what seemed like genuine welcome, was about her age and seemed like a lovely person. Better yet, she hadn't asked more than the usual questions about a prospective tenant, questions for which Sophie had had well-rehearsed answers. In another lifetime, they might have become friends.

"Since she swore you were the cutest baby she'd ever seen, she's obviously a very discerning lady," Sophie murmured to her daughter bending to kiss the crown of Jessie's silky head. But not too discerning, Sophie hoped fervently. Darlene had drummed it into her over and over—"Act natural, as though you have absolutely nothing to hide."

Before she'd left Portland, she'd spent endless hours reinventing the bare bones past of a woman named Sophie Reynolds. And then, one by one, she and Darlene had added enough details to make that past believable. It wasn't all pretense. She *was* a widow, and she *was* twenty-eight. But she wasn't from Billings, Montana, and she hadn't spent the past year keeping house for an elderly rancher in a neighboring town.

She'd lost track of the number of times Darlene had grilled her on her new identity. Her cover story had to be flawless, with no furtive looks when she was questioned, no obviously evasive answers when she replied. Her answers were instinctive now, and she was able to give them easily, without even a smidgen of hesitation.

Darlene had been a good friend to her, perhaps the best she'd ever had. It had been Darlene who had arranged for her new social-security card and a false birth certificate for Jessie, Darlene who had suggested the South as a place to establish her new identity. Sophie herself had picked Clover because she'd liked the name and the sense of peace and safety it had conjured up in her mind.

"We're safe now, Jess," she whispered, watching the baby's face closely for a sign she was coming to know her mother's voice. "No one will find us here, I promise. And if anyone gets suspicious, we'll just move on."

Jessamine gazed up at her with the distinctive brown gold eyes of her father, and Sophie's breath caught. Wells had been dead for more than a year, and yet she still flinched when she heard a voice that sounded like his or caught a sudden glimpse of a tall, well-built man with sandy hair.

During the fourteen months since his death, she'd had plenty of time and opportunity to wish she'd stayed home to study for final exams instead of going with her roommate to listen to the Portland Pops play Gershwin under the stars. If she had, Wells Manwaring, Jr., wouldn't have seen her sitting there on her blanket, never would have offered to share his bottle of expensive French wine with her, never would have swept her off her feet and into the glittering world of Portland's upper crust before she'd had a chance to catch her breath.

But he *had* seen her, and she *had* married him. Because she'd loved him, she'd tried to make the marriage work. It hadn't, and now she was the one being punished for its failure.

She still remembered the numbness that had come over her at his funeral. She'd been in shock, unable to sleep, unable to eat. She could still hear the minister who had married them eulogizing Wells for his generous donations to charity and his wide circle of friends. Everyone had loved Wells, especially the students and faculty at the junior college where he'd been Vice President. She'd been the only one to experience his black moods and possessive rages, the only one to bear the full brunt of his constant demand for reassurances of her love and loyalty. Just thinking about how wrong she'd been about him had chills cascading down her spine.

"You'll like Clover," she murmured, rubbing Jessie's satiny cheek with a hand that was still far too pale. She'd waited so long to be able to touch her own child that each time she did it felt as though she'd just received a precious gift.

"Did you notice how warm it was outside, even in September? And it's such a pretty place." And as far away from Portland as the money she'd scrounged for their escape had allowed.

Jessie gurgled, then succumbed to a huge yawn that wrinkled her tiny forehead and made Sophie smile. "Looks like it's bedtime for my darling girl," she murmured as she gently laid the baby in the middle of the bed and got to her feet.

They'd been on the bus more than thirty hours, and she was grimy and stiff. Traveling with a six-month-old infant had been more trying than she'd expected, but somehow she'd managed to keep Jess well fed and clean. She, herself, however, had eaten sparingly in an effort to save her money, and she was beginning to feel light-headed.

"Maybe I should try some of your yummy formula," she crooned to Jess, who was beginning to fuss. It wouldn't be long before Jessie made her wants known, and when her little girl got wound up, her crying could shake walls, even in an antebellum house built to last forever.

"It's coming, sweetie," Sophie murmured as she hurriedly opened a can of formula and poured it into a bottle. Knowing she would be traveling, she'd purchased the kind of bottles with disposable liners and a larger-than-usual diaper bag. Carrying it and a squirming baby from the bus station to the rooming house had tired her back and strained her shoulder. Tomorrow, first thing, she would have to find a way to bring her things from the station where the ticket agent on duty had agreed to keep them overnight. And then she would find a job. Any job. She wasn't proud. In the past year, she'd scrubbed toilets and washed dishes until her hands bled, just to keep her body active and her mind numb.

"First thing tomorrow, Jessie Bear, you and I are going to buy a newspaper and scour the want ads," she murmured as she slipped the nipple into the baby's eager little mouth. Jessie's tiny fingers opened and closed against her mother's hand, and her brown eyes looked up with her perfect trust. Sophie's chest swelled with love until it ached.

Nothing was more important than Jessie. Not the words uttered by some coldhearted judge in a Portland courtroom, nor the determination of dispassionate officers of the court sworn to enforce those words. Not even the teachings of the parents she'd adored.

Without Jessie, she had no life, no reason to open her eyes every morning, no hope. No matter what hardships she had to face or lies she had to tell, she would never let anyone take her child from her again.

Chapter 1

It was 6:20 on a raw Monday in early December when Sophie felt the air change and knew that Sheriff Ford Maguire had just walked into Peg's Diner.

She'd been working at Peg's for nearly three months now, and just about every morning at twenty past six he walked through the front door, looking grumpy and intensely male in his always-crisp khaki uniform, his stride more swagger than hurry, a lethal-looking .45 on one lean hip, and a small gold badge glittering on the left side of his wide chest, just above his heart.

To her dismay Sophie was finding it difficult to dislike the man, even though he was a living, breathing, intensely masculine symbol of all that she feared. Something about the way he kept part of himself distant from others, even when he joined in the morning banter, had touched her deeply—like the lone wolf who patrolled the perimeter of the camp on the darkest, coldest nights so that those he guarded stayed warm and safe.

No matter how drawn to him she might find herself, however, she needed to remember that he was an officer of the law and, therefore, a man to be avoided at all costs. Unfortunately, that was exactly what she couldn't do when he sat at her station every morning.

Grabbing a quick breath, Sophie reached for the coffeepot and turned to greet him. Keeping her hand steady even as her stomach did its usual clenching routine when he was near, she took her time pouring steaming coffee into one of Peg's oversize mugs and set it carefully in front of him.

"Looks like it's fixin' to blow up a storm out there this mornin'," he drawled in a scratchy baritone uniquely his, like flint scraped over hide, she'd decided one morning when she'd been in a whimsical mood.

He dropped his winter Stetson on the counter and unzipped his down vest before settling his lean length on the stool. Unlike his sister, Lucy, who had an almost Madonna-like paleness about her, Ford had thick black hair without a hint of curl, an aquiline nose and sun-bronzed skin, suggesting an Indian branch or two on the Maguire family tree. His mouth, though, was pure stubborn male, only just saved from cruelty by the added fullness of his lower lip.

"Miss Rose Ruth is convinced it's going to be a bad winter," she murmured as she sat the pot on the gleaming countertop and pulled her order pad from the pocket of her apron. "She claims she saw the leaves outside her window shivering this morning when she took Beau out for his constitutional."

Ford cocked his head and gave her a wry look that crinkled the corners of his eyes into sun-weathered lines. "Beau? Is that old hound dog still alive?"

She flipped to a clean page in her pad and took out her pencil. "He was this morning when I left."

His smile was slow forming, taking a long time to reach his eyes. "That old hound has to be goin' on sixteen years if he's a day."

"Seventeen. He just had a birthday." Sophie had bought the nearly blind dog a soft chew bone as a present from Jessie who loved to pull the elderly basset hound's floppy ears.

Turning to the side, Ford stretched out his long legs awkwardly, making her wonder why he had chosen to sit at the counter instead of a table where he'd have more room.

"I remember when she got that old dog. It belonged to a man by the name Boone who used to live out by the landfill. Had him a good recycling business going, turnin' half-rotten potatoes into moonshine in the back room of his cabin. Finally had to arrest him when he ended up damn near poisoning a half dozen of his best customers, old Judge Calhoun among 'em."

She laughed, then hastily bit her lip when she realized she was attracting curious stares. Peg Jones, the "Peg" of Peg's Diner, had worked hard to make the large room seem more like a family kitchen than a restaurant, with the Jones family ancestral pictures lining the walls and gingham covering the windows and tables. That Peg had succeeded was admirable, but sometimes the sense of family tended to press too close for someone like Sophie who had to guard her privacy so zealously.

"You're making this up," she accused in a low voice.

He shook his head. There was a small half-moon scar right below his lower lip, and his hair seemed to fall into a natural part that was endearingly off center. Though she'd heard a lot of comments about him in the past weeks, not once had she heard a single soul praise him for his looks. Somehow, though, when he was teasing her in that slow, somber way of his, his too-angular, too-rawboned face had a way of making her forget his lack of conventional sex appeal.

"No, ma'am, that would be lyin' to you, and I was taught never to lie to a lady."

Or anyone else, she suspected, especially if all the stories she'd heard about Clover's straight-arrow sheriff were true. "What about the dog?" she reminded him.

His mouth slanted. "Well, it's like this. When His Honor got over having his stomach pumped, he ordered me to arrest Boone and haul his sorry self into jail. Darned if this little bitty pup didn't jump in the squad car with the old man. I tried to get him out, but he set up such a howl, I just took him along for the ride. Nobody wanted him, he was such a wrinkled-up bag of bones, so I took him to Miss Rose Ruth. She's just naturally a pushover for helpless things."

"Yes, I know," Sophie murmured before asking him what he wanted for breakfast.

Wondering what he'd said to put her back up all of a sudden, Ford glanced over her left shoulder at the blackboard where Peg had printed the breakfast specials in brightly colored chalk every morning since he couldn't remember when.

"Guess I'll have the biscuits and gravy," he said, working up a smile, which was as close as he ever came to flirting with a pretty woman.

"Good choice," she returned politely before collecting the coffeepot and leaving. Not being one to miss a chance to enjoy female beauty from all angles, he watched her walk away from him, her too-skinny hips swaying just enough in the pink uniform skirt to send his normally well-disciplined mind running to hot summer nights and cool sheets.

Not that he intended to do more than look, he reminded himself, downing half his coffee in one greedy gulp. He'd never cared much for small women, especially one like her who was on the thin side. From the time he stopped reading comic books and started sneaking looks at the magazines in brown wrappers behind the counter at Cliff Phelps's Pharmacy, he'd liked his women tall and built generous. And when he wasted more than a second look, it was almost always a green-eyed blonde who'd caught his eye.

Mrs. Sophie Reynolds wasn't any of those things. Her hair was more brown than blond, the color of prime tobacco right before it was picked, and her eyes were so blue they seemed almost purple at times. 'Course she did have nice legs, what there was of them, which wasn't all that much since she was a little thing, not more than five-two would be his best guess, and maybe a hundred pounds after a good soaking, with a bosom that wasn't hardly worth that first look, let alone a second.

Sipping his coffee, he let his mind absorb the conversations going on around him, his gaze skimming the familiar faces without really seeming to. Two minutes later he knew that Brod Eggers had a dandy of a hangover and that the Yankee honeymooners staying at the Old Magnolia Bed and Breakfast were glaring at each other as though they were already working on a divorce. He'd also heard Roy Dean Stevenson and Gator Haley at the "regulars" table wrangling over which fishing hole to try later, but even as he watched Sophie heading his way with his breakfast, he still hadn't figured out why he kept thinking he'd seen her somewhere before.

"Looks good," he said, watching her instead of the food she set before him. He guessed her to be around Lucy's age—twenty-six, twenty-seven, something like that—though her eyes were much older.

"More coffee, Sheriff?" she asked, holding the heavy pot a few inches above his almost empty mug.

"Yes, ma'am," he said, pulling his plate closer before picking up his fork. "Looks like you've done this kind of work before."

"A few times."

"Close by, or up north?"

"In Montana. I'm from Billings."

Ford figured most folks wouldn't have noticed the split-second hesitation before she'd answered. He'd noticed because it was his job to notice. He didn't figure it mattered much why she'd had trouble with the question. Still, it didn't hurt to file away the fact that she had.

"Findin' Peg pretty demanding, are you?"

"A little, but I like to know exactly what my employer expects." Her smile was restrained, her answer cautious. He understood caution, even respected it. He just didn't find it very often in Clover.

"That's Peg, all right," he drawled, deliberately holding her gaze with his. "Taught my sister and half the females in Clover at one time or another how to wait tables and bring home big tips without losin' their virtue."

"Believe me, Sheriff, I'm beyond the stage where I worry about my virtue." He watched the bitter curve of her lips and wondered about that, too. Before he could scare up more conversation, however, she was off again, filling mugs and removing dirty plates.

Ford rubbed the back of his neck and gave some thought to the way she'd deflected his questions. It could be that she was as wary of sharing private information as he was, but most folks he knew loved to talk about themselves. Even those who didn't were usually enough intimidated by the uniform and badge to tell him just about anything he wanted to know.

Sophie didn't look like the kind of person who had anything to hide, but still, he couldn't afford to give a newcomer too much slack. Even a small-town cop learned right quick to expect the worst and act accordingly.

More than once Lucy had let fly at him for always looking at the dark side of human nature. Each time she took out after him, he kept his mouth shut and let her have her say. Since that day when he'd been nine and held her in his arms only hours after she'd been born, he hadn't been able to deny her that first little thing. That didn't mean he'd let her change him any, though, and she knew it. He deeply and firmly believed that a day—or more likely a night— would come when his refusal to take anyone at face value would save the life of a more trusting soul, maybe even his own, flawed as it was.

Not that he thought Sophie was a danger to him or anyone else, he hastened to remind himself. For sure, the feeling he got when he watched her was different from the tightness he got in his belly when he spied a couple of local toughs hanging out down at the old forge. It was more like an itch he couldn't scratch—or the hot-wired irritability that came on him when he'd gone without sex for too long a time.

He was still mulling that over when Abraham Washington claimed the empty stool to his right. "'Mornin', Ford. Looks like we got us a real winter day workin' out there, don't it?"

"Yes, sir. Might be one of the coldest we've had so far this December."

Close to eighty, Bram Washington had been the janitor at the Clover High School for as long as Ford could remember. Retired now, he spent his time teaching his grandson, Charles Thomas, how to coax a succession of wily old mud cats out of the ooze of Yahoo Creek and onto his fishing hook.

Ford had grown up with little C.T.'s daddy, Charles, Sr. They'd fished together most summers, run traps in the winter and shared cheap cigars behind the schoolhouse whenever Charles managed to swipe a decent-size butt from his granddaddy.

Ford had thrown passes to Charles for three years at Clover High and they'd gotten hammered together on 'shine graduation night. The next day Ford had sat in the front row of the pretty white Baptist chapel out on Charleston Road when Charles had married his sweetheart, Mareena Sue.

Two weeks later Charles had stood next to Ford in the rain while the minister of the Community Church had read the burial service over Ford's parents, and through the years Charles and Reeny had served as uncle and aunt to Lucy when she'd been growing up. It had been a sad day a year ago when Ford had been forced to arrest Charles for nearly killing Reeny in a drunken rage.

Some folks still held that Ford should have let his friend off with a stiff warning instead of hauling him off to jail. Others claim Ford did right to arrest the man, but owed it to Charles to put in a good word with the judge at the trial instead of testifying for the prosecution. Those same folks blamed Ford for the stiff sentence Charles had received. What earthly good was a conscience to a man

if he couldn't make it bend in a good cause? they'd asked one another over a beer at Fitzgerald's Bar and Grill or a cup of coffee at
Peg's.

There were times during his all-too-frequent sleepless nights
when Ford wondered if those folks weren't dead right. Maybe it
would have been better to bend the rules by which he ran his life in
order to keep the next best thing to a blood brother he'd ever had.

"How's C.T. doing with his trumpet playin'?" he asked when
the old man had settled his bones. "Still fixin' to be the next Louis
Armstrong?"

The old man chuckled. "Way he's apracticin', he'll be that, sure
enough. Last time I saw Charles we spent the entire hour takin'
turns braggin' on C.T."

Ford thumbed the thick handle of his mug and thought about
the one and only time he'd gone to visit his old friend. Charles had
called him every name in a very thick book before making it plain
that Ford wasn't welcome to visit again. And Reeny, who worked
for Ford as a night dispatcher for the sheriff's and fire depart-
ments, treated him more like an employer than a friend these days.

"How's Charles doin'?"

The old man sighed. "Middlin'. It's hard for him to be caged like
he is."

Ford winced inwardly, but habit kept his facial muscles immo-
bile. "Is he still takin' those college courses?"

"Says he is."

While C.T.'s granddaddy studied the menu he knew by heart,
Ford watched Sophie serving ham and grits to a slick-looking
stranger in a shirt and tie at the far end of the counter. Ford
marked him as a salesman, and harmless. When Sophie laughed at
something the guy said, however, Ford found himself scowling at
that good ole boy like a jealous lover.

Disgusted at himself, he jerked his gaze back to his plate.
Mooning over a woman he barely knew was a risky way to start out
his day.

"Good morning, Mr. Washington. What are your bunions saying today?"

Lost in his own dark thoughts, Ford hadn't seen Sophie approaching. Glancing up, he caught her smiling at Bram with more
warmth than he'd gotten on his best day. His mood edged from
grumpy to foul. Too much coffee, he figured. Or not enough sleep.

"Well, I tell you true, Miss Sophie, I haven't heard a peep from those bunions at all this mornin'." The old man's eyes twinkled brightly in his brown face, and Ford could tell he approved of Peg's latest hire. It wasn't exactly the kind of scientific evidence most cops swore by these days, but Ford had never known Bram to be wrong about a person's character. Heck, he'd been the first to support Ford's decision to arrest Charles. And he'd never once voiced even the mildest criticism since.

"What can I bring you this morning, Mr. Washington?" Sophie asked, her pencil poised over her pad. One of the first things Ford had noticed was the bare ring finger of her left hand. According to Lucy, who'd been at Kate's house when she'd arrived, she had her a child to support, a little baby girl, he seemed to recall.

Maybe the sadness he caught in her eyes now and again had to do with her husband's death. Ford had seen others go plum crazy from grief after the loss of a spouse, which was one reason he'd made up his mind to live and die a bachelor.

The other reasons were a lot more personal—and a lot more painful. He'd grown up listening to his parents arguing, then fighting, and finally hurling bitter insults and accusations at each other. After a while, he'd learned to sleep with his head under his pillow instead of on it.

During the day, however, he'd had no such protection. His mama had cried a lot, and Ford had tried to comfort her. He still winced when he remembered coming home from school one fall when he'd just turned twelve to find her gliding downstairs in her best dress, smelling like summer roses. "Hurry and wash up, honey, 'cause I'm takin' my best beau out for a late lunch," she'd ordered in that shivery Charleston drawl he still heard sometimes in his dreams.

They'd gone to Clarke's Steakhouse. He could still remember how heads had turned when they'd walked in. And how the men at the bar had stared at his mother's legs.

When she'd given him money to attend a matinee at the movie house while she did some boring old shopping, he'd never once suspected that she'd been carrying on with Race Clarke in the room above the restaurant. Or that the pink he'd noticed in her cheeks when he'd met her back there after the movie let out had been caused by whisker burn instead of fast walking the way she'd claimed.

He was smart enough now to know that not all women were like his mama. He just wasn't sure he was smart enough to pick one who wasn't.

"Guess the number three would go down right this mornin'," Bram answered after due reflection. "I like my eggs over hard."

Sophie glanced up from her pad and narrowed her gaze. "You had eggs yesterday. Remember your cholesterol count."

"Hmm, can't say as I do."

"Two sixty-five." Leaning forward, she pointed with the pencil to the number six breakfast. "How about some oatmeal and fruit?"

"How about grits instead?"

She shook her head. "Too much butter."

Blatantly eavesdropping, Ford had to work at keeping his poker face. Bram was as stubborn as the gray-haired mule he kept in a pen behind his place. It seemed that Sophie had some of that same stubbornness hidden behind those solemn blue eyes.

"A mess of hash browns, then," Bram bargained, his eyes taking on a cagey glint.

"Whole-wheat toast would be better."

Bram shared a look of pure misery with Ford before grudgingly giving in. "That toast better come with some of Peg's strawberry jam," he added in a last-ditch effort that had her soft lips curving. Sucker punched by a sudden yearning to feel that sometimes-sad mouth moving under his, Ford concentrated on his coffee. Hell, he didn't have a problem with wanting to take the woman to bed. He just wanted to make sure he was calling all the shots.

"Someday I'll have to introduce you to my daughter," she chided Bram as she took back the menu. "The two of you have a lot in common."

"Now that would be a pleasure, yes, ma'am," Bram answered, grinning. "How old is that young un' of yours, anyway?"

"Nine months, and growing like a weed."

"Most likely one of our Carolina wildflowers, if she's like her mama."

She blushed a pretty shade of pink, but her eyes narrowed. "Now, Mr. Washington, that is a charming thing to say," she said, smiling so sweetly Ford felt something ease inside him. "But don't think you can sweet-talk me into bringing you grits, because someone has to watch out for you, and it's sure not you."

Before she left, she glanced Ford's way. "More coffee, Sheriff?" she asked politely. She didn't waste a smile, sweet or otherwise. Is that all she had to say to him—*More coffee, Sheriff?*

"No, ma'am, but thank you for asking."

"You're welcome." Calmly, efficiently, she collected his dirty dishes and headed toward the kitchen, her tidy little backside catching his attention one more time.

He felt another slam of sexual interest, stronger than before, and not as easily dismissed. Damn, he thought, downing the rest of his coffee in one bitter gulp before getting to his feet.

"Something botherin' you, son?" Bram asked, lifting one bushy eyebrow.

"Nothin' special. Just figured it was time I did somethin' to earn my salary today."

Maybe it was also time to take him a trip down to Clay City. Get in some Christmas shopping while he was at it, and treat green-eyed, blond-haired Sissy Tyrone to one of those expensive dinners she liked so much. If history repeated itself, she'd invite him back to her place for brandy and a wild few hours on those silk sheets she fancied.

He dropped some bills on the counter next to his empty plate, aware that he was tipping way too much. He figured a widow with a baby to support needed the money more than he did, and besides, it was the least a man could do for a woman he'd just decided to get into his bed, come hell or high water.

Jessie's laughing brown eyes followed the spoon as Sophie made circles in the air, coming closer to her daughter's mouth each time.

"Zoom, zoom, zoom," she buzzed, then beamed as Jessie imitated her eagerly, "Zoo', zoo'."

"Here comes the airplane, Jess," she murmured. "Get ready now . . . zoom, zoom, zoom!"

Jessie laughed, clapping her chubby hands excitedly. Laughing, too, Sophie shoved the spoonful of pureed peas into the rosebud mouth.

"Uh-oh," she muttered as Jessie's silky eyebrows drew together in a furious frown and her lips puckered. Hastily, Sophie set the jar of peas on the table and grabbed the towel she'd readied just in case. Sure enough, out came the peas, helped along by Jessie's little pink tongue.

Sophie and Miss Fanny exchanged looks over Jessie's curly head. "Gracious, how that child does hate anything green," Miss Fanny murmured, her faded blue eyes mirrors of distress.

Once lauded as the belle of three counties and now well into her seventies, Frances Beaulieu Bedford was the last living member of two of Clover's four founding families.

Though well-educated and well-read, she'd been gently but persistently guided by her genteel mother toward the express goal of marrying well. Now almost sixty years after the fact, Sophie still heard accounts of the joy that had spread through the town's best families when eighteen-year-old Fanny had become engaged to John Raymond Hampton IV, the scion of another of Clover's first families.

But Johnny Ray had died at Anzio during the Second World War and Miss Fanny had put her heart into lavender-scented storage along with her heirloom wedding gown. She'd spent fifty of those lonely years giving piano and deportment lessons to other people's children and now filled her days with volunteer work at the library and the hospital.

As soon as she'd heard Sophie questioning Katie about day-care for Jessie, she'd volunteered her services as a live-in sitter, and Sophie had wholeheartedly accepted, only to realize soon thereafter, that by accepting Miss Fanny's offer, she had unwittingly offended Miss Rose Ruth Adamson, the third resident on the top floor, who'd been about to offer *her* services. As a result, the ladies took turns caring for the baby and everyone, especially Sophie, was satisfied.

None of them, however, had been able to entice Jessie to swallow that first bite of peas or green beans or spinach, and as Sophie swiped the last of the peas from Jessie's now pouting mouth, she fought down a rush of panic. At her last checkup, Dr. Gossely had wondered aloud if Jessie wasn't just a tad overweight. More vegetables and less fruit had been his prescription, and Sophie was determined to follow his advice to the letter.

"You have to eat your veggies, sweetheart," she crooned to her now red-faced daughter.

"How about mashin' up some of the zucchini squash I canned last year?" Katie suggested, looking up from peeling potatoes for the evening meal.

"Rose Ruth and I tried that first," Miss Fanny assured her in a soft-spoken drawl. "Didn't we, sugar?" she added in an aside to the baby who started to wail.

"And *I've* tried everything else the grocery store had on its shelves. Peas were my last hope." Sophie quickly opened a jar of strained plums and offered Jessie a spoonful. Furious now, Jessie turned her head to the side and wailed louder.

"Now, now, sugar, don't fuss, hear?" Miss Fanny captured one of Jessie's flailing fists and attempted to pat it. Jessie refused to be distracted.

"She's never been a fussy eater before," Sophie said, sharing a helpless look with her elderly friend.

"Do you think she's sick?" Katie asked anxiously, leaving the sink to hover next to the other two women.

"She seemed fine when I got home from work." Just in case, Sophie touched her fingertips to her daughter's cheek, then shook her head at the others. "It doesn't feel as though she has a fever."

"Aunt Peg mentioned something about a bug goin' around," Katie said, still holding a half-peeled potato in one hand and a paring knife in the other.

"Maybe I'd better call Dr. Gossely just in case." Without bothering to hide her fear, Sophie plucked Jessie from the chair and settled her on her lap. Jessie let out one more wail, hiccuped a few times before planting her minuscule thumb firmly in her mouth and nestled against Sophie's breast. Soon she was jabbering away in a language all her own.

"Why the little dear just wanted some cuddlin' from her mama," Miss Fanny asserted, beaming first at Jessie and then at Sophie.

Katie's mouth popped open, and then she laughed. "I think I'd hold off on callin' Doc Gossely if I were you," she commented before returning to the sink.

"I believe I'll just take that advice," Sophie decided, hugging Jessie close. It felt so good to have the warm weight of her baby pressed against the breasts that had ached for weeks after they'd taken Jessie away.

Her grief had been bottomless, and Darlene had feared for her sanity. The days had blurred together in an smothering black haze, broken only by frequent bouts of uncontrollable sobbing. Only when Sophie had come up with the plan to get Jessie back had she begun to come alive again.

She'd been terrified, and yet determined. It had been surprisingly easy to gain admittance to the Manwaring house while Anita and Wells, Sr., had been attending a political gala, even easier to slip past the nanny who'd been watching TV in her room. Jessie hadn't been discovered missing until early the next morning, by which time Sophie and the baby had already crossed three states.

She knew there were people looking for her. The Manwarings had plenty of money and, more importantly, political clout. All Sophie had was her determination to keep Jessie from growing up in the same sterile, repressive, joyless house that had produced Wells.

Bending her head, she kissed Jessie's shiny curls before breathing in the sweet scent of her. "Mama loves you dearly, my sweet precious baby," she murmured as she nuzzled Jessie with her chin.

A pale brown at birth, the baby's hair was slowly but surely turning darker, like hers. Jessie had her chin, too. And her slanting eyebrows. But Jessie's eyes were very like her father's.

Sophie felt a wave of deep sadness pass through her. She and Wells had started their marriage with such high hopes—at least she had. After all that had happened, she would never be sure that she'd known what Wells had felt about anything, even her.

Glancing up, she discovered Miss Fanny gazing at her with sad longing. "If my dear Johnny Ray hadn't gone into the service in 1941, I would have filled our lives with babies," she murmured. "He wanted at least nine, for a baseball team, you see. My Johnny was right partial to baseball."

Sophie smiled, her heart going out to the older woman who had treated her with generosity and kindness from the moment they'd met. "He sounds like a wonderful man, Miss Fanny. No wonder you loved him so very much."

"Aunt Peg remembers him from when she was a girl," Katie called over her shoulder. "She said he and Lucy's grandfather were the two handsomest men in Clover County."

Fanny pursed her lips and took her time thinking that through before nodding slowly. "I do believe my Johnny was a mite better looking than Buchanan Maguire."

"Old Buck must have been something, though, you have to admit." Katie dropped the last potato in the boiling water on the back burner of the big stove and adjusted the fire. "Has Aunt Peg ever told you about him, Sophie?"

"No, although she's mentioned Miss Fanny's Johnny Ray."

Katie dried her hands before carrying a mess of winter peas and a large bowl to the table. Before she sat down, however, she poured herself a glass of iced tea and then refilled Sophie's glass for her. Miss Fanny preferred her tea hot, and the teapot was still half-full under the knitted tea cozy.

"Old Buck could have stepped right out of a Civil War novel, drooping cavalry mustache, swaggering walk, shiny boots and all," Katie continued, settling into her chair. "What was he, Miss Fanny? Six feet seven?"

Miss Fanny's eyes took on a reminiscent sheen. "In his boots, taller than that. I remember because I danced with him once when I made my debut, and my nose was just even with the middle stud of this beautifully ironed dress shirt."

"Do girls still have coming-out parties in the South?" Sophie asked curiously.

"Very rarely," Miss Fanny said with a sigh. "It's such a shame, too. In my day a girl looked forward to her debut almost as much as she did to her wedding."

"Do y'all still have debutante balls in Montana?" Katie asked, snapping open a pea pod.

Sophie shook her head. At least none of the girls she'd met in the six weeks she'd spent working on a ranch there when she'd been a sophomore at Oregon State had mentioned being a debutante.

Still cradling her now-sleeping baby, she reached for a handful of peas and set about shelling them into the bowl. Initially reticent to stray far from her room unless she was taking Jessie for an outing or preparing her bottles, she had gradually come to feel at home in the big old kitchen with frilly yellow-and-white-checked curtains at the tall windows and a redbrick fireplace taking up one wall.

Though neither of the others would ever know it, just sitting with them in the homey kitchen helping to prepare supper was as precious to her as any fortune.

"I do believe Ford resembles Buck more the older he gets," Miss Fanny mused after a moment's silence. "Of course, he's not nearly as tall, but he has the same rebel look about him." She clucked her tongue. "That poor boy, he was such a devil when he was coming up, with a laugh that fairly rattled the windows when he let loose."

Katie looked thoughtful. "I still hear folks marvelin' at him becoming sheriff when half the town was sure he'd end up in prison or shot dead pullin' some prank."

"He was simply high-spirited. That's always been the nature of the Maguire men."

"Except for Ford's daddy," Katie mused. "Aunt Peg told me once that he was the most unfriendly man she'd ever met."

"That's because he married the wrong woman. Before he met Susannah, he was full of beans and vinegar. Ford favors him greatly."

Katie didn't look convinced. Glancing Sophie's way, she asked casually, "What do you think of the last of the Maguire men?"

Sophie felt a familiar tightening in her stomach. "He's a generous tipper," she hedged.

"He should be," Katie said, laughing. "It's not like he has anything else to spend his money on but that old airplane he's so crazy about."

"That poor boy never had a day's ease," Miss Fanny muttered, clucking her tongue. "I swear, Morgan Maguire had him doing chores around that place of theirs before he was old enough to go to school."

Katie took a sip of tea, then scowled. "I wonder if he ever thinks about the air force anymore?"

Sophie fought a quick battle with herself—and lost. "Was Ford...Sheriff Maguire in the air force?" she asked nonchalantly.

"No, but he wanted to be," Katie said as she got up to switch on the overhead light. It was a week before the shortest day of the year, and dusk came shortly after five.

"Aunt Peg said she remembers him studying day and night to keep his grades up so he'd have a chance at an appointment to the air force academy." She checked on the potatoes before returning to her seat.

"He must have been terribly disappointed when he didn't get it," Sophie remarked.

"Oh, he got it, all right. First time anyone in the county ever came close to qualifying. I was only eleven then, but I remember how excited he was the day the telegram came. Whirled Lucy and me around their living room until we were all three dizzy."

Sophie thought about a man with unsmiling gray eyes and a hard, controlled mouth and tried to imagine him happy enough to dance around a room. No matter how hard she tried, however, she couldn't picture Ford Maguire unbending even a fraction.

"What happened?" she asked, knowing she shouldn't. "Did he flunk out?"

"Never went."

Jessie stirred, and Sophie resettled her into a more comfortable position before glancing up to ask, "Why ever not?"

The two women exchanged looks. "Right after Ford graduated from high school, his father killed his mother and her lover, then killed himself," Katie said soberly, "and Ford gave up his dream so he could take care of Lucy."

Fanny expelled a long sigh, her expression terribly sad. "Ford found them, you see. He was asleep in his room this one morning when Lucy woke him up to tell him their mama and daddy weren't in the house. Nobody knows how he figured out they were out at the airport, but that's where they were, sure enough. The coroner decided that Susannah and the colonel, that's Colonel Tim Shields, the owner of the airport, were carrying on in the colonel's office in the back of the monstrous old hangar when Morgan caught them, er, in the act, so to speak. Ford found the bodies."

It took Sophie a moment to realize she was staring at Katie, her breath dammed in her throat. "I...didn't realize, I mean, I shouldn't have pried..." she stammered, instinctively drawing Jessie closer to her heart. She felt the room tilt as memories surfaced to claw at her, then slowly right itself as she fought them off.

"This is Clover, sugar," Katie said with a forgiving smile. "Pryin's just about our favorite pastime, so secrets don't last long around here—especially the messy ones. But I wouldn't mention anything about this particular mess to Ford or Lucy. Far as I know, neither one of them ever talks about that morning."

In spite of the kitchen's cozy warmth, Sophie felt chilled to the bone. "No, of course, I won't," she promised quickly. Too quickly. "Everyone's entitled to privacy." If only they knew how fervently she hoped to preserve her own.

"I remember seeing his face when he brought Lucy to stay with Aunt Peg and me," Katie confided. "It was like he'd aged twenty years. And his eyes were so empty, like a dead man's.'' She shuddered. ''One minute he was packin' to leave for Colorado, and the next he was makin' funeral arrangements. The day after he and Lucy buried their parents, he asked Sheriff Doherty for a job, sent his regrets to the air force, moved Lucy back into the house his daddy had left him and never looked back.''

''As far as you know,'' Sophie murmured, feeling sick inside. No wonder Ford carried the look of a lone wolf on those broad shoulders.

''Yes, as far as I or anyone else knows,'' Katie echoed, then sighed. ''When I was a teenager, I was terribly in love with him. I used to lie awake at night and plan ways to make him see me as a woman instead of Lucy's best friend. I just knew I was that one special woman who could make him forget all about the past.''

''What happened?'' Sophie asked almost reluctantly.

''He still treats me like another baby sister, and I fell in love with someone else.'' After standing abruptly, she carried the beans to the sink and began washing them, leaving Sophie with a lot to think about.

Sophie finished winding her thrift-shop alarm clock and returned it to the nightstand with a deep sigh. Across the room, Jessie was finally asleep in her crib, still sucking her thumb.

Downstairs, some of her fellow boarders were gathered around the gleaming rosewood piano Miss Rose Ruth had brought with her three years ago when strained finances had forced her to give up her ancestral home.

Smiling to herself, Sophie closed her eyes and let the faint strains of ''Silent Night'' wash over her. Outside her window Christmas lights festooned an enormous Norfolk pine, casting a multicolored glow over the entire garden.

Just yesterday, with much ceremony and laughter, her fellow boarder Roy Dean Stevenson had installed a new birdbath there, his gift to what the former high school math teacher had termed ''Katie's extended family.''

This morning Sophie had noticed a male cardinal gobbling his fill next to the cute little brown wrens that offered a serenade outside her window every morning. Unlike the proud and strictly monogamous cardinal, the cheerful wrens were prone to have more than one mate at a time and didn't much care who knew it.

Like Wells, she thought, her smile fading. She'd lost count of the number of times he'd accused her of cheating on him, even as he himself had been juggling at least two mistresses. And they were only the ones she'd known about.

She'd been seriously considering a separation when she'd found out she was pregnant. She hadn't expected Wells to be pleased, but she hadn't expected her announcement to be greeted with a blast of icy rage, either. After all, Wells's mother, Anita, had been periodically lamenting the lack of grandchildren, and Wells had always given his parents everything they'd demanded of him— including a college-trained, suitably pedigreed wife.

When he'd accused her of carrying another man's child she'd been dumbfounded. Yes, he'd used protection, but even the best measures sometimes failed. The child was his. She'd never had another lover. Not before their marriage nor during.

She still cringed whenever she thought about the names he'd called her—vile, ugly names that had shredded the last of her love for him. Still, it was only when he'd ordered her to abort the baby that she'd fought back.

Settling back against the twin pillows piled against the headboard, she drew up her knees and hugged herself until the sick feeling of revulsion faded.

No looking back, she reminded herself, watching the colored lights twinkling against the night sky. She'd gone through hell, yes, but without the hell, there would have been no Jessie. Closing her eyes, she let her mind drift. When she found herself thinking about Ford Maguire, she snapped them open and reached for the library book on her nightstand. It was a thriller by one of her favorite authors. Usually engrossing from the first page, she found herself reading the same paragraph over and over while the conversation in the kitchen ran through her mind.

This is Clover, sugar. Secrets don't last long around here— especially the messy ones. Katie hadn't meant to turn her blood to ice with those words, but she had.

She closed the book and drew a ragged breath as she returned it to the nightstand. In a moment of macabre humor she wondered how the ladies would have reacted this afternoon if she'd told them *her* secret?

She could imagine the shocked look that would have come into Miss Fanny's kind eyes. As for Katie, no doubt she would have ordered Sophie to leave her house that instant—or worse, called Ford Maguire to come and arrest her.

Sophie cringed at the thought of his sexy gray eyes going cold and condemning at the very sight of her. There wasn't a chance in the world he would understand the anguish and worry that had driven her to kidnap her own child, she thought as she turned out the light and slipped her tired body under the covers.

It was a long time before she managed to sink into sleep. Before consciousness faded, however, she had renewed her vow to stay as far away from Ford Maguire as possible—even if he did have a touchingly shy smile and a way of looking at her that said he understood loneliness as much as she did.

Chapter 2

Normally a slow weekday, the last Wednesday before Christmas had been endless and backbreaking, and Sophie was worn-out. Evangeline, the young mother of five who worked the supper shift, had stayed home to care for a sick child, and Sophie had worked her own shift and Evie's, too.

And then, worse luck, the cook had gotten sick in the middle of the dinner rush and gone home as soon as orders had eased off to a trickle, leaving Sophie to do double duty for the final hour of her shift.

Fortunately, the last customer had left a good twenty minutes before the eight o'clock closing, and she'd been able to wipe down the tables and scour the grill without interruption.

Trying not to notice her aching feet, she was daydreaming about a long hot bath and a lovely bedtime cuddle with Jessie when the bell over the door jangled, and a man in soiled work clothes and filthy boots lurched inside. She shot a quick glance at the clock, hoping against hope that it was past closing time.

It wasn't. Not for three more minutes.

Heart sinking, Sophie pasted a polite smile on her face and reached for a menu. Peg insisted on her employees treating every customer with courtesy, no matter how scruffy, but she was so tired her head was buzzing, and her face felt numb.

"Good evening," she murmured, hoping against hope that the obviously intoxicated man had come in for coffee to go.

"Miz Jones in the back?" he snarled, darting a bloodshot glance at the door to the kitchen behind her. "I come to git my pay for some work I done for her."

"I'm sorry, she's not here tonight."

"She ain't? Then who's helpin' y'all with the cookin'?" The closer he came, the stronger the stench of stale whiskey and sweat became.

"I'm afraid the kitchen's closed for the night." It wasn't exactly a fib—more like a slight exaggeration. But she figured Peg would understand. "I'd be happy to brew you some coffee to take with you, and we have some doughnuts left," she added when he continued to stare at her without speaking. "On the house."

"Reckon I don't want nothing to eat or drink."

Sophie drew a determined breath. "In that case, I'm afraid I can't help you."

"Maybe you can, little lady. Maybe you can."

"I don't think so," she asserted, edging backward. All of a sudden she didn't like the look in his eyes.

"Tell you what, I'd be obliged if you'd just open that till there and hand me out the hundert thirty-two dollars I'm owed." He grinned at her, displaying large yellow teeth mottled with chewing-tobacco stains.

Sophie stared at him, her tired brain only beginning to understand exactly what he was saying. "I can't do that, but I'd be happy to leave a note for Mrs. Jones to call you first thing in the morning."

He shifted his sloppy wad of chew to the opposite cheek, swiping at a dribble of juice with a filthy sleeve. "Guess you bein' a Yankee, you don't understand how things are done in these parts."

"I understand that we're closed, and you're trespassing."

A dull red flush spread along the stubbled jawbone, while at the same time his thin lips pulled back in a snarl. "Outta the way, missy. Old Man Ducette's made him a prime batch of 'shine, and I aim to get more'n my share afore it's gone."

"Looks like you've already had more than your share," she muttered, as angry now as she was tired. To her surprise, he threw back his head and brayed a laugh at the ceiling.

"That's a good one, all right. Yes, ma'am, it surely is." His gaze narrowed, then took on a sly glint as he slowly looked her up and down. "For a Yankee woman, you're not half-bad. Maybe a little on the skinny side, but like the man says, the closer the bone, the juicier the meat." He reached out a grimy hand to squeeze her breast. She slapped him away, and his eyes slitted.

"Now that ain't neighborly, missy," he whined. "A man might get the idea you had it in for him, just 'cause he come claiming what was his by right."

He turned his head to one side and spit. Sickly yellow tobacco juice spattered over her clean floor, turning her stomach. It was all she needed.

"Get out now before I call the sheriff," she ordered, her voice shot with revulsion.

"Git me my money, and I'll go."

"I am not giving you one red cent unless Mrs. Jones tells me to personally."

"Then git outta my way." He barged past her, using his elbow to shove her aside. Without thinking, she shoved back. Surprised, he stumbled, arms flailing like a scarecrow, but he managed to keep his footing.

As soon as he turned toward her, she realized her mistake. However ludicrous it might seem, this filthy buffoon of a man just might be willing to kill her to get his one hundred and thirty-two dollars. Keeping Peg from losing far less than a day's take wasn't worth losing her life.

Spinning around, she took off toward the door. Faster than she would ever have guessed, he lunged after her, catching her by the bow of her frilly white apron, and jerked her backward so hard she lost her footing and careened sideways into a table.

His filthy fingers dug into her flesh, spinning her around. Desperate, she cried out, and at the same time she brought her knee up, aiming for his crotch.

Drunk as he was, he managed to twist just enough to take the blow on his thigh. At the same time, he drew back his fist and took aim. Instead of connecting with her jaw, however, he ended up flying sideways to land in a crumpled filthy heap against the base of one of the counter stools.

The moment his shoulder had made contact with Ransom Talley's rib cage, Ford remembered why football players wore pads.

The jolt had gone to the bone, stretching out the same ligaments he'd torn twenty years earlier.

"Damn you, Rans," he grated, getting slowly to his feet to take a few testing breaths. "Why couldn't you stay on the wagon like you promised me last time you got liquored up?"

Talley lay prone, his mouth opening and closing like a carp, one miserable-looking excuse for a man. Wincing at the hot pain knifing his shoulder, Ford reached behind him for the handcuffs dangling from his gun belt. Talley didn't even protest when Ford rolled him to his belly and cuffed his grimy hands behind him.

Sophie had been knocked aside and was trying to sit up. Ford called her name, and she looked up blankly, her face as white as the silly ruffled apron Peg made all her waitresses wear.

He hesitated, then knelt next to her and touched her shoulder as gently as he could. And felt her flinch. Instantly, he withdrew his hand, afraid to spook her.

"Sophie, listen to me, you're safe now," he assured her, deliberately using the same tone he'd once used to soothe Lucy when she'd awakened in the night, screaming with another of a long series of bad dreams.

To his relief, it seemed to work, and a semblance of life returned to her frozen features. Like a diver surfacing after too long beneath the surface, she blinked her way back to clear focus, drawing her eyebrows together slowly.

"He came in to see Peg about some money he's owed, and when I told him she wasn't here, he decided to steal it," she declared firmly, with only a faint tremble to her voice. Even as he registered every word she said, along with the way she'd said them, he couldn't help noting that her lips looked softer without the glossy stuff women love so much and had a definite wobble in spite of the brave thrust of her chin.

"Did he hurt you?"

"I think I ripped my apron," she muttered, fingering a torn ruffle with obvious disgust. Ford ran his gaze over her, checking for cuts and bruises. She looked worn-out, but uninjured.

It struck him then how much she resembled the fragile glass angel he'd won for Lucy at the county fair the year he'd turned thirteen and she'd been four.

He still didn't know why he'd told her it was a *guardian* angel, but he had, and Lucy, far too trusting even then, had believed her big brother. Now that she was all grown up, she knew better. But darned if she didn't keep that little angel safely behind glass in their mama's old china cabinet.

Every time Ford saw it, he was reminded of the vow he'd made to keep his little sister safe and secure all the days of her life. He'd never felt that way about anyone else—until now.

It wasn't a realization he particularly liked. In fact, it made him damn irritable. He'd figured out a long time ago that a man was better off confining his feelings for a woman to the basics, like sex—or in a few select cases, friendship. He'd never managed to put the two together and wasn't at all sure it was even possible.

"Do you think you can stand?"

When she nodded, he extended his hand. She hesitated, then with obvious reluctance, accepted his help. As soon as she could, she withdrew her hand. At the same time, she darted a quick glance toward the miserable heap of humanity on the floor.

"I might be just an ignorant Yankee," she muttered, "but I had the distinct impression that moonshine stills were illegal in this country."

"Yes, ma'am, they are."

"Perhaps you'd better tell that to someone named Old Man Ducette, because according to that person on the floor there, he's just produced a prime batch."

"Is that a fact?" Ford shot a look Talley's way. He and Rans had run together some as boys. In those days he'd been the one getting into trouble while Rans had hung back to watch the fun when he'd gotten caught.

He called Rans by name, then waited patiently until he had the man's full attention. "I gotta tell you, son, it would sure do me a big favor if you'd tell me where Frenchy's set up this time."

"Aw, Ford, you know I cain't do that." Talley tried to work up a spit, and failed. "Damn, now you made me go and swallow my chaw."

Ford grinned. "Probably the most nutritious thing you've eaten all day."

Talley offered him a sloppy grin. "You got a cigarette you can spare?"

"Don't smoke."

"Do so. I recollect you and me sharin' a whole carton once under Carston's Bridge."

"Yeah, when we were twelve and stupid." Ford had given up cigarettes when he'd decided to try for the air force academy. According to the manual he'd devoured from cover to cover more than once, cadets were prohibited from drinking on academy grounds and discouraged from smoking. Besides, he'd planned to make the football team his freshman year and hadn't wanted to diminish his stamina.

"It's like this, Rans," he said, suddenly out of patience. "You and me need to make us a deal here. You tell me where Frenchy's set up again, and I'll talk to the country prosecutor about a suspended sentence."

Talley tried spitting again. "Maybe you don't recall how talented old Frenchy is with that pig-sticker of his'n."

Ford recalled all too well. He'd been in the ambulance when Roy Dean Stevenson's youngest boy had bled out his life after getting in the way of Frenchy's murderous temper. Roy Dean, Jr., had been nineteen that summer, and Roy Dean had never been the same after the boy's funeral.

Since that time, Ford had tried every trick he'd learned in his eighteen years of law enforcement to amass enough evidence to convict the hulking bootlegger, but Frenchy had too many people terrified of talking.

"Rans, hear me and hear me good. You have forty-eight hours before my report goes to the town clerk to be processed and sent on. After that, you're riding a one-way train to prison. If I were you, I'd give some thought to what it's gonna be like, spending the next year or so locked up behind bars."

Fear leapt in Talley's eyes like a roach on a hot griddle. "Git on with you. You done arrested me for drunk and disorderly twice before, and I didn't get no jail time."

"This time the charge is attempted robbery and assault."

"A man cain't rob what's his by right, sure enough, and it seems to me I'm the one who got assaulted on." He shifted his attention to Sophie, who stiffened, before Ford deliberately moved into Talley's line of sight. "Me'n this sweet little Yankee gal was just fixin' to have us a party when she up and changed her mind is all."

"That's ridiculous and you know it," she declared hotly.

Ford felt his mouth relax into a grin. So the lady had a habit of getting testy when her blood was riled, he thought, and wondered how she would react if he suddenly covered those pouty lips with his. He let his mind linger over that for a split second before he iced down his unruly libido.

"Won't wash, Rans," he said, heading for the phone by the cash register. "Give me a minute to get the duty deputy over here to tend to Rans, and I'll drive you home," he told Sophie as he punched out the number of the sheriff's office.

"Please don't bother, I like the walk," she answered quickly.

"Be better if you rode, just this once."

Sensing the steel beneath the polite words, Sophie gave in. "I'll just finish up in the back," she told him before fleeing to the kitchen.

Ford leaned against the cluttered counter in the rooming house kitchen, sipping coffee he didn't want but couldn't politely refuse and wondering how long he was going to have to wait before Sophie appeared again. At the moment, she was upstairs in her room putting her daughter to bed while Miss Rose Ruth and Miss Fanny fussed over her.

Katie had been in the midst of baking Christmas cookies when he'd brought Sophie home. Once she'd made sure Sophie was un-injured, she'd ordered Ford into the kitchen and plied him with questions until finally, and to his great relief, she'd run out of things to ask.

"Someone should have shot Rans Talley years ago," Katie muttered, her green eyes blazing. "You, for instance."

Even as Ford shrugged, he wanted to tell her that he hoped he never had to kill Talley or anyone else. Since he'd walked into Tim's office at the airport and seen the blood spattered from the floor to the ceiling, he'd gotten sick to his stomach at the sight of blood.

The thought of actually inflicting that kind of carnage, even in the name of the law, made his knees shake. So far he'd been lucky the few times he'd had to pull his gun.

"Rans isn't all bad," he said, studying the coffee left in his cup. He'd known better men who'd been driven to do worse things—like his old man, God rest his tormented soul.

"I wish Sophie would have let me call Doc Gossely. At least he could have prescribed a tranquilizer for her, if nothing else."

Ford slugged down the remaining contents of his cup before shrugging. Pain seared his shoulder, and he scowled.

"Somethin' bothering you?" Katie asked quickly, her knife poised over the roll of cookie dough she was busy slicing onto another greased tin.

"More like puzzlin'," he admitted, pouring himself a refill from the big pot.

Katie shrugged. "I sure would have enjoyed watching Sophie kick old Rans in the privates," she admitted, her eyes sparkling the way they used to years ago when she and Lucy ran together like little hellions.

"It was a sight to see, sure enough." He could have added that, in his professional opinion, Sophie's common sense didn't stretch quite as far as her courage.

Sober, Ransom Talley was just about the nicest guy in all of Clover, but when he got liquored up, he turned into two hundred pounds of pure mean. Ford had arrested him twice before, and both times Rans had tried to take his head off with one of those hamlike fists.

Old Rans didn't quite believe it yet, but he'd just run out of second chances. He figured he could talk Peg into pressing charges. With Sophie testifying to what Rans had told her and him telling the judge what he saw, old Rans was sure to get more than a hand slap this time.

That settled, he attempted to rub some of the soreness out of his shoulder and watched Katie take another tray of Christmas cookies from the oven. He smelled cinnamon and orange, and his stomach growled. Dinner had been hours earlier, and he'd missed supper entirely. Figuring he was entitled, being a public servant and all, he filched the fattest of the cinnamon Santas and received a sour look and a muttered warning for his trouble.

"Did Sophie mention why she happened to pick these parts to settle?" he asked between bites.

"Not that I recall."

"What about her kin?"

Katie wrinkled her brow. "I'm not sure she's ever mentioned family, but then Yankees aren't like us, spilling out our entire history at the drop of a hat."

"Did you ask?"

Katie slanted him a disbelieving look before sliding the tray onto the slate counter. "Have you forgotten where you're livin' all of a sudden? Of course, I asked. She just wasn't answerin'."

He gave that some thought. So he wasn't the only one Sophie shorted in the conversation department. "You didn't happen to notice what kind of mail she gets, or how much?"

After taking a bowl of green icing from the refrigerator, Katie placed it on the counter to soften before answering. "So far she hasn't gotten all that much, just a bank statement every month, and a bill from Doc Gossely a month or so back."

"Has she been sick?"

Katie shook her head. "She took Jessamine for a routine visit shortly after they arrived." A smile played over her mouth. "I might not know much about Mrs. Sophie Reynolds's personal affairs before she came here, but one thing I do know, Ford. Her daughter is her life. Sophie wore the same three outfits for a month after she got here, but Jessie had the best of everything. Whatever she needed, she had. Even when Sophie's dead tired after working nights and mornings both, she makes sure Jessie gets an afternoon airing and playtime at the park. And love?" Katie's eyes turned starkly envious. "All you have to do is see them together to feel the love Sophie pours into that baby."

Ford shoveled another cookie into his mouth and swallowed it damn near whole. He wasn't as ready as Katie to bestow sainthood on a woman he scarcely knew. He'd seen too many cases of public saints who were private devils.

"Who watches the baby while she's working?"

"Miss Rose Ruth or Miss Fanny, and sometimes both. It depends on what shift Sophie's working."

Ford slugged down the rest of his coffee and walked to the sink to rinse his cup. "What about phone calls?" he asked, upending the cup in the dish drainer.

"Not many. Aunt Peg calls sometimes about work, and now and then one of the other waitresses calls, wanting to swap shifts or some such."

He dried his hands and tried not to think about the nice soft bed waiting for him at his place. The holidays were always busier than usual, especially when he'd been shortsighted enough to let Sig Roberts have two weeks off to be with his girlfriend down in Charleston.

"What about men?" he asked, turning to lean his backside against the counter again.

Katie regarded him critically. "Maybe we'd better establish who's asking these questions before I say anything more."

"You're lookin' at him, aren't you?" Ford retorted, his patience thinning more rapidly than usual.

"Don't narrow those gray eyes at me, Fordham Maguire," she exclaimed with a disgusted look. "I was around your place so much when I was growing up I was practically family, so I know what a pussycat you are under that mean old face you put on along with your uniform of a morning."

Ford grunted his displeasure. There weren't but a handful of people in the whole county who could call him a pussycat to his face—or much else for that matter—and get away with it. Katie just happened to be one of them.

"Katie, I'm tired, and I've got at least an hour of paperwork to do on this arrest before I can call it a night, so I suggest you just answer the blasted question."

Katie relented with a good-natured smile. "Okay. Only I forgot the question."

Ford watched the second hand of the Regulator clock tick its way through ten long seconds before he got ahold on his patience. He'd been awake since five, and had spent most of the day wrestling with budget projections the town council liked so much, and he sure as hell wasn't looking forward to another hour doing paperwork.

"Does Sophie have men callin' her here?"

"As in lovers?" Katie inquired with an innocence so exaggerated he was tempted to forget they were both adults and bend her over his knee for a hard swat the way he'd done when she was a kid and he was the closest thing to a daddy she and Lucy had.

"As in men friends," he grated.

"So far there haven't been any. Not as far as I know, anyway." She tested the temperature of fresh-baked cookies with a fingertip, then reached for a spatula. "According to Miss Fanny, Sophie was widowed before her baby was even born. Maybe she's not ready to date again."

Ford tried to imagine what that had been like for her. Rough as hell was as good a description as any. "Any idea what happened to her husband?"

"Perhaps you should ask me that question, Sheriff Maguire." Still dressed in her uniform, now sadly wrinkled and soiled, Sophie was standing stiff and unsmiling in the doorway. He didn't need a second look to tell him that she was very angry.

He wasn't surprised. Ford had spent half his life wearing a badge and carrying a gun. He was used to folks swearing at him one minute and yelling for his help the next. Taking the heat for a long list of imagined sins—and some that were real enough by anyone's standards—that went with the job.

He liked what he did for a living, and he was honest enough to own up to a certain pride in doing it well. There were times, however, when he wondered if he'd worn that badge so long he'd lost the ability to take it off, even on those rare occasions when he found himself damn near chasing his tail over a woman.

"Consider it asked," he drawled, watching her mouth tighten.

Ignoring her thudding heart and suddenly dry throat, Sophie looked first at him and then at Katie before declaring flatly, "My husband fell down a flight of steps and broke his neck. I was six weeks' pregnant at his funeral."

She could have added that she'd nearly lost the baby that same night and, as it was, had had to be hospitalized for shock. But what would be the point? Even during the worst of the ordeal that had followed, she'd never sought sympathy, only understanding. In the end, she'd gotten neither.

"How terrible for you," Katie murmured, her tone thick with sympathy. "No wonder you don't like to talk about it."

"It's easier now," Sophie lied.

"I hope you believe me when I tell you I don't usually discuss my tenants' private business."

"I'm sure you don't." Sophie was almost too worn-out to care.

Checking on Jessie and answering first Miss Rose Ruth's and then Miss Fanny's anxious questions had sapped what had been left of her reserves. Simply walking from the door to the butcher-block table in the center of the kitchen was an exercise in willpower.

"I made coffee," Katie told her, smiling tentatively. "But it wouldn't take me but a minute to brew some herbal tea if you'd prefer. And I just took a fresh batch of cookies out of the oven. Best help yourself before Ford wolfs them all down."

"Nothing for me, thanks," she murmured. "I just came down to ask if anyone has thought to tell Peg what happened."

Sophie's side was beginning to ache where she'd slammed against the table, and though she'd snatched a moment to wash her face and run a brush through her hair, she felt grimy and disheveled. At the moment all she wanted was a long hot bath and an uninterrupted night's sleep.

"Ford called her while you were upstairs. She should be here any minute." Katie cast an anxious glance toward the backyard. Her aunt lived three doors down on the other side of the alley. "Come to think of it, it doesn't usually take her long. I hope nothing's happened."

Kate shifted her attention to Ford, who sighed. "One problem at a time, Katie. Besides, if I know your aunt, she's got half the phone lines in Clover tied up by now."

"I have a feeling you're right about that," Katie admitted with a quick shake of her head.

Relieved that she'd fulfilled her obligation to her employer to the best of her ability, Sophie was about to excuse herself and return to her room when Ford suddenly pinned her with a look. His tired eyes were friendly enough, in an impersonal sort of way, but Sophie found herself going tense to the bone. Even without the badge he was a man she couldn't easily ignore. With it, and backed up by the gun hugging his right hip and the quiet air of command he wore so comfortably, he was the enemy personified.

"If you feel up to it, I have a few loose ends I need to tie up for the arrest report." Straightening, he pulled a pad and pencil from his back pocket. The badge pinned to his wide chest flashed in the overhead light, and she felt a stab of icy fear.

"As long as it doesn't take too long," she murmured, glancing up at the clock. "I don't like to leave Jessie longer than necessary."

"I'd be tickled to sit with her," Katie offered. "It's not often I get the chance, what with the ladies always fussin' over who gets to hold her next."

Touched, Sophie offered her a grateful smile. "If you're sure you wouldn't mind?"

"Heavens, no! Nothin' I'd like better, in fact."

"She was sleeping when I came downstairs, but Miss Fanny said she's been fussing on and off all evening long."

"I'll call you if she wakes up," Katie promised, putting down her spatula. "Help yourself to the cookies," she added before heading for the back stairs. "Just leave me enough to fill a plate."

"Depends on the size of the plate," Ford called after her, and received a very unladylike comment in return. Chuckling, he pulled out a chair and waited for Sophie to seat herself before doing the same.

"Probably help us both if you just go ahead and tell me what happened any way that suits you," he suggested, leaning back and stretching out his legs. "Start anyplace you want. If you leave any blanks, I'll ask you to fill them in when you're finished."

Over the years he'd found that he more often than not learned more from the way a story was told than the specific details.

Sophie was silent for a moment, then began talking, reciting the details of Talley's arrival a few minutes before closing time and the events that followed dispassionately, as though she were describing a play she'd seen.

He took a few notes, mostly to show he was paying attention, and wondered what she was doing in a backwater town in South Carolina waiting tables for a living, when she was obviously well-educated and pretty enough to get married again a dozen times over.

Most folks new to town had kin somewhere close or, like the new pastor of the Community Church, a job bringing them to the area. The way it had been told to him she'd just stepped off the Greyhound one Monday evening and gone looking for a place to live. She didn't seem like the wandering type, but he'd read folks wrong before—especially women.

"—and then you came in," she concluded, then frowned as though she'd suddenly remembered something important. "Why *did* you come in so late?"

"I was on my way home when Dexter Bobo flagged me down to tell me he'd seen Rans driving that old pickup of his all over the road. I saw it parked outside Peg's and, bein' the nosy so-and-so I am, I just naturally had to find out what was goin' on inside."

"I never thought I'd be grateful to see a policeman come barreling through that door, but I have to admit that, in this case, I was."

"Sounds like you're not too partial to lawmen."

She shrugged. "I got a speeding ticket that wasn't my fault once."

"Happens that way sometimes, even in Clover. Strange as it seems, I've had folks take one look at me and form an instant dislike."

"Imagine that."

"Amazin', isn't it?" he drawled, scanning his notes for holes that needed filling. He came up empty. She'd been concise and thorough, twin talents his deputies had yet to master completely.

"You ever done any teaching?" he asked as he returned pad and pencil to his shirt pocket.

Her gaze flickered, then fell away. "That's an odd question to ask, isn't it?" She toyed with the edge of the quilted place mat, and he filed away the fact that she'd deftly worked around the question without answering. He knew enough about himself and the way his mind worked to know that the need to find out why would stick to him like a burr to a mongrel's tail.

"I reckon it does sound that way, yeah. But I asked because you have a knack for stating facts better than any of my deputies. Probably better than me, if you come right down to it. Might be you'd share some of your secrets."

Her pale lips curved, but he sensed it was an effort. He nudged his estimation of her strength even higher. Soft velvet over a steel core, he thought.

"Actually, I think this whole evening is just engraved on my brain." She shivered suddenly, as though remembering. "If he'd just waited a few more minutes, I would have finished closing up, and none of this would have happened."

Ford shifted. "One thing I've learned in this job is the futility of second-guessin' yourself or anyone else."

Her expression clouded. "How do you keep from doing it?"

He shrugged. "I guess by doing the best you can with what you have, and letting the rest go."

"That's a skill I've yet to perfect," she murmured, getting wearily to her feet.

Rising, too, he thought about the years he'd spent beating up on himself for the things he'd done wrong. He hadn't even tried to forgive himself for the things he hadn't done right.

"If you think of anything else in the next hour or so, I'll be down at the station typin' up my report."

She nodded, and some of the stiffness eased out of her pale face. "It occurs to me that I've been so wrapped up in my own problems I haven't even thanked you for showing up in the nick of time. Please forgive the oversight, and know that I am very grateful."

"All part of the service," he said, watching the play of the overhead light on her hair. He had a hunch it was just as soft as it looked and was tempted to find out for himself.

She had freckles, he noticed, tiny flecks of pure gold meandering up and over the slight bump at the bridge of her nose. They made him think of Tom Sawyer and Becky Thatcher. He'd been a kid when he'd read that book. Ten maybe, or eleven, old enough to wonder when he would meet his "Becky" and feel the same breathless tightness in his chest that Tom had felt. He never had—until he'd walked into Peg's one morning and seen a scrawny little Yankee stranger with ageless eyes and the sexiest mouth he'd ever laid eyes on smiling at one of the customers.

It had taken him by surprise, like a left hook delivered in a dense fog. It wasn't love at first sight because he didn't believe in love, but it had rocked him harder than a simple jolt of sexual desire.

Far as he knew, Tom had never ended up with Becky. And he didn't expect anything permanent to happen between him and Sophie. But that didn't mean he didn't intend to make love to her. Still the timing wasn't right. He wasn't much of a horseman, but he knew enough not to rush his fences.

"What will happen to him?" she asked, glancing up, then away, as though she had trouble meeting his gaze.

"Like I told old Rans himself, he'll probably remain a guest of the state for a spell."

"Will there be a trial?"

"Most likely, unless the lawyer he's entitled to under state law convinces him to plead guilty."

She very carefully slid her chair under the table. "Does that mean I'll be called to testify?"

"Would that be a problem?" he asked so mildly she was tempted to believe he didn't care one way or the other what she thought. And perhaps he didn't. Perhaps she had only imagined that quick flash of something lethal in his eyes earlier, when he'd laid out Talley's future for him so succinctly.

"I admit I'm not looking forward to it," she hedged, straightening suddenly tense shoulders.

"No sense worrying about something that might not happen. Best thing for you to do now is get on up to bed and forget all about tonight."

Her eyes softened, and she nearly smiled—before she seemed to think better of it. "That does sound tempting."

Ford was a man of careful habits and meticulous ways. He never gave in to impulse or took action that hadn't been carefully considered. So the fact that he found himself wanting to gather that small, tired body into his arms and carry her upstairs to her bed had him backing down hard.

"You'll need to read through your statement after it's typed and make any corrections before signing it."

"Fine."

"I work seven to four tomorrow if you want to stop by the office. If I'm out on patrol, the dispatcher can always reach me. Or I could bring it by here after you get off work. Whatever's easier for you.'

"I'll stop by the office. I have errands to run after work, anyway."

Ford accepted that without comment, and without repeating his offer to conduct their business less formally. If she wanted to take a chance on cooling her heels in the smelly, dusty basement of the city hall, that was up to her. He had other things to do than wait on her, he told himself as he took Katie at her word and filled the pocket of his jacket with Christmas cookies.

They left the kitchen together and had just reached the foyer when he noticed Sophie stiffening and then heard a baby crying so faintly he first thought Myrtle Baughman's cat was stuck in a tree again.

Sophie hurried toward the stairs just as Katie appeared at the top. "Sophie! I was just comin' to get you. Something's wrong with the baby."

Chapter 3

In a panic, Sophie raced up the stairs as fast as her tired legs would take her. Behind her she heard the front door open, and the sound of Peg Jones calling her niece's name.

"Don't worry, I'll fill her in on what happened," Katie said as Sophie passed her on the stairs.

"Thanks," Sophie told her gratefully, slowing only slightly. As soon as she reached the third flight, she saw Miss Fanny and Miss Rose Ruth peering over the third-floor railing like pale ghosts in nightclothes and slippers. As soon as they spied her, they both began talking at once.

"Poor little thing's teething," Miss Fanny asserted confidently.

"Colicky," Miss Rose Ruth countered just as confidently. A former elementary teacher, Rose Ruth Adamson was the quintessential Southern maiden lady, always proper, always well-groomed and neat, and extremely generous to everyone who crossed her path. She was also the teeniest bit bossy and Fanny's lifelong friend, though a casual observer would be more than likely to conclude the opposite.

Fanny drew herself up straighter. "Now, Rose Ruth, that's nonsense and you know it. Jessie's always been an excellent eater."

"Until that old fool Hammond Gossely put her on vegetables way too soon, which she very rightly has been refusin' to eat."

Reaching the top, Sophie paused to catch her breath. The ladies meant well, but she was in no shape to arbitrate, even if she'd known which of the two was right.

"A nice warm hot-water bottle is all she needs," Miss Rose Ruth declared firmly, "and a bottle of weak sassafras tea for the tummy cramps."

"Bourbon whiskey on those sore gums," Miss Fanny stated.

Sophie left them still arguing and hurried into her room. Before she'd gone downstairs, she switched on the ceramic clown night-light she'd bought for Jessie out of last week's tips. Even before she reached Jessie's crib, she realized that the baby's little cheeks were flushed.

"Shh, sweetie, Mommy's here," she murmured, scooping the squirming, screaming baby into her arms. Jessie stiffened and, instead of calming, cried even harder. Frantic, Sophie laid her cheek against Jessie's and felt scalding heat.

"She's burning up!" she cried anxiously to the ladies who were now hovering just inside the door.

"I'll call Hammond," Miss Fanny decided before disappearing.

"Now don't go telling him any nonsense about teethin'," Rose Ruth ordered as she, too, disappeared. Through the open door. Sophie could hear them arguing all the way down the stairs.

"Miss Fanny says you're just teething, and Miss Rose Ruth swears it's those peas I tried to make you eat, and I'm scared it might be something a lot worse," she murmured, laying the baby on her back. "Let's just make sure it's not some nasty old bug, okay?"

Jessie wasn't about to be placated, making it an exercise in patience just to get her out of her diaper long enough to take her temperature. By the time Sophie finished, she was nearly in tears. Discovering that the baby had a fever of a hundred and two didn't help. Knowing she had to do something fast, she got to her feet and carried Jessie to the dresser she'd converted to a changing table.

"Don't cry, sweetie," she crooned, pulling open the top drawer with one hand while awkwardly cradling the screaming, kicking baby who was now pulling at her right ear with frantic little fingers. As far as she knew Jessie had never suffered from ear problems before, but then she knew almost nothing about the first six months of her daughter's life.

Guilt nearly swamped her as she thought about the upheaval she herself had brought about in Jessie's short life. Only the certainty that it had been necessary had enabled her to live with the guilt, and even then she'd sometimes lain awake at night in a cold sweat, worrying that she might be causing Jessie more harm than good. Every one of the dozens of books she'd read on child care in the past year had stressed the need for stability and security during a child's first few years.

No, she thought fiercely. It can't be wrong for a mother to want her own child. No one could love Jessie as much as she did. Or fight any harder to keep her happy and safe.

"Sophie?"

Glancing up, she saw Ford standing just outside the open door, watching her. For the first time she realized that he was by nature an observer, with the air of someone who wouldn't tolerate interference or invite intimacy.

"Miss Fanny sent me up to let you know Doc Gossely's goin' to meet us at his office."

It took a moment for his words to sink in. "Us?" she asked, staring at him.

He shrugged. "You need transportation. My car's still outside, remember?"

Sophie fought down a quick flutter of panic. Somehow she'd kept her nerves under control, even when he'd turned those thoughtful gray eyes her way. But now, with Jessie's frantic cries pounding in her head, she knew she was close to snapping.

"Thank you, but I've imposed enough. Besides, you said you had a report to write, and I don't want to take up any more of your time," she hedged.

"Why don't you let me worry about that?" The steel was back in his voice, and she realized that arguing with him would be a waste of energy.

"I'll just be a few minutes more," she said instead, reaching for a warmer outfit for the baby.

Jessie squirmed and fussed, making it difficult to hold her still and dress her at the same time. Sophie's fingers were suddenly all thumbs, and she took twice as long as she should to get the baby zipped into a one-piece sleeper.

Wells had always accused her of being too disorganized and scatterbrained to be entrusted with a baby. He'd also told her that all pregnant women were grotesquely ugly and he didn't intend to share his bed or his life with ugliness. She'd stopped listening to the words after a while, but the hurt had remained.

"All done," she assured Jessie with a bright smile that only seemed to upset her daughter even more.

"I'll take her while you get your things," Ford said, lifting Jessie into his arms.

"No!" she exclaimed before she could calm herself.

"Don't worry, I won't drop her." He tucked the baby against his shoulder with the skill of a practiced father, his big, brutal-looking hand surprisingly gentle as it made soothing circles against Jessie's tiny back.

"It's not that," Sophie explained quickly. "It's just that she's shy around strangers."

Not as shy as her mama, Ford thought, wondering about the flare of panic in Sophie's eyes. Instinct told it was more than a first-time mother's worry over her sick child. And Jessie was her child. The resemblance was obvious, especially around the mouth. Give baby Jessie a few years and she'd have a trail of lovesick, broken-hearted boys behind her, he thought with a cynical smile he kept to himself.

"You just hang in there, sugar, you hear?" he drawled. "Doc's treated a lot of sick little ones in his time. He's even patched me up a time or two."

Jessie blinked and then stopped crying as though the sound of a man's voice had startled her into a sudden silence. Still pulling at her ear, she stared into his face intently. Tentatively, she touched his mouth, and he felt his heart tumble into those tiny little hands.

"I know we haven't been formally introduced, but I know your mama so don't you be getting worried that some strange man's got his arms around you, okay, sugar?"

"Her name is Jessamine," Sophie told him with the tiniest hint of a smile surfacing briefly in her worried eyes.

"Pleased to meet you, Miss Jessamine," he drawled solemnly, giving her tiny hand a little tweak. "I'm called Ford—when folks are thinkin' kindly of me. No need to tell you what they call me when they're not."

Sophie felt tears press her throat. No matter what name he answered to, Ford Maguire wasn't nearly as cynical and hard-nosed as he wanted people to think. Under that rough, less-than-handsome exterior was a very softhearted man who'd clearly adored her daughter at first sight. In spite of the malady making her fretful, Jessie, too, seemed smitten with the dark-haired man speaking to her in a husky drawl. She couldn't ever imagine him ordering the woman who'd conceived his child to have an abortion. Or threatening to kill her and the baby if she didn't.

"Sophie, what's wrong? If you're afraid I'll drop her—"

"No, I..." She blinked back the tears and with them the horrible images in her head. Ford wasn't Wells, but neither was he Jessie's father. And he never would be. "I just wanted to tell you I'm ready to go."

Hammond Gossely was a sturdy, rotund man with pink cheeks and a tonsure of frizzled white hair. She'd been right to suspect an ear infection, he'd told Sophie after examining Jessie with all the thoroughness of any big-city clinic. Fortunately, she'd caught it at a stage where it could be easily and swiftly treated, he'd told her with a benign Santa Claus smile that only partially relieved her fears. So after he'd prescribed a liquid antibiotic and baby aspirin, he'd patiently answered Sophie's anxious questions for the next twenty minutes or so until she finally allowed herself to be reassured.

It was almost 1:00 a.m. when he escorted her from the examining room. Nestled against Sophie's shoulder, Jessie was still restless, but the sharp cries of pain were now muted to an occasional whimper.

In the neat but dated waiting room Ford was sacked out on a narrow Naugahyde sofa, his arms folded over his chest and his feet, shod in very large, very scuffed boots, propped on the arm. His jaw was shadowed by a day's growth of thick black whiskers, and his ebony hair was mussed, as though rearranged by an impatient hand. All in all he was the picture of a nineteenth-century wild-West outlaw snatching a quick nap between stage robberies. The moment they entered, he opened his eyes and sat up, instantly alert and ready to move.

"Everything under control?" he asked, his voice graveled from sleep.

Sophie nodded. Even though she knew the concern he'd showed her was strictly impersonal and prompted by his strong sense of duty, there was something reliable and solid about his calm eyes and resolute mouth that tempted her to walk into his arms and lay her head on his shoulder. Instinctively, she knew he wasn't the kind to welcome a woman readily or without thought, but once he'd taken her into his arms, he would risk even life itself to keep her safe.

Fighting a sharp pang of loneliness, she turned to the doctor and smiled. "Thank you again for seeing us so late."

"You are quite welcome, my dear, and I meant what I said about calling me at any hour if you feel the need."

"I will, I promise."

Sophie was suddenly close to tears. With the exception of Ransom Talley, every single soul she'd met since arriving in Clover had been unstintingly kind to her and Jessie. The contrast between the past few months here and the year that had gone before was so marked she sometimes marveled that she'd actually survived those hellish months with her sanity intact.

"Thanks, Doc," Ford said, shaking the older man's hand. "If we're done here, I'd best get these two tired ladies home."

"Give me a minute to call a couple of prescriptions into Cliff Phelps before you head out," the doctor said before disappearing into his office. Finding herself suddenly alone with Ford, Sophie felt her heart start to race.

"She looks better already," he said, smoothing Jessie's soft curls with a long forefinger. There was an awkward gentleness about him that drew Sophie in, even as she fought to maintain an emotional distance.

"The doctor said ear infections are common in babies this time of year and not to worry." Even as she repeated Dr. Gossely's words, she knew that she would be awake and watchful for the remaining hours of the night.

His lived-in gray eyes crinkled, adding unexpected charm to his dark bandit's face. "Easy to say, hard to do, I reckon."

"You reckon right, Sheriff," she murmured, wanting desperately to be back in her tower room, just Jessie and her.

"Hmm, Miss Sophie, you wouldn't be making fun of this ole boy's accent, now would you?"

"Oh, no," she exclaimed with genuine dismay. Dangerous as he was to her peace of mind, he had been there for her when she needed a friend. Certainly he deserved more than a polite thank-you, though she wasn't quite sure what, exactly. "To tell you the truth, I'm not sure I'm even making sense."

"Tired?"

"I passed that hours ago," she admitted before shifting the drowsing baby from one shoulder to the next. Lashes fluttering, Jessie whimpered a protest around her soggy thumb before letting those feathery little lashes close again.

Guilt-ridden in spite of the doctor's soothing words, Sophie dropped a kiss on the hot little forehead and tried not to think about the advantages her wealthy in-laws could have provided for their only grandchild. A child needed more than money to make her feel cherished, she reminded herself yet one more time.

"It's not your fault, you know." For an instant she was certain she'd spoken her thoughts aloud, and panic rushed her veins. It made little difference to tell herself to calm down. The longer she was with Ford, the more she was risking. She'd always known that he was dangerous. Now she added perceptiveness to a lengthening list of reasons to avoid him at all costs from now on.

Sensing movement behind her, she whirled, only to find that the doctor had returned and was now regarding her with concern in his eyes.

"Cliff will meet you down to the drugstore," he said to Ford instead of her. "Promised he wouldn't charge extra for openin' special, but you might have to prod him a tad to remember that."

Ford nodded. "He knows what to give us?"

"He does, and make sure he includes the extrastrength vitamins for Mrs. Reynolds."

"Really, that's not necessary," Sophie said quickly, thinking of the twenty-eight dollars and forty-two cents left in her checking account.

"I think it is, my dear," the doctor said gently, his smile kind but firm. "You're far too pale and, I suspect, underweight, as well. It wouldn't do either of you any good if you collapsed from exhaustion."

Sophie straightened her aching back. "I'm stronger than I look," she assured the fatherly physician, and then fervently hoped that she was.

"So long, Doc," Ford said, holding the screen door open for her.

" 'Night, Ford, Mrs. Reynolds."

"Good night, Doctor, and thanks again," Sophie murmured, moving past Ford without looking at him. Outside, the air had grown colder. Shivering in her light jacket, she drew Jessie's hood over her head and pressed her close.

Doc's house had a wide wraparound porch like the others on the tree-lined street. Unlike those, however, it had a wheelchair ramp sloping to the sidewalk as well as steps and a wide driveway leading to the rear parking lot. Someone had strung Christmas lights along the eaves, and across the street Santa and his reindeers were outlined in red lights on the lawn.

Sophie drew a breath, drawing in the familiar scent of burning logs. From the time she'd been a small child, she'd loved the smells and flavors of Christmas. Last year it had come and gone without her taking much notice.

"Must be nice to have a little one this time of year." Ford offered an easy smile as he slipped the heavy diaper bag from her shoulder and slung it over his own.

"It is," Sophie admitted, thinking briefly about the room full of stuffed animals and toys in the nursery Wells's mother had had professionally decorated in their riverfront mansion in Portland. As far as she knew, everything was still there, waiting.

"From the things Miss Fanny and Miss Rose Ruth keep saying, I'm not sure Santa will be able to find room under the tree."

"I imagine he'll work it out,"

Casually, as though he'd known her for years, he dropped his free arm over her shoulder and led her slowly down the ramp. Sophie stiffened and would have drawn away, but the look he gave her was anything but suggestive. Besides, it felt so good to feel the warmth of a human touch after so many months of shutting herself off from everyone but Jessie.

"Now you take my sister, Lucy, she just loves the holidays," he drawled as he opened the passenger door to the black-and-white squad car. "It's a wonder that big old house of hers doesn't crumble under the weight of all those lights she strings on just about anything that can't move out of her way. No matter how many times I tell her she's goin' too far, she just gives me one of those looks of hers and keeps on doing things her way."

Before Sophie knew how he'd done it, he had buckled her and Jessie into the seat and had gone around to climb in behind the wheel. Sophie was too tired to do more than hug Jessie close as he started the car and made a deft U-turn.

"Your sister sounds like my mother," she murmured, knowing he wasn't really interested, but needing a distraction from the confusion in her head. "As soon as Halloween was over, she was hauling the ornaments down from the attic and sorting through her cookie recipes."

"Imagine you generally had yourselves a white Christmas where you grew up."

Sophie started to shake her head, then remembered that she was supposed to be from Montana. "I've always loved winter." That at least was true.

"Were you raised on a ranch?"

"No, in town," she murmured, feeling a hard little ball of nerves forming in her stomach.

"Ever think of goin' home for the holidays?"

"There's no home left to go to. My father died while I was away at college, and my mother died last May." She remembered the suffering in her mother's eyes the last time they'd talked.

The pain of that memory was no longer razored, but still sharp enough to cut through the pitifully thin walls she'd tried to shelter behind since Wells's death.

"Sounds rough." His tone was burred with understanding and she thought about the things she'd learned from Katie about the way he'd lost his parents.

"It was," she murmured, cuddling Jessie closer. "Jessie was named for her."

"Did she get a chance to see her grandbaby born?"

Sophie drew a ragged breath. "No. She died six weeks before I delivered. An aneurysm." If she had lived, things might have been different.

Suddenly exhausted and lulled by the warmth of the car's heater and the hum of its powerful engine, she closed her eyes and let herself drift. It felt good to blank her mind and relax her body, if only for the few minutes it would take Ford to drive them home.

Home. Hearing the word echo in her mind gave her a bitter-sweet feeling of loss mingled with sadness. She drew in a lung full of damp Southern air and wondered if she would ever really be able to provide a real home for herself and Jessie instead of a corner room in someone else's house.

It didn't have to be fancy—a few rooms would do just fine, as long as those rooms came with big squishy chairs that invited cuddling and windowsills wide enough for pots of flowers and herbs. In the best of the dreams she'd conjured up during the darkest of many dark nights, the windows would have a view of water, maybe not a river as majestic as the Columbia but a stream would do nicely. Or even a pond where she and Jessie could keep a family of ducks, and maybe some fish.

She'd always loved to fish, especially for the glorious king salmon. Jessie would want to throw them back, just as she had, and together they would watch the imperious king flick his tail at the pure joy of freedom before plunging into the swirling water.

Her father, bless his heart, had never quite understood how he, an avid fisherman, could have produced a daughter who loved releasing a prize catch more than she relished keeping it. He would have adored Jessie, she thought, and Jessie would have adored him.

It struck her suddenly that Ford was a great deal like her father—not in looks, of course, since Sven Gundersen had been blond with blunt Nordic features—but like him in the quiet, steadfast way Sven had stood behind those he loved. She didn't know Ford well, nor could she let herself know him better than she did at this moment, but she knew with absolute certainty that he gave far more than he received.

"Are you warm enough?"

"Mmm?"

Watching her lips curve drowsily had Ford kicking himself for disturbing her. Feeling the familiar rush of desire low in his gut had him grinding his teeth and resigning himself to a cold shower when he finally called it a night.

"I can turn up the heat if you're cold," he said when she opened her eyes and looked at him like a very sleepy, grown-up version of the baby sleeping in her lap.

"No, I'm fine," she murmured, licking her lips and trying hard to focus. Her hair had gotten mussed in the hurried trip and fluffed around her face, its dark sheen contrasting markedly with the pallor of her skin. In the shadowed light, her eyes seemed more purple than blue, her lashes sweeping up and down with the lazy concentration of someone not yet fully awake. He had a hunch she would look just like this when she woke in the morning—or when she'd just made love. Both images had his hands tightening around the wheel and his mouth firming into a hard line.

He was too old and too experienced to waste time mooning over a woman he scarcely knew. A woman he was certain was dead wrong for him. He liked long-legged blondes, and he liked being a bachelor. Just because he found his mind running along different lines now and then didn't change the fact that Sophie was a mama first, and a woman second. Not once in twenty-some years of dating had he ever found himself more than fleetingly attracted to a woman with children. It was too hard on kids when a relationship ended.

Lucy had been a mature-for-her-age nine when they'd lost their parents, and he could still remember the nights he'd held her while she'd sobbed out her grief. He'd been helpless to do more than utter words of comfort neither of them believed.

No, he would never risk letting a child become attached to him. But every time he looked at Sophie, he felt like scooping her into his arms and riding off into the sunset like the matinee cowboys he used to watch on the old black-and-white TV he'd found in the dump and fixed up from parts scrounged from Amos Lincoln's repair shop.

Hell of it was, while he wanted to make love to her, he also wanted to hold her in his arms and tell her things he'd never in his life told another living soul. Like the soft feeling he got inside when he watched a doe lovingly nudge her still-wet fawn to its wobbly little feet, then lick it dry, or the longing that sometimes came over him to feel a woman's arms welcoming him back to the warmth of their bed after a long terrible night at the scene of a bloody accident.

It wasn't love he was feeling. He knew himself well enough to accept that he wasn't remotely capable of caring that deeply about anyone but his sister. But he was honest enough to admit it was more than mere sexual attraction, and that's what had him riled up whenever he thought about getting to know her better.

It was the same helpless, infuriating feeling his friend Mike Flint had described once after a few beers when they'd been talking about women and the things they could do to a man's peace of mind without really trying too hard. And look at old Mike now— about to take that long, fateful trip down the center aisle of the Community Church over on Jackson Street.

Ford didn't begrudge Mike his happiness with Emma. She was a real nice lady, and even he had to admit she lighted up like sunshine whenever Mike was around. As for Mike, he was almost stupid with joy these days. He'd damn near bawled the day he'd asked Ford to be his best man.

What the hell, Ford thought, turning onto the street leading to Phelps's Pharmacy, maybe Emma and Mike would be the first to beat the odds and actually end up happy together for more than a few sex-crazed years. As for him, he'd pretty much figured out the way things worked in the real world.

Sex was the most honest exchange between a man and woman. Every woman had a price for her favors, and the honest ones let the man know what it would cost him right up front. The starry-eyed romantics like his sister wanted a man to recite certain words before she let him into her bed, and the more practical ones like Emma Wynn demanded the security of a double-ring ceremony and all the nonsense that went with it, like showers and bachelor parties.

And then there were women like his own mother who used her beauty and her sexy body to steal a strong, decent man's heart and then take great delight in slowly ripping it to shreds. When his old man had found out she'd been sleeping with half the adult males in Clover, he'd snapped. Ford didn't intend to end up the same way.

He parked in front of the narrow brick building that had been in the Phelps family since reconstruction and killed the engine. Light blazed around the posters and notices taped to the front window, illuminating the sidewalk in a crazy quilt pattern.

"Wait here," he ordered, giving Sophie a glance that had her mouth tightening. "I'll be right back."

"You'll need money," she said, reaching for her purse with one hand while trying not to jar the baby into waking.

"We'll settle later," he said before getting out and leaving the door ajar.

Haphazardly dressed in running clothes and bedroom slippers and looking surprised to see Ford standing there, Cliff admitted him almost immediately.

"Doc didn't tell me you'd be bringing the lady by," he said over his shoulder as he led the way to the prescription counter in the back.

"I happened to be at Katie's when the baby got sick."

"On business or purely pleasure?" Cliff asked with a suggestive grin as he slipped behind the counter.

Ford ground his teeth and thought longingly of the anonymity of a big city where no one cared about your family tree or your private business. He'd always wanted to travel. Maybe someday he would.

"Rans Talley took a notion to clean out the cash register at the diner and Ms. Reynolds did her best to disabuse him of that same notion," Ford told Cliff.

"Sounds like ole Rans was dippin' into the jug again."

"Frenchy Ducette's finest, I hear."

Cliff chuckled as he typed out a label on an old manual typewriter. The rest of the staff used the computer Cliff had been talked into buying last year, but Ford had heard it said that Cliff himself had sworn never to touch the blasted thing.

"Sure would have liked to see that little bitty Yankee girl givin' ole Rans what for," Cliff declared, still chuckling. "Must have been a sight."

"It was a sight all right," Ford said, shoving his hands in his pockets. He doubted that Sophie realized just how close she'd come to serious injury, but he did. And it gave him a sick feeling in his belly to think about what he might have found if he'd shown up a few minutes later than he had.

"Understand she's a widow," Cliff commented, glancing at Ford over the top of his half glasses. "Must have been hard on her, bein' left with a baby like she was."

"Guess so."

"She's a hard worker, I'll say that for her. Peg was sayin' just the other day how she'd have to give her a raise so's she wouldn't lose her to the five-and-dime or that fast-food place out on the state highway."

Cliff pasted the label on the bottle of pink liquid, then dropped the bottle into a small white paper bag before repeating the process one more time with a vial of yellow pills while Ford prowled the aisles, too restless to stand and wait. At the same time he made sure he kept the squad car in sight.

"You fixin' to buy yourself some protection, Ford?"

Ford was annoyed to discover he'd stopped in front of a large array of condoms. "No need," he said, heat climbing his neck. He wasn't a prude, and he'd never pretended to live a celibate life. He just preferred to take his pleasure in private.

"Yessir, that sure is one sweet-looking little Yankee girl," Cliff commented solemnly, his mouth twitching ever so slightly. "Make some man a fine wife, according to Miss Fanny and Miss Rose Ruth."

"Provided a man was lookin' to get himself a wife," Ford muttered, reining in his temper with more difficulty than usual.

"There is that," Cliff agreed. " 'Course, a man pushing forty hasn't got that many good years left to him if he's fixin' to be a daddy."

Ford scowled, far too aware that Cliff Phelps and Morgan Maguire had played football for Clover High School together. His father hadn't hung on to many friends during his later years, but he'd made fewer caustic remarks about Cliff than most. Because of that, he owed Cliff a certain respect, but that didn't mean he had to listen to nonsense in the middle of the night.

"How much do I owe you?" he asked, hauling out his wallet.

"Forty-seven fifty, including the vitamins Doc prescribed."

Ford slapped down a fifty, then waited impatiently while Cliff made change. "You paying the lady's bills these days, Ford?" he asked before counting it into Ford's hand.

"You know better than that, and I'd appreciate it if you didn't tell folks I was."

Pocketing the change, Ford grabbed what he'd come for and headed for the door. By tomorrow noon it would be all over Clover that Ford Maguire was bird-doggin' the new waitress at Peg's. He could almost hear the telephone wires buzzing already. By supper time, half the ladies in town would be planning the wedding while the other half would be wondering how best to warn Sophie off from getting involved with a man carrying his kind of history.

It wasn't as if they hadn't had enough practice at doin' both. The ladies of Clover over a certain age had been trying to marry him off since the day he'd become solely responsible for his sister. He'd offended more than his share of matchmaking ladies, and he was sorry about that, but his temper tended to shorten when folks messed with his private life.

After a lot of years of failure, though, even the most persistent had pretty much given him up as a lost cause, for which he'd been enormously grateful. Now the talk was bound to start again, stirring up the ugly gossip. Setting his jaw, he climbed into the car and dropped the bag between them.

Sophie was resting her head against the seat, her features relaxed and vulnerable, her arms cradling her baby protectively against her breast. The instant he closed the door, however, her eyes snapped open again, and she forced life into her face.

"How much do I owe you?" she asked, her Northern accent muted by weariness.

"The receipt's in the bag," he said, firing the engine to life and backing up in one motion.

He said nothing more as he navigated the dark streets, his face set in hard lines. What had the druggist said to him? Sophie wondered anxiously. Something about her? About something he'd heard or suspected?

Every day since she'd left Oregon, she'd been on guard, searching the eyes of strangers for a startled look of recognition or a shadow of suspicion. Clover was a long way from Portland, and she'd covered her tracks well. But she could never allow herself to think that time and distance would keep her safe.

Even though she knew she was behaving irrationally, she was nearly frantic by the time Ford pulled into the narrow driveway next to the boarding house. Without so much as a glance in her direction, he opened the door and climbed out, circling behind the car to open the passenger's door. Lights blazed from the downstairs windows, illuminating the scowl on his face.

"I *did* offer to take a cab, if you'll recall," she muttered, speaking in a low voice so that that she didn't wake the baby.

"What does that mean?" he demanded, his tone polite, but his scowl deepened.

"Never mind," she said, climbing out.

"Go on up to the house," he ordered. "I'll bring the rest of your things."

Biting her tongue to keep from telling him not to bother if it was so darn much trouble, she headed up the walk toward the deep front porch. As soon as she set foot on the bottom step, the door opened to reveal her two elderly friends, still in their night attire.

"We just spoke with Hammond, and he told us about that nasty old ear infection," Miss Fanny exclaimed, clearly worried. Her thinning white hair was confined into a long braid that hung over one shoulder, and her eyes were shadowed with weariness.

"No wonder our little angel was fussin' so," Miss Rose Ruth added, stepping back so that Sophie could enter. "I was just fixin' to make us all some hot milk. I'll bring it up when it's ready."

"Please don't bother making any for me," Sophie said with a tired smile. "I'm going to give Jessie her medicine and put us both to bed."

"Nonsense, child. Hot milk is just the thing to ward off a chill this time of year." Without giving Sophie a chance to answer, she turned and headed for the back of the house.

"I'd best help Rose Ruth with that milk, or she's liable to burn down the house," Miss Fanny proclaimed as she ushered Ford in and closed the door.

"While you're at it, splash some brandy in that milk, and I'll have a cup, too," he drawled, glancing toward the stairs.

Miss Fanny managed to look flustered and offended at the same time. "Now, Ford Maguire, you know Katie does not allow spirits in her house."

Sophie caught the quick flash of amusement in his eyes before he shifted his gaze from her face to Miss Fanny's. "Yes, ma'am, that's true," he said gravely. "But I also remember you once telling me that spirits used as medicine weren't in the least sinful, or did I misunderstand you?"

A delicate pink bloomed in Miss Fanny's cheeks, reminding Sophie of faded rose petals. "Don't get sassy with me, young man. I used to wipe your bottom when you weren't any bigger than that sweet little angel in her mama's arms, and you'd do well not to forget that, you hear?"

"Yes, ma'am," he said, his grin flashing even as he ducked his head like a chastised little boy.

Sophie wasn't fooled. There was a man's strength in that tired, not-quite-handsome face, and a lifetime of experience in those cynical gray eyes. She'd learned tonight that he also had a stubborn streak bordering on a form of masculine dominance that unsettled her—just one more reason to avoid him.

Avoiding him was one thing, ordering her body to ignore the purely male signals of sexual interest he kept sending out was something else again, she discovered, listening to the thud of his boot heels as he followed her up the stairs. He smelled like soap and the night air, and his rangy body moved with a restrained, sensual grace that had her imagination spiking and her blood heating whenever he walked into Peg's.

Her room was the only one on the right and looked out over the street. "Looks like you're already thinkin' like a Southerner," Ford said when she simply turned the knob and pushed open the door.

"Sorry?" she murmured, drawing her brows together.

"Folks around here are so used to leaving their doors wide open in the summer months it's hard to remember to lock 'em when it turns chilly." He offered an easy smile that erased much of the cynicism from his face. But not all—nor the subtle hint of loneliness around his mouth. "I keep raggin' at 'em to take more precautions but some habits are hard to break."

"It's easier for the ladies when they're baby-sitting if I leave it open."

The clown lamp was still burning, and the room was just as she'd left it, with the exception of Jessie's blanket, which had been folded neatly at the bottom of the crib.

"Where do you want this?" Ford asked, indicating the diaper bag. The anger she'd sensed in him when he'd stalked out of Phelps's Pharmacy had disappeared. Or perhaps he'd simply willed it not to show, something she suspected he did often and very well.

"On the dresser, please," she murmured, laying Jessie on her back in her crib. The baby fluttered her lashes and whimpered, but she didn't wake, even when Sophie stripped off the furry pink jacket. Sensing his presence, she glanced up quickly to find him standing behind her right shoulder, watching the baby with anxious eyes.

"Cliff said to be sure and get her to drink as much water as possible while she's taking the antibiotic," he said when he realized she had looked his way.

"I could have sworn she was perfectly fine when I went to work," she murmured. "Otherwise, I never would have left her."

"Seems to me my sister had an ear infection when she was just about Jessie's age. Doc pulled her through just fine."

It would be easy, she realized, to get used to the way his eyes warmed when he spoke of his sister. Too easy.

"In other words, give her the medicine and stop acting like an hysterical mother," she murmured, reaching for the pharmacy sack he'd set next to the diaper bag.

"You're not hysterical, far from it. And you'd be a sorry excuse for a mama if you weren't worried."

"I can't help worrying," she admitted before reading the instructions on the small pink bottle.

What if it had been something worse? she thought on a wave of pure panic. What if Jessie had had to be hospitalized? Or required surgery? She couldn't even afford a few bottles of medicine, let alone expensive treatment.

"Oh, *hell!*" she murmured, turning away before he could see the tears already filling her eyes.

"Hey, none of that," he said, gripping her shoulder just hard enough to turn her his way. "No reason to be embarrassed for cryin', not after the night you've had." He brushed a knuckle over her cheek and it took all of her strength to keep from turning toward that gentle touch.

"If something happened to Jessie—" Her voice broke, and she clamped down hard on her lower lip with her teeth.

"It won't, Mama. Not with you on the job." He rubbed his callused palms over her shoulders in a gentle friction more soothing than erotic. It felt good, just to be touched again, even though she'd made herself so numb, she wasn't sure how long she'd be able to accept even the gentlest of human contact.

"Sometimes raisin' a youngster all on your own can get mighty lonely, though, especially when there's no one around to lean on now and then."

"Who did you lean on?" she asked, seeing shadows darkening his eyes.

"Southern men aren't real big on askin' for help."

Stunned by the tension in the small, rigid shoulders, Ford concentrated on lightly massaging the tight muscles of her neck with only his fingertips at first, and then as she accepted his touch, more intensely.

"Northern women sometimes have trouble, too," she murmured, swaying under his ministrations like a half-hypnotized, but still touch-wary, barn kitten.

"Relax," he urged, careful to keep his voice low and easy. "You're carryin' a lot of weight on these little bitty shoulders."

"Not so little," she said, her lashes fluttering.

Ignoring the heat that was slowly but surely pooling between his legs, he massaged her shoulders with slow, even movements, until he saw the knot between her silky eyebrows ease and her lips part in a half smile of pure pleasure.

It moved in him to kiss her then. Just thinking about rubbing his mouth over that sulky curve had tension skating along his shoulders before settling in the hollow between his shoulder blades. In her relaxed state she was more receptive than she might ever be again. Only a few inches separated his mouth from hers—and a sense of honor he couldn't quite make himself violate, though he was sorely tempted. Too tempted. Abruptly, he withdrew his hands before he forgot the oath he'd taken to protect victims, not take advantage of them for his own selfish reasons.

"Better now?" he asked, his voice hoarser than usual.

"I didn't mean to unload on you," she murmured, lifting her lashes with obvious difficulty as though she were only now coming back into her body.

"Feel free to do it again anytime." Watching a smile crinkle the corners of those ever-watchful eyes gave Sophie a fast little jolt, and she realized that, just for a moment, she had thought of him as a man instead of the sheriff of Clover. A man who was solid and reliable and, in his own reserved way, disturbingly sexy.

He would be a thoughtful lover, she was sure of it. And he would have a beautiful body, with long roped muscles and lean, agile hips. She saw herself lying next to him, her hands running over his tanned skin, feeling the veins throbbing beneath the surface, trapped between pliant skin and hard muscle. And she saw him touching her, his callused hands gently kneading her breasts instead of her shoulders, his fingertips caressing the aching nipples, then slowly trailing lower to her belly, her thighs, lower. Needs she had successfully quashed for a very long time suddenly surged to life again, stronger than ever. Mortified, she felt heat rush to her face and quickly lowered her gaze to the bottle in her hand.

"Uh, before you go, I need to give you a check," she said, setting the medicine on the dresser before reaching into the bag for the receipt. As soon as she saw the amount, her heart sank. "I can give you half tonight and the rest on Friday when I get paid. Maybe earlier, if my tips are good."

"Be easier if you just waited till Friday."

Sophie stiffened her spine. "Not for me."

Frowning, he waited while she wrote him a check for exactly half the amount. "I want your word you'll cash this tomorrow."

The subtle shift in his expression told her he'd intended to do just the opposite. "I knew my sister was kin to a mule, but I believe you've got her beat," he muttered, drawing his eyebrows together in an impressive frown.

"If you're suggesting I'm stubborn, you're right," she admitted, walking him to the door. If she hadn't been stubborn, she most likely would be dead by now.

Ford glanced back at the pretty white crib with a bunch of wild-looking parrots swinging from some kind of contraption hanging above it. Across the room, Sophie's bed was still neatly made, big enough for two. He didn't belong here. He didn't even want to be here, so why was he all of a sudden wanting to stay?

Dumb question, Maguire, he thought, jerking his gaze back to Sophie's face. He wanted to stay because he was a man and she was a woman, and somehow she just naturally had the knack of making him remember that every time she turned those bluer-than-blue eyes his way.

"You get some sleep, you hear?" He jerked open the door and left before he forgot how tired she really was.

Chapter 4

It was just past eight when Ford pulled into the driveway of Katie's house. He'd finished typing out his report at half past three the night before and taken it home with him, intending to show it to Sophie over his morning coffee. But Peg had been behind the counter when he'd walked into the diner at his usual time. Sophie had taken the day off in order to take care of Jessie.

Never one to mince words, Peg had lit into him but good for not locking up Rans Talley before he could cause trouble, then proceeded to give him a double order of bacon on the house for shoving his shoulder into Talley's gut in the nick of time.

He'd let Peg talk herself out, then spent the time it had taken to wolf down his breakfast trying to convince himself he wasn't in a black mood because Sophie wasn't there to refill his cup or chide Bram Washington for ordering eggs again.

Exiting the squad car, he scowled again, just thinking about the way a woman could mess with a man's mind—if he wasn't the careful type, that is.

Katie answered his knock at the back door, her smile quick as always. "What brings you around so early?"

Ford held up the manila folder. "Wanted to get Sophie's signature on this statement I typed up from my notes before I made it official."

"She's upstairs changing the baby," she said before once again expressing her opinion of Rans Talley's character.

"How's the little one feeling this mornin'?" Ford asked, grinning at Katie's less than genteel choice of words.

"Almost as sweet as usual. Sophie's the one who needs lookin' after. I don't think she got a wink of sleep all night, what with givin' Jessie her medicine every four hours and walkin' the floor with her when she fussed."

Ford frowned. "Guess it was a good thing she took the day off."

Katie sneaked a quick glance over her shoulder. "I've never seen a woman more upset than Sophie when she called Aunt Peg to ask for the time off. I swear she was shaking like a leaf. Told me afterward she didn't know what she would have done if Aunt Peg had fired her." She shook her head. "She offered to make up the time by working double shifts when Jessie was well again."

"Did Peg take her up on her offer?"

"Come to think of it, Sophie didn't say exactly. What I do know, though, is that she's very relieved to still have a job. It's got to be hard on her, supporting herself and Jessie on waitressin' pay like she does." Katie sighed, then glanced at her watch. "Go on up if you want. As soon as I finish the breakfast dishes, I'm meeting Emma at her place and we're drivin' over to Charleston to look for bridesmaid dresses."

"Sounds like fun."

"Ford Maguire, you lie like a rug!" Setting her hands on her hips, she eyed him disapprovingly. "I don't suppose you've given any thought to the bachelor party you're supposed to be having for Mike next month, have you?"

"Some." Actually he'd been trying to figure a way around having it at all without making Mike mad as sin at him.

"Like what, exactly?" she demanded, going back to stacking the dishes in the dishwasher.

"Like figurin' I'd pay the bills and let you women do the plannin'."

Katie snorted. "That's exactly what Lucy and Emma and I thought you'd say."

"What's wrong with that?"

She put the last of the plates in the bottom of the washer and closed the door. "It's lazy, that's what."

"Lazy, hell, it's pure self-defense," he muttered, wondering if Sophie had been in on the discussion of his shortcomings. "I know my sister, and I know you. Doesn't matter what I decide to do, one or the both of you will just change it, so why not cut to the chase and save myself the aggravation."

Katie punched a button, and the dishwasher groaned into action. "If you had your way, you'd serve that horrible Texas chili you're so fond of and beer with whiskey chasers, and half the men in the wedding party would be sick as dogs during the ceremony."

"A blatant exaggeration," he declared, more than a little annoyed that she was close to being dead right. He'd figured on topping off the chili with some of that new peanut-butter chocolate ripple ice cream from the convenience store.

"Take my advice, and hire yourself a caterer. I hear there's a new one just opened for business." Grabbing her purse, she shot him another disgusted look before heading for the door. "I have a hunch she's going to be very busy, what with the wedding and all, so you'd better book her quick."

"What new caterer?" He didn't like the glint in Katie's eyes. She was up to something, and he had a hunch he wasn't going to like it.

Katie pulled open the back door. "Her name is Sophie Reynolds. Everyone I know is tired of Miss Clara Barnwell's pimento cheese loaf on soggy white bread, and Sophie has some really clever ideas. If you're very nice to me, I might just put in a good word for you."

He figured he must have some dumb look on his face because Katie was giggling as if she was fifteen again and tickled at the success of a joke she'd just played on her best friend's gullible big brother. Ford muttered his favorite curse word, the one he only used when he was alone or in exclusively male company, before heading toward the stairs. If he'd had any sense, he would have planned to take a good long vacation right around the time Mike and Emma were walking down the aisle.

The third floor seemed deserted. Only the door to the bathroom stood ajar. The other three were firmly shut, and he wondered if all three ladies living on the top floor were catching up on their sleep. Correction, four ladies, he thought, remembering tiny Jessie snuggling against her mama's soft, warm body when he'd driven them home. He suspected that was a picture he would carry with him for a long time.

He had to knock two more times before Sophie opened the door, her eyes still drowsy from leftover sleep, and her skin dewy from the warmth of her pillow. She was dressed in a pale yellow running suit at least two sizes too big, and her feet were bare.

Ford's mind made a fast trip into a life where morning kisses were slow and lazy and got a man's day started off right. How long had it been since she'd awakened in a man's arms? he wondered, and then knew that sooner or later he was going to feel that small, ripe body snuggled up next to his. And when that happened, he would make darn sure there weren't any baggy sweats to come between his flesh and hers.

"Sheriff. I meant to call you." She blinked, but her eyes were still dream dark. "Last night you mentioned something about needing my signature?"

"On your statement," he amplified. She smelled like soap and baby powder, and her hair swooped over one pale cheek, just begging for a man's hand to smooth it back.

"Would you mind if we talked downstairs?" she murmured, glancing over her shoulder at the sleeping baby. "She just dropped off to sleep a few minutes ago."

"How's she feelin'?" he asked as he took a step backward to allow her to exit.

"Much better, thank you," she said, closing the door behind her. "She's been taking her medicine like a good little girl."

"How about her mama? Has she been taking her vitamins like a good girl, too?"

"If you mean those horse pills the doctor prescribed, yes, when I can force them down my throat."

"I noticed they were on the large size."

Sophie heard a low throb of amusement in his tone and shot him a quick look. Sunlight flooded the upper floor through a large window fronting the stairwell, and the bright light was anything but kind to his windburned face. And yet, when he cocked his head and crinkled his eyes in her direction, she thought of sex, the tempestuous kind that made a woman's heart pound and her throat go dry. Turning abruptly, she headed for the stairs.

He is not your friend, she warned herself firmly, concentrating on each step. He's the enemy, remember that. It doesn't matter how nice he seems or how fast he makes your heart beat or how slippery you feel inside when he looks at you. He wears a badge on that wide, deep chest that looks so sexy in a uniform, and he's very good at his job.

The parlor was empty, but someone had turned on the Christmas tree lights, and they twinkled like brilliant chips of sunlit glass. One of the delicate glass balls that Katie had unwrapped from its nest of tissue paper so carefully only a week before had fallen to the carpet, and Sophie hastened to return it to an uppermost branch of the huge Douglas fir for safekeeping.

The branch was still supple, the needles crisp and smelling of winter snow and clean mountain air, even if the tree itself was sitting in a sprawling old-fashioned dowager of a house only twenty miles or so from the Atlantic Ocean. She found herself smiling at the thought of waking up Christmas morning to sunshine and balmy air instead of gray skies and rain. She turned around to find that Ford was watching her.

"It's a nice tree, don't you think?"

"Very nice." His drawl was whiskey and smoke, but it was the sudden heat in his eyes that had her thinking of a man's hot mouth skimming her breasts and a man's hard thigh nudging hers apart.

Even as she moved to the nearest chair and sat down, a sensuous heat was spreading inside her skin, pooling in warm secret places to taunt her.

"Guess you know the word's already out about the run-in you and I had with Rans last night," he said as he took the chair opposite and opened the folder.

"No, actually I didn't. I haven't been out of the house."

"Don't worry, sooner or later word will get back to you. Probably won't even sound remotely like what really happened. Before some of the gossips in this town get done, you'll probably end up being to blame for the whole thing."

Is that what happened when his parents died? she wondered. Speculation and innuendo taking the place of truth? She knew all too well how easily the truth can become distorted into a grotesque lie.

"I guess that's one of the bad things about living in a small town."

"Among others."

Ford selected a single typewritten page and handed it to her. "If you come across any inaccuracies, you can make your corrections in the margin," he said, offering her the pen he'd unclipped from his shirt pocket. Taking it, she discovered that it was still warm from the heat of his body.

Bending her head, she began to read. After only the first few lines, she found herself admiring the terse, unemotional style of a skilled observer. He'd organized her words into a cogent, accurate description that carried none of the terror she'd felt at the time, yet managed to convey Talley's underlying ruthlessness and intent to hurt her to get what he wanted. Remembering his filthy fingers clawing at her shoulder, she shivered in spite of her warm clothing.

"Something wrong?"

Glancing up, she found Ford studying her again, this time with a frown on those hard lips. "I was just thinking about what happened." Instinctively, she lifted a hand to rub the still-sore flesh his fingers had bruised so easily.

His eyes went still, and she found herself tensing. She'd known bigger men. Men with more money, and men with more charm. But she'd never met one who exuded such quiet, unassuming authority. She knew suddenly that he was a small-town sheriff because that's what he'd chosen for himself, not because it was all that was available to him.

"He won't hurt you again," he said quietly. "You have my word."

Even though she believed that unequivocally, there was no need to say so. Ford wasn't looking for praise for simply doing his job. In fact, she suspected it would offend him.

"What about the man who sells the moonshine? Do you have any idea where he's, um, doing business?"

He shifted, stretching out his long legs as though suddenly restless. "My guess would be Deadman's Slough. The vegetation's thick as any jungle in there, and Frenchy knows every hill and hollow. It would take an army to find him, and even then, a search would make so much noise he and his still would be long gone."

Ford watched her absorb his words silently, her eyes growing larger as she reflected on them for a moment before returning to the report he'd given her. And then he watched the morning sunlight shimmering over her hair and imagined her small, lush body straining against his, skin against skin, lubricated by the sweat of a passion neither of them could control.

"No changes, no addition?" he asked when she returned his pen and the report.

"Not a one," she said, rising.

"That's a first." He tucked the pen into his pocket and reached down for the folder. After giving her signature a cursory glance, he returned the statement to the folder and stood.

"Sure there's nothing that needs changing?"

"You covered everything I told you without adding anything I didn't," she said, lifting her gaze to his.

"Did you think I would?" Though his tone was mild, his eyes were suddenly alert and trained intently on her face. It was as though he were probing her thoughts, her soul, searching for a flaw in her story or a secret evil in her heart. Even though she knew she was reacting more to the past than the present, her stomach roiled, and it took all her willpower to curve her lips into a casual smile.

"Actually I was trying to pay you a compliment, but somehow it came out sounding like I was critiquing a research paper. I guess it's just habit. Sorry," she said.

He regarded her in silence for a moment before his mouth relaxed into another of his almost smiles. "I have to tell you, Sophie, you sure don't look like any of the English teachers I had when I was sweatin' through high school."

She drew a quick breath, and tried to calm her suddenly galloping heartbeat. "Oh, but I told you I'm not a teacher," she insisted, trying hard to sound truthful without overdoing it. "I'm a waitress."

"A waitress who knows Voltaire from Virgil and can discuss the fine points of Shakespeare's more obscure plays with Camilla Martin over eggs and grits and hold her own just fine."

Sophie felt her jaw drop. "How do you know what I discuss with Mrs. Martin?"

He shrugged, drawing her attention to the breadth of those muscular shoulders. "I listened."

"Guess I'd better not spill any secrets around you," she said lightly.

"Depends on the secrets."

Careful, she warned herself silently. Whatever you do, don't overreact. "I'm not sure I have any, but if I do, they're bound to be pretty boring."

"Now that *is* a shame," Ford drawled, busy wondering what had put the stiffness in her shoulders all of a sudden. "'Course, what's borin' for one isn't always borin' for someone else."

"Believe me, Sheriff, I've lived a very mundane life." She paused to clear her throat of a sudden tightness. "Now you, I imagine your life has been a lot more exciting. Even Clover has its share of big-city crime and violence."

Ford had to admire the smooth way she'd managed to shift the attention away from herself. He'd seen Lucy do the same thing when she'd been busy feeling guilty about something she didn't want him to discover.

"Not so exciting," he told her with perfect candor. "For instance, I've never packed up and moved clear across the country with a baby in my arms and no job waiting for me when I got there."

Her eyes flickered, a mere whisper of movement that he noted but didn't acknowledge. "Is this an interrogation, Sheriff, because if it is, I suggest you read me my rights." She was smiling, but her voice had come out a little more rushed than usual.

"Sorry, force of habit. Cops are just naturally nosy, I reckon."

"So I've noticed."

A car pulled into the driveway. A quick look told Ford it was only Arnie Maxwell's taxi. "Miss Fanny's home from her morning at the county food bank," Sophie murmured, her gaze softening into affection. "She and Miss Rose Ruth take turns helping out."

Ford watched her lips slide into a smile and felt his blood quicken. She had a passionate mouth, and a habit of gnawing at one corner when she was nervous.

"I hope nothing's wrong," she murmured, gazing intently through the window at Arnie's prized Impala. Reluctantly, Ford shifted his attention from her mouth to the window.

"Knowing both Miss Fanny and Arnie, I suspect they're not done tradin'."

Drawing her eyebrows together, she turned to look at him. "Trading what?"

"Gossip. If there's anything interesting going on within a fifty-mile radius of the town square, Arnie will know about it before nightfall."

"Oh, I see," she murmured, her expression clearing momentarily before clouding again. "So what's Miss Fanny trading him, then?"

"Most likely, her latest remedy for a bilious belly. Arnie tends toward problems in that general area. Last I heard, he was partial to a cup of aniseed tea mornin' and night."

"Aha," she exclaimed softly, her hand stealing toward her lips as though stifling a need to laugh.

Ford drew a breath, then shifted, suddenly restless. Who would have figured the scent of plain old Ivory soap could have the power to play hell with a man's imagination? he thought, feeling desire crawling into his belly.

He wanted desperately to strip off that baggy sweatshirt and run his hands over the warm soft skin underneath, lingering over the sweet, round breasts for a very long time before tracing the tidy curve of her waist, the flare of her hips, lower. He could almost feel the slippery barrier of her panties—

"I'll be goin' now," he said a bit too abruptly. "The county prosecutor will want to interview you before the arraignment. If you have any questions before then, feel free to call." Without waiting for an answer, he tucked the folder under his arm and fled.

Sophie had long since stopped asking Ford every morning if he wanted more coffee. It had taken her a few weeks to realize that, in spite of the early start he made on the day, he wasn't by nature a morning person. He needed coffee to wake up, lots of it. When he'd had his fill, he would let her know. Until then, she made sure she passed by with the pot every few minutes while he was eating his breakfast.

"How's Jessamine?" he asked the next morning as she was re-filling his cup for the third time.

"When I left she was stuffing her mouth with banana and re-galing the ladies with this fascinating story about trees."

"Trees?" He wrapped his big hand around the brimming cup and pulled it closer.

Sophie glanced at the counter where the cook put the food when it was ready and saw no sign of the biscuits and gravy Ford had ordered. Since Ford was her only customer at the moment, she rested the pot on the counter and treated herself to a breather.

"We *think* she was talking about trees," she explained. "Although I have to admit, we're not sure. Brilliant though she is, Jess hasn't quite mastered all the intricacies of English pronunciation."

His mouth slanted, and she was struck again by the subtle strength in his face. No doubt about it, he wasn't a handsome man. His face was too angular, his mouth too hard, but when he cocked his head and crinkled those deep-set eyes into an almost smile, it didn't matter.

"How do you know she's speakin' English?"

"I guess I don't," she acknowledged, then grinned. "Come to think of it, a lot of her words do sound more like Polish than English. Or maybe German—anyway, something with a lot of syllables strung together."

"There you go, then. For all you know, she's recitin' beautiful poetry, and you're just sittin' there thinkin' it's gibberish."

"Oh, no, I never said that," she exclaimed, laughing. "I just said I couldn't understand the words. Not that they weren't wonderfully clever, because of course, they are. Not that I'm prejudiced, you understand."

" 'Course not."

"I'll have you know, Sheriff, that I am completely objective when it comes to my daughter."

"Is that right?"

"It just so happens that I've produced the world's cutest, cleverest, most beguiling child." Though her tone was light, she meant every word she said.

"A man would be a fool to argue with that, especially if he was settin' up to ask that child's mama to have supper with him tomorrow night."

Sophie felt emotion run through her. It felt like excitement. She told herself it was merely surprise. "That's very kind of you, but I don't date."

"Anyone, or just me?" When he tilted his head and looked up at her the way he was doing now, she wondered what it would feel like to see herself reflected in those steady gray eyes an instant before he kissed her. This time there was no mistaking the emotion she felt. Once experienced, the rush of sexual heat was unmistakable.

Before she could formulate an answer that wouldn't hurt either of them, the bell over the door tinkled, drawing his quick glance. The woman entering was tall, with sun-streaked blond curls cascading to her shoulders and the kind of taste in clothes and jewelry that came with old money and careful training.

Pausing just inside the door, the newcomer swept the room with a deliberate gaze, comfortable with the knowledge that she herself had become the object of all eyes. As soon as she saw Ford, she started toward him, a sexy, suggestive smile on her glossy lips.

"There you are, sugar. That cute little Vietnamese deputy down at your office told me you'd be here."

His smile came even more slowly than usual and had controlled edges. Sophie suspected that he was less than thrilled to be greeted so familiarly in public, especially when he was on duty.

"Somethin' special I can do for you this mornin', Ms. Tyrone, or are you just passin' through?" Ford asked.

"Passin' through. I'm on my way to Charleston for a weddin', but since you asked, there might just be one little old thing you can do for me better than anyone else. If you catch my drift."

Without giving Ford a chance to respond, she bent suddenly to plant a kiss full on his mouth. He froze, his eyes going glacial for an instant before turning lazy again. Shifting to one side, he dragged a folded white handkerchief from his pocket.

"Cecelia Tyrone, meet Sophie Reynolds," he drawled, before wiping the lipstick from his mouth.

"Call me Sissy," the woman said amiably.

Sophie managed a polite smile as those strikingly green eyes focused on hers. She decided that the vivid color had to be the result of tinted contact lenses, and then castigated herself for being catty.

"Can I get you a menu, *Sissy?*"

"Why sure thing, hon. And a cup of coffee with real cream, too, if it wouldn't be too much trouble."

"No trouble at all, especially for a friend of Sheriff Maguire's."

Sophie plucked a menu from the holder at the end of the counter and set it on the paper place mat as Sissy took the seat next to Ford's, managing to brush his shoulder with her breast as she slipped past him.

"Why that's right nice of you, Sophie. Thanks a bunch."

"Cut it out, Sissy," Ford ordered curtly. "You sound like you've been reading *Gone With the Wind* again."

Sissy shrugged. "What can I say? I'm just a dumb little old Southern belle?"

Ford caught Sophie's gaze. "Sissy makes her living selling real estate to rich Yankees lookin' to retire in the sunny South. Trudging around those dusty old houses down Clay City way has warped what little brain she had left after her daddy wasted half his considerable fortune on some fancy school in Switzerland."

"Now, Ford," Sissy declared petulantly, swatting his big hand. "Don't you go insultin' me. You know all you tall, dark and silent Southern boys like a little sugar with your mornin' grits." Smiling, she glanced at Sophie again and winked. "Right, Sophie?"

"Actually, Sheriff Maguire's the only tall, dark and silent Southern boy I've met so far," she said, picking up the coffeepot. "And he's issued strict orders never to serve him grits. Since he carries that big old gun with him everywhere he goes, I'm not about to argue with him."

Sissy's mouth popped open, and then she laughed. "Touché, sugar," she exclaimed easily. "As one smartass to another, I'd say you're gonna fit in right nicely down here in Dixie."

"I'm trying," Sophie said as she tipped the last of the coffee into Ford's cup, dregs and all. "I'll be right back with your coffee, Sissy. The real cream is in the kitchen."

"Take your time," Sissy said, giving Ford an arch look. "I'm in no hurry."

Sophie started to leave, but Ford stopped her by wrapping his hand around her wrist. She tried to pull away, but he exerted just enough pressure to show who was in control. His palm was warm and dry and callus-rough on the heel.

"I asked you a question a while back, remember?"

"I gave you my answer."

One side of his mouth lifted, but he let her go. "As I recall, we weren't real sure exactly what that answer meant."

She shifted her gaze to Sissy and manufactured a bright smile. "In case you're wondering, Sissy, Ford had just asked me to dinner a few minutes before you walked in. I turned him down, but he doesn't seem willing to accept my answer. Perhaps you might have better luck convincing him that he doesn't have any other choice."

Sissy's eyes darkened, then began sparkling with curiosity. "Lord almighty," she drawled, curving her glossy lips into a sexy grin that she turned on Ford like a spotlight. "So she's the one who's got your mind running hot? I figured it had to be someone like her. Sweet, and wholesome, you know? Just the opposite of your mama."

Ford's face flushed a dark red. "Be very careful what you say next, Sissy."

He sat back, his body language suggesting a man at ease and just a little amused. Sophie knew better. She'd heard the ice crystallizing his voice, and seen the cold creep into his eyes until the gray irises seemed frosted over.

Hadn't she heard once that a man slow to anger almost always proved to be the most dangerous foe of all? She believed that of Ford. So, apparently, did Sissy, because she drew a long breath, then laughed nervously.

"Okay, I get the message. I thought, since I was passin' through, I'd give you one last chance to make love to me. Like the man said, nothing ventured, but, hey, no hard feelings." Shifting her attention to Sophie, she let her smile fade. "If you're worryin' about Ford and me, don't bother. Last time he was down my way, he very nicely, very sweetly called things off between us. Didn't even avail himself of my hospitality, if you know what I mean. I figured it was on account of him fallin' in love with someone finally, though God knows, he's goin' to wear you out tryin' to understand him."

Sophie blinked, conscious that Ford had shifted slightly and was now watching her with those chilly eyes. "You're mistaken if you think I'm the reason for whatever has happened between you. Ford and I scarcely know each other."

Sissy lifted sleek eyebrows, her eyes a little sad, a little amused. "Maybe not now, but you will. Ford might like folks to think he's not much more than a slow-witted country boy with the ambition of a slug, but take my word for it, sugar, he's got this way of gettin' exactly what he wants when he wants it."

She kissed Ford gently on the cheek before slipping from the stool with a serene grace Sophie admired. "Merry Christmas, y'all," she murmured, easing back her shoulders. "And remember, Ford, if it doesn't work out with your pretty little Yankee, you know where you can find me."

He rose, his expression shuttered, his mouth tense. "Are you all right?" he asked in a rough voice.

She drew a breath, then reached up to touch the spot she'd kissed earlier. "You know me, Ford. I'm so shallow nothin' gets me down for longer than it takes me to buy something shiny and expensive." Offering Sophie a smile that seemed oddly sweet, she turned sinuously on four-inch heels and walked to the door.

Sophie saw at least three men across the room sit up and take notice, and Jimbo Stevens actually dropped his jelly doughnut into his coffee. She should be amused. Instead, she found her stomach doing flip-flops and her hands clenching around her order pad.

"Guess if I'd gone to college I'd be comin' up with somethin' real clever to say right about now," Ford drawled, drawing her attention.

"Don't bet on it," she murmured, thinking of her bachelor's degree in education.

Ford shifted again, then rubbed his hand over his flat belly. "Sophie, about the things she said—"

"Please, Ford, you don't need to explain your private business to me of all people."

He lifted his eyebrows. His eyes were clear as smoked glass now, though the dusky color prompted by Sissy's imprudent mention of his mother still lingered on the rise of his angular cheekbone.

"I didn't intend to."

Hands on hips, he glanced around, causing more than one pair of eyes to skitter in another direction. "Look, Sissy didn't mean to embarrass you." A sardonic smile tugged at his mouth. "It was me she was after, but that's just Sissy. She's spoiled rotten and used to getting her way, so it takes her longer than most to let go of... things." He plowed strong brown fingers through his thick hair, leaving it untidy and wildly sexy. "Aw, hell, I don't want to talk about Sissy. I want to talk about you."

"What about me?" Fear skittered down her spine, and she realized she'd come very close to forgetting all the reasons why she'd vowed to keep conversation between Ford and herself to a minimum.

"For one thing, why won't you let me treat you to dinner tomorrow night?"

The look in his eyes was pure frustrated male and should have made her smile. Instead, it only served to make her more uneasy.

The last thing she wanted to do was make him angry with her over something so trivial as a refused date.

"I've promised to help Katie wrap Christmas presents," she said, relieved to have the weight of perfect truth behind her words.

"Tonight, then."

"Tonight I'm helping to decorate the Sunday school rooms at my church."

"No problem. I string a mean rope of that tinselly stuff myself. What time should I pick you up?"

Sophie cast a fast glance around, hoping to see a customer in need. Instead, she saw only contented faces, heard only the buzz of lazy Saturday-morning conversation layered over the plaintive wail of a Christmas carol done to a country beat. Not even crotchety, demanding Jimbo was looking her way. She'd never thought she'd be longing for a sudden rush of business that would have her feet aching and her head spinning, but she was.

Chin up, she let her gaze find his. "Please believe me, the last thing I want to do is hurt your feelings." She stopped abruptly, aware of the stilted quality of her voice and the banality of her words. "I'm not good at this," she muttered.

Emotion flickered in his eyes, quickly absorbed. It wasn't danger she sensed from him, but it shivered her skin nonetheless.

"Would it help if I told you I didn't break it off with Sissy because I was in love with you or anyone else?"

"Of course you're not," she hastened to agree. It was ridiculous to even consider such a possibility. "Sissy was hurt, that's all. She needed to blame something, someone . . ."

His mouth moved. "Don't waste any sympathy on Sissy," he drawled, an odd look in his eyes. "Before we started out, I told her what I was willin' to give, and it wasn't love."

"Which makes it her problem if she gets hurt, is that what you're saying?" she couldn't help challenging, even though she suspected he wasn't nearly as cold and calculating as he sounded.

"That about sums it up, yeah."

She took a deep breath. "And what speech did you intend to give me over this dinner you were offering?"

"No speech, though I can't promise I won't try to steal a good-night kiss."

Sophie let the image of his hard mouth coming down on hers linger for only an instant before forcing it from her mind. "As I said, I don't date."

"Don't date me, or anyone?"

"Anyone."

"Are you still grieving for Jessie's daddy?"

Sophie drew a breath. She knew what he was asking, just as she knew what her answer had to be, but even as she opened her mouth to answer, the lie she needed to tell him for her own safety and maybe even for his stuck in her throat.

"I was married for almost five years," she hedged, forcing herself to keep her gaze level on his. "I'm still not used to being a widow."

He narrowed his eyes and stared into hers. "You figure cutting yourself off from dating again will help get you used to it?"

"Well, no...that is, I'm not cutting myself off—exactly."

"Sophie, I'm not much good at flirting. Always seemed like a waste of time." His eyes crinkled. "But I have to tell you straight, there's no way I'm gonna stop buggin' you till you agree to go out with me at least once."

She blinked at him. He was becoming too important to her, she realized, panic dawning. "And if I don't?"

He shook his head, his mouth twitching. "Then you'd better prepare yourself to see a grown man pining away to a shadow right before your eyes."

She tried to imagine that superb body diminished in any way, and realized her pulse was speeding. "I doubt that very much," she said, picking up the menu Sissy no longer needed.

"Like I said, you are one stubborn lady," he drawled. "But I've been known to be a little mule-headed myself."

"I'm sorry," she said, feeling more and more miserable. "But I'm just not interested in taking Sissy's place in your bed, especially when the sheets are probably still warm."

His eyes took on a deadly flatness. "Is that the kind of man you think I am?"

"I don't know what kind of a man you are, and I...don't want to know. As far as I'm concerned, you're one of Peg's best customers and a friend of many of my friends. And that's *all* you are."

"Forget the breakfast," he said, dropping a couple of dollars on the counter. "I've already wasted too much time hangin' around here as it is." He grabbed his hat, nodded curtly and walked out. Watching him go, Sophie felt like putting her head down and crying.

Chapter 5

Ford heard a sharp rap on his half-opened office door and glanced up, furious at being interrupted, a reaction that was unusual for him. But he'd been restless and moody since he'd given up on a sound night's sleep around 5:00 a.m., and left his solitary bed for an early-morning jog.

Running hadn't helped his mood or his sleep-starved muscles. Nor had chopping a quarter cord of wood for the fireplace he only rarely used. In the back of his mind he had a feeling what was digging at him. He'd acted like a jerk with Sophie yesterday, and he owed her an apology he was too mule-headed at the moment to make. So he was punishing himself by doing paperwork on the most beautiful Sunday morning they'd had in months.

"I thought you were on patrol," he said to Eli Grover, who started to grin, then thought better of it.

"Sorry to bother you, Sheriff. I can come back later if you're busy."

Ford threw down his pen and settled back in his chair. Eli was the closest thing to a son he figured he'd ever have.

A few years younger than Lucy, the kid had grown up in a tar-paper shack on the wrong side of Yahoo Flats, the eldest of four. His father, Gresham, had been a Vietnam vet and, when a badly injured back had allowed him to work, had been a whiz at rebuilding gasoline-powered engines. He'd also been a falling-down drunk, using cheap wine to numb the ache in his back and his soul.

Eli's mother had been Vietnamese, a tiny wisp of a woman who cleaned other women's houses until her hands bled and her hopes for a good life for her children shriveled. Still, she never complained. Nor did she ever smile—or so Eli had told Ford at her funeral.

Gresham had disappeared a few months later, his already tenuous hold on reality snapped by the loss of his wife. Eli had been twelve, his youngest sister just starting school. For six months he'd managed to keep his father's desertion a secret, even from Ford, who'd stopped by periodically to check on the family's well-being.

By working at two paper routes and a lawn-mowing business, he'd kept his sisters fed and clothed and in school, but when he himself had been turned over to the juvenile authorities for chronic truancy, the report had ended up on Ford's desk. He'd gone to the shack and discovered the kid worn-out and much too skinny, trying to fix a lawn-mower engine with the few broken tools his old man had left behind.

Enlisting the aid of a sympathetic social worker, Ford had found a foster home that would take all four kids, then discovered that Eli was refusing to leave the rat-infested shack that had been his only home. When reasoning with the boy hadn't worked, he'd locked Eli in his squad car and burned the place to the ground.

At the time Eli had called Ford a long list of insulting names in a mixture of English and Vietnamese. Six years later he'd invited Ford to his high-school graduation and asked him for a job. Ford had ordered him to go to college first. Eli had resisted. They'd compromised on a two-year degree.

Eli had been a member of Clover's twenty-two-man sheriff's department for almost two years now, and Ford was generally satisfied with his performance. There were times, though, when he wondered if Eli wasn't a bit overly zealous in tracking down deadbeat fathers.

Ford understood his reasons. He also understood the parallels that some people had drawn between his life and Eli's. They figured he'd felt sorry for Eli the way half the town had felt sorry for him, which was one of the reasons he'd wanted Eli to grow up in another town where he wouldn't always have to drag around the baggage from the past he'd neither created nor could control.

"Since you've already got my attention, you might as well tell me what you need," he drawled, glancing at his watch.

Eli added a thick folder to the stack threatening to topple out of the in basket. "Here's another batch of wanted posters. There's a couple you might want to check out on top, nothing really urgent, though."

Ford stifled a sigh. "Thanks. Anything else?"

"Yep. Got me a call from a lady out near Deadman's Slough. Says she's been smelling mash cookin' when the wind's from the south. I figured to take a run out there this afternoon after I get relieved at the duty desk and poke around a bit."

Ford nodded. "Don't forget to move slow and soft while you're doin' that pokin'. And if you get a lead on Frenchy, don't try to take him down yourself. Get on back to the car and call for backup."

Eli looked crestfallen, and Ford had a hunch the kid was setting himself up to play hero. "I mean what I say, Eli. Frenchy's a crack shot, plus he's a mean hand with a bowie knife. Last thing I want to do is tell that sweet little wife of yours you made her a widow right before she's fixin' to become a mama."

It was the right thing to say. Just thinking about his wife and the baby she was about to deliver had the bloodlust fading from Eli's eyes.

"Good thing you mentioned Ellie, 'cause I almost forgot the most important reason I came in just now. We're havin' us a party New Year's Eve, and we'd be proud if you'd attend."

"Thanks, but I'll probably pull duty that night. Let you young folks do the celebratin'."

Eli looked genuinely disappointed. "Maybe you could drop in for a few minutes, anyway. Ellie really wants you to see the house, you being the one to lend us the down payment and all."

Ford sat up straight and picked up his pen. "Tell Ellie I'll try to make it, but not to be disappointed if I don't."

"Yes, sir." Eli took the hint and left, leaving the door half-open. Ford's men knew he was always available to them, even when he was off duty. They also knew he didn't second-guess every decision or monitor their every move. Some folks called that his style of managing. He didn't much care about labels. He just knew it worked, just as he knew most of the credit went to his deputies.

He had a good crew, he thought, signing the recommendation for promotion passed up the line by his next in command. There were half a dozen senior officers who could do his job as well as he could, all trained by him. And the youngsters coming up were all sharp and dedicated.

Too bad Lucy hadn't fallen in love with one of them instead of that Dooley character. Ford frowned, just thinking about his baby sister mixed up with a man who not only aroused Ford's protective instincts, but also his suspicions.

Dooley's story seemed too pat to his thinking, almost like a bad movie plot. As long as Ford could remember, Hannah Franklin had claimed to be the last of her line. And then, six months after her death, Dooley shows up claiming to be her long-lost great-nephew and, coincidentally, of course, her heir.

While the lawyers wrangled, Dooley had taken up residence in the big old house on Highgate Road, behaving for all the world as though the rumors about Hannah's having hidden away a fortune were true.

Ford had his doubts about that, all right, but as far as he'd been able to determine, Dooley didn't work at anything much except charming gullible young women into thinking he was the best thing walking on two legs so he must have been getting his money from somewhere.

He was a good-looking bastard, Ford gave him that, but he had shifty eyes, the kind that couldn't quite hold steady on yours for more than a second or two. As soon as he'd found out Lucy was mooning over the man, Ford had wanted to run a routine check on his background. If Dooley had turned up clean, no one would have ever had to know Ford hadn't trusted the guy. But fool that he was, he'd made the mistake of telling his sister what he'd planned to do.

She'd threatened never to speak to him if he so much as sent out a motor-vehicles check on Joe Dooley or any other Dooley, and Ford had been dead afraid she'd meant what she'd said. Still, he hadn't quite abandoned the notion to do some discreet checking on the man, just shelved it for a time in order to let Lucy cool down some.

Lord a'mighty, it was tough dealing with women, he thought. A man never knew what they were going to do next. Now take Sophie, he thought, sitting back again, a scowl playing over his face and his gut tightening.

He'd been turned down for a date before. Hell, since the first time he'd worked up his nerve to ask Robin Sue Bobo to the church picnic when he'd been thirteen, he'd been turned down more than he'd been accepted. He figured that went with being homely and mostly uneducated and stained by his old man's madness. Sometimes he'd been flat out crushed to find out the lady of his choosing didn't share his interest. Sometimes he'd been ticked off, but mostly he'd shrugged it off the way he managed to shrug off most things he couldn't change.

So why the hell couldn't he get Sophie out of his head?

He swiveled his chair to the left and shot a disgusted look at the photo board showing his officers and the chain of command. It wasn't as if he was pining away of loneliness or any such nonsense like that. In fact, he had a pretty great life. Maybe law enforcement hadn't been his first choice, but mostly he liked what he did. Though not a man to brag in public, he was privately proud of the job he'd done building a solid, reputable force. If he wasn't universally liked, he was generally respected, and he slept easy every night knowing the people under him knew their jobs and did them honestly and with pride. Since he'd exchanged the silver shield of a deputy for sheriff's gold six years ago he hadn't lost a man, and the only injuries had been minor ones.

Closing his eyes, he ran his hands over his face, more tired at half past eleven than he would have been if he'd been picking cotton all day long. What the hell, Maguire, haul your butt over to Sophie's place and apologize to her.

But damn, she'd been dead wrong about him. He might not be the most tactful guy who ever walked the dusty streets of Clover, but he'd never held much with the tomcatting some men held with.

He'd been celibate for more than a year when he'd met Sissy at a board meeting for a child-abuse prevention group they both belonged to. They'd gone out for coffee afterward, at her invitation and at her place, and she'd been on him like a sweat in a heat wave. She'd been bored and mad at her daddy for cutting back her spending money, and an affair with a poor country sheriff was just the thing to make Daddy choke on his Havana cigars.

Ford might not have a college degree, but he sure as hell knew when he was being used. He figured that was her game and he'd play it, just so long as she knew he was playing that game by his own rules. And that meant no strings on either of them and no false promises.

He'd broken it off because he'd found himself thinking of Sophie while he was making love to Sissy, and to his way of reckoning right from wrong, he wasn't playing fair.

What the hell did Sophie want him to do? Marry Sissy just because she couldn't stand losing one of her playthings? Muttering a curse, he opened his eyes and sat up. No matter how many times he told himself a man was just asking for trouble wanting a woman who didn't want him, Sophie kept showing up in his dreams dressed in nothing but his imagination, waking him up so worked up he'd ended up taking an icy shower in the middle of the night two nights running. Not that it did more than put an edge on his already filthy mood.

"Son of a bitch," he grated, gritting his teeth. Work was supposed to keep his mind off of her, not drive him up the wall because all of sudden he was imagining how her skin would warm under the friction of his hand, or how her mouth would sigh and open under his. Cursing again, he grabbed the folder Eli had just delivered and slammed it open. He was just reminding himself that he was a bachelor because he liked being alone when he heard the outside buzzer indicating someone seeking admittance.

He started to get up, then heard Eli's boots on the bare floor. Thinking vaguely that he hoped it wasn't trouble, he returned his attention to the wanted poster on top of the stack, a new addition to the FBI's "ten most wanted." Mean looking bastard, he thought. Wanted for murder one, escaped from a small-town jail in Idaho while waiting transport back to Florida.

"Sheriff Maguire's office is the first one on the left, ma'am. Just go on in. He won't mind a bit."

Ford groaned aloud, wishing fervently that Southern hospitality had died a slow death years ago. He was preparing himself to hear about some domestic disaster or other when Sophie appeared in the doorway with Jessie, who was bouncing up and down in her small folding stroller. But it was the baby's mother who had his heart rate speeding and his spine straightening. Dressed in a tailored skirt and high-necked blouse, with a touch of makeup darkening her lashes and glossing her lips, she looked nothing like the harried waitress he saw every morning but Sunday at Peg's. Nor was she offering him the usual welcoming smile. In fact, she was gazing at him with a distant coolness in her dark blue eyes that squeezed his heart.

"Your deputy said that it was all right to come in," she said, glancing nervously at the four walls of the small space, as though unsure it was safe to enter. Since his bare-bones office was anything but intimidating, he figured it was him she was wanting to avoid.

"It'd be a poor sheriff who wasn't available to the people who pay him," he said by way of reassuring her. It seemed to work. Her slender shoulders lost some of their stiffness, and her gaze settled, if not exactly on him, at least on the bulletin board behind him.

"It was such a nice day. Jessie and I decided to walk home from church, and when we passed the town hall, I saw your car out front. I can come back if you're busy."

"I'm not doing anything special, nothing that can't wait, anyway," he said, getting to his feet. Jessie immediately stopped chattering to look up at him in that curious way she had. Dressed in Christmas colors, from the top of her red-and-green hair ribbon to the tips of her tiny red sneakers, she was just about the cutest thing he'd seen since Lucy had been a baby. Because he realized Sophie's unexpected appearance had shaken him, he concentrated on the baby instead.

"Mornin', Miss Jessamine," he said, sinking to his haunches in front of her. "Have you and your mama been out for a walk on this pretty Sunday?"

"Mama?" Jessie echoed anxiously. She had long lashes like her mama, and a tiny cleft in her chin that matched Sophie's perfectly.

"Yeah, Mama's still here." Ford glanced up to find Sophie watching him almost as warily as her daughter. "Looks like your daughter doesn't remember me."

"Don't take it personally," she said, looking only marginally more comfortable. "Sometimes I feel like I need to introduce myself to her when I come home after a double shift."

Ford found it remarkable that she could laugh about having to work as hard as she did. Or maybe he just wanted her so badly he found everything about her remarkable. At the moment he wasn't quite sure how he felt.

"What can I do for you two ladies?" he asked, straightening to his full height. He noticed then that Sophie was wearing high heels, bringing her mouth to just the perfect height to be kissed by a man six feet tall. She was wearing perfume, too, something light that reminded him of spring showers. Though he knew it was just chemistry, her scent had his body reacting as though she'd suddenly brushed her soft body against his in a blatant come-on.

"I came to give you the rest of the money I owe you for the medicine," she explained, opening her purse.

"Guess it wouldn't do me any good to suggest waitin' to settle up until after Christmas, would it?"

She smiled then, a quick curving of her lips that didn't last nearly long enough to suit him. "No good at all."

"In that case, you'd best use my desk while I try to coax a smile out of Miss Jessamine."

"Thanks." Sophie pushed the stroller a few more feet toward the center of the cluttered office. Just setting foot in a police station had her stomach roiling with sick memories, but she'd been determined to repay her debt to Ford as quickly as possible. Now she realized the enormity of her mistake. Seeing him behind the desk framed by the flags of South Carolina and the United States brought the nightmare to the surface again. The sooner she finished her business and left, the better.

Ford closed the folder he'd been examining and moved it to the side, out of her way. Slipping into the chair that was still warm from the heat of his body, she opened her checkbook and accepted his offer of a pen.

While she wrote, he hunched down and began talking to Jessie in a gentle voice that had Sophie remembering the things she'd heard about how smitten he'd been with his sister when she'd been a baby. And how totally he'd devoted his life to her care after they'd been orphaned. She didn't want to think of him as a good man. She just couldn't seem to think of him any other way.

Finished with the check, she tore it from the pad and placed it on top of the folder, automatically reading the words printed in large block letters on the tab. WANTED FUGITIVES—CURRENT (FBI National and Local Jurisdiction). Her breath stopped, and she felt the blood draining from her face. Was there a sheet on her in that stack? she wondered.

Panic swept through her, and her first thought was to grab Jessie and run. But somehow she managed to sit perfectly still, even as her heart pumped frantically beneath the cover of her second-hand blouse.

She drew a breath and told herself to think. But the institutional green walls were suddenly too smotheringly close, too terribly familiar.

"We'd better be going," she said, standing quickly, desperately needing space.

Ford glanced up, the offer of a cup of coffee he was about to make forgotten as soon as he saw the alarm in her eyes. Wondering what had set her off, he stood quickly, instinctively putting himself between her and the door.

"Is something wrong?" he asked, feeling some intense emotion coming off her slight body in chill waves. A quick glance told him that her skin had paled and her hands were balled into fists against her thighs.

"Actually, no," she said, her voice audibly strained. "I'm a bit claustrophobic, and there aren't any windows in here."

Ford glanced around, trying to see the office through the eyes of someone who feared closed places. It did seem on the smallish side, he decided, especially crammed with filing cabinets and the biggest desk he'd been able to scrounge from the county warehouse.

"Guess I'm so used to the place I never really thought about how confining it might be to someone else." He grinned, trying to reassure her. "Mostly we live like moles down here. There's a legend that one of my predecessors had a squabble with the town council about somethin' or other. Made himself so unpopular the council just up and moved the whole darn department to the basement, and we've been stuck down here ever since."

She laughed, but the wild-eyed look of panic had only diminished, not disappeared. It showed in her eyes, in the faster-than-usual cadence of her breathing. She was good and spooked, yet doing her best to hide the extent of her fear. He understood that kind of courage, though fear wasn't one of the emotions he allowed himself. Not because he doubted its existence, but because it got in the way when a man needed to be at his best.

"Just the same, we'd better go," she said, glancing at the door. "Jessie will be wanting her dinner, and when she decides she's hungry, she can threaten walls—windows or no windows."

"I'll walk you out."

"No, that's not necessary—"

She was interrupted by the sounds of a commotion in the duty office next door. From the shouts and thuds coming through the wall, she concluded that someone was complaining loudly and profanely about being arrested.

"Excuse me just a minute," Ford said over his shoulder as he headed out. "Be right back."

Left alone, Sophie's immediate instinct was flight. And then she remembered the reason for her panic—the folder on the desk. Hastily, she flipped it open and paged through. Finding the posters alphabetized had her breathing a quick prayer of gratitude, even as a mixture of guilt and dread fluttered in her stomach. Ears straining to detect the sound of returning footsteps, she paged through quickly to the *M*'s.

Seeing her own face staring up at her sent shock knifing through her, even though she'd thought herself prepared. It was the picture they'd taken when they'd booked her into the country jail, and her eyes were glazed over with shock and disbelief.

The sights and sounds of that terrible day came back to her vividly, nearly sending her to her knees. The police had waited until she'd been walking out of the church after Wells's funeral before they'd stopped her and read her her rights. She still remembered the humiliation of having her wrists shackled together in front of her friends and fellow teachers.

Dazed and disbelieving, she hadn't understood at first that they'd been accusing her of deliberately pushing Wells down those stairs. Instead of sympathizing with the terror she'd felt as she'd struggled to save herself and her baby, they'd actually believed that she'd set out to kill him in order to inherit his money.

Trembling, she snatched the paper from the stack. It crackled accusingly as she folded it and quickly shoved it to the bottom of her purse. Somehow she managed to regain her composure as she closed the folder and made sure it was in the exact place on the desk.

Clutching her purse, she turned the stroller with one hand and was preparing to leave when Ford returned. "Sorry about that," he said, raking a hand through his untidy hair. "Looks like Frenchy's still doin' a land-office business out there in the Slough."

"I take it that was another of his customers doing all that shouting about police brutality," she commented lightly, though she was certain her cheeks must be stained with guilt.

Ford nodded. "From the looks of him, a *real* good customer." He scowled suddenly, turning his face to a hard mask of danger-ous determination. "Hope Frenchy's savin' his money, 'cause he's about to close up shop—permanently this time."

Sophie felt the undercurrent of anger that seethed like molten steel beneath the laconic promise. Ford might walk slow and talk slower, but the more she was around him, the more certain she be-came that the easygoing manner hid a sharp intellect and a will of razored flint. A man like that would make a relentless hunter—and a deadly adversary. Just realizing the risk she was taking by steal-ing the poster with her name on it had her going cold all the way to the marrow.

Averting her gaze, she took a tighter grip on the stroller. She had to have been out of her mind to think she could hide for more than a few months at a time in any one place. "In that case, Jessie and I had better leave you to do whatever it is you need to do about him."

"I'll see you to the door."

She started to protest, then changed her mind. It didn't matter how she escaped this place, just as long as she got out. Even though she wasn't under arrest, she felt like it as Ford walked next to her through the station. Most of her memories of that time were blessedly blurred, but she could still remember the smells of burnt coffee and stale cigarette smoke that had lingered on her clothing when they'd locked her in a cell with six other women, four of whom were prostitutes caught in a sting while the fifth had been a heroin addict going through the first stages of withdrawal, the stench of her vomit filling the cell. Shuddering, she tried to con-centrate on putting one foot in front of the other in order to block out the too-vivid image of that day.

"From the expression on your face, I figure you're not inter-ested in a tour," Ford stated, drawing her from her own thoughts with a start.

"It's . . . picturesque," she said truthfully.

"It's usually a lot busier," he replied, casting a quick look around. Sundays they worked with a light support crew, one dis-patcher handling 911 calls instead of two, one traffic officer in-stead of three and their two detectives on call only. "And cleaner," he muttered, spying the remnants of someone's take-out lunch on one of the desks.

"Do you enjoy police work?" she asked, glad to be diverted from her black thoughts.

His expression turned thoughtful as he opened the door to the stairway leading up to street level. "Been doing it since I was eighteen, so I guess I must," he said with a shrug.

"Katie said you had intended to go into the air force."

He lifted one eyebrow. "Been talkin' about me, have you?"

This time the heat that burned her cheeks had to do with a different kind of guilt. "Katie has," she murmured, already regretting her rash admission. "Since I'm a polite person, I felt compelled to listen."

"Is that so?" He held the door until she'd pushed Jessie over the threshold, then followed her into the foyer and closed the door behind him.

"Sophie?" His hands were on her shoulders before she could answer. Strong fingers turned her so that they were facing each other squarely. As soon as her eyes melded with his, he dropped his hands.

"Damn," he muttered, feeling about seven years old and stupid. Now that he had her attention, he was wondering how fast he could get the words out and find something to kick.

"Okay, I'm sorry about the way I acted yesterday," he said, plunging in. "I felt pushed, and I pushed back. By the time I hit the street, I knew I was out of line. I just didn't have the guts to turn back around and tell you so."

The relief that came at the end of the impromptu speech died the instant he saw the tears shimmering in her eyes. His immediate thought was that those pretty blue eyes weren't made for crying. Knowing that he'd put tears there had him swallowing acid.

"Why are *you* crying, damn it?" he grated, feeling heat climb his neck. "I'm the one who damn near choked on that mouthful of crow."

"I'm not crying," she declared fiercely. She almost managed to hold it together. And then he smiled one of those slow, crooked, impossibly sweet smiles, and she felt as though her stomach was trying to digest ground glass.

When she and Darlene had talked about the lies she would have to tell, she'd managed to smother the voice of conscience by telling herself she had no choice. Lying in a good cause couldn't be wrong, she'd told herself over and over. Everyone lied—the press, the politicians, even her in-laws when they'd sworn she'd been the one who'd wanted to abort the baby, not Wells. She could still see the hatred on Anita Manwaring's face when she'd sworn that Wells must have been trying to stop her when *she'd* pushed *him* down the stairs. But now, suddenly, it hurt terribly to lie to a man who had swallowed a lot of pride along with that crow in order to right what he considered a wrong he'd done her.

"I should be apologizing to you," she murmured, feeling more and more miserable the longer she stood there.

"No, you were just standin' up for what you thought was right. Once I cooled down, I couldn't find fault with that."

"Please, Ford, don't say nice things to me. I don't deserve them," she whispered, his face blurring.

"Matter of opinion, but I sure wouldn't want to get myself in any more trouble, so here goes." He cleared his throat. "Sophie Reynolds, you are one scrawny, sorry-lookin' woman..." He touched her face with the pads of his fingers, and she felt heat. He moved closer, his thighs nudging hers, and his hand fisted in her hair.

"Just because your hair looks like sunshine and smells good enough to drive a man to drink doesn't mean diddly when you go and wear it short as your daughter's there. And those blue eyes of yours, well, shoot, honey. They just have to be hiding a mean-as-sin disposition, sure enough."

His hands framed her face, and his eyes grew dark. "'Course there are those of us who like vinegar with our greens."

"Don't," Sophie managed to choke out, but his head was already lowering toward hers.

He touched his mouth to hers gently and felt her tremble. Pulling back only a little, he opened his eyes and saw uncertainty in hers. A gentleman would retreat, giving her time to decide if she wanted more. He wasn't a gentleman. Never had been, never would be. At the moment he was glad. Slowly, deliberately, he slid his arms around her waist. Her eyes turned quizzical, her breath came a little faster.

"I have to go," she murmured. "The baby—"

"—is fine. At the moment, she's taking a little siesta, lookin' just like a sleepy little angel."

He'd checked. He'd also thanked whatever lucky star had fallen on him all of a sudden that they were in the basement where no one came unless they had business with his department, which on Sunday wasn't all that often.

"But—"

"Shh, now." He ran his hand up her spine, and felt her give. Needs he hadn't allowed for a long time threatened to erupt, but he kept them leveled. A woman like Sophie was made for sweet words and gentle loving, both of which were difficult for him.

"The more I look at you, the more I think I might have been wrong about you bein' on the scrawny side."

Sophie felt a low, urgent humming in her head. Like the quiet power of the sea pounding the Oregon coastline. It came to her that he wasn't going to let her go until he kissed her, and she braced for the savage assault that was in his eyes.

Instead, his hands ran slowly up the length of her spine to cup the nape of her neck. He didn't drag her into his arms, but instead drew her closer so gently she was pressed against him before she could find words to stop him.

"I've never kissed a Yankee lady before," he murmured, his voice rough. "Might be interestin' at that." He moved one hand lower to rub the tender hollow at the base of her spine, and she drew in air on a sudden spike of pleasure.

His eyes stayed open and riveted on hers as he brought his mouth to hers again, slowly, gently at first, then with an absorbed possession that had her lowering her lashes on a sigh of need that wasn't to be denied. Her arms were around his neck before she'd admitted the need to be closer. Her mouth was moving under his before she wondered if that was wise.

Expecting power, she'd been charmed by a strong man's awkward tenderness. Ready to repel force, she'd been beguiled by unexpected restraint. He didn't pressure her for more, so she gave willingly. He didn't push, so she yielded. He savored, and she savored more. Even knowing that she was being slowly, sweetly, but surely seduced, she was helpless to resist the demands of her own awakening needs.

Ford heard the low throaty moan coming from her creamy throat and knew that he could push her up against the wall and take her hard and fast, satisfying both of them physically. But he knew that once unleashed, the part of him urging him on would ultimately destroy them both. Still, drawing back from the edge while she was so soft and pliant and willing in his arms tested the self-control he'd honed through long years of practice. His body burned for her, and his blood was running hot. When his mind turned cloudy, and the ache in him turned to pain, he stepped back and opened his eyes, supporting her until she came slowly back to reality.

Slowly, dreamily, she opened her eyes and he saw that they were dark as midnight and misted with desire. All that was male in him cried out for him to pull her to him again and finish what he started. But he'd learned a long time ago just how destructive passion without thought could be. And she looked so easily shattered, with her lips still parted and her eyes only now finding focus.

"I . . . You . . ." Realizing she was having trouble forming a coherent thought, Sophie paused, running her tongue over her lower lip. "*We* shouldn't have done that," she managed finally.

His grin slanted, not quite as slow as before. "You don't like kissin' a Southern boy?" he asked, arching one lazy eyebrow.

"No boy kisses like that," she muttered, and then felt her skin flame.

His eyes crinkled, adding a nearly irresistible charm to his dark, angular face. "Why, thank you, ma'am. We aim to please."

"In that case would you please promise me you'll never do that again?" She ran an unsteady hand through her hair, while at the same time smoothing the other over her skirt. She felt disheveled and shaken and . . . thoroughly kissed.

Glancing up, she saw him watching her, the smile gone from his mouth and his eyes. "I can't make you that promise, because I'm aimin' to kiss you as often as you'll stand still long enough for me to catch."

Even as excitement began to flutter in her stomach again, she was shaking her head. "It's best we just forget the past few minutes ever happened."

"Do you really think you can?"

"I don't have a choice." Her heart was beating too fast, and her palms were sweating.

His mouth lost the last of the softness remaining after he'd ended the kiss. "There are always choices. Sometimes they're just a bit limited."

"In this case, there's only one."

"Why?"

Tell him the truth, a little voice urged. He might believe you. Maybe he'll even let you go.

"Sophie? Talk to me, honey. Tell me what's so wrong in your life that you're shutting yourself off like a nun."

His voice flowed over her, a bit rough but gentle. The need to put her head on his shoulder came again, stronger this time and driven by a desperate need to confess her guilt. Not just for stealing the flyer, but for betraying every principle of right and wrong she'd lived with for so long.

"Sheriff, I—"

"Mama," Jessie suddenly piped up, obviously awake and kicking her feet so hard she shook the stroller.

Sophie exhaled, stunned by the risk she'd been about to take. Ford might want her sexually, but he was also sworn to uphold the law, and she was a wanted felon.

The panic returned full force, deepened by the knowledge that she was far too vulnerable to him. And his kisses. No matter what, she had to keep her vow to stay far, far away from Ford Maguire.

"Jessie's my first priority, my *only* priority," she said, putting as much force in her tone as she could. "I don't have room for anything or anyone else."

His expression turned impatient. "We can make room. Hell, I'm already crazy about her, and—"

"Are you asking me to marry you, Sheriff Maguire?"

The shock on his face should have made her laugh. Instead, it only deepened the shame she felt for deceiving him.

"What kind of question is that?" he demanded. It didn't take more than a look into those suddenly flint-hard eyes to know that he could be a very violent man if pushed too hard. Still, she would risk violence and more to keep her daughter with her.

"The kind a single mother has to ask before she even considers a relationship with a man," she said, feeling a deep, unexpected pang of regret even as the words left her mouth.

She bent to mutter a few soothing words to the baby, but not before Ford had seen something in her eyes that had him backing down hard on a sudden surge of icy rage. Not much for words, he couldn't quite put a name to the emotions shimmering in those blue depths. Sorrow might come closest. The kind that stripped away a person's defenses and left them raw and bleeding inside.

"Here, let me do that," he said when he realized she intended to carry the baby, stroller and all, up the stairs.

He moved fast, needing to distance himself from her long enough to fight through the memory of another time, another place, when he'd felt that same kind of helpless sorrow.

"There you go, sugar," he said, setting the stroller carefully on all four wheels. "Ready to burn rubber again."

Jessie kicked her feet and regarded him imperiously as only a female could. Taking one tiny hand in his, he brushed his lips over the satiny skin. "You be good for your mama now, you hear?" he ordered with a mock sternness that earned him a toothy grin.

"Mama," Jessie pronounced firmly.

Straightening, he turned to look at Sophie who was shading her eyes from the sudden glare. She looked so fragile and defenseless in the harsh light, and yet, he suspected that she was anything but.

He shoved his hands into his pockets while he still had some control, and offered her a polite grin. "Guess I'll see you in the morning."

"Yes, 6:20 on the dot."

She shifted her purse from one shoulder to the other, then took a firm grip on the umbrellalike handles of the stroller. He let her get almost to the corner before he called her name, feeling his heart start to gallop again as she turned to look back at him.

"Tell you one thing, Sophie, if I *was* a marryin' man, I sure would give some serious thought to your proposal." He turned quickly and disappeared into the building.

There was a storm in the Atlantic, and the tail end had come ashore to drench the Carolinas in a cold, dreary rain that had begun shortly after Sophie had taken Jessie upstairs for her bath. What had started as a gloriously sunny, springlike morning had turned into a depressingly sodden evening. Not even the blurred twinkle of the Christmas lights outside could brighten Sophie's mood. By ten o'clock she was more than ready for the oblivion offered by sleep.

The third floor was quiet as she returned to her room from the bathroom and closed the door. Her head buzzed with exhaustion as she tucked the quilt more snugly around Jessie's chunky little bottom.

"I love you so much," she whispered, leaning over the crib's high side to breathe a kiss on her sleeping baby's cheek. Her little girl was thriving. Everyone said so. And she seemed to have adjusted beautifully to a communal life-style, better even than Sophie had dared hope. Katie and her boarders had become an extended family, as loving and supportive as her own had been when both her parents had been living.

Sighing, she crossed to the bed and sat down. She'd been so lucky to have grown up in a stable home and a traditional life-style. It had been almost embarrassingly idyllic. One mother, one father, one little girl they adored, just as she'd adored them.

Her father had told her not to marry Wells. "He's got eyes like a dog we had on the farm when I was growing up," he'd warned. "Good-looking cow dog, he was, and smart, but he had a possessive streak, that one. Killed a kitten of mine once because it was sitting on my lap, broke its back with one bite. Couldn't stand to share, you see."

Sophie still remembered the sorrow in her father's eyes when he'd told her that story—and the sudden intensity that replaced that sorrow when he'd urged her to call off the engagement.

"Judge and Mrs. Manwaring are fine people, don't get me wrong. They do a lot of good in the community, but from what I've seen, they have a blind spot when it comes to Wells. I'm not saying he's not an intelligent, well-mannered young man, because he is, but he's never been taught to share the way you have."

But she'd known better. Wells simply appeared overly possessive because he loved her. Once they were married and he knew for sure that she was his, he would relax.

Sophie drew a long breath, staring at the rain spatters on the window. It had gotten worse, not better. First he'd objected to her friends taking so much of her time, so she'd declined more invitations than she accepted until finally she found herself isolated from everyone but her family and his.

Then it was her job that was coming between them. Why was she spending so much time at night on lesson plans when they should be together? What was so pressing she had to stay late after classes were over for the day? Maybe it wasn't teaching she loved, but another teacher? A *male* teacher.

Tired of his constant suspicions and questions, she'd suggested counseling. She'd seen his rage for the first time then. The words he'd flung at her hadn't stayed in her mind, but the meaning had. Wells Manwaring was incapable of admitting he was wrong about anything, even the smallest detail.

There seemed to be nothing she could say or do to placate him, short of quitting her job and devoting all of her time and attention to him. It had been an agonizing dilemma. She'd still loved Wells, in spite of his faults. Certainly she had faults of her own, but she couldn't make herself believe that a love of teaching could be wrong.

When she'd found she was pregnant, she'd been so sure Wells would be thrilled. Instead he'd resurrected the old accusations about her and some phantom male teacher. It was *his* baby she was carrying, not Wells's.

Sophie dropped her face to her hands. "Oh, God," she whispered, shuddering. It had been so ugly that night. A nightmare. Hell on earth. She could still see the virulent hatred in his eyes as he reached for her, the ugly snarl of his mouth as he ordered her to kill the baby.

She struggled, tried to run from the names he called her, from the madness that had come over him. And then, he was falling away, the killing rage in his eyes changing to a vacant stare as his neck snapped. Sophie cringed, her eyes stinging with hot tears. *Dear God, you know I didn't want him to die. I would never want him to die.*

Drawing a shaky breath, she fought for calm. *Why are you torturing yourself like this?* she asked herself. But the question was a foolish one. She knew why.

It was because of the poster she'd stolen.

Sick inside, she crossed the room and opened the door to the closet where she kept her purse. The poster was still there, waiting.

Her hands shook as she unfolded it and stared at the cold black letters. SARAH SOPHIA GUNDERSEN MANWARING—Wanted For Child Stealing And Parole Violation. The facts were all there. Her conviction of involuntary manslaughter, the dates dispassionately detailing the year she'd spent locked away from everything that mattered to her like some kind of vicious animal.

Sick inside, she ripped it in two, then tore those to bits no larger than confetti before letting the pieces sift through her fingers into the wastebasket by the dresser.

When her hand was empty, she continued to stand statue still, staring at the small pile of paper in the bottom of the basket. Is this what I've become? she thought sadly. A common thief, stealing from a man who's only shown me kindness?

"Oh, Ford," she murmured, her voice catching. "If only you knew how very much I wish things were different."

Chapter 6

Perched on the edge of Katie's double bed, Sophie measured out a length of paper with candy-cane stripes and reached for the scissors she'd placed on the nightstand beyond Jessie's reach.

With only two days to go until Christmas Day, the two women were in Katie's bedroom on the ground floor, wrapping the needlepoint ornaments Sophie had made to give to the kids in the Sunday school class she taught.

Oblivious to the two adults and the carols playing on Katie's CD player, Jessie was busily crawling around at Sophie's feet, happily playing with the scraps of paper and bits of ribbon littering the carpet. Nearby, Katie sat back on her heels and arched her back, a grumpy look on her face.

"Every year I swear I'm not going all out for the holidays, and then along about Halloween this fool stranger takes over my body, and the next thing I know I'm knee-deep in wrapping paper and Christmas cookies."

"And you love every minute of it, too," Sophie told her with a grin.

"I suppose I must," Katie admitted with a sigh before reaching for more ribbon. "These sure are cute ornaments, Sophie. Maybe next year you'll have time to make a few more for your friends, like yours truly, for instance."

Friends. Sophie liked the sound of that. More importantly, she no longer felt like an outsider in the house, or even in the town itself. It was a nice feeling to be able to recognize a goodly number of the people she met in the market or at church or during the hours she spent at the diner.

"I never thought I'd like doing needlepoint, but I love it." It was also surprisingly soothing, probably because it required so much concentration she couldn't think about anything else while she had that murderously sharp needle in her hand.

"Miss Fanny tried to teach me once," Katie muttered. "Turns out I'm hopeless at anything having to do with a needle and thread."

"Well, you saw my first attempts, so you know I'm close to hopeless myself. If it hadn't been for the kids and wanting to give them some little thing for Christmas, I would have given up after my first bloody finger."

The third floor had been in turmoil for weeks, and the "ladies" had nearly come to blows over which color yarn to use. Somehow, however, the three of them had managed to finish twelve perfect miniature pillows in time for the Sunday school party tomorrow night.

"No, no, Jessie. Ribbons aren't for eating, sweetheart." Sophie plucked the silvery ribbon from her daughter's hand a split second before it would have become a bedtime snack. "Ribbons are for tying up pretty packages to put under the tree."

Jessie jabbered something profound, and Sophie burst out laughing. "Here, chew on this," she said, handing Jess a teething ring in the shape of a dog bone.

"Has Ford asked you to cater his party yet?" Katie fluffed the bow she'd just tied and sat back to admire her handiwork.

"No, and I don't expect he will. After all, I've only had one catering job so far, and it hardly counts, since it was Miss Fanny who hired me."

"It does so count," Katie declared firmly. "And it was a lovely tea. All the ladies said so."

Sophie watched Jessie scoot crablike under the bed, her little hand reaching for something. Bending, she caught the baby's fat little foot and pulled her into the open again. Squealing, Jessie immediately brought her hand to her mouth.

"Oh, no, you don't," Sophie muttered, plucking something shiny from the baby's fist. It was a silver earring.

"I think this belongs to you," she told Kate, dangling the hoop from her thumb and forefinger.

"I wondered where that went." She gave Jessie a little hug before putting the earring with its mate in a Chinese lacquered box on the dresser.

Keeping one eye on Jessie, Sophie began gathering the leftover paper. "I still wish you'd let me pay you for the use of your kitchen."

"You've already paid me by organizing that mess I call my recipe collection." Katie wound up the last of the ribbon and returned it to the large shopping bag containing the rest of her wrapping supplies. "By the way, Lucy called while you were bathing Jessie. She sends you her best."

"Did she get over that awful cold?"

"More or less, although she's still coughing. She's not sure she's going to be able to make it to the party at church tomorrow night, so just in case, she asked me to oversee the refreshment table."

"Why don't I do that for you? You have enough to do coordinating the nativity play."

Katie frowned. "That would be a real help, true enough. If you're sure you wouldn't mind?"

"Of course, I wouldn't," she said as she lifted Jessie onto her lap for a quick snuggle. It was nearly bedtime for both of them, and she was tired, even if Jessie wasn't.

"Remind me to bake an extra sweet-potato pie for Christmas dinner," Katie said as she stowed the shopping bag of supplies in the back of the closet. "It's Ford's favorite."

Sophie felt a shiver run down her spine. She'd seen him twice since Sunday, both times for breakfast. Both mornings she'd kept herself too busy to do more than serve his food and refill his coffee cup.

"Is that what you're giving him for Christmas, a sweet-potato pie?" she asked with feigned nonchalance.

"I guess it is, in a roundabout way. He and Lucy are coming for Christmas dinner." Katie slanted her a look. "Didn't I mention that to you already?"

"No, I don't think you did." Keeping her face hidden, Sophie kissed the top of Jessie's sweet-smelling curls before letting her crawl away.

"It's the strangest thing," Katie mused as though to herself. "I've been running this boarding house for six years come next June. And for six years I've been inviting Lucy and Ford to Christmas dinner. Every year Lucy comes, and Ford doesn't, claiming he has to work, which never surprises anyone who knows him because if there's one thing Ford hates it's social obligations."

"Maybe he just got tired of working every Christmas."

"Not just Christmas. Ever since Lucy was old enough to be on her own, he's worked *every* holiday, plus Saturdays and a lot of Sundays. When he's not working, he's out at the airport fiddlin' with that old airplane of his. Lucy swears he goes out there and works on it at the oddest times, like sometimes in the middle of the night, when no one's around. She worries about him, you know?"

"I'm sure he can take care of himself."

Katie yawned, then stretched. "Sure he can, but even a solitary soul like Ford needs some comfortin' now and then. My instincts tell me you're the one person who can do just that."

Sophie knew exactly what her friend was thinking. She and Ford were both alone and emotionally unattached to anyone else. Why shouldn't they end up together?

Sophie drew a careful breath, her skin warming everywhere he'd touched, as though her body remembered what she'd tried so hard to forget. But just the thought of lying next to that long, lean body while those sensitive hands roamed over her had her going weak with longing.

She hadn't slept well for the past two nights, and when she did sleep, she dreamed about him, and the slow, sensuous brush of his mouth over his. And then when she woke up, tangled in the sheets and breathing hard, she couldn't stop thinking about that same clever mouth moving slowly over her breasts, his tongue slowly swirling around the sensitive nipples.

She nearly moaned aloud, but caught herself in time. "Then your instincts are seriously out of whack," she declared firmly as she scrambled to her feet and swung Jessie into her arms. "I'm not Ford Maguire's type, and he's definitely not mine."

But even as she said good-night to Katie and carried Jessie up the two flights to their little nest, she was thinking about Ford Maguire and the soft, sweet smile he'd put in her heart for a few blessed minutes, just by kissing her.

It rained Christmas morning, but by the time the rooming house residents had watched Jessie open her presents and then exchanged small gifts with each other, the showers had moved on, and the sun was shining.

While Roy Dean and the other two gentlemen in residence took a morning constitutional and the Misses Fanny and Rose Ruth amused Jessie, Sophie helped Katie and her Aunt Peg with the turkey and trimmings.

By noon the house was filled with the wonderful aroma of roasting turkey, the table had been set with heirloom china and flatware, and everyone but Lucy and Ford had gathered in the parlor to have a glass of champagne and the canapés Sophie had insisted on providing as her contribution to the feast. She was just returning to the kitchen for another tray of crab puffs when the doorbell chimed.

"I'll get it," she called, setting the empty tray on the entry table before reaching for the vintage glass doorknob.

"Merry Christmas," Lucy sang out before giving Sophie a hug. "You look marvelous. Ivory suits you."

"Thank you," Sophie murmured, knowing that she looked more dowdy than marvelous in the simple rayon blouse and tan wool skirt. Since it was the best she had, however, she refused to feel depressed.

"And you look fantastic," she told Lucy truthfully. "Very festive."

Lucy was wearing a raw silk shirtwaist in a rich shade of blue that seemed to have become her favorite color of late.

"Bless you, dear," Lucy exclaimed, glancing over her shoulder at Ford. "My overprotective big brother thinks the skirt is too short."

Sophie cast a second, longer look at the skirt, noting that the soft folds ended at a far-from-daring two inches above Lucy's knees.

"I think that length is very flattering on you," she said honestly. "You have great legs, so why not show them off."

"That's what Joe said," Lucy replied, her cheeks turning a pretty shade of pink.

Sophie had heard about Joe Dooley's recent interest in Lucy and hers in him. She'd also heard that Ford wasn't pleased about either and hadn't been shy in telling Lucy so.

"Where is Joe today?" she asked politely.

"He had other plans," Lucy said, her expression revealing her disappointment.

"So he said," Ford interjected, drawing a pained look from his sister and a curious glance from Sophie.

Instead of the uniform she expected to see, he was wearing a dark blue business suit that she suspected had to have been custom-tailored to accommodate those extrawide shoulders and long legs. His shirt was the latest in trendy stripes, the paisley silk tie impeccably conservative, his cordovan loafers mirror shiny. For once his thick black hair had been blown back from his face, falling into a sexy thatch that looked soft to the touch. He looked so devastatingly appealing that she found herself unabashedly staring.

"Something wrong?" he asked, quirking a raven eyebrow.

"I've never seen you in anything but your uniform," she admitted, drawing a breath.

"You almost didn't today, either!" Lucy exclaimed. "He showed up at my house in ratty old jeans and this horrible faded work shirt that should have been in the ragbag years ago. For a formal Christmas dinner, yet. So naturally I refused to be seen with him unless he changed into something respectable."

"This is Clover, not Charleston," Ford grated. "If a man is clean and doesn't smell bad, he's respectable."

"Don't pay any attention to him, Sophie. He's gone and gotten himself into a bad mood over something or other, and heaven only knows when he's gonna snap out of it."

Ford resisted the urge to tug at his tight collar. Since he'd been elected sheriff that first time, he'd only worn a necktie twice—once when the governor swung through town on a campaign trip and insisted that Ford sit next to him on the speaker's platform in the town square, and once when he'd attended the funeral of the man he'd replaced.

"Are we gonna stand out here all day?" he groused, already second-guessing his decision to take the afternoon off.

"Oh, for heaven's sake, Ford, stop acting like Scrooge and give Sophie a Christmas hug like a good boy," Lucy ordered imperiously before disappearing inside.

Sophie felt a flare of panic, but managed to level it before it showed. "Don't worry, I won't hold you to it," she teased.

"Didn't figure you would."

She turned to follow Lucy. He moved closer. They didn't really collide, but suddenly Ford hooked a steely arm around her waist and spun her around until she was slammed up against him. Solid with muscle, his big chest didn't give an inch. Before she could react, his mouth was heading straight for hers.

Sensations surged through her so fast there was no time to separate one from the other. Outrage, pleasure, a delicious hunger—feelings, impressions and a swirling, intoxicating need for more. He let her go as suddenly as he'd pulled her to him, and she rocked back on her heels, her head swimming.

"I told you not to do that again," she murmured, unable to put more than token anger into her voice.

"And I told you I wasn't about to make a promise when I knew there was no way under God's blue sky I could keep it."

His grin flashed, but his eyes were liquid fire as he reached past her to open the door Lucy had closed behind her. "After you," he said politely.

Sophie walked inside without answering. She had a sinking feeling that nothing she could say would matter to him in the slightest, anyway.

Jessie had obviously finished her dinner and let her mother know by banging her cup on the tray of her high chair.

"Just a minute, sweetheart, and Mama will get you down." Sophie put the last plate into the dishwasher, then closed the door and switched it on.

"Now for those sweet-potato pies I promised everyone," Katie said, reaching into the cupboard for more plates to dirty.

"The coffee's ready." Sophie wiped Jessie's face with a clean washcloth, then kissed the still-damp little cheek. "How about it, toots? Ready to go night-night for a while?"

As if she understood, Jessie shook her head.

Sophie glanced at the clock over the refrigerator. The hands read half past two, a full hour past Jessie's usual nap time. "Just a little while," she proposed in her most persuasive tone.

The baby continued to shake her head.

Sophie and Katie exchanged looks. "Guess that means I'll pour the coffee," Sophie said, laughing.

Jessie let out a screech, holding up her arms so that her mother would pick her up.

"Okay, but no more pulling ornaments off the tree, you hear?" Sophie lifted the baby free of the chair and gave her a hug before setting her on her padded bottom.

"How long do you think it'll be before she's asleep in Roy Dean's lap?" Katie teased as she opened the refrigerator door and peered inside.

"Ten minutes tops," Sophie asserted with total confidence. "Unless one of the misses gets to her first."

"Don't forget about Aunt Peg. I've never seen her so taken with a little one—not even me. And I was adorable."

Laughing, Sophie began piling coffee things on a serving tray Katie had filched from the diner. "What in the world are you looking for in there?" she asked when she noticed Katie shifting cans and containers from one shelf to the other and then back again.

"A carton of whipping cream," Katie muttered. "I know I bought some, but it's disappeared."

Sophie winced. "Uh-oh."

Katie swiveled on the balls of her feet and gave Sophie a pointed look. "Uh-oh what?"

"I used it for the mashed potatoes," Sophie admitted. "That's the way Peg has us make them at the diner, and I guess I just assumed you made them that way, too."

Katie grinned. "No wonder they were so good!" she declared, closing the fridge. "You noticed there wasn't a scrap left."

Sophie put the last of the cups on the tray and reached behind her to untie her apron. "If you'll keep an eye on Jessie, I'll just run down to Shepherd's Market and get some more. They're open for a while yet. It won't take but a minute."

"Since I'm older than you, I'll just let you do that running while I save my energy for pie. Just charge it to my account."

Sophie knew it would be useless to argue, but neither did she expect Katie to pay for her mistake. "Speaking of energy, maybe I'll take Jessie with me. She hasn't been outside today, and it's a beautiful afternoon."

Katie cast a longing look at the patch of blue sky outside the kitchen window. "Great idea. She might even nap a little on the way. I know ridin' always makes me sleepy."

Sophie opened the door to the back porch and retrieved the folded stroller she'd stored there. She was just scooping Jessie into her arms when the door to the dining room swung inward and Ford walked in, looking far too appealing in shirtsleeves and tailored trousers.

Not that she'd wanted to notice, she told herself. She just hadn't been able to ignore the way the pale-blue-and-white shirt had deepened his tan to a sexy bronze or the way the rolled-up sleeves just naturally drew her attention to his impressive biceps whenever she happened to glance his direction.

"My little sister sent me to ask if you two needed help," he drawled, glancing from one to the other casually. Too casually, Sophie suspected. If asked, she had a feeling he could describe the room and everything in it in meticulous detail—including the flush on her cheeks.

"Is Lucy offering her help or yours?" Katie asked, grinning.

"Depends on what needs doin'."

Katie cast a speculative glance Sophie's way. "Sophie's just volunteered to run down to Shepherd's for some whipping cream."

His gaze took in the baby clinging to her neck and the stroller leaning against her leg. "Be best if you had a police escort, I reckon."

"Please don't bother," Sophie said quickly. "It's only a few blocks."

"Truth to tell, Sophie, I've been feelin' so guilty for takin' the day off I'd be grateful if you'd let me walk along with you two ladies. Maybe I can trick my conscience into thinkin' I'm doin' somethin' useful."

Sophie felt her heart sink. Making a fuss would make her appear petty—or worse, afraid to be alone with him.

"Guess we can't have the sheriff's conscience kicking him on Christmas Day," she murmured before shifting her attention to

Katie who had obviously been listening with unabashed interest. "Is there anything else you need?"

"Can't think of a thing." Katie's expression was too innocent for Sophie's peace of mind.

"We won't be long," she said, dodging Jessie's head as the inquisitive little girl suddenly took a notion to dive into Ford's arms.

"Whoa there, sugar," he said, catching her before she slammed into his hard chest. Terrified that the rambunctious baby would fall, Sophie hadn't quite let go, so that in the confusion Jessie ended up wedged between them, with Ford's hand pressed hard against her breast. Startled, she drew a sharp breath and stepped back. He tightened his hold on Jessie and did the same, leaving a good two feet of tense air between them.

"Ready?" he asked, his already deep voice lowered an octave. Nodding, she picked up the stroller and walked ahead of him to the back door.

"Have fun, children," Katie called after them.

Ford muttered something under his breath that had Sophie biting her lip, very grateful that Jessie was too young to understand more than a few basic words.

Outside, the air had the just-washed freshness that invariably followed a rain. A few pillowy clouds floated lazily overhead, and Roy Dean's beloved garden seemed even more vividly green after the morning shower.

Sophie waited until they were beyond the back gate before suggesting that Ford put Jessie in the stroller. He agreed without argument, then insisted on pushing her himself while Jessie chattered away, waving her arms at passing birds, and calling out greetings to neighborhood dogs.

To Sophie's enormous relief, Ford behaved as though the demanding kiss he'd given her on the porch had never happened. Not once did he glance at her suggestively or maneuver on the narrow sidewalk so that his body "accidentally" touched hers.

"You can slow down some now," he said, easily matching his long strides to hers. "Folks watchin' are gonna think something's happened to put a fire under you."

Something has, she thought, and his name is Ford. "What watching folks?" she asked, casting an uneasy glance at the small, neat houses on either side of Clover Street.

"It's only an educated guess, but I'd say damn near everyone along this stretch of street."

"Oh, Lord."

Ford glanced at the lace curtains fluttering in the dining room of the Patterson place and imagined that Sally Patterson was already racing to the phone to alert her mother-in-law three doors up to look out through *her* lace curtains.

He was tempted to drop his arm around Sophie's shoulders, just to give the two devoted gossips something really juicy to chew on. Part of his reason had to do with the streak of pure cussedness he'd learned to tame over the years, even though he'd never quite rid himself of it completely. Mostly, though, he just plain wanted to touch her again.

The more he saw of her, the more she reminded him of a shy, slender-necked doe he'd seen in the Florida Keys once, ready to bolt at the first sign of danger. And yet she wasn't a timid woman. Far from it.

For reasons that she kept private and he intended to respect until he had cause not to, she'd arrived with almost nothing, yet managed to provide everything her little girl could possibly need, including love.

She worked long hours, yet no matter how tired she might become, she was always willing to listen to Miss Milly Culpepper rattle on about long-dead beaux or to prod Catfish Williams into spinning one of his yarns for her, the ones that have long since driven most local folks into yawning boredom. And she'd handled Rans Talley *and* a sick baby in a span of a few hours with a gutsy strength that had impressed the hell out of him.

A gleaming 1949 Packard turned the corner and came toward them at a snail's pace, the tiny white-haired driver peering intently through the steering wheel as she concentrated on controlling the enormous sedan. As the big black car drew abreast, the driver glanced their way, then did a double take. Hiding a smile, Ford nodded and lifted a hand. Sensing Sophie's curious glance, he turned toward her. She looked lovely with her hair burnished to a deep golden brown by the sun and her eyes reflecting the clear blue of a nearly cloudless sky.

"I hope you know we're both gonna be ducking polite questions for a good week or so," he informed her solemnly. "If you get tired of answerin', just refer all questions to the sheriff's office."

"I just might do that." She smiled, and he remembered the feel of that sweet mouth against his. For an instant, right before she'd jerked away, she'd been kissing him back. At least, it had sure felt that way.

His body stirred, and he felt his neck growing hot. Good thing he'd had plenty of practice at keeping his appetites under control, he thought as he opened the door to Shepherd's for her. A damn good thing.

"...and fourteen cents is your change." Mr. Shepherd closed the cash drawer and counted the money into Sophie's hand. "I thank you, and Merry Christmas to y'all."

"Merry Christmas to you and Mrs. Shepherd," Sophie returned, stowing the whipping cream in the stroller's seat.

"I'll pass that along to the missus sure enough," the congenial grocer assured her kindly. "She'll be sorry she missed seeing that cute young 'un of yours. Sure has growed some in the last month. And gettin' prettier all the time, just like her mama."

Returning his smile, she glanced around uneasily. Speaking of Jessie, where had Ford taken her? She could hear Jessie's high-pitched jabbering and Ford's deep-throated answers coming from the rear of the cluttered market, but she couldn't see them anywhere.

As soon as she'd pushed Jessie over the threshold, her little girl had started screaming bloody murder. It was as though she'd taken a sudden and intense dislike to something in Shepherd's only she could understand.

To Sophie's dismay, none of the tried and true methods she'd used in the past had succeeded in soothing the obviously unhappy baby. It was then that Ford had simply plucked the little girl from the soft stroller seat, settled her firmly in the crook of one strong arm and strode off, talking to her in a low, calm voice, leaving Sophie standing by the counter with her mouth open. By the time she'd made a fast trip to the dairy department, Jessie was no longer screaming.

"Don't worry, Miz Reynolds. Ford knows all about amusin' fractious babies. Learned right early, he did, when his mama used to make him look after little Lucy so's she could—" He stopped abruptly, his face rapidly turning from pasty pale to hot pink. "Well, no sense saying out loud what it was that Ford's mama did, rest her soul. Point is, Ford pert near had full charge of his sister from the time she was no bigger'n your Jessamine, so don't you be worryin' when she's with him."

"Oh, I'm not worried," she said, craning her neck for a better look at the rear of the cluttered market. "It's just that Katie is waiting for the whipping cream."

"Knowing Katie, I reckon she'll find somethin' to occupy herself until you get back."

Mr. Shepherd angled a stringy hip against the scarred counter and crossed his arms over his bony chest. "Never did know a girl who could stay busy the way she does. Why, I recollect the time she was in her last year of high school or was it her second to last . . . hmm, let me think a minute . . ." Lips pursed, he paused to search his memory, and Sophie grabbed the opportunity to excuse herself and hurry toward the rear of the cavernous store.

The sound of delighted baby giggles led her through the stockroom to a screen door opening onto a large fenced-in enclosure. Relief ran through her as she caught sight of Ford's broad back.

He was crouched in front of a large rabbit hutch, with Jessie perched like a pampered princess on one strong thigh. One arm encircled her back, holding her secure, while he cradled a baby rabbit in his cupped hands. Crooning nonsense syllables, Jessie was busy rubbing her cheek against the baby's soft white fur. It didn't take a mother's eyes to see that Jessie obviously adored the fat little creature. Sophie was certain she hadn't made a sound, but suddenly Ford looked her way.

"Shopping all done?" he asked.

Nodding, she pushed open the door and joined them by the hutch. "I didn't realize the Shepherds raised rabbits."

He nodded. "For as long as I can remember, anyway. I used to bring Lucy here when she was about Jessie's age."

She swept her gaze along the row of neat cages, laughing at the bewhiskered bunny faces, with their soft, vulnerable brown eyes and pink wiggling noses. Crouching, she touched a finger to the baby's oversize ear.

"Well, hello there, Peter," she murmured. "How are you today?"

"Bun," Jessie asserted, her eyes sparkling.

Sophie's heart turned over. "You like the bunny, don't you, sweetheart?"

Jessie bobbed her head vigorously.

"Give the bunny a kiss good-bye."

"No, no!" Jessamine bounced up and down on Ford's hard thigh, her eyes full of snap and determination.

Ford's mouth twitched. "Stubborn little thing, isn't she?"

"I guess she's decided Peter belongs to her."

"It does seem that way."

Jessie jabbered something in her special jargon, drawing her feathery eyebrows together and looking indignantly from one adult to the other. At the same time, one fat hand smacked Ford on the side of his hard jaw, and Sophie bit her lip.

"Whoa, there, slugger," he drawled, laughing as he captured the flailing little fist in his. "Can't have you puttin' the sheriff down for the count. Might give some bad guys around these parts ideas."

"Here, let me take her," Sophie murmured, reaching for now wriggling little girl. "Say bye-bye to the bunny, sweetheart. It's time to go home."

"No!" The baby flung her arms around Ford's neck and held tight. He looked startled, but pleased.

"We'll come back and see the bunny lots of times," Sophie promised with a coaxing smile. "Tomorrow, even. Okay?"

Jessie turned away, her small square chin set at exactly the same angle as her mother's.

"Guess she's comin' to trust me, even if her mama still has doubts," Ford drawled smugly.

"Or she just knows a gullible ally when she finds one."

Fighting back a grin, Ford tucked Jessie against his side and got to his feet. Instead of returning the rabbit to its cage, he snuggled the furry little body against his belly and wondered how the hell he was going to get the three of them out of this mess.

"Might not hurt her to have a pet to take care of," he ventured, testing the waters.

"Ford, she's only nine months old! Besides, there's Beau. He'd take one look at Peter here and see his next meal."

In her agitation, she'd used his given name for the first time. He told himself he'd crossed an invisible line she'd drawn between them, though he sure as the dickens didn't know how he'd managed that, just being himself like he was.

"I get your point," he admitted reluctantly, "but I have a feeling it's gonna be a mite difficult explaining the brutal realities of the animal kingdom to your daughter."

Sophie had only to look at the rapture on her daughter's face as she petted the tiny rabbit to know that he was simply stating fact. Reluctantly, she lifted her gaze to his. She wanted to be angry with him for introducing Peter in the first place, but she didn't have the heart. Besides, how could she fault him for wanting to spoil her little girl when she had to fight every day to keep from doing the same thing?

"I'm open to suggestions," she said, trying not to think of Beau's sharp teeth. In spite of the aged dog's fading faculties, he could still get around surprisingly fast when the mood struck him.

"We could always keep Peter at my place."

"That's very generous of you to offer, but—"

"Generous, hell," he muttered. "I'm just trying to figure out a way to make Jess here happy without making you mad as a little hornet in the bargain."

"I'm not mad," she murmured, smiling at Jessie because smiling at him seemed too intimate all of a sudden. "I realize you were only trying to do a good deed."

It was the wrong thing to say. His mouth drew tight, and his eyes flashed. "I'm no Boy Scout, Sophie. Whatever I do, I do because I want to, not because I'm tryin' to pile up a bunch of points."

"That's not what I meant at all," she declared, her voice rising and her cheeks heating.

"Just so's that's understood."

"Perfectly!"

"Fine." He shifted Jessie to a more comfortable position, then whispered something in the little girl's ear that had her giggling.

"Here, hold Peter a minute," he said, handing Sophie the wriggling rabbit. As soon as his hand was free, he slipped it behind Sophie's back and drew her against him. He was kissing her before she could think, arousing her before she could push him away.

His hand flattened against her back, urging her to curl against him while he patiently, gently explored her mouth with his. She felt infused with new energy, new life, as she strained against him. Her breasts swelled and throbbed against the muscular wall of his chest, tangible signs of the urgency building inside her.

It was as though her deadened senses had suddenly come to life, blossoming under the stimulation of his mouth and his body.

Distantly, in the back of her mind, she wished he didn't have Jessie tucked against one lean hip, keeping him from pressing the hard length of his body against hers. All that was womanly inside her longed to feel his hands stroking bare skin, to feel the heat of a hard, masculine arousal filling her, soothing old hurts, healing old wounds.

When he finally lifted his mouth from hers, she swayed, and felt the muscles of his forearm bunch, supporting her until she managed to stiffen her suddenly liquid spine. Her senses were swirling, her mind clouded. Lifting her lashes took effort. Focusing on his face took concentration. When her vision cleared, she all but gasped aloud at the violent need she saw reflected in his dark eyes.

"You were saying?" he drawled, his voice hoarse and a little breathless.

"I won't be coerced," she murmured, dropping her gaze to his mouth. He had strongly molded lips, with a sensuous fullness that she hadn't noticed before. The corners, though, held a tension that she suspected never completely relaxed, even when he slept.

"Into what?" he demanded, his eyes the color of storm-drenched flint.

"Whatever you're trying to coerce me into," she replied lamely, her mind suddenly muddled.

"Now that's what I like, a decisive female."

"Oh, shut up," she muttered, bending to set Peter on his four furry feet.

"Yes, ma'am." So quickly she found herself frozen, he'd deposited Jessie on her padded bottom next to Peter and was pulling her into his arms again.

"No," Sophie murmured, but his mouth was already finding hers. This time he wasn't so patient, nor as gentle. This time the hunger she tasted was sharp and insistent, as though he was no longer capable of restraint. His arms pressed around her as his tongue urged her lips to part.

Dimly aware of Jessie's soft patter, she fought for sanity, fought to push him away, only to find her arms stealing around his neck. The sounds she heard came from her now, soft moaning pleas that invited the invasion of his probing tongue.

He lifted a hand to her hair, fisting his fingers there to hold her still while his mouth tasted. Pleasure ran along her spine to gather in a hot pool low and deep inside her. As though feeling the same sensations, his body shuddered, his thighs going rigid against hers. A groan broke from his lips, and he pulled his mouth from hers.

"I've always had rotten timing," he said, drawing a long stream of air into his lungs. "But it's goin' to happen. Sooner or later we're goin' to make love." He rested both hands lightly on her shoulders, not trapping her so much as steadying her. Or perhaps himself.

She shook her head, a feeling very close to despair pressing in on her. "No, Ford, we're not."

His smile was lazy, his hand just as lazy as he brushed the rough pad of his thumb over her lower lip. Her mouth trembled, before she firmed her lips, igniting a flare of heat in his eyes.

"Oh, yeah, it'll happen. And when it does, it'll be because it's what we both want." He held her gaze for a long moment before he released her.

Turning away, she crouched next to Jessie, who was still sitting where Ford had settled her, contentedly sucking her thumb as she watched the little white rabbit munching tufts of grass at the edge of the concrete.

"Time to go bye-bye, sweetheart," she said, scooping Jessie into her arms. Instantly, the baby went rigid, then began screaming.

"I don't think she wants to leave quite yet," Ford drawled, watching Sophie struggle to control her squirming, frantically kicking child.

"She...*ouch!*" Jessie's heel caught her in the solar plexus, and though the pain didn't last, it was momentarily intense enough to make her flinch.

Scowling, Ford snatched the baby from her and hoisted her high above his head. Sophie opened her mouth to shout a protest, when a sudden silence descended. Instead of screaming, Jessie was now staring at Ford intently with something like astonishment shining in her chocolate-colored eyes.

"That's better," Ford said gently, bringing her into the shelter of his body.

"How did you know to do that?" she asked, halfway expecting Jessie to start yelling bloody murder any minute.

"Trial and error. Lucy used to be a holy terror at this age, too. Darn near had me ready to wring her neck more than once. Guess it was providence that had me shovin' her up in the air one day. I think the shock of finding herself all but suspended in midair drove the cryin' right out of her."

Sophie tweaked Jessie's toes. "Whatever, I'm glad it worked."

Jessie yawned, her eyes sleepy. She rested her head on Ford's shoulder and poked her thumb in her mouth.

"Better get her out of here before she starts up again," Sophie said, glancing uneasily at the rabbit. The quick frown crossing Ford's tanned face told her that he'd forgotten all about the cause of Jessie's tantrum.

"Good idea. You take her, and I'll put Peter back in his cage."

She took the baby, who fussed a little at leaving Ford's arms. Another mark against him, she told herself while knowing that it was just the opposite.

"Let's go find the stroller," she said, turning toward the store. Behind her she heard Ford mutter a curse, followed by the sound of scuffling. Turning instinctively, she nearly laughed aloud at the sight of Ford's supremely conditioned, marvelously male body sprawled flat on the concrete. As for the rabbit, all she saw of him was a fluffy white tail as Peter streaked for the bushes in the corner of the yard.

"Are you all right?" she asked, her voice suspiciously unsteady.

He flipped to his back, then sat up. Why did he have to look so adorable with his hair flopping over his forehead and a smudge of dirt on his chin? she wondered, her nerves beginning to unravel.

Narrowing his eyes, he glared up at her. "I'll be just fine, provided you swear never to tell a solitary soul what you just saw."

She struggled to hold back a grin. "Actually, I didn't *see* anything—"

"Good." His expression cleared. "Could be my luck's changin' for the better." He got to his feet and brushed the dust from his front.

"—other than our illustrious sheriff spread-eagle on the ground," she continued when his gaze leveled on hers again.

His mouth pulled up at one corner. It wasn't really a smile, but it still had her stomach fluttering. "Something which you will never reveal."

"I won't?"

"No." He advanced on her, his movements slow and deliberate, like a boxer setting up an opponent. She took a step backward, her arms tightening around the baby.

"You wouldn't attack a woman with a child in her arms, would you?" she protested plaintively.

"Oh, yes, ma'am, I would. Maguire men have no scruples at all." His eyes grew dark and turbulent, and his jaw set. She took another step backward, only to find her back against the building. She was reminded again of a wolf on the prowl as he stopped in front of her and braced both arms at the level of her shoulders.

"Want to argue some more, or shall we get right to New Year's Eve?" he asked, slow and easy.

"New Year's Eve?" she asked, peeking past Jessie's curls.

"One of my deputies is having a party. He's invited me to come, and I tried like hell to get out of it, but you know these young bucks. Won't take no for an answer, so I'm stuck. I want you to go with me."

He leaned closer, his voice a menacing growl, but she noticed that he was careful not to crush Jessie's small body between them. She felt heat radiating from his skin, saw it in his eyes. For an instant she had a vivid image of the two of them locked together on clean, smooth sheets, his mouth on her breast, her hands tangled in that thick, tousled hair. Like a persistent ache, need spread through her until she felt heavy and hot inside.

"I'm, um, busy."

"It wouldn't be a date," he persisted as though she hadn't spoken. "It would be a favor, and though I hate to bring it up, you do owe me one for driving you and Jessie to Doc's in the middle of the night."

Neatly, deftly trapped, she sneaked a peek at Jessie's face. It wasn't nice to hope her daughter would suddenly take a notion to throw another tantrum, but she was hoping just the same. Traitor that she was, the little dickens was sound asleep, and Sophie nearly groaned aloud.

"It wasn't exactly the middle of the night, and in case you've forgotten, I offered to take a taxi," she grumbled, "but you're right. I do owe you a favor, and if you want me to go to the party, I will."

Ford felt elation run through him with the same fiery kick as Frenchy's finest, but he kept his expression controlled as he stepped back.

"I'll pick you up at eight."

"I'll be ready." She shifted the sleeping baby from one side to the other and waited for him to open the screen door. "Don't forget the rabbit," she replied over her shoulder as she sailed past him. "And wipe the dirt from your chin before you head back to Katie's."

His sudden rumble of laughter stayed with her all the way home.

Chapter Seven

Christmas in the South was different, Sophie discovered, and it wasn't only the warm weather and bright sky that distinguished Christmas Day from the ones she remembered. It seemed that Christmas dinner lasted all day. After the sweet-potato pie, Katie served coffee and homemade mints, followed by an offer of turkey-and-cranberry-sauce sandwiches. Between courses, the ladies "visited" and the men played cribbage.

By seven-thirty Jessie had finally succumbed to the bustle and excitement and had fallen asleep on Ford's shoulder. Over his quiet protest Sophie had taken her up to bed, grateful for the respite from so many conversations flowing at once.

It was close to eight when she came downstairs again, determined to plead fatigue in order to make it an early night. Ford was waiting for her in the foyer, holding Beau, who was enthusiastically licking Ford's hand.

"You and I have been nominated to take Beau for his nightly constitutional," he said when she was nearly to the bottom of the stairs.

"I'm afraid I'll have to decline that honor tonight," she murmured, rubbing Beau's ears. "I just came down to say good-night to everyone."

"Aren't you feelin' well?"

"I'm fine, but I *do* have the morning shift tomorrow."

The old dog made a rumbling noise of pleasure in his throat and closed his eyes, and Ford found himself in the infuriating position of envying an old hound dog.

"A turn in the night air is just what you need to make you sleep like a baby," he drawled, knowing it was damn thin as reasons went, but he was desperate. If he didn't kiss her again soon, it was a good bet he'd spend the rest of the night wishing he had.

"No, really, Ford. I'd rather just call it a night."

"Humor me, honey. Beau and I never were the best of friends, and if I bring him back in a bad temper, Miss Rose Ruth will blister my ears but good."

Sophie couldn't help laughing at the image of the tiny septuagenarian blistering anything of Ford's without his permission. "Oh, all right, but only for a few minutes. I'll go get a jacket."

"No, you can use mine." He hooked a hand under her elbow and drew her to the door.

"But what'll you wear?" she protested, but he shoved Beau into her arms and opened the door, hooking his jacket from the brass hall tree as he ushered her out onto the porch.

"Nice night," he said as he took Beau's leash from his pocket and clipped it to the old dog's new red collar. "Here you go, old son," he said, lifting the dog from her arms only to deposit him on the porch floor.

"Now you hold on to this," he said, handing her the leash.

"Ford—"

"Here, slip into this before you get chilled." Before she could make him understand, she found herself wrapped in his suit coat, her free hand tucked into his, and a very anxious Beau straining at the leash she still held in her left hand.

"You're impossible, you know that?" she said as Ford led her down the porch steps.

"But lovable, right?" His teeth flashed white in the glow from the porch. He seemed younger tonight, and more relaxed than she'd ever seen him.

"Lovable isn't exactly the word I'd choose," she admitted, pausing to let Beau sniff the azalea bushes by the steps.

"Irresistible, maybe?" He bent his head to nuzzle her neck. Pleasure chased down her spine, followed by an invasive warmth.

"More like irritating."

"Good thing I'm not sensitive, or my ego would surely be hurtin' about now," he said, his breath warm on her neck.

When she realized she was in danger of wanting more than a few lazy, teasing kisses, she tugged Beau away from the flowers. The old dog gave an annoyed, "Woof," and then settled into his usual shambling rhythm.

This time they headed north, toward Clover's business district. Clover Street itself was deserted, but Christmas lights blazed from every house along the tree-lined thoroughfare, giving the night a festive air.

At the corner, Beau decided to turn left, taking them down Atlantic Avenue. It was one of Clover's older areas, and the houses were all one of a kind. Nearly all of the yards were beautifully landscaped, many surrounded by ornate iron fences.

"I really do love it here," she murmured. "Everything's so different, so interesting. The people, the antebellum architecture— just walking down the street is a living history lesson." She took a breath, then laughed self-consciously as she lifted her gaze to his. "I guess I must sound pretty naive."

"Not to me."

"Wells always said I was a sucker for old things. In a way I suppose he was right." She laughed as Beau detoured toward his favorite tree, intent upon marking his territory with the frantic fervor of a pup.

"Was your husband from Montana, too?" Ford asked when they'd walked almost a block in silence.

"Yes," she said, staring straight ahead.

"Where'd you meet?"

"In school."

Ford cursed himself for being a nosy bastard, but the need to know her feelings about her dead husband was like a painful knot in his belly.

"Guess you must miss him a lot this time of year."

When they reached the circle of light from the next street lamp, she stopped short. "Please, Ford, don't ask me any more questions about my marriage," she said, turning to face him.

His first instinct was to wrap himself around her and hold her close. Because it wasn't sex that motivated him, he hesitated. The same fragile look was back in her eyes, as though she would shatter if he touched her.

"Just tell me one more thing," he said quietly. "Are you still in love with your husband?"

Her gaze flickered. "No," she murmured. "I'm not in love with him, but I haven't forgotten him, either, or the pain I caused him and his family."

Without planning it, he stepped closer—physically, emotionally. He was touching her hair before he gave himself time to weigh the reasons—or the consequences. When she didn't protest, he skimmed his mouth over her temple, breathing in the spring-rain scent of her shampoo.

"Tell me what I can do to make you happy tonight," he murmured, easing her into his arms.

"It makes me happy to know that you cared enough to ask." She tilted her head back so that she could see his face. "I think you're a very nice man, Ford Maguire. Even though you don't smile nearly as often as you should."

Ford lifted his eyebrows. Since he'd been no taller than a thistle weed, he'd put up with people he cared about pointing out his faults to him, but that wasn't one of them.

"How do you know how often I smile when I'm not around you?"

"I don't," she admitted, lowering her gaze from his eyes to his mouth and pursing her lips. It was all he could do to keep from covering that provocative pout with a kiss. He couldn't remember ever wanting a woman as much as he wanted Sophie—or found himself as willing to wait for her.

"Are you telling me it's my fault you scowl more than you smile?" she demanded softly.

"Must be. Nobody else in thirty-six years has ever complained. But just for you, I'll try not to scowl so much."

"Starting now?"

When he continued to scowl at her, Sophie pushed at the tight corner of his mouth with her fingertip. Obediently, he curved his lips, looking self-conscious, and yet disturbingly attractive. Without warning, she felt desire gathering again, stronger this time, based more on emotion than sexual excitement and thus harder to resist.

"You really do have a gorgeous smile," she murmured before she could stop herself.

She saw surprise in his eyes, and hunger, and then his mouth was covering hers and warmth was spreading inside her. His mouth made gentle demands, and pleasure exploded. His arms drew her closer, and she responded by pushing to her tiptoes, needing the pressure of his chest against her suddenly tingling breasts.

She heard whimpering, then knew that it was her making the small greedy sounds. His mouth lifted, and she forced open her eyes.

"More?" he whispered hoarsely, his eyes glittering between thick black lashes.

"Yes," she murmured, scarcely recognizing that sultry panting voice as her own.

Even though Ford was driven to take her there and now, in the soft earth beneath the fragrant winter azaleas, with the sounds of Christmas carols ringing in their ears, he managed to curb the savagery of his own need, even as he deepened his kiss.

It stunned him to realize that he wanted more from her than one night. And knowing that, admitting that, had him banking fires he'd never banked before.

Drawing back, he waited for her to open her eyes. They were the color of deep twilight in the glow from the streetlight and glazed with pleasure he'd put there.

"I think it's time we headed back. Otherwise, I'm not sure we'll make it before sunrise."

Sophie was still sleepy when she went to work the next day at 6:00 a.m. The morning rush was lighter than usual, something Peg had already warned her usually happened when December 26 fell on a weekday. A lot of the people who worked in Clover's business district had the day off.

Because she'd needed the money, Sophie had jumped at the chance to work Evie's shift again so that Evie could spend Christmas with her husband's family in Atlanta. But now that she was actually at work and looking at a long day, she was wishing she'd said no when Evie had asked.

It didn't help that Peg seemed grumpier than usual. Did she wish she were somewhere else, too? Sophie wondered when she entered the pantry for another jug of blueberry syrup and found Peg muttering to herself over the year-end inventory.

"Instead of caterin' to make money on the side, why don't you buy this place so's I can get me some rest," Peg grumbled when she spied Sophie entering. "I'll make you a real good deal."

"Thanks but no thanks," Sophie said, reaching for the syrup. "I'm having enough trouble trying to figure out what to charge for my catering services."

"Did you have those flyers printed up yet?"

"Not yet. Friendly Printers wants to be paid up front."

"Not very friendly, are they?" Peg drawled.

Sophie laughed. "No, but they are the cheapest. That's why I picked them."

Peg gave her a sympathetic look before returning her attention to the shelf of canned vegetables. "Oh, I almost forgot," she said as Sophie was on her way out. "Ask Ford to stop by to see me before he leaves, will you please? I got this letter from the prosecutor's office I need to ask him about."

"He hasn't come in yet," Sophie said, glancing at the hands of the nearby time clock. To her shock, she discovered that it was almost eight o'clock.

Peg raised her eyebrows in obvious surprise, then shrugged. "I guess he's entitled to sleep late one day of the year."

"I'll give him your message when he shows up," Sophie promised before shutting Peg in. But even as she filled one of the pitchers she'd carried into the kitchen she was thinking about Peg's words.

In her mind's eye she saw him asleep, his arms hugging the pillow, his body not quite relaxed, his face still taut with tension that didn't ease, even when he closed out the world. Even though she knew he hadn't lived the life of a cloistered monk, and Sissy certainly proved that, she pictured him lying there alone. Always alone.

Perhaps that was the reason she kept imagining him as that proud solitary wolf, taking on the heaviest burdens, accepting the loneliest of tasks so that others would be free to live as they wished, just as he'd shackled himself to a small-town job and a small-town life so that his sister could grow up feeling secure and protected. And loved.

For all her gentle complaining, Lucy knew that above all. Ford might fuss about the length of her skirt and her choice in men, but he would always let those choices be hers. And, Sophie suspected, he would always be there for her, no matter what mistakes she made.

Smiling to herself, Sophie exchanged a full pitcher for an empty one, and tipped the heavy bottle over the lip. Her parents had loved her without reservations, the way Ford seemed to love Lucy. Perhaps that's why she hadn't understood how devastating it could be when love came with conditions. Conditions she hadn't been able to meet, no matter how hard she'd tried.

A small shudder ran through her as she remembered the frustration seething in Wells's eyes when she'd refused his repeated demands that she give up teaching for a full-time job as wife, mistress and hostess.

Gradually, like a virus sapping her strength, she'd realized just how pathologically insecure he'd been under that glossy, constantly refined image of the powerful, dynamic, sophisticated professional. He'd been all flash, and no steel. Just the opposite of Ford Maguire, she thought, licking a drop of sweet syrup from her finger before switching to the next pitcher.

Ford seemed tough because he *was* tough. It wasn't simply a matter of steely muscle and sinew, though he was a magnificent man in the physical sense, no doubt about that. No, his toughness came from some inner code that wouldn't allow him to bend a rule he considered fair or violate a principle he believed just, no matter what personal grief he might suffer.

Such a man would never flinch from duty.

Such a man would be impossible to ignore, and even more impossible to love. There was a third "impossible," she realized, stunned into immobility. It was all but impossible to keep from loving such a man once you'd found him.

"Good gracious, child, where *is* your mind?"

Jerked back to reality by Mrs. DuPuis's incredulous tone, Sophie was mortified to discover the pitcher she'd been refilling had overflowed onto the fussy cook's spotless counter. Gooey syrup the color of ink was already dripping onto the equally spotless linoleum.

"Uh, guess I was daydreaming," she told the imperiously majestic cook with an apologetic smile.

"Must have been some daydream, that!" Mrs. DuPuis retorted, a smile flitting across her teak brown face. "I recollect one or two of those myself, especially after I first laid eyes on my Henri.''

Feeling her face flame, Sophie hastily put down the jug and grabbed a towel. It took *three* towels and a great deal of elbow grease and liquid soap before the last of the sticky syrup had been wiped away. By the time she was finished, she'd convinced herself that she couldn't possibly be in love with Ford Maguire.

He came in at ten, looking tired and out of sorts. His long rope-muscled body was dressed in the familiar khaki uniform, the well-cut trousers laundered to a chamois softness that only made the hard musculature of his legs and calves that much more noticeable.

Only a few of the tables were still occupied, and none of the counter stools. Presented with a choice of seats, he nevertheless headed straight for the last stool on the left, walking with a loose, easy stride that only enhanced the air of command he wore as easily as the blue steel pistol on his hip.

Sophie drew in one deep breath, then let it out again, trying to relieve a sudden and definitely unwanted case of nerves. Instead of easing the annoying flutters in her stomach, it only seemed to make them worse.

"Good morning." Sophie set a brimming mug of steaming coffee in front of him before readying her pad for his order.

'' 'Mornin'.''

He favored her with a far-from-seductive look as he lifted the mug to his mouth. Waiting for him to finish, she noticed suddenly that the back of his hand was crisscrossed with angry red scratches.

"What happened to your hand?" she asked, indicating the superficial wounds with a pointed look.

His gaze followed hers. "Tangled with some briars down at Deadman's Slough. A couple of my boys and I went lookin' for Frenchy this mornin'.''

She winced. "Any luck?"

He shrugged. "Some. We found where he'd been set up only a short time back. Figured he'd relocated when Talley was arrested.''

"Speaking of that, Peg would like to speak with you before you leave, something about a letter from the county prosecutor. She's in the back.''

His mouth firmed, giving him a harsh, angry look. Outside, a semi rumbled past, shaking the window glass. "Looks like Rans is gonna get out on bail today. Word around the courthouse is that the same someone who put up the money for bail also hired him a big-city lawyer."

"Any idea who that someone might be?" she asked, dreading the answer.

"My first guess would be Frenchy. Be my last guess, too, come to think of it."

Sophie's felt a chill. "Should I be worried?"

His mouth softened slightly. "Not as long as Rans stays away from the booze."

"What happens if he doesn't?"

"If he stays inside his place, nothing. If he even looks like he's leavin', he'll find himself headin' back to jail, like *right now.*"

Sophie drew a breath. "How would you know if he was drinking?"

His eyes narrowed. "Because he's being watched." He glanced past her at the blackboard, his expression nonthreatening. Only someone observing him closely would notice the taut pull of his jaw muscles.

"Who's cookin' this morning?" He shifted his gaze to her face, pinning her. It was then that she noticed the ice in his eyes.

"Mrs. DuPuis."

He leaned back, drawing his coffee closer to his flat belly. "In that case, I'll have some of her fried bread and sausage."

"Toast and juice?"

"Might as well."

"Anything else?" She glanced up, her pencil still poised.

"Now that you mention it, yeah." He tilted his head, a cynical smile playing over his hard mouth. "Now that you and I are gettin' on so well, I'd like to hire you to handle the doings for Mike Flint next month."

"I should have said no," Sophie muttered, rummaging through the sparse contents of her closet. "No to the party, no to the catering job."

While Jessie watched from her favorite spot on the floor, Sophie pulled out her ivory blouse and held it against her while inspecting her image in the mirror affixed to the closet door. Almost new when she'd found it at the resale shop, the blouse was a lovely color, a classic design and... "Frumpy," she muttered, suddenly more dispirited than ever.

It didn't help to remember the lovely, silky gowns she'd had before she was married. Her mother had helped her make them, and each one was special. She had no idea where they were now. After she'd been sent to prison, Anita Manwaring had taken it upon herself to sell everything left in Sophie's house. Sophie had had to sell the house itself in order to pay her legal fees. The few dollars that had been left over had gone into a trust for Jessie.

"It's hopeless, Jess," she muttered, returning the blouse to the rod. "I don't have anything festive enough for a party."

Jessie furrowed her brow as though deep in thought, and Sophie laughed. "Yes, I know. It's not a date, and no one will notice what I'm wearing, anyway."

Bored with watching her mother, Jessie flipped to all fours and crawled to her crib. Using the bars, she pulled herself to a standing position, then glanced over her shoulder to see if her mother had been watching.

"What a clever girl!" Sophie exclaimed softly, clapping her hands.

Distracted by her own giggles, Jessie blinked, then lost her grip and fell hard on her bottom. Her face started to crumple, and Sophie scooped her into her arms.

"Don't be ashamed of falling down, Jessie Bear," she murmured, kissing the baby's crown of curls. "That's how we learn. The important thing is to keep on trying, no matter how badly you want to quit, and before you know it, you'll be walking all over the place."

With a sore heart, Sophie realized that her little girl would soon be talking more, too, and asking question after question in the way of all children—about everything and nothing. Why is the sky blue? Where does the sun go at night? Why didn't she have a daddy or grandparents or any family at all besides her mother?

Sophie drew a shallow breath, feeling sick at heart. A lot of children grew up with only one parent, she told herself staunchly as she carried Jessie to the bed and sat down.

"Look at Katie," she said to Jessie brightly, cradling her close. "She was raised by her Aunt Peg and she turned out just fine. And Lucy, she lost her parents when she was only nine. You couldn't ask for a nicer, more well-adjusted person." She drew a breath. "Ford must have been a good father to her, don't you think?"

Jessie gurgled something indistinct and started playing with Sophie's watch. "Yes, I know you like him a lot. I do, too, but we have to be very careful not to let ourselves become too fond of him."

She bounced Jessie's foot in her hand, remembering Ford's gentleness with Jessie. And with her, though she knew full well that there was another side to that good-natured, slow-walkin', slow-talkin' way he had.

"If he knew the truth, he'd arrest me, Jessie," she murmured with a sigh. "Maybe he wouldn't like doing it, and maybe he'd do it as privately as he could, but he'd still arrest me. And he'd turn me over to the Portland police because that's what he's sworn to do."

Her throat tightened, and she swallowed hard. "See, the thing is, Jess. I think I might be falling in love with him, and—"

A knock at the door kept her from finishing the sentence—and the thought. "It's Fanny, dear."

"Come on in, Miss Fanny," she called, curving her lips into a welcoming smile.

"I just came in to see if you'd like some hot milk," Fanny said as she entered and closed the door behind her. "Oh, dear, you're not leaving, are you?"

Sophie drew a blank. "Sorry?"

"The clothes," Fanny explained, gesturing to the outfits strewn over the bed and chair. "You're not packin' to leave us, are you?"

"Oh, no," Sophie exclaimed, smiling. "I was just trying to decide what to wear to a New Year's Eve party."

Fanny's pale eyes brightened. "Ah, I see. You have a social engagement with a young man."

"Well, no, not really," Sophie hastened to explain. "Ford was invited to a party by one of his deputies, and he asked me to go along. That's all."

Fanny offered her a genteel smile. "I do believe things must have changed more than I thought over the years, because that surely does sound like a social engagement to me."

"We're just friends." She gave Jessie a quick kiss, then set her on the floor before rising to hastily gather the discarded outfits.

"I confess I'm sorry to hear that. You see, I was so sure I noticed a certain chemistry between you and Ford during Christmas dinner and, well, I was so hoping you two might find the happiness denied Johnny Ray and me."

Sophie's heart went out to the old woman. How sad to be so alone with only memories for such a very long time. "Not everyone is as lucky to find that special person the way you were," she murmured around the lump in her throat.

Miss Fanny picked up a cotton turtleneck and began folding it carefully with her gnarled hands. "I hear a terrible sadness in your voice, Sophie. I don't mean to pry, but if there's anything I can do to help, I hope you'll let me at least try."

Sophie felt tears sting her eyes, but she managed to will them from falling. "Thank you, Miss Fanny. I wish you could help, but you can't. I have to solve my own problems."

"And bear your own burdens?" Fanny asked gently.

Sophie smiled. "Something like that, yes."

"Like Ford," the old lady murmured on a heavy sigh before brightening. "There is one thing I can do, however, and that's to lend you the perfect dress for tomorrow night."

Sophie felt alarm stiffen her face. "Oh, I couldn't—"

"Don't worry, dear. It's not one of these old-lady frocks I wear these days," she declared, lifting her skirt with her hand. "It belonged to my mother, and I've kept it all these years because it was just too lovely to part with."

Sophie hung the last of her clothes in the closet, then turned to accept the folded turtleneck from Fanny. "I'd love for you to show it to me, Miss Fanny, but I couldn't wear your mother's dress."

Miss Fanny simply smiled. "It's in the trunk in my room. Why don't you bring Jessamine with you, and we'll all three take a look at it."

"Did you hear that, Jessie Bear?" Sophie said, stowing the folded shirt in a drawer before lifting her daughter into her arms. "Miss Fanny is asking us to a fashion show."

Jessie blinked her feathery lashes, then yawned. Sophie shared a smile with Miss Fanny as they left the room.

On the way, Fanny paused to knock on Rose Ruth's door, but there was no answer. "Rose Ruth is certainly proving the adage about there bein' no fool like an old fool," she said peevishly as she opened her own door. "Told me she was goin' to the library tonight, but I'll bet you dollars to doughnuts she's with Hammond Gossely at his place right this minute."

Sophie stared at her. "I . . . you mean they're, um, dating?"

Fanny sniffed. "At the very least."

Amazed and amused, Sophie deposited Jessie in the corner where Fanny kept some of the baby's toys for the times when she watched Jessie during the day.

"Can I help?" she asked as Miss Fanny lifted the lid of the old metal steamer trunk at the foot of her bed.

"If you'll just lift out that top tray for me, please," Miss Fanny said, hovering eagerly. "That's it, put it on the bed. It won't hurt that old quilt any."

Sophie did as she was told, then watched, bemused, as Miss Fanny lifted an amazing collection of old letters, rumpled clothing and other odds and ends from the stuffed trunk.

"Ah, here it is," she murmured, lifting out a dressmaker's box with reverent care. "It's been years since I packed this away, but, thank the good Lord, silk is practically indestructible."

The box was tied with a pink satin ribbon. Inside, the contents were swathed in tissue paper and smelled of lavender. Sophie found herself leaning closer as Miss Fanny drew back the last layer.

"I'd forgotten how heavy this was," the old lady murmured as she lifted out a bead-encrusted chemise of shimmering champagne silk.

"Oh, Miss Fanny, it's exquisite!" Sophie murmured with an excitement she couldn't quite keep inside.

"It is, isn't it?"

Miss Fanny lovingly stroked the low-cut silk bodice with gnarled fingers. Row after row of beaded fringe caught the light, sparkling like bubbles in wine. Sophie drew a shaky breath. The longing to slip into the sleek sheath was close to irresistible. But the delicate silk seemed too fragile to risk.

"Did you ever wear it yourself?" she asked, unable to tear her gaze away from the beautiful gown.

"Yes, once. It was the night Johnny Ray asked me to marry him." Miss Fanny's smile was ethereal, contrasting with the very real tears suddenly filling her faded violet eyes. "It would give me great pleasure to see you wearin' it tomorrow night."

"Oh, but I couldn't," Sophie murmured, regret and longing fighting for dominance. "What if I spilled something on it? Or... or got the fringe caught in the car door?"

"We both know that's unlikely, my dear," the old lady chided gently, pressing the gossamer chemise into Sophie's hands. "And I won't take no for an answer, so let's hear no more nonsense."

Before Sophie could utter another word, Miss Fanny was on her feet and heading for the ornate highboy in the corner. From the top drawer she drew a flat jewelry case covered in faded maroon velvet.

"Something very simple would be best, I think," she muttered, opening the case. She hesitated, then from the satin interior she drew a single teardrop pearl on a thin gold chain and held it up to the light. Like a delicate pink prism, it splintered the light into a muted pastel rainbow that had Sophie's breath catching.

"It would be perfect," she admitted softly, "but truly, I can't—"

"Of course you can," Miss Fanny declared, her expression turning beatific. "I can hardly wait to see Ford Maguire's face when you come floatin' down the front stairs in that dress. Likely he'll need help rememberin' his own name."

Chapter 8

Getting Jessie ready for bed, and then herself ready for an evening out, had been an exercise in patience, not to mention stamina. First Jessie had decided to practice her flutter kick during her bath, drenching both the bathroom and Sophie, which meant Sophie had to wipe down the floor and several of the walls before she herself could bathe.

With Jessie's interested help, it had taken her half a dozen tries to get her eye makeup on straight and her hair fixed just so. Then Katie had come in to offer the use of her pearl earrings, followed almost immediately by Miss Rose Ruth, who'd spent a good twenty minutes debating aloud which comb would look best with Sophie's brown hair—the one studded with eye-catching rhinestones or the more sedate mother-of-pearl. By the time Katie had kidnapped Jessie, and the two misses had retired to the parlor for several bracing sips of medicinal wine, it was nearly eight o'clock, and Sophie was wracked with nerves.

Holding her breath, she carefully lifted the dress over her head and let it slither down her upraised arms. The silk was skimming soft and hugged her hips with not even a fraction of an inch to spare. In spite of the flapper flavor, it was the most sophisticated dress she'd ever worn—and the most provocative.

"I might as well wear a sign," she muttered as she zipped up the low cut back. "Lonely widow seeks a strong, honest and infinitely gentle man to love her just as she is, without asking questions she can't answer."

Love? Who was she kidding here? Ford didn't love her. Nor did she want him to. But he *does* want to make love to you, a voice at the fringes of her mind reminded her. *And you want to make love to him.*

The silent admission gave rise to another, stronger flutter of nerves. She was making a terrible mistake, she realized, on a wave of pure panic. Agreeing to go anywhere with Ford had to be utter lunacy. Greeting him at the door in the sexiest dress she'd ever laid eyes on was an invitation to disaster. Every time she moved, the beads swayed and shimmered like steamy August heat, and the silk caressed her skin like the hand of an adoring lover. Simply walking across the room made her think of rippling male muscles and a strong man's lonely eyes.

"Oh, Lord," she moaned as she nervously affixed Katie's pearl studs to each ear. Her hair had been tousled into a casual bob, caught above one ear with the mother-of-pearl comb Miss Rose Ruth had decided would be the crowning touch. Before she had a chance to settle her suddenly sizzling nerves, she heard the distant chiming of the doorbell. The clock on the dresser said 7:59.

Of course he would be on time. He'd said eight o'clock, so he'd meant eight o'clock—not a fashionably late eight-fifteen, followed by an excuse subtly crafted to impress her with his busy schedule and infinite importance, a power game Wells and his friends had played to perfection.

Ford didn't play power games. He didn't have to, she reminded herself grimly as she snatched up Katie's wrap and Miss Fanny's black satin evening bag.

By the time she made the turn at the second-floor landing, her pulse was roaring in her ears. She hadn't been this nervous at her first senior prom, or even, she realized with a bittersweet pang, at her wedding to Wells.

Ford was waiting for her in the foyer, along with the two elderly fairy godmothers and Katie. Jessie was there, too, held high in Ford's arms, her head resting against his shoulder. Even though this time she was prepared to see him in civilian clothes, she hadn't expected him to look so sophisticated. He was wearing a tweed jacket in shades of brown and a creamy hand-knit sweater that did marvelous things for his tanned skin. Her lips twitched when she noticed the snug jeans and boots, both obviously clean and, in the case of the boots, polished to a high gloss.

"Happy New Year," she murmured when his gaze came to hers and held. She was two steps from the bottom, which put them eye to eye. Perhaps that was why she was able to see eyes darken to the color of smoke.

"Evenin'." His voice had that same slightly raspy quality to it she'd noticed right before he'd kissed her the last time. Taking a tight grip on her composure she descended the two steps to the tiled foyer floor. "Uh, I'll just take Jessie upstairs and put her to bed, and then we can go."

"You'll do no such silly thing," Rose Ruth chided. "Fanny and I will tuck Jessie in good and tight—"

"After her bedtime story, of course," Fanny chimed in, beaming at Jessie, who seemed perfectly content to snuggle against Ford's big chest and suck her thumb.

"Don't worry about a thing, dear," Rose Ruth admonished cheerfully. "Run along and have a good time with your friends."

Sophie smiled her surrender. When the ladies ganged up against her, it was usually more prudent to give in than fight. "I'll just kiss Jessie good-night, then."

While the two misses argued about whose turn it was to tell the bedtime story, Katie plucked Jessie from Ford's arms and gestured toward the door. "Have a great time," she ordered, her smile brilliant and only a little strained.

"Count on it," Ford grated, propelling Sophie toward the door with the firm pressure of his hand against her spine. Before opening the door, however, he surprised her by taking the shawl from her arm and wrapping its soft folds around her shoulders.

"Ford Maguire, y'all drive careful now," Catfish Williams called from the parlor door where he and Roy Dean were hovering like overprotective fathers.

"Yes, sir," Ford muttered, jerking open the front door.

"Night-night, Jessie Bear," Sophie called over her shoulder as she went with Ford into the cool night air.

The moon was on the wane, but still bright enough to light the way to the driveway. There was an unfamiliar vehicle parked there. When she got closer, she realized that it was an older, powerful-looking midnight blue Camaro, riding low and gleaming as though recently waxed.

"I'd rather wrangle with a whole passel of skunk-mean moonshiners than face a woman's family on a first date," Ford muttered.

"It was a bit overwhelming," she admitted, risking a glance in his direction. "And this isn't a date," she added belatedly. For a few minutes, she'd forgotten all about caution and self-preservation and prudence.

"Thanks for remindin' me," he drawled, looking her way.

As he stepped past her to open the car door she caught a whiff of sandalwood. It wasn't a scent she would expect a small-town sheriff to favor, and yet she was beginning to realize that no matter how provincial his rearing, Ford had the instincts of an aristocratic gentleman. He would have made a superb air force officer, she thought as he slipped behind the wheel.

"Do you ever regret not going to the air force academy?" she asked, giving in to impulse as he was backing the Camaro onto Clover Street.

"Why regret what you can't change?" His answer came so readily she suspected he'd said the same thing to himself more than once.

"True enough," she said, shifting position.

"Something wrong?" he asked, shooting her a quick look. He drove with the relaxed skill of someone comfortable with his own ability, but she sensed a tension in his big body that had nothing to do with driving.

"Let's say I've just made an important discovery," she replied, shifting again.

"Which is?"

"Sitting on beaded fringe is definitely uncomfortable."

His laugh was as startling as an unexpected caress. Offering an answering smile, she realized that she wanted more of both. She was still trying to tell herself otherwise when Ford turned onto a quiet street in a modest residential area where the homes were small but clearly well-kept.

Lights blazed from the third house on the right, and the sound of music drifted on the winter-crisp air. Cars lined the street on both sides for a good block on either side of the house, and Sophie groaned inwardly.

"Hope you're up for a hike, 'cause this is as close as we get," Ford said, maneuvering deftly into a space only a few feet longer than the car.

"I like to walk," she fudged. She hadn't worn high heels in months, and she had a feeling her legs would be sore when she woke up in the morning.

"You said this was just a small gathering of friends," she chided as he helped her from the car.

"What can I say? Eli and Ellie have a lot of friends."

"Eli and Ellie?" She slanted him a disbelieving look. "You can't be serious."

"Dead serious. This is the South, remember?" His grin was fleeting, but powerfully male nonetheless. And she felt its impact, even as it faded.

"Mind the steps," he said, taking her arm. The tiny house was clearly in the process of remodeling, and most of the porch railing was missing. The party was in full swing, requiring Ford to ring the bell twice before the door swung open to reveal a slightly built young man in a bright red shirt and tight jeans. He was clean-cut and handsome, with slanting brown eyes suggesting Oriental blood, and a cleft in his square chin. It was the same deputy who had admitted her to the sheriff's department a few days before Christmas. Somehow he had seemed older in his uniform.

His face lighted up when he glimpsed Ford standing there. When he smiled, he seemed even more boy than man, but the hint of authority riding his shoulders reminded her of Ford.

"Sheriff! Good to see you, sir." He hesitated, then reached out to shake Ford's hand. Sophie found the deputy's awkwardness endearing and wondered if Ford realized that Eli was afflicted by a bad case of hero worship.

"Evenin', Eli. I reckon you already know Sophie Reynolds."

"Ma'am. Good to see you again."

"You, too, Eli," she said, shaking his hand. He had a strong grip and a direct gaze. His eyes were filled with a lot of questions she suspected he wouldn't ask. She decided she liked him very much.

"Come on in and make yourselves to home," he urged, ushering them in eagerly before closing the door. "The booze is in the kitchen yonder and lots of it, so pour heavy if that's your pleasure, and Ellie made enough food to feed half the county. Oh, and the bedroom's at the end of the hall."

Sophie stiffened, her gaze instinctively meshing with Ford's. "For the coats," he confided in a low tone. "Or in your case, that shawl you've been huggin' to you like armor."

"Don't exaggerate," she murmured, feeling the heat searing her cheeks as she slipped free of the shawl.

"Here, let me, Ms. Reynolds," Eli offered, taking the wrap from her. "Y'all just make yourselves at home, okay?"

"I can see why he's so popular," she said, watching Eli exchanging friendly banter with the other guests on the way to the bedroom. "He's got a generous heart."

Ford glanced at his deputy with narrowed eyes. "How can you tell?"

"He has sweet eyes."

"Sweet, huh?" His mouth twitched. "Guess that's somethin' only a woman would notice."

Glancing around, Sophie drew a nervous breath. Everywhere she looked, she saw color—twinkling lights on the trees, garlands of red and green crepe paper, candles in colorful holders. It was a young crowd, and the music had a pounding beat. It came to her that she couldn't remember the last time she'd been to a party without engraved invitations, tuxedoed waiters and a lot of bored faces.

"C'mon, help me find the bar." Ford had to lean close to be heard. Though his breath was warm, she felt a shiver run through her.

"Okay."

He led the way, stopping now and then to introduce her to one of the other guests. She was surprised at the number of familiar faces she saw. With Ford's help, she was soon matching names to faces and feeling much more at ease.

The kitchen was empty. With the door closed, the music was reduced to a muted throb, and the temperature was a few degrees cooler than the crowded living room. As Eli had promised, the kitchen counter was practically sagging from the weight of bottles, along with a plentiful supply of ice in a plastic bucket and an array of plastic glasses.

"Somehow I thought people didn't drink much in the Bible Belt."

"Only on special occasions," Ford told her solemnly. "Like the first and last day of the month and the thirty or so days that come between."

"Aha. Sounds like timber country."

He glanced at her curiously. "I thought folks in Montana considered themselves cowboys."

Sophie felt a quick stab of anxiety. "Some do."

He nodded, seemingly satisfied, but her throat was suddenly dry, though, paradoxically, her hands felt revealingly damp.

"What would you like?" Ford asked, still watching her with eyes that were very clear and very steady.

"Something soft, please," she murmured.

"Ginger ale okay?"

"Fine."

While he poured, she wandered over to the window overlooking the floodlit backyard. Azaleas were blooming beneath the window, their bright red blossoms clearly visible through the lightly misted panes.

"I still can't get over it," she murmured. "Flowers blooming on New Year's Eve."

"Guess it's gotta be depressing up north around this time," he said, handing her a glass. He gave off waves of pure male energy, carefully controlled.

"Yes," she said. "Very depressing." She'd spent last New Year's Eve heartsick and pregnant, lying in her narrow prison bed when the calendar had clicked over to a new year.

"Guess you know I damn near swallowed my tongue when I saw you in that dress." His voice was suddenly a half octave deeper than usual, and her pulse was at least a dozen beats faster.

"It belonged to Miss Fanny's mother. When I saw it, I wanted to roll back the rug and do the Charleston."

His grin flashed. Finding his eyes, it lingered. "Seems fittin'."

She shook her head. "No, the mood's all wrong," she declared with a mournful sigh.

"It is?" Though not as broad, his smile still played at the corners of his mouth. It suited him, she thought, that restrained way he had of handling amusement.

"Oh, yes. We should have had to give Eli the secret password before he let us in." She took a sip of her drink and let the bubbly ginger ale slide down her throat. "And we should be drinking bathtub gin out of teacups instead of ginger ale and . . ." She glanced pointedly at the drink in his hand.

"Scotch." He drank it neat, and he knew his capacity to the sip.

"Scotch," she repeated, smiling. "Not some of Frenchy's finest?"

"Not with most of Clover's police force just outside that door."

"Ah, but you're the boss. You can break the rules."

"I can, but I don't."

"Never?"

"Never." Ford wondered if she had any idea what she was doing to his control every time she moved. If there was anything but silky warm skin under that dress, it was whisper thin. Just imagining how it would feel to shimmy that scrap of material, beads and all, over those sleek feminine curves was doing serious damage to his self-control.

Already seriously tempted to make some excuse and spirit her away to someplace private and quiet, good manners be damned, he couldn't for the life of him figure out how he was going to make it to midnight without going stark staring mad. Scowling suddenly, he took a hefty swallow and waited for the liquor to blunt the sharp edges of need.

"How about something to eat?" he asked, gesturing with his drink toward the door.

"Sure," she said, curving her lips, even as the playful softness faded from her eyes. "Maybe I'll pick up some new catering ideas."

She walked out of the kitchen ahead of him, her hips teasing him with every step. He'd disappointed her. He didn't know why, though it didn't particularly surprise him. He hadn't been a particularly lovable little boy, though he'd tried to be for a lot of years, and he wasn't a lovable man. Once he'd accepted that, it had gotten easier to accept the solitary life everyone just naturally believed he'd deliberately chosen for himself.

"Ford! Is it really you, you old hermit, you?"

Ford nearly groaned aloud as Deputy Mervin Grimes's wife, Karen, charged toward him. "Happy New Year, Karen," he said, turning his head at the last minute so that her exuberant kiss landed on the flat of his cheek. It didn't help his mood to see three of his so-called good buddies closing in around Sophie before he could stop them.

"I swear I called Merv a liar right to his face this afternoon when he said you'd promised to show up tonight," Karen gushed as was her wont. " 'You've got to be jokin' with me,' I told him. 'Ford never goes to parties.' "

He lifted his glass to his mouth and took a drink. Over the rim he saw Sophie laughing at something Nick Fielding had just told her. For a man supposed to be grieving over a failed marriage, old Nick was spending a lot of time looking at Sophie's dress as though he couldn't wait to strip her out of it. Not that Ford could blame him much. It wasn't much more than a scrap of fabric and a bunch of little bitty beads that stopped just a full hand's width above the knee.

She had pale satiny thighs to go with the sleek calves he'd already decided were the sexiest thing he'd seen in a coon's age, and just enough curve to her hips to boost a man's blood pressure a good ten points. If the surge of hot blood in his veins was any indication, his was rocketing toward the red zone.

"Ford?" Karen's plaintive voice jerked his gaze back to her face. She was a nice woman, he reminded himself, and Mervin had been sober these past five years mostly because of her.

"How's the family?" he asked, knowing that she would tell him. And that he would listen politely until she ran out of things to say.

By the time Merv came looking for his wife, taking her away in the midst of a detailed replay of Merv, Jr.'s last wrestling match, Ford's glass was empty, and Sophie was nowhere in sight.

Ellie Grover was as plain as Eli was handsome, with flaming orange hair, pale skin dotted with freckles and a charmingly crooked smile. Small-boned and dainty, with golden eyes and pale, pale lashes, she was hugely pregnant with their first child, and when she'd found out that Sophie had a daughter, she'd insisted on showing her the nursery.

"I made the curtains myself, but my mama and sister helped me with the quilt."

Sophie fingered the soft coverlet draped over the rails of the shiny white crib and fought down a wave of bitterness. When she'd given birth to Jessie, the prison officials hadn't even let her keep the baby with her overnight.

"I love the colors. I didn't realize there were so many different shades of pink."

"Eli wanted our first to be a son, but I think he's finally gettin' excited about seein' his daughter." Ellie Grover rubbed a caressing hand over her bulging tummy, her eyes lit with so much love Sophie had trouble breathing.

"I'm sure he'll adore her," she murmured, hoping she was right.

Ellie smiled. "Did your husband want a son, too?"

Sophie felt her stomach twist. "We never really had a chance to talk about the baby very much before he died. In fact, I'd only just learned I was pregnant."

"Oh, I am sorry," Ellie said, her pretty face registering genuine dismay. "I could just bite my tongue for speakin' so thoughtlessly."

Sophie touched the hand Ellie rested on her stomach. "Please don't give it another thought."

"How long has it been since he died?"

A lifetime, and yet not nearly long enough to enable her to forget that horrible night. "Almost eighteen months."

"It must be hard raisin' your little girl by yourself." Ellie drew a breath.

"It's had its moments, but I've been fortunate to find good friends here to help."

Though Ellie smiled, Sophie sensed that something was troubling her. About the baby? she wondered. The delivery?

She remembered how frightened she'd been those last few weeks before she'd delivered. And at the same time, how eager to see the face of the child she'd already come to know and love. Her cell mate by then, Darlene had held her hand during the long hours of labor she'd been forced to endure without medication or medical attention until the last possible minute. And it had been Darlene who had heard her sobbing out her nearly unbearable anguish when a hatchet-faced social worker had taken her baby from her only a few hours after delivery.

"When are you due?" she asked casually.

"In two weeks. Eli's already arranged with the sheriff to take time off. At first he was sort of afraid to, for fear that Sheriff Maguire would think we were ungrateful, him lending us the money for the down payment on this house and all so soon after giving Eli the job."

"I'm sure that even Sheriff Maguire understands how special babies are."

"Oh, he does," Ellie was quick to reply. "Eli said he's even delivered one himself. Or maybe you heard the story?"

Sophie shook her head. "No, but I'd like to."

"The mama's name was Alice Freedlander, from up on the mountain? Her husband got killed in an accident at the rock crusher, and when Ford went up to tell her the news, he found her about ready to deliver, poor woman. It was her first, and the baby was shifted all wrong."

"Did everything turn out all right?"

"Yes, praise the Lord, although it was a near thing. Being winter and all, those mountain roads were really dangerous, even with four-wheel drive. Sheriff had to park at the bottom of the Freedlanders' lane and hike two miles to the house. Had to carry Alice and the baby back those same two miles. Got himself a good case of pneumonia for his trouble, too. Alice swears he saved her life, and Doc Gossely pretty much agreed. Alice even named her little girl Fordene."

Sophie blinked. "Oh, my."

Ellie giggled. "Awful, isn't it?"

"It's unusual, to say the least," Sophie admitted, choosing caution over brutal honesty. "Was Ford . . . the sheriff pleased?"

"I hope to shout! He fairly doted on that sweet little girl. Grieved some when her mama got married again and moved to New Orleans. Folks swore Alice was really in love with the sheriff, and would have married him in a minute, only everyone knows he's not the marryin' kind." Ellie bent forward to rearrange the pile of stuffed animals in the corner of the crib. "Guess you know you've got folks wonderin' if he's changin' his mind about that."

Sophie drew a breath. "If you're asking if Ford and I are involved, we're not."

"Truth to tell, I didn't think you were, but Eli, he and the other deputies were hopin' the sheriff had finally found a woman who could put up with him. Sort of mellow him out some, you know?"

"They don't like working for him?"

"Oh, no, it's not that," Ellie said, managing to look guilty and worried at the same time. "It's just that, well, he's a perfectionist, you know?"

"That can make things difficult sometimes."

"Very!" Ellie glanced around nervously, then leaned closer. "He fired a deputy once for not arrestin' a man for drunk drivin' because he was a judge. Said some innocent person might have gotten hurt or even killed because of that."

"He's right."

"Sure, but that poor old deputy had three kids at home and a brand-new house. I mean, everyone's entitled to a second chance, don't you think?"

"I believe that, yes. But I also know that life doesn't always work that way."

"That's what Eli said." The young mother-to-be drew a long breath. "Guess we'd better get back to the party before Eli starts worrying about me."

Ford was sorting through the CDs lined up neatly on a shelf near Eli's sound system when he saw Sophie and Ellie emerge from the hall, laughing together. For an instant, his mind played him dirty, mixing the two so that he could suddenly see Sophie in the full bloom of pregnancy, her belly swollen with his child.

Faster than he could take a breath, his stomach muscles twisted into knots. A man who'd given up a dream learned never to dream again. But now, suddenly, he saw himself standing next to Sophie in a nursery like the one Ellie was so proud of, maybe decorated in blue for a son. His son.

A longing so great swept over him, nearly sending him to his knees. He could almost see himself teaching the boy to fish for mud cats on the bank in front of his place. And Jessie, too, he thought, smiling to himself at the thought of becoming that little hellion's daddy. But first, he had to convince Sophie that he would be a good one.

Drawing a breath, he watched her head for the buffet table, her dress shimmering and swaying with every step she took. It was just possible he'd been all wrong about marriage being as good as prison for a man like him, especially when he had a woman like Sophie in his bed every night. Because he was tempted to throw her over his shoulder and head for his place at a fast trot, he made himself concentrate on the CDs he still held in his hand.

When he came to vintage Johnny Mathis, he grinned to himself. He wasn't the greatest dancer in the world, but he could manage to keep from bumping into the furniture for a dance or two. And if his luck held, he might not have to do much moving around at all.

Sophie was piling pimento cheese spread on a cracker when she felt a funny little tickle run up her spine. "Good recipe?" Pitched low to carry over the music, Ford's voice rumbled through her like unexpected desire.

She took a moment to let her pulse settle before lifting her gaze to Ford's. His gaze had lost none of the directness she'd come to associate with him.

"Try it and see." Feeling just a little daring, she held the cracker close to his mouth, offering him the bite she'd been about to take for herself. His gaze flickered, grew wary, but he allowed her to feed him.

"I'd rather have chili," he said, running his tongue between his lips.

Sophie laughed. "Your sister warned me I'd have trouble with you."

"My sister has a vivid imagination and a big mouth."

"And you love her very much, big brother."

His face took on a sudden flush. "Sometimes." He shifted his attention to the center of the room where several couples had started swaying to the music.

"How about it?" he said, feeling fourteen and dry-mouth scared he was going to be turned down.

Her gaze followed his. "I haven't danced for years," she murmured, looking sad and eager at the same time.

"About time you did, then," he said, taking her hand. He led her to the darkest spot he could find, then swung her into his arms.

"We fit," he murmured, drawing her closer. "Must be an omen."

He hadn't held a woman for the pure pleasure of feeling her body gliding against his since he couldn't remember when. She was all silk and sheen, melting in his arms. Her skin was glass smooth where his hand rested against her back, and her hair smelled like roses.

"Everyone's watching," she murmured when he lowered his head to nuzzle her ear. He knew damn near everyone in the room was watching. He knew what they were thinking. He didn't give a holy spit what they thought.

"Let 'em watch. Tomorrow morning I'll line up every man that's here tonight and make 'em swear they'd spent the whole evening struck blind."

She sputtered a laugh. Damn, even her laughter had a sexy sound, he thought, conscious of the hot fingers of desire spreading inside him. He closed his eyes, knowing that he was vulnerable then, something he normally made a point to avoid at all costs. It annoyed him a little that he would be willing to break his own rule for her. It didn't surprise him. Ever since he'd met her, his carefully ordered regimen had taken more than a few hard shakes.

Tomorrow he'd get himself on track again, he thought, feeling her thighs moving against his. Tomorrow he'd sort out his options and plan his campaign. Definitely tomorrow, he thought, drawing in the warm, sensuous scent of her perfume. She was so softly alluring, so feminine. And he'd gone to bed alone too many nights lately.

He held her shamelessly close, his movements slow and sinuous, each shift of lean hip and muscular thigh sending pulsing jolts of desire into Sophie's bloodstream. She'd always loved dancing, but she'd never felt quite so *dominated* on the dance floor. His arms were like steel, and yet she felt wrapped in cotton wool like one of Katie's delicate glass ornaments, as though she were a treasure to be protected at all costs. It was a lovely feeling, almost as lovely as the slide of his hard thighs against hers and the press of his callused hand against her spine.

Snuggled tightly against him, she reveled in the feeling of his muscles straining against hers, her excitement growing with each gliding move, each small shift in direction. Gradually she became acutely aware that he was as aroused as she was.

"Sophie?"

Suddenly aware that he'd stopped moving, she fluttered her eyes open and looked at him, aware that she was blushing.

"Either we leave now, or I'm going to end up making love to you right here and now."

"You wouldn't," she whispered, suddenly unsteady on her feet. Looking helplessly into those dark, unerringly focused eyes had her drawing an equally unsteady breath. She wasn't a woman given to swooning, but suddenly she felt overwhelmed. Dizzy.

"I never say anything I don't mean," he murmured, his voice graveled. " 'Course, if you'd care to test that—"

"No, I'll take your word," she said quickly, her body still throbbing in newly awakening places. "Besides, it must be getting late."

He slanted her a rueful look, then led her to an empty chair and eased her into the cushy seat. "Wait here, I'll get your shawl."

She was almost certain she could speak coherently, but just in case she was wrong, she simply nodded. He returned almost immediately, moving like a man intent on a mission and determined not to be diverted. Even in civilian clothes he had the rangy look and fluid walk that came from lean muscle and steel sinew working together in perfect marriage. And his shoulders were as wide as any she'd ever seen, even in the northwest where big men were the norm.

"Ready?" he said when he was still a few feet away.

"Something tells me it doesn't matter if I am or not," she teased, rising. Sensing the impatience in him, she took the shawl from him and draped it over her shoulders before allowing him to steer her toward their host, who was perched on the arm of a brown plush sofa, his hands measuring the air in what Sophie took to be a whopper of a fish story. Spotting them approaching, he broke off immediately and leapt to his feet. He didn't exactly come to attention, but as close as he could get.

"You give a great party, son," Ford told him, extending his hand.

"Yes, sir. I mean, thanks for comin'." His gaze darted to Sophie. "You, too, ma'am."

"Thank you, Eli. You have a lovely home, and the baby's room is adorable."

"Ellie gets the credit for that. I just tacked up the pictures and such."

Sophie glanced around, but Ellie was nowhere in sight. "Please thank Ellie for me, as well. Tell her I'll call her tomorrow for those recipes we talked about."

"Yes, ma'am, I sure will." He darted a glance toward the other side of the room. "I think she's in the powder room. She does that a lot these days." His face got beet red, and Sophie wanted to hug him.

"I understand." She extended her hand. "Happy New Year."

Two minutes later they were back in Ford's car and heading away from the party.

"What a nice young couple," she murmured. "I liked them both."

He shot her a curious look. "You're not all that much older than either one of 'em."

Maybe not in years, she thought, drawing her shawl tighter. "Neither are you."

"I've got a few hard years on all of you." His voice was shaded with an emotion she didn't recognize.

"Not that many."

"Enough so those youngsters you met tonight refer to me as the 'old man' when they think I can't hear 'em."

Sophie slanted him a curious look. "Perhaps that's more a term of affection than a description."

His gaze sliced her way briefly, edged with the same impatience she'd sensed in him earlier. "If it is, I'm not doin' my job."

Sophie watched the trees whizzing past the car. "Don't you want to be liked?"

"It's not a matter of wantin'. It's a matter of makin' sure the streets are safe and folks sleep easy every night."

He braked for the intersection where Clover crossed Lost Creek Road. Instead of turning left, however, he shifted to neutral and turned to face her. "I can turn left and you'll be home and tucked into bed by midnight. Or I can turn right and take you to my place, which means that we'll both be awake to see the new year in properly."

Sophie's heart took a violent tumble. "I'm not sure your idea of 'proper' is the same as mine."

His grin flashed. "Champagne and clean sheets?" He sounded so pathetically hopeful that she burst out laughing.

"How about coffee and conversation instead?"

He groaned. "I guess that's a start," he said, and spun the wheel to the right.

Chapter 9

Sophie stood in the middle of the pine-and-glass living room and turned a slow circle, noting the bookshelves covering one wall and the huge stone fireplace taking up the one opposite. In between was a wall of windows overlooking what she assumed was the Lost Creek of Lost Creek Road.

The room itself was small, and her immediate impression was one of meticulous order and restraint. Nothing was out of place, suggesting impulse or haste. The colors were muted, reflecting the taste of a man who preferred the melancholy browns and golds of autumn over the more frivolous shades of the other seasons. Though of good quality and generous proportions, the furniture seemed more appropriate for a hunting lodge than a home and, though not shabby, had been well used.

"It's bigger inside than it looks," she remarked when her gaze settled on his again.

Ford shrugged out of his jacket and tossed it onto a muddy brown easy chair. "It wasn't much more than a shack when I bought it. Probably paid more than it was worth, but I liked the view."

"I imagine it's marvelous."

"You'll have to come back in the daytime and check it out."

Sophie smiled, grateful that he hadn't suggested she see it in the morning—from the bedroom window.

"How long have you lived here?" she asked, walking to the center of the largest window to look out at the night. A thicket of trees was silhouetted against the dimly lit sky, lending an air of isolation she wasn't sure she liked.

"Goin' on nine years. As soon as Lucy turned eighteen, she wanted to try livin' on her own, claimed I was still treatin' her like she was nine and helpless."

"Were you?"

His grin flashed. "Probably." He ambled across the room to stand next to her. "She went through a rough patch for a while. Kept tellin' me she was seein' things before they happened."

"You sound as though you didn't believe her."

He shrugged. "I think she got things a little mixed up in her mind. Doc Gossely told me that happens sometimes when a person's had a violent shock, especially a child who's missin' her mama and daddy. After a while we got it straightened out."

"Something tells me you went through a rough patch of your own."

"If you're askin' me if I'm still carryin' baggage from years ago, I'm not."

"No one escapes the past," she murmured sadly, "but if you're warning me not to ask you questions about yours, I'll make you a bargain. You don't ask me questions and I won't ask you."

He narrowed his gaze, seemingly reluctant to agree. "Am I at least allowed to ask you if you take regular or decaf?"

Sophie felt the knot in her stomach ease. "Regular. Otherwise, I might not even make it to midnight."

"Don't worry. If you fall asleep, I'll make sure you wake up in time." He gestured toward the far end of the room. "Coat closet's next to the bathroom—in case you want to use either one."

She used both, returning to find he'd lit a fire in the fireplace and was in the process of adding another log. He looked up when he heard her heels clicking against the plank flooring.

"Figured that since it was almost January, a fire would be a good idea."

"Seems appropriate to me." Suddenly she was nervous, and not really sure why. To calm herself—and, she admitted, to put some distance between them—she wandered over to the bookshelves.

There seemed to be an even mix of paperbacks and hardbound and all seemed well-read. Lightly running her fingers along worn spines, she read some of the titles. He seemed to favor westerns and thrillers—and a lot of very dry-looking volumes on military history.

"How come I don't see any police procedurals?" she asked, looking back at him.

"Too boring." He watched the flames greedily lapping at the seasoned oak for a moment before closing the mesh screen.

"How about you?" he asked, joining her. "What do you read?"

She felt the rigid line of a shelf pressing into her spine and realized that she'd taken a step backward. "You mean besides books on child rearing?" she murmured, smiling ruefully.

"And cookbooks," Ford reminded her, fingering a bit of beaded fringe. The delicate, shimmering beads were surprisingly warm to the touch, though not nearly as enticing to a man as the warmth of a woman's skin.

"I forgot about the cookbooks," she admitted, shaking her head.

He noticed that she'd changed her hair. Curled it some and pulled it back from her face so that the vulnerable curve of her throat seemed more accessible.

"Any ideas about Mike's party?" he asked, letting his fingers toy with one of the shimmering curls.

"A few." His fingers brushed her jaw and she drew a quick, nervous breath. "The coffee smells ready."

He glanced toward the kitchen. He'd forgotten he'd set a pot to brewing. Coffee and conversation. She'd made the rules, and he believed in rules.

"How do you take it?" he asked, stepping back.

"Black."

"Have a seat. I'll just be a minute."

"Anything I can do to help?"

He'd told himself he wasn't going to rush her, yet he found himself stepping closer.

"Come to think of it, there is. You can put this old boy out of his misery."

Her eyes grew wide, and her lips parted. Though he wasn't an expert by any means, he knew enough about body language and facial expressions to know that she was aroused, perhaps as aroused as he was, but even a wisp of fear in those bottomless blue eyes would have had him backing off instantly. That her gaze remained drowsy and just a little excited had his own need swelling.

"We shouldn't," she murmured, even as he was framing her face with his hands. She seemed as fragile as her daughter, and as innocent somehow.

"It's all the way right," he murmured, his voice hoarse with a need so violent it left him feeling raw inside.

"I don't want you to care about me," she whispered, her soft lips trembling.

"Too late, sweetness, way too late," he grated before his mouth closed over hers. He'd intended the kiss to be brief, a release of tension, a leveling of need. Instead, he found himself craving more than a taste, needing more than the simple pressure of her mouth against his. His mouth grew greedy, his hands close to frantic as they framed her face, stroked her neck, moved down to caress her breasts. He probed her lips with his tongue, impatient, driven. When she parted her lips, he tasted deeper, his hunger growing more razored, his senses more clouded. The need grew unbearable, his control stretched to the last tenuous thread. Drawing back on a harsh, shuddering groan he neither planned nor could prevent, he fought to clear his head. She, too, seemed shaken.

"I think you should get that coffee now," she murmured, drawing a shaky breath.

Ford drew a long breath of his own, shaken to find that she could make him drunker with just one kiss than a gallon of Eli's best Scotch.

"I want to make love to you, Sophie. Not just tonight, but as often as we can arrange it." He found himself holding to a razored line between asking and taking. It was painful and terrifying and he wished like hell he'd read a few of those romantic novels Lucy liked so much. Maybe then he'd know how to talk straight to a woman without sounding like a horny bastard or a damned wimp.

"I guess what I'm askin' is for you to tell me if I'm goin' too fast or pushin' too hard."

Sophie was suddenly powerless in the face of such honesty. "I'm scared," she admitted. "Oh, not of you," she hastened to add when hurt shot into his eyes. "But of . . . consequences," she finished lamely. How could she tell the man she was beginning to love very deeply that she didn't want to draw him into her web of deceit? Not only for her own protection, she realized suddenly and with shock, but for his.

He used his left hand to trace the curve of her mouth. "I'm not carryin' anything contagious, if that's what's botherin' you. If you want proof, I can get it. Everyone in the department is required to have a complete physical on his birthday."

"That's not it," she assured him quickly, deeply touched.

"I won't make you pregnant. If you want me to wear a condom, I will. I don't promise I won't complain mightily, however. I hate the thought of anything comin' between us."

"It's not just a little piece of latex or whatever that might come between us," she admitted, determined to tell him as much of the truth as she dared without compromising Jessie's safety. "There are things in my past that I can't tell you about, things that if you knew—"

"Don't," he murmured, pressing hard fingertips against her lips. "We agreed to forget the past."

If only they could, she thought sadly, but perhaps, for a time, she could pretend the past really didn't matter.

"I don't want to hurt you," she cried softly, her hands going to his chest. Instead of pushing him away, however, her fingers clutched at his sweater, curling and uncurling against the thick wool like kitten claws. Longings rose in him, powerful and compelling, and not easily mastered.

"I'll risk it," he murmured, testing the softness of her cheek with the back of his hand.

"I'm not free," she whispered. "I have obligations, debts."

Ford thought about the obligations he'd once carried. "Maybe I can help."

"I wish you could, but you can't. No one can."

Even without knowing the details, he wanted to tell her to trust him with her problems and her pain, that he would take care of her. But once made, promises like that had to be kept, and he wasn't sure how much he had in him to give.

"I'm not askin' for more than tonight."

Sophie felt something catch and tear inside her. Perhaps if she been dealing with only her own desire she could have resisted. But the rough burr of need in his voice touched her heart as nothing but Jessie's smile had been able to do in months.

"It's been a long time," she told him, her voice catching. "Since before Jessie was born."

Something changed in his eyes. "Then we'll go as fast or as slow as you need," he promised, touching his mouth to hers in the gentlest of kisses. "Tell me what you want, honey."

"More of the same," she murmured, waiting for a smile to find his eyes.

"My pleasure," he drawled, kissing her again, harder this time and longer before he drew back. "Your turn," he invited, his eyes dark as the night beyond the windows.

Yielding not only to him but to her own craving to feel those hard lips against hers again, she rested one hand on his hard shoulder and brought her mouth up to touch his. He stood motionless, his body tense but passive. His hand remained tangled in her hair but exerted no pressure.

There was no rush, no demand, to deepen tenderness to passion, and yet she felt the connection between them in every part of her. Even as she ended the kiss, she felt her body sway toward his, felt his arm come around her, his strength like a warm blanket on a cold, lonely night.

His chest was hard under the soft wool, his hands comforting as they stroked her back. She clung to him, feeling relief and pleasure run through her. He was strong enough to hold her up when her knees went weak, secure enough to accept her desperate need to keep her secret, even from him. Especially from him.

Holding her, his desire spiking close to his ability to ignore, he felt the last of her resistance melt away, leaving her warm and vulnerable in his arms.

This time it was he who brought his mouth to hers, he who increased the pressure. Using his tongue Ford traced the line of her lower lip, testing its softness, savoring its sweetness. Her body was warm and pliant against his, the beaded fringe on her dress whispering sex with every movement she made.

He needed to absorb that warmth, to draw in the subtle shifts and twists of emotion that fascinated him, even as he worked at shoring up walls he didn't dare let her breach.

His mind, usually so well-ordered, spun with impressions and sensations he hadn't felt in years. Perhaps had never really felt. His senses, too, seemed beyond his control, driving him beyond the bounds of reason.

He'd never known another woman like her, so strong, so resil-
ient, and yet utterly feminine and giving, a creature of passion and
emotion, of feelings that flowed over him like sweet spring rain,
soothing the parched, aching wounds on his soul.

It was dangerous to need so completely, so desperately. But even
as he fought to pull back, to keep himself apart from her, he knew
it was too late.

What control he'd managed to hoard in reserve splintered,
leaving him defenseless. Terrified, and yet committed, he plunged
his hands into her hair, desperate to feel the softness swirling
around his fingers, clinging to his skin. He took her mouth over
and over, until he felt the blood pooling dangerously hot in his
loins.

Dragging his lips from hers, he buried his face against her throat,
waiting for the need pulsing for immediate release to ease off.
When he took her, he wanted it to be with the care and gentleness
of a first-time lover.

When his mouth left hers, Sophie murmured a protest, only to
gasp as his lips trailed moist kisses along the curve of her throat.
Instinctively, she drew back her head, giving him more intimate
access to her throat. On her lips was the lingering taste of the
Scotch he'd drunk, still potently intoxicating, though not nearly as
intoxicating as his kisses. Nestled against him Sophie sensed his
struggle for control, her own needs churning in a delicious whirl-
pool deep inside her.

No one had ever needed her like this before. No one had ever
made her need so wildly in return. She had known pleasure before—mild and sweet and all mixed up with a need to nurture and
protect. But nothing she'd ever experienced with Wells had prepared her for the all-consuming violence of the demands Ford was
making on her body, on her soul. Nor had she expected her own
needs to grow stronger with each kiss, each touch of his hand.

He muttered something against her skin she didn't understand,
and then he was nibbling at her ear. The scent of sandalwood and
aroused masculinity seemed to envelop her, as though pulsing from
his pores. And then he was claiming her lips again, his hard mouth
hot and drugging while his fingers slipped beneath the fringed hem,
seeking skin. Sensations bunched and gathered inside her until she
thought she would shatter.

When his hand went to her breast, she moaned. And then he was stepping back, his glittering gaze running the length of her.

"That's one hell of a dress, honey, but it sure makes it rough on a guy tryin' his best not to look like a fool gettin' you out of it."

The raw frustration in his voice had her biting her lip, trying not to laugh, even as the thought of appearing naked before him had her throat going dry and nerves rioting in her stomach.

"I promised Miss Fanny I'd be very careful." It was difficult to speak, more difficult to think clearly. "I . . . if you could help with the zipper," she managed to get out, turning her back to him.

The dark behind the windows turned them to mirrors, and she found herself watching as he stepped closer. His hands were erotically slow as they traced the curve of the silken straps from her shoulders to the gown's low center. She saw the sheen of his black hair as he dipped his head to press a kiss to the nape of her neck, felt the sliding pressure of his hand as he slowly drew the zipper down to the spot where her spine curved into her backside.

The dress fell open from its own weight, needing only a nudge from his hands to fall away from her shoulders. Even as he was very carefully laying the dress over the back of the brown chair, he was devouring her with his eyes.

"Damn if I wasn't right," he murmured, almost reverently. "You weren't wearing anything underneath." No slip, no bra. Just sinfully sheer panty hose that had cost her a day's tips.

"It has its own bra built in," she murmured, feeling herself trembling. Already her bare breasts were growing heavy from the weight of desire for him.

"Pretty slick," he said, his voice hoarse. Bending, he kissed one dark nipple, then the other before lifting his gaze to her face.

"You deserve candlelight and roses," he murmured, brushing the back of his hand over her hot cheek. "And a poet to say all the things a woman needs to hear."

"The way you're looking at me right now is all I need," she whispered, her voice trembling.

Ford swallowed hard. It felt like years that he'd been aching for her. Now that she was only a thrust of his body away, her eyes soft and yearning and her lips so close, he was suddenly afraid he'd made promises with his kisses he wasn't skilled enough or experienced enough to keep.

"I've never wanted anyone the way I want you," he admitted when her gaze turned questioning. "The first time I saw you, before I even knew your name, I wanted to make love to you. I damn near drowned in coffee day after day just so I could watch you."

"Oh, my," she murmured, bemused and touched. "And here I was thinking you were addicted to caffeine."

"I'm addicted, all right. But not to caffeine."

He kissed her fast and hard, then stepped back to rid himself of his sweater. His boots came next, and then his hands were working the buttons of his jeans.

Fumbling only a little, Sophie removed her panty hose and let them fall to the floor. Then transfixed, and a little frightened, Sophie watched him, letting her gaze flow over the powerful structure of chest and shoulder, the long, muscular arms and wrists, the lean washboard torso tapering to a flat belly.

He glanced up, his expression rueful. "Never saw it fail. In the movies, those guys can get out of their breeches as smooth as you please."

The flash of vulnerability in his eyes had her heart opening even as she smiled. "Could be 'those guys' don't wear their jeans as tight as you do."

He kicked the jeans away, then stripped off the pale blue briefs that were already straining to contain him. Proudly aroused, and definitely not shy now, he advanced on her.

"Are you sayin' I'm fat?" he asked just before he took her into his arms.

"I think I'd better take the fifth on that," she murmured, feeling the heat of his body enveloping her far more seductively than the crackling fire behind the screen.

"Wise decision, honey." He brought his mouth down hard, yet she felt no pain, only elation. Arching upward, she dug desperate fingers into his hard shoulders, pressing her aching breasts against his chest.

His arm circled her waist, pulling her upward, until they were thigh to thigh, belly to belly, need to need. Shifting position slightly, he drew her even more intimately to him until she was astride the hot, rigid shaft of his sex.

He shuddered, his groan a long hoarse sigh of need that she felt all the way to her womb. Driven beyond reticence, she moved back and forth, feeling herself grow soft and moist, as tiny shivers of pleasure shook her faster and faster.

"Hang on to me, sugar," he demanded hoarsely as she rode him faster, harder. She dug her fingers into his shoulders as she came to an unexpected climax, so dizzy she was reeling.

She cried out, then arched her head back as he replaced his body with his fingers, driving her ruthlessly, relentlessly to yet another shuddering release.

Half-crazed, Ford saw the rapture bloom on her face, and felt the blood in his loins surging to an almost unbearable pressure.

His mouth still hotly welded to hers, he drew her to the floor, the taste of his need on her tongue and her lips. As her back pressed against the rough carpet, she found herself clutching him with frantic fingers, unable to lie still, her need a wild demon within her.

"Now," she panted, desperate to feel again that glorious crescendo of sensation and emotion he'd created in her.

He drew back, the savage side of his nature rawly visible in eyes that were no longer calm, no longer patient. This man, with fierce eyes and hands that could bruise as easily as arouse, was capable of cruelty as well as kindness. Once freed, the warrior side of his psyche would be impossible to control or resist.

She felt an instant of fear, and then she was reaching for him again, glorying in the primitive, crystalline emotions pouring from her after being repressed for so long. All that she'd denied herself cried out for him.

"I need to feel you," she whispered. "Please, Ford. I hurt inside."

"Oh, baby, so do I!" he exclaimed on a groan before he broke free to draw his jeans to him. His fingers shook as he plucked his wallet from the back pocket. Nearly sobbing, she lay back, her body throbbing, her breath coming in frantic pants, impatiently waiting as he readied the protection he'd promised to use.

Sheathed now, his own need driving him, Ford sought her mouth with his yet one more time, plunging his tongue deep. Shackling her wrists above her head with one hand, he ran his palm over the silk of her breasts, her waist, her belly, feeling the tiny tremors running under the skin wherever he touched. Inside he burned for her. Only her.

She was quivering for him. He was throbbing for her.

Crying his name over and over, she arched toward him, her hands frantic. Driven to the edge, he slammed her legs apart with his knee. Desperation urged him to drive himself into her, but some last thread of sanity had him remembering that she'd borne a child since she'd made love the last time, and he made himself ease into her, feeling her take him in with difficulty at first, and then more easily until he was fully inside her.

She cried out, and he felt her tighten around him in yet another climax. Exulting, he experienced a primitive jolt of possessiveness, spurring him to mate this woman who made him feel strong and wise and powerful.

Bracing his hands, he arched back and drove into her again and again, his need spiraling with barbed edges. He felt that first burst of heat, and then he was sucked into the blinding flash of pleasure, years and years of need pulsing out of him.

Exhausted, and yet soaring, he collapsed, his body blanketing hers as he fought for breath, all his strength in her now. Still exultant, he struggled to draw into himself again, only to discover that the place where he went when his secret soul felt threatened had sealed over. Pouring himself into her had changed him forever.

Fear ran through him almost as fiercely as the need to make her his. She was part of him now, and he was part of her. Nothing would be the same, and he wasn't sure he was man enough to handle the demands that put on him.

Closing his eyes, he sought to calm his raging pulse. Beneath him she was still trembling, her breath coming in small pants. Realizing that he was crushing that small body with his, he attempted to lever himself off her, only to have her reach for him. "Don't leave me," she whispered, drawing him to her again.

"I won't," he promised, turning them both so that she was cushioned atop him now. Cuddling her close, he stroked her hair with a hand that wasn't as steady as it should be, and stared at the ceiling. Was this what it felt like to want to love someone? he thought. This wild, aching hunger to keep her next to him always? This vicious, desperate need to keep her safe at all costs?

Suddenly, he was pierced with regret that honor had driven him to protect her. With all his lonely heart and soul, he wished that even now she was carrying his seed deep in her body.

Next time, he thought, closing his eyes. But even as he let himself savor the possibility of a child of his growing in her womb, a part of him knew that it was only a dream. And he'd given up dreaming a long time ago.

Chapter 10

Sophie lay in bed, listening to Jessie jabbering to her teddy bear in the crib across the room. It wasn't yet seven, but she'd been awake for hours, thinking about Ford. Even now, in the harsh light of day, the need for him hadn't diminished. If anything, her need for him had only increased during her fitful sleep.

"Stop torturing yourself with what can't be," she murmured, dragging herself from the warm blankets. He'd asked for one night, and that night was over.

Today was the start of a new year, but the harsh circumstances that defined her life hadn't changed. She was still a woman on the run, and he was the one man who could destroy the new life she'd made for herself and Jessie. No matter how much pleasure she might find in his bed, how much solace they might share, she couldn't take the chance of losing Jessie.

The next time she saw him she would be pleasant, even friendly. They were both adults, after all, she rationalized as she slipped into her robe and tied the sash. And if he asked her out again, she would simply decline, politely but firmly. Very firmly.

Sensing movement, Jessie turned over and sat up, her arms automatically reaching for her mother. Sophie drew a resigned breath as she slipped her feet into her scuffs.

"Good morning, sunshine," Sophie crooned, lifting her free of the bars. "You're bright eyed this morning. We'll go visit Peter after breakfast, but first Mama has to change that soggy old diaper."

Jessie cooed and chattered while Sophie changed and dressed her in tights and a warm shirt. "Sometimes life can be very complicated," she told Jessie sadly. "Sometimes it hurts to find out how much you care about the wrong person. I cared about your daddy until I realized he wasn't the man I thought he was. Now I'm pretty sure I'm in love with Ford, and that means you and I have a big problem."

Jessie watched solemnly while Sophie tied her tiny sneakers. "We may have to move on, Jessie Bear. I know you'd hate that. I would, too, but staying here, feeling the way I do about Ford, it's going to be so hard."

She was just brushing the bouncy baby curls into some kind of order when someone knocked on the door. "Come in," she called, lifting Jessie into her arms.

It was Katie, looking harried and flushed. "Sorry to bother you before you're even dressed, but I just heard it on the radio. Ford and some of his deputies went after Frenchy Ducette early this morning, and Ford's been shot."

Part of a state highway, Clover Street ran the length of Clover, from the southern limit to the northern. Katie's rooming house was no more than a half mile from the town hall, an easy walk on a pretty day, but as she hurried toward the business district, Sophie was oblivious to everything but the fear pounding in her heart and the uncertainties still whirling in her head.

Katie had made call after call, allowing them to piece together the bare facts. Two local teenagers, members of prominent families, had gotten liquored up on some of Frenchy's finest and had decided to drag race on a lonely strip of road outside of town. One of the boys had been killed, the other grievously injured.

Ford had been called out around 2:00 a.m. By three, acting on information he'd gotten from the seventeen-year-old survivor, he and four of his deputies had flushed Frenchy from his well-hidden digs in the densest part of the woods bordering Deadman's Slough. Shots had been exchanged, and both Frenchy and Ford had been rushed to the hospital by the fire department ambulance. Frenchy had been dead on arrival. Ford's condition wasn't known.

Eli Grover was just stepping from his squad car in front of the fortresslike town hall when Sophie approached. Turning at her call, he waited, tight-lipped and tense, until she reached his side.

"How's Ford?" she asked without bothering with more than a cursory greeting.

"Last I heard, he was still at the hospital."

"Did you see him?"

The young deputy shook his head. "Doc wouldn't let any of us see him. I figured Ford wouldn't want me cooling my heels in the waiting room on taxpayers' time, so I went back on patrol." He glanced toward the building. "Come on in, and I'll see what I can find out for both of us."

"Thanks."

Clearly she wasn't the only one seeking information. The basement offices were crammed with local reporters and curiosity seekers. Following the officer to Ford's office—according to Eli, the only place where they could speak privately—Sophie spotted Clover's mayor talking with the editor of the newspaper and another man she didn't know.

"I'll be right back," Eli said, leaving her alone in the office.

Too nervous to sit, Sophie paced, stopping in front of the various plaques and photos on the walls without really seeing them.

He's not dead, she told herself for the umpteenth time, pausing to stare at the collage of photos representing the chain of command.

Ford's photo was at the top of the ragged pyramid. All the photos were similar, the background the same for all. Most of the men were young, though not all. Some were handsome, some homely, some merely nondescript. None of those faces had the same combination of strength, integrity and compelling depth that Ford's had.

"You are so special," she whispered, caressing that seamed, angular face with her gaze. If only she'd met him first, she thought, feeling sadness well inside her.

Hearing Eli's footsteps, she turned to face him, her spine braced.

"Sorry to keep you waiting, ma'am," Eli said, closing the door behind him. "According to Mayor Fall, the sheriff left the hospital about two hours ago, and no one's seen him since." He checked his watch, a worried frown creasing his forehead.

"Does that mean he wasn't badly hurt?" she asked on a rush of hope.

"Gettin' shot is always bad." Eli stared down at a stack of reports waiting Ford's signature. "The sheriff got lucky this time, is all. The bullet went clear through his shoulder. Doc said it was loss of blood that made him pass out. He damn near pleaded with the sheriff to stay in the hospital at least overnight, but Ford wasn't havin' any of that. Got up from the table after Doc pumped some blood in him and sewed him up. Just took off."

"Maybe he's at home." Eli picked up the phone and punched out the number he'd obviously memorized. Many unanswered rings later, he hung up.

"Maybe he's at his sister's place," he said suddenly, reaching for the phone.

"Yes, maybe he is, although Katie and I have taken turns calling Lucy's house since we heard what happened. There's been no answer."

"Maybe I'll have better luck," he said, flipping through Ford's Rolodex for the number. Too nervous to sit, Sophie paced while he punched the number. The result was the same. No answer.

"It all happened so fast," Eli grated as he hung up. "Frenchy had the place booby-trapped and, dumb me, I stepped wrong, settin' up this god-awful racket. Frenchy came out shootin', and woulda got me for sure if the sheriff hadn't shoved me on my ass— beg pardon, my posterior." He cleared his throat, obviously shaken, and Sophie indicated that she understood.

"The sheriff dropped old Frenchy with one shot, right through the heart. None of us knew the sheriff had taken a bullet until he just...folded up." His fingers plowed furrows in his short hair. "I don't mind admittin' I was damn scared." He lifted his gaze to hers, and they shared a look of misery.

"At least he's alive."

Eli drew a noisy breath. His face was abnormally pale, and his eyes were red-rimmed ànd weary. "Maybe he's sleepin'. Doc said he needed rest more'n anything."

"You're probably right."

"Ford's one tough son of a gun. He'll be fine."

"I'm sure he will." She glanced at the ceiling, remembering the last time she'd been in the office and the crime she'd committed. A fresh surge of guilt ran through her, followed by a resurgence of worry. Dropping her gaze to Eli's face, she saw the same worry mirrored in his dark eyes.

"Maybe it wouldn't hurt to check on him, though," she suggested. "Just in case."

"I'm off duty in another few minutes. I'll run by his place on my way home."

She expelled a relieved breath. "If you don't mind, I think I'll ride along."

His mouth curved in a sympathetic smile. "I reckon that's what you had in mind all along, isn't it?"

She nodded, her stomach knotted with nerves. "It's just that I don't have a car or a driver's license—"

"Don't apologize for worryin' about him, Miss Sophie. Ford's been waitin' a long time for the right woman to come along. I'm right glad it's you that did."

Eli said very little on the drive to Ford's house, and Sophie was grateful for the silence. She'd been jumpy and on edge since Katie had brought her the news.

"Is that Ford's car?" she cried as the sun glinted off something shiny beyond the trees.

"Looks like," Eli said, expelling a long breath.

The woodsy clearing surrounding the house seemed to be sleeping in the bright winter sunshine filtering through the trees. The house itself seemed deserted, its large windows opaque with reflected sunlight.

Eli parked the squad car behind its twin and killed the engine. Silence settled once again. "You want I should come in with you?" he asked, instinctively casting a quick look around.

"No, I'll just slip in quietly and see if he's sleeping."

"I'll wait."

Sophie opened the car door and stepped out. "I won't be long," she said before closing it quietly.

Crossing the lawn, she heard the sound of water rippling over rocks, but Lost Creek itself was hidden from view by thick underbrush lining the banks. She paused at Ford's front door, struck by a moment of uncertainty. It was one thing to be frantic with worry, another to barge into a man's home unannounced and uninvited.

Glancing over her shoulder, she saw Eli watching her through the windshield. She offered a reassuring wave, then grasped the doorknob. The door was unlocked, and she pushed it open far enough to permit her to see inside. The living room was as she remembered from the night before. It was also empty, the lingering scent of wood smoke reminding her of the fire Ford had lit and all that had happened between them.

Taking a quick breath to boost her courage, she stepped over the threshold, leaving the door ajar. Her canvas sneakers made no sound on the bare wood as she walked down the short hall toward the room at the end. As she suspected, it was Ford's bedroom. The door was ajar, revealing rumpled uniform trousers in a heap on the floor, along with his boots and a bloodstained shirt.

Her heart beating at a frantic pace, she pushed the door open, terrified at what she might find. Her breath caught as she glimpsed his long, lean body sprawled atop the rumpled sheets, dressed only in briefs, white ones this time. He was asleep, his face half-buried in the pillow. A large gauze bandage wrapped his right shoulder.

She thought about calling his name, then decided against it. Instead, she tiptoed to the bed and bent closer. His skin was flushed, suggesting a fever. As soon as she touched his forehead, she felt the heat radiating from his pores.

"Oh, no," she cried softly, but not, she realized immediately, soft enough as he opened his eyes. The pupils were huge, the focus unsteady at first. And then he frowned.

"Sophie?"

"Yes, it's me, Ford. I...we were worried when we couldn't reach you by phone so Eli drove me out to check on you."

"Eli?" He rolled to his side, then sucked in quickly, as though a sudden pain had lanced through him.

"He's outside in the car."

He grunted, his lashes lowering as though he were sinking into sleep again. Holding her breath she waited, only to have him rouse himself to offer her a crooked grin. "Believe I like wakin' up to find you lookin' at me with those pretty blue eyes," he murmured, his voice slurring.

"I can't believe Doc Gossely let you leave the hospital," she muttered, seeing his struggle to remain alert. "You're not nearly strong enough to be alone."

His mouth moved. " 'Kay, you stay."

"Don't be silly. We're going to get you dressed, and then Eli and I are going to take you back to the hospital where you belong."

"The hell you are." His voice was weaker than usual, but his determination to resist was as powerful as though he'd boomed it out.

"Be reasonable, Ford. Trauma can do strange things to a person's immune system."

"You smell good." He eased over onto his back, then skimmed his left hand slowly up her arm and back again.

"Ford, you should be under a doctor's care—"

"Feel good, too," he murmured, wrapping his fingers around hers. Her pulse leapt, even as she uttered a soft protest. His lips curved, and his eyes grew drowsy. "Tell you what, if you promise to stay and be my nurse, I promise to be a model patient."

Sophie nearly moaned aloud. His tone had been lazy, even teasing, but she sensed it would be useless to argue with him. Whatever his reasons, he was determined to fight through the pain and weakness on his own. Even though it was frustrating to accept, she understood the pride that prompted that decision. During the worst of her torment, she'd drawn inside herself to heal, shutting out even Darlene's offers of help.

"Define model patient," she demanded softly, already knowing that she couldn't leave him alone.

"No joggin', no arm wrestlin'."

"Ford, be serious. I'll stay, but only if you promise to let me call Dr. Gossely for instructions, and then follow those instructions to the letter."

His brow creased, and his eyes slowly took on a sharper focus. "No hospital," he stated firmly.

"No hospital," she agreed.

"And no Jell-O. I hate Jell-O."

Sophie burst out laughing, her heart so full of love it ached. "Agreed, but I'm holding firm on chicken soup. My mother swore it kept me from having scars when I had chicken pox."

He frowned, his eyelids drooping again. "It's a deal."

Sophie squeezed his hand, then slipped hers free. First she needed to tell Eli that she was staying on awhile, and then she would phone Dr. Gossely to find out what she needed to know about nursing a victim of a gunshot wound. After that, she would give Katie a quick call to check on Jessie and let Katie and the others know what was happening. After that, she would play it by ear.

Eli had just climbed from the car when she came out of the house. They met halfway up the walk.

"How is he?" the young deputy asked anxiously, his affection for his superior obvious.

"Groggy, and a bit feverish, but okay, I think. You were right. He was asleep."

"Damn, he should be in the hospital."

"Just what I told him. He doesn't agree."

Eli's mouth twitched. "Guess I figured as much." He squared his shoulders and looked toward the house. "So what do we do next?"

"You go home and tell that sweet wife of yours how much you love her, and I'm going to stay here with Ford until I can get reach Lucy."

"Sure you're not goin' to need help managin' him?"

Sophie laughed softly. "Don't worry. I'll tie him to the bed if he gives me too much trouble."

Eli looked startled, then a grin spread over his face. "Now that's a sight I sure would like to see. Yes, ma'am, it surely is."

Sophie shook her head. "Don't give me any more trouble than I already have, Eli Grover, or I'll report you for disobeying an order."

He chuckled, then sobered. "If you need anything, you be sure to call. I'll be home the rest of the day, and I'm only five minutes from here. Less than that with siren and lights."

"Thanks. I'll remember that." Giving in to impulse, she leaned forward to kiss his cheek. "Now, scoot. I have phone calls to make."

"On my way." Still looking worried, he turned and headed for the car. Sophie watched him go for an instant, then hurried back to the house, wondering what she'd gotten herself into.

* * *

Sophie closed the novel she'd been reading and laid it on the floor by the chair she'd brought in from the kitchen. Arching her back, she lifted her arms over her head and stretched, then checked the time.

It had been nearly four hours since she'd managed to shovel a bowl of soup into Ford along with a glass of juice and two of the pills Doc had sent home with him, then held his hand and distracted him with stories about her childhood until his eyelids had gotten heavy and he'd drifted off to sleep.

He was still sleeping, stretched on his back with one hand fisted above his head. Some men looked as docile as little boys when they were asleep, but not Ford. The texture of his face was decidedly adult male, the angles sharply molded, the lines bracketing the hard mouth deeply embedded. His hair was sweat tangled, and the black stubble did little to soften an already stubborn jaw.

Leaving her chair, she crept closer, measuring his breathing by the rise and fall of his big chest. The bandage protecting the wound the doctor had sutured front and back was a vivid swath of white against his tanned skin, bisecting the triangle of soft black hair that narrowed to a fuzzy black line leading to his navel and beyond.

Under the thin sheet the outline of his lower body was clearly discernible—lean hips flowing into long muscular thighs and sturdy calves. A sculptor's dream. And a woman's, she thought, letting her gaze rest on the distinctive bulge that showed him to be partially aroused, and very much a man.

She drew a careful breath, conscious of a gentle tightening between her thighs.

"Like what you see?" The sudden rasp of a hoarse male voice flashed her attention to his face. With his eyes only partially opened and his hair mussed, he looked sleep-rumpled and grumpy.

"Yes, you're breathing much easier now." Though surprise and guilt had her pulse running out of control, she managed to keep a straight face.

Those deep gray eyes, now so very alert, crinkled with amusement. "Funny, when I opened my eyes just now I could swear it wasn't my chest you were studyin'."

Sophie felt her face burn and cursed the Irish genes she'd gotten from her mother. None of her Gundersen cousins blushed. Only her.

"Swear all you want," she bluffed in a haughty tone she had to force, "but you'd still be wrong."

He reached out a hand and took hers, tugging her closer until she was forced to sit on the bed or risk falling on top of him. Looking a little drowsy, a little smug, he laced his fingers with hers and brought their entwined hands to his chest. Beneath her hand she felt the rough band of the gauze and the hammering of his heart.

"You wouldn't lie to me, would you, Sophie?" he asked, his voice silk and smoke.

Her breath stopped. "Why should I?"

"Could be you're feelin' a little shy about wantin' me to make love to you again."

"I'm not a bit shy," she declared firmly.

"But you *do* want me to make love to you, don't you, honey?"

"No, I do not."

"Liar."

She froze, feeling a sharp pain twisting inside her. "Don't say that," she whispered, her voice rasped with a guilt she couldn't share. "I hate lying. That's what cowards do when they can't stand the truth."

She slipped her hand free and leapt to her feet before he could reach for her again. "I'll make you some more soup," she said, unable to look him in the eye as she hurried from the room.

By the time she reached the kitchen she was trembling badly. Her fingers were icy, her face numb. At the moment, she hated herself as fiercely as she'd once hated the prosecutors who sneered at her for pleading with them to believe her. They'd called her a liar then. And in court they'd made the jury, and even the judge, believe it.

"I hate lies," she whispered, hugging herself in a vain attempt to stop the violent tremors shaking her. It was getting so hard to keep telling them, so terribly hard. Each time, she hated herself more, but what else could she do?

"Sophie?"

She jerked around, only to find herself being gathered into his arms. He'd pulled on an old blue bathrobe that smelled of soap and tickled her nose where her face was pressed against his shoulder.

"Oh, baby, I'm sorry," he whispered hoarsely. "Please believe me, I was only jokin' with you."

Squeezing her eyes shut against a flood of sudden tears, she bit her lip, struggling to regain her composure, but calm suddenly seemed beyond her. Too much had happened too quickly. Her mind was overloaded, her heart vulnerable and aching.

She didn't want to spend the rest of her life—and much of Jessie's—looking over her shoulder, always fearful, never being able to set down roots. Never feeling at ease or safe or comfortable. Never being able to express her love for the tough, kindhearted, impossibly sweet man holding her so tenderly, stroking her so gently, wrapping her in a feeling of safety, his warmth sinking into all the cold, lonely places she'd held inside since they'd locked her away from all she loved, all she longed to have again.

She felt herself melting into that longing, allowing herself to rest for just a few minutes. Just until the shaking stopped.

Ford felt the increase of her weight against him and closed his eyes in relief. He hadn't meant to upset her. He'd slice off half his tongue before he'd put that raw look of pain in those blue eyes again.

Thing was, he didn't know what to say to make things right. He never had—not to his mother when he'd tried to tell her how much it hurt his daddy when she went with other men, not to Lucy when she was hell-bent on falling in love with the wrong man. And not to the woman he was coming to care for more than he'd thought possible.

The word *love* drifted through his mind again like smoke from cornstalk twists, filling him until he felt raw inside. His mother had claimed to "love" his father, even as she was destroying his manhood inch by bloody inch. His mind told him there were women who didn't cheat and who didn't lie when they said those words. Women like Sophie. He wanted to believe that with all his heart and soul. Maybe he even did a little. Maybe that's why he felt so foul because he'd hurt her.

Because he didn't know what else to do, he smoothed his hand down her back, petting her the way he'd helped Jessie pet the baby rabbit. Beneath the shapeless shirt she was wearing, her skin felt nearly as smooth as Peter's fur. He flattened his palm, enjoying the sensation running over his skin.

She was so small, so precious. A treasure he hadn't really believed existed. Not for him. Never for him. Drawing a breath, he savored the musky allure of her shampoo before pressing his cheek against hers.

He felt her sigh, then strain against his arms. Reluctantly, he eased his hold and lifted his head. "Better now?" he asked gruffly.

Sophie lifted her gaze to his and nodded. His smile was crooked, his eyes probing, yet gentle. "I don't usually give way like that," she murmured, knowing that she should step from his arms, yet unable to make herself move.

"Everyone's entitled," he said, his eyes crinkling. "'Specially when a jackass like me says something stupid. I truly am sorry for that."

She felt a smile trembling her lips. "You were entitled, too. I really was staring at, uh, you know."

He cocked his head, his expression part arrogant male, part tickled little boy. "You know?" he echoed solemnly.

Her cheeks felt scalded. "I think it's time I made you that soup."

"I don't want soup. I want to make love to you again." He drew her close and smoothed his palms down her spine, setting up a chain reaction of shivers.

"You should be in bed," she said, lifting a hand to stroke his whisker-rough cheek. He turned into her hand and kissed the palm before capturing the hand with his.

"You should be with me." It was a simple statement, simply stated in the raspy Southern drawl she was coming to adore. No matter where she went, or how long she lived, she knew she would never again hear the lazy cadence and slurred vowels of Southern speech without aching inside.

"All right, but only to sleep," she conceded, struggling to hang on to the little authority he'd already granted her.

He narrowed his eyes, and shook his head. "No way. If we go back into that bedroom together, we're goin' to make love."

A thrill ran through her, dancing along her nerves, warming inside and out. "But your shoulder. You're still recovering."

He ran his hands down her back, then drew her closer and, at the same time, spread his legs so that suddenly she felt the hard bulge of his arousal pressing intimately against her.

"From where I'm standin' I don't know how much more recovered I can get," he drawled ruefully, but his eyes were liquid fire.

"I see what you mean," she said, choking off a laugh.

"Figured you would."

The electric shock at feeling his full arousal faded into an urgent need to feel him inside her, filling her so completely. Curling up against him, she clung to his neck, and he groaned.

His mouth took hers greedily, his hands roaming her back, her hips, his fingers cupping her bottom, urging her hard against him.

His kiss became fevered as he concentrated on exploring her mouth, his lips hot, his tongue tempting hers.

She returned the kiss eagerly, running her hands through his hair, feeling its silky thickness sliding coolly over her fingers. Delicious, erotic sensations spun through her, driving her more and more frantic. He groaned, then dragged his mouth from hers.

"Lord help me," he exclaimed hoarsely, pressing his hot cheek against hers. His breathing was raspy, hers more so as her lungs demanded oxygen. Finally he drew back, his expression fierce, a dusky flush layered over the tan.

"I need you, Sophie," he murmured, his voice rough with emotion. "It scares the spit out of me how much."

Her breath seemed dammed by her suddenly aching throat. "I need you, too," she admitted when she could find her voice again.

He drew a long breath, then stepped back and held out his hand. "Come with me, darlin'. It's time we took ourselves to bed."

Chapter 11

Day had slipped into dusk while they'd been in the kitchen, and the bedroom was bathed in pale light shining from the west window. Above the trees the beginning of a glorious sunset was faintly visible, though Sophie had little chance to enjoy the view as he turned her away from the window and into his arms.

"Happy New Year, sweet Sophie," he murmured, and she smiled.

"Happy New, ah, Year," she murmured on a rush of pleasure as he brushed the sensitive skin beneath her ear.

"You smell good," he whispered, nuzzling her gently. "Like woman."

"Ah, what?" She eased her head back, tangling her fingers in his hair.

"Woman," he repeated thickly before touching his tongue to her throat. "My woman."

He drew back, but only to align his mouth with hers. He tasted and tempted with his lips and his tongue, while his hands stroked and molded. She pressed her palms against his spine, feeling the hard flesh beneath the terry cloth, remembering the texture of skin and flex of muscle. His kiss grew more demanding, more fevered, until both were out of breath, but still he wooed her, exploring the contours of her throat with his mouth until she was quivering and her thighs felt like water. Swaying, she clutched his shoulders for support.

With a harsh sound he drew back, his eyes narrowing. It took her a moment to realize his face had gone paper white. The word he ground out with a tight jaw was anything but poetic.

Searching his face with anxious eyes, she expelled a shaky breath, somewhere between a laugh and a sob. "I knew we shouldn't have started this," she declared, her voice sounding like a stranger's to her ears. "You're in pain, and don't try to deny it."

"I'll be in worse pain if you get all noble on me," he said, holding his right arm against his chest.

"It's past time for your pills," she said as firmly as her galloping senses would allow. "I'll get you another glass of water."

He looked grumpy. "Forget the pills."

She snatched up the glass by the bed and was already halfway to the door before he had a chance to stop her. Two seconds later she returned to the bedroom with a full glass of water to find him trying to untie the sash of his robe.

"I was never very good with my left hand," he muttered, working at the knot. Hastily, she put the glass on the nightstand and went to help him.

"Here, let me." She pushed his hand away and finished the job he'd started. His robe fell open, revealing the hard contours of his chest—and the bandage that she'd all but forgotten.

"You're impossible, and I'm irresponsible," she muttered, helping him out of the soft terry cloth. Naked now, save for the skimpy briefs, his body exuded heat, causing her to curse herself for being so selfish.

"No, you're not," he declared, his voice deeper than usual. "You're adorable and sweet and sexy, and for the moment, all mine."

"Not until you take your medicine." She shook two tablets from the small vial and held them out to him.

"They'll make me sleepy," he groused.

"So?"

"Be reasonable, Sophie."

"Open your mouth."

"If I do, will you undress for me?"

"That's blackmail," she protested, helpless to stop the shiver that ran through her at the look of intense longing in his eyes.

"Undress for me, Sophie," he demanded harshly. "Let me see you again."

She licked her lips, her nerves leaping and jumping. "Ford—"

"Please," he coaxed. "Just this once. For me."

"You'll take the pills?"

Instead of answering, he took the tablets from her outstretched hand and threw them to the back of his throat, swallowing without water. "Okay, your turn," he demanded, his crooked grin a little wicked, a little vulnerable.

Sophie felt a surge of tenderness for him, and the last of her resistance crumbled away. She knew the risks involved, the searing heartache she would feel when she had to leave Clover forever. She would face the pain when she had to. Not now. Now belonged to Ford. Whatever he wanted from her, she would give willingly and with all of her heart.

"Sit down first," she murmured.

"Why?"

She shot him a look, and he grinned. His eyes, however, took on a heated intensity. "Okay, I'll sit. But I'm not promisin' to stay put."

He sat down on the bed, his gaze flowing over her as she worked the buttons of her shirt cuffs and slipped out of her sneakers. Terrified, and yet determined, she undid her belt and unzipped her jeans, then tugged her shirt free, the sound of fabric sliding against skin unnaturally loud in the electric silence.

One by one she undid the buttons, then slipped the shirt free of her shoulders, letting it fall in a heap at her feet. Before her courage failed her, she slipped off her jeans and kicked them away, leaving her with only her bra and panties. His eyes flamed, and his nostrils flared, and for a moment she faltered.

"In those movies you were speaking of last night the women are always wearing lacy underwear instead of industrial cotton," she murmured self-consciously, glancing down at the plain white underwear she'd bought because it was cheap and durable.

"Do you hear me complainin' any?" he rasped, his dilated pupils and strained breathing revealing his impatience as he let his gaze run very slowly, very thoroughly, over her near nakedness. She couldn't prevent a shudder from running through her, and she drew an agonized breath.

"I'm not very good at this. I'm sorry."

"Oh, baby, don't be sorry," He got swiftly to his feet and folded her into his arms again. "You have a perfect body."

"I'm too flat chested," she whispered, her face buried against his shoulder.

"Not by my reckonin'," he said, stroking his left hand over one throbbing breast. She drew air, pleasure flaring through her. Taking his time, he lowered his mouth to the nipple outlined against the cotton, swirling his tongue over the tip. She moaned on an indrawn breath, arching her neck back, her hands digging into the firm flesh padding his hard shoulders.

"Easy, baby," he murmured, gliding a finger over the curve of each breast, his expression absorbed, as though hers was the first woman's body he'd known.

"I can't seem to breathe properly," she murmured, sucking air.

"We can fix that. Turn around."

In a daze she obeyed, gasping suddenly as his fingers slipped beneath the clasp of her bra. His hands were gentle as he slipped the straps over her shoulders, freeing her breasts. He drew the bra from her quickly and sent it to join her blouse at their feet. Still behind her, he drew her against him until his arousal rested between her legs, and cupped his hands over her breasts.

She was incapable of moving, unable to speak, even to think. With his voice and his hands and the reverence in his eyes, he was making her feel like a woman again. Desirable, feminine, and so wonderfully adored. The lingering insecurities Wells had put in her seemed far in the past, no longer able to touch her.

Needing to see him, she turned in his arms until they were face-to-face. Steeped in love and pleasure, she ran her hands down the long stretch of his back, kneading the firm flesh, absorbing warmth, imparting tenderness. He groaned, and she felt his arousal stretching the fabric of his briefs.

His kiss exploded against her mouth, his tongue sliding into her mouth to taste and tantalize. His hands roamed over her with maddening slowness, his early weakness seemingly forgotten. Fires kindled wherever his fingers stroked, spreading wildly through her until she was no longer capable of thought. Only feelings mattered. Only sensations registered, swirling, tantalizing, consuming her.

"I need you under me," he murmured, slipping his fingers beneath the elastic of her panties.

"Yes, oh, yes," she cried, helping him slip them free. And then she was helping him remove the briefs until he was as naked as she was. Hooking his arm around her waist he drew her to the bed. The sheets were cool against her back, his chest hot against her breasts. He seared a kiss against her shoulder, and she cried out.

When he slipped a hand between her thighs, she caught her lip between her teeth to stifle the cry of ecstasy. Unable to lie still, she tossed her head from side to side, desperate to escape the exquisite pressure building inside her. With each stroke of his fingers, she became more frenzied, driven to the brink time and time again, only to fall back. Sobbing in frustration, she clawed at his unbandaged shoulder, needing to feel him inside her, desperate for release. Murmuring something harsh, he rolled her over until she was lying atop him. She started to protest, then remembered his injured shoulder.

"In the nightstand," he rasped. "Protection."

Stretched across him, she somehow managed to get the drawer open without pulling it completely free of the frame. Her fingers were frantic, her breathing as labored as his as she found the small box. Finding it sealed, she whimpered at her inability to get it open quickly. He took it from her, his own efforts far from effortless as he removed a packet.

"Damn, I hate these things," he muttered, tearing it open. Biting her lip, she waited until he was ready for her, then clumsily, driven by her own frantic impulses, she managed to position herself above him.

"That's it, baby," he cried, his eyes dark and dangerously wild. Framing her hips with his hands, he helped her settle slowly over him, her body accepting his with hot, moist welcome.

Ford shuddered as she fitted herself to him, his body beyond even his iron will to control. His woman had taken over his mind, his soul. His need for her had gone beyond physical before he'd realized he'd spent a lifetime hungering for more from a woman.

It didn't take long to realize that she wasn't skilled at taking the lead. He didn't care. Not when she was tight and smooth around him, her movements driven by the passion he'd put in her. Arching his back, he dug his head into the pillow, his blood sizzling, his mind fragmenting. Dimly he was aware of other parts of his body—a stinging in his shoulder, a roaring in his head—even as the hot pressure coiling and uncoiling in his groin grew more punishing.

He wanted to please her, to imprint his body on hers until she remembered only his lovemaking, his face, his name. Instead, she was branding him with hers, warming the stark, frozen wasteland inside him with her fire, soothing the still-raw hurts with her hot, honeyed sweetness.

Sophie was beyond thought, awash in sensations, dizzy with need, greedy to go higher, faster. Urgency built, grew more intense, driving her, enveloping her, until she felt sensation gathering, pulsing. It seemed forever that she was poised on the brink, and then there was nothing but a blinding explosion of feeling, a star burst of indescribable ecstasy.

Ford felt her body tighten around him, tiny spasms shivering, building, until he was being squeezed in a warm vise. Opening his eyes, he saw the passionate sheen on her skin, the rapture in the eyes seeking his as she moved faster now, for him this time. Only for him.

Never taking his gaze from her face, he bucked toward her, driving himself into her with a desperate, helpless need. His release was cataclysmic, sending savage pleasure into every part of him. He cried her name, the world a chaotic swirling star burst of colored lights. She collapsed on top of him, breathing rapidly, her eyes closed, her expression pure bliss.

He'd never felt so strong, so fulfilled. Nothing he'd done in his life until now had touched him as fiercely as the dreamy smile on her lips as she rested trustingly against him.

"You're mine now," he murmured, wrapping his arms around her possessively. "No other man will ever touch you again."

She woke slowly, her face buried in Ford's pillow, a feeling of delicious lassitude lying heavy inside her. It was a new experience to find herself smiling, even before she was fully awake. In spite of the lethargy gripping her, she felt wonderfully refreshed. It took her only a moment, however, to realize that she was alone.

Though it was dark in the bedroom itself, the hall light was burning, and she heard the sound of water running in another part of the house. Still groggy, she eased to her back, wincing at the dull throbbing between her legs. What had happened with Ford was beyond anything she'd ever experienced with Wells, beyond anything she even hoped to feel.

Pulling the sheet higher, she trailed a hungry gaze around the room where they'd created true magic together. Soon, so terribly soon, she would have to leave Clover, and when she did, she would take only memories with her. Dear, special memories of dear, special friends. And one very dear, exceptional man who for a few brief, precious moments had loved her. As she loved him—passionately, totally. She knew enough about herself now to know that she would always love him. She knew enough about him to know that his feelings were more easily controlled, more readily rationed. But for a time, he'd given her all of himself. Body and soul. And heart.

It was enough.

It had to be enough.

She drew a shaky breath, then sat up and ran nervous fingers through her hair. The clock by the bed read 7:25. She'd been away from Katie's and from Jessie for nearly nine hours. As soon as she made sure Ford wasn't suffering any ill effects, she would see about rounding up some transportation back to the rooming house.

The sound of running water stopped abruptly, and she found herself easing the sheet higher. It didn't help to tell herself that she was in love with the man who usually occupied this big, soft bed. She could talk to herself until she ran out of words, and she would still be bone-rattling nervous.

"Hey, you're awake," he said as he came into the room, still stark naked and grinning, carrying a tray. The combination of the darkened room and his dark skin and dark eyes had her thinking of marauding pirates and bare-breasted native girls. And wild, savage seduction.

He set the tray on the nightstand, then eased in next to her and kissed her hard. "I wanted to wake you with a kiss, like Snow White."

"Sleeping Beauty," she corrected, her heart leaping.

"Damn, I must have read those stories to Lucy a hundred times. Guess I'm just not much for fairy tales."

"Most men aren't."

Ford saw the quick swipe of her tongue over her lower lip and figured she was suffering from morning-after nerves. He knew how she felt. He'd climbed out of bed feeling jittery as a first-time lover, not knowing which way his lady was going to jump.

"Hope you like your eggs scrambled hard, 'cause that's the only way I know how to make them."

She stared at him. He'd shaved, combed his hair and, from the fresh scent of soap clinging to his skin, bathed. Either the man was superhuman or he was crazy.

"You were cooking?"

"Sex makes me hungry."

"But your shoulder—"

"Is just a little achy, nothing to worry about."

"You shaved and took a shower."

"Bath. Doctor's orders, until the sutures come out."

He handed her a napkin, then took one himself. "Sorry I don't have one of those fancy bed trays. Never needed one before." He handed her a fork, looking for all the world like a very contented man.

"I should call Katie."

"Already done. She said to tell you Jessie's fine. Ate all her dinner, except for the vegetables, which Katie led me to believe ended up on the floor while her back was turned."

Sophie felt a laugh bubbling. "Oh, no. Katie's probably pacing the floor, waiting for me to get home." She took a bite, wondering how fast Maxwell's taxi could get to Ford's place.

Ford drew the sheet to his waist, then settled the plate on his thighs. "Good, huh?" he said, watching her all but devouring the eggs.

"Terrific," she said, swallowing so fast she scarcely knew what she was eating. "Uh, maybe I should try Lucy again."

He gave her a puzzled look. "Why?"

"To tell her you're okay, of course. I don't know why she hasn't called before now, but surely she has to be worried about you."

He snorted, his mouth taking on the same intimidating line she used to fear. "I doubt it. That shyster Dooley has her so besotted, she can't think of anything but him. Besides, she's in Charleston until Friday."

She blinked at him. "Why didn't you tell me earlier?"

"You didn't ask." He smothered his eggs in Tabasco, then politely offered the bottle to her. She shook her head impatiently.

"I distinctly remember mentioning to you that I'd been trying to call her," she persisted.

"No doubt you did. I probably heard you, too." He forked eggs into his mouth and chewed, a look of intense enjoyment spreading over his rugged features.

"Then why didn't you tell me she was in Charleston?"

"Because you also said you were only goin' to stay until you got ahold of her, and I didn't want you to leave." His sudden grin was unabashed, and the lines of strain bracketing his mouth softened, leading her to imagine the boy he'd once been. She had a feeling he'd been a lot like his sister then—quick to laugh and to trust, until life had turned ugly.

"Don't look so proud of yourself, Maguire," she teased, her throat aching for that long-lost boy. "As soon as I finish this culinary feast, I'm calling for a taxi to take me home."

"No need. I already told Katie you were spending the night."

He felt a jolt of satisfaction as her fork hit her plate. "Oh, Ford, you didn't!"

"How many times do I have to tell you, woman? I never say anythin' I don't mean." He leaned forward to touch his mouth to hers. She tasted hot sauce and need, and her heart began speeding.

"Now shut up and eat. Somethin' tells me we're both goin' to need our strength."

Ford willed himself awake, the scream he'd bit back still echoing in his head. Jackknifing to a sitting position, he threw back his head and tried to drag air into his lungs. Nausea stung his throat, flavored with the horror of what he'd just seen.

"Ford? What's wrong?" The anxious question came out of the dark, startling him. He stiffened, ready to fight off an attack, and then he remembered that tonight he wasn't alone.

"Nightmare," he muttered. "Be okay in a minute." He was breathing easier now, but from past experience he knew the queasiness wouldn't fade quickly. More accustomed to the dark now, his eyes took in the pale shape of Sophie's face. Her eyes were huge, and silvered with worry.

"Can I help?" she asked, touching his arm. "I could get you some water, or maybe some juice?"

"Nothing,"

"At least let me change the sheets," she murmured. "They're soaking wet, and so are you."

He started to refuse, then realized that he wasn't the only one who'd be spending the rest of the night sleeping on clammy sheets. "Clean ones in the hall closet," he muttered, rolling away from her.

His head spun as he got to his feet, and he shivered in the sudden chill. Careful to keep his head up, he made his way to the bathroom and turned on the tap. Nausea spun in his head and ground in his belly as he lowered his face to the sink and splashed cold water on his head and neck, then drank from his cupped hand until he felt able to stand without a cramp bending him in two again. It had been years since he'd felt this sick. He wanted to believe it was too much hot sauce on the eggs, not the long-buried feelings making love to Sophie had stirred to life in him.

Sensing movement, he glanced up to find Sophie watching him from the doorway. She'd pulled on her shirt, but left it hanging open.

"I saw some brandy in the kitchen," she murmured, hugging herself as though she, too, felt the same chill. "Why don't I pour you a glass?"

"Liquor makes it worse." Embarrassed, he pulled a towel from the rod and wiped his face, leaving it in the sink when he was done.

"Then come back to bed," she urged, moving from the door to come to him. Steadier now, he let her put her arm around his waist, and together they returned to the bedroom. His shoulder was hurting badly, and his knees felt more wobbly than secure. He'd had worse tussles with the all-too-familiar nightmare. He just couldn't remember any offhand.

She'd turned on a light and left it burning. She'd folded the sodden sheets and left them by the door. All very tidy, very neat, like the bed she'd remade. That she'd had to do anything at all had him wanting to kick something hard.

"Don't scowl," she murmured, her voice husky. "Everyone needs help sometimes."

"Trouble is, I'm the one who's supposed to do the helpin'." He climbed into bed and watched her do the same.

"Who says?"

"The people who elected me sheriff."

She gave him an incredulous look. "Seems to me that's exactly what you were doing when you went after the man who'd sold those boys rotgut."

"If I'd found that still a week ago the youngest McEwin boy would still be alive, and LeRoy King wouldn't be facing surgery."

"You don't know that."

"I know I didn't do my job." He slipped between the sheets, furious with himself for ruining damn near the best night of his life.

"Of course you did." She drew a breath. "You're not perfect."

His face twisted. "Now that's an understatement."

"You saved Eli's life."

Damn that kid's hide, he thought. Probably spreading that all over town, which just meant he'd spend the next month having to listen to people telling him how brave he was. Yeah, right. He was brave, all right, a real cool head who passed out cold at the sight of blood. Disgust clawed at his throat, worse than any sickness.

"Look, can we talk about somethin' else?"

Sophie understood the haunted look in his eyes all too well. The nightmare had reminded him that there were things he couldn't control, no matter how strong he made himself or how tightly he sealed himself off from his emotions.

"Okay, tell me about the nightmare."

"No." Just like that, he had shut her out, as though the intimacy they'd shared meant nothing. It hurt that he could push her aside so easily.

"Since I'm already wide-awake, I think I'll just have a quick shower and be on my way." She offered him a friendly smile, which wasn't returned.

"You're runnin' away 'cause I won't open a vein and bleed all over you, aren't you?"

"No, I'm going home because I have to be at work in less than two hours. I just hope Arnie Maxwell doesn't mind an early wake-up call."

His frown wasn't unexpected. The quick flash of something very like pain in his eyes was.

"Tell you what," he said, taking her hand and lacing their fingers. "I'll take that shower with you, and then drive you into town myself. Save you taxi fare."

"Thanks for the offer, but you're off showers at the moment, remember?"

Ford caught the anxious look she flicked at his bandaged shoulder and consigned Frenchy Ducette to an eternity of fire and brimstone.

"So we'll take a bath." He brought her hand to his lips and enjoyed the sudden leap in her eyes. "A nice long bath."

"No time," she murmured, trying to tug free. "Ford, let me go, please."

"Not until I get a good-mornin' kiss from my lady." He attempted to draw her closer, only to stop dead by the sudden sheen of tears in her eyes. "Sophie?"

"I'm not your lady, Ford," she said, her voice vibrating with emotion. "Not when you're only willing to share your body with me and nothing more. So let's just agree we had great sex and let it go at that."

Ford narrowed his gaze and studied her face. He'd learned never to trust the look in a woman's eyes, or even the tears that she might squeeze from them on command. But the hurt radiating from her was too sharp and too vivid to be anything but real. He drew in air, cursing his lack of education and limited vocabulary for the feeling of helpless frustration ripping through him.

"You know that past we keep talkin' about?"

She nodded, her expression still wary. The need to draw her against him was painfully real, as real as the hurt he still sensed in her.

"I reckon you know how my mama and daddy died?"

Sophie nodded again, watching his face. Something had changed, something intangible and important. "Katie told me that you . . . found them."

"Found the bodies, you mean." His mouth twisted. "But that hadn't been the first time I'd been out to the hangar that night."

Because she knew nothing she could say would change the pictures he saw in his mind, she simply took his hand and held it. His fingers stiffened, and then slowly curled around hers until he was gripping her tightly.

"I'd been working on this Cessna for Tim and needed a part from the factory. On my way home I stopped at the post office to pick it up, then went home to look after Lucy while Mama went to a meetin' at the church."

Sophie found the lack of emotion in his voice more chilling than the most violent expression of emotion. "My old man was workin' late, so I hung around the house with Lucy till he came home, then decided to go on back to the hangar and get in a few hours more work. I parked around back and was about to let myself into the office so I could turn on the hangar lights when I saw my mama and Tim." He shook his head, his mouth taking on a bitter line. "I'd never seen my mama naked before. At first I didn't believe it could really be her I was seein' on top of my best friend, doin' a whore's work."

Sophie flinched. "Perhaps she was in love with him."

"Love." His voice gave the word an ugly, obscene twist that tore at her. "Mama used to talk about that a lot. About how Daddy came home from the war and swept her off her feet. How much in love they were until I came along and ended the honeymoon."

He turned his head to look at her. His eyes were bleak as a winter sea. "I bought a jar of 'shine on my way home and drank until I passed out. The next thing I remember was Lucy comin' into my room with that damn ring she got from Daddy's mama in her hand, tellin' me that Mama and Daddy hadn't come home."

"So you went back and found them."

"What was left of them, yeah. Daddy was always a crack shot, but this time he used a shotgun. I never knew why for sure. Maybe because he was afraid his hand would shake when he got Mama's head in his sights."

"Oh, Ford, I'm so sorry." Her hand trembled slightly as it came up to smooth the sweat-rumpled hair from his forehead. Ford saw the anguish in her eyes and realized that he'd never told another soul what he'd just told her.

"That's what I see, Sophie. My mother splattered all over that office. And then I wake up, knowin' I could have prevented three people I cared about from dyin' like that."

A shiver chased through Sophie at the vicious sting of self-hatred in his voice. "You don't know that," she said gently.

"I could have stopped them before Daddy got there," he said in a tone without any emotion at all. "All I had to do was open the door and walk in, but I couldn't. I was afraid my mama would end up hatin' me." He looked at her with eyes so haunted he couldn't quite keep all the hurt hidden. "Folks think I'm some kind of hero for stayin' home to take care of my sister. Now there are two of us who know I'm not.''

"I know that you're much too hard on yourself, Ford Maguire. Perhaps you *could* have prevented what happened that night, though I think at best you would have simply postponed the inevitable. More probably you would have ended up as dead as everyone else. And then Lucy wouldn't have had anyone to hold her when she woke up screaming.''

Sophie saw that she'd touched him in some small way and wanted to weep for the torment he'd put himself through all those years.

"You really believe that, don't you?''

"With all my heart.''

She felt a slight easing in the terror tension holding him captive. "How'd you get to be so wise?''

"I'm not wise,'' she whispered, her voice thick with conflicting emotions. Though he would never know, she had her own bloody memories. Memories that still woke her in the dead of night. Memories that had the power to batter at barriers that she suspected weren't quite as solid or as permanent as his. "I just don't want you to hurt anymore.''

"I don't, not when I'm with you,'' he murmured, cupping his hand around her slender neck. He kissed her lips before she had a chance to refuse. He eased her to her back before she could protest.

Passion flared in her quickly this time, needing only the taste of his mouth to send her blood surging. Was it so selfish to want what only he could give her? Was it so terribly wrong to need another memory to take with her when she left? Even as she argued with herself, she let her head fall back, giving him access to the pulse throbbing in her throat.

His gaze welded to her face, he watched her eyes go soft and cloudy before her lashes fluttered closed. On a sigh, she whispered his name, sending his own need spiking. But this time was for her, only for her. To that end, he leveled his own desire, using all the skill he'd learned to control his body as well as his mind.

It wasn't as easy as it should be, nor as utterly successful as he might wish, but the sharp flare of urgency slowly diminished to a bearable ache as he slowly, thoroughly explored the soft contours of her breast, using his lips and tongue and, when he had her trembling, his teeth to gently nip the tender nipple that had once suckled a child. When he felt her hands fisting in his hair, he shifted his attention to the other breast, tracing the fullness with his tongue before taking the nipple into his mouth. At the same time he trailed slow, caressing fingers along the inner fullness of her thigh, feeling the soft warm flesh quiver beneath his fingertips.

She breathed his name, her hands frantic, her body moving restlessly. Schooling himself to patience, he moved lower, pressing slow, moist kisses in a meandering line from her breasts to her navel, feeling the muscles contract beneath his lips.

Using his tongue, he enjoyed a leisurely exploration of the swell of her belly, lapping at the shallow indentation before tracing the downward slope of warm silken flesh to the downy triangle of sable curls between her legs.

For his own pleasure as much as hers he rubbed his face in the luxuriant softness, drawing in the scent of rose-flavored bath powder and the intensely erotic hint of womanly musk. Barely leashed desire clawed his loins, threatening to override his control, and he tightened his grip on her hips, willing the savage hunger to ease its grip.

Buffeted with a wild wanting, she felt him freeze, his breathing a hot rasp against her thighs. Frustration ran through her, prodding her to arch upward, needing release from the urgent tingling turning her soft and hot and tense inside. Helpless, she tossed her head from side to side, her lip caught between her teeth to keep her cries from exploding into the room. Her hands pulled frantically at his hair, urging him to finish what he started. Blood roared in her head, and sang through her veins. Everywhere her body touched the sheet beneath her was sensitized, the pressure nearly unbearable. Desperate, she moaned, his name coming from her lips in a long keening cry, blending with the hoarse groan of a man in pain.

But before she could focus her thoughts, he was nudging her thighs apart, his clever fingers already seeking, now stroking, now rubbing, until she was sobbing helplessly, desperate to feel him inside her.

"Easy, darlin'," he urged, his voice hoarse. He moved, his hands sliding down her thighs, then up, his breathing a tortured sound.

His tongue lapped where his fingers had stroked, and she cried out, lost in a frenzy. Helplessly, instinctively, she bucked upward, increasing the pressure, heightening the pleasure, until release came in a hot, hard wave, shuddering through her in one wave after another.

Ford felt the spasms shaking her, and felt his own body react. Before he could prevent it, he was shuddering, powerless to prevent his own orgasm, and his seed pulsed onto the sheets. Crying out, he held on, riding out the most intense wave of pleasure he'd ever felt.

Long moments later, he lifted his head from the soft pillow of her thigh and looked at her. Her eyes were closed, the dark lashes contrasting with the flush of arousal still blooming on her cheeks. Her lips were passion full, the corners still soft and dreamy, giving them the look of a woman who had just been thoroughly kissed.

Satisfaction rocketed through him, followed more slowly but surely by a rare easing of thought that he could only label contentment. He wasn't a particularly generous man, but suddenly he wanted to shower her with gifts, beginning with the security of knowing that no one would ever hurt her again.

"Wake up, Sleeping Beauty," he murmured, easing himself into position to press his mouth to hers lightly. Her lips curved slowly, sweetly, her lashes fluttering up to reveal passion-sated blue eyes.

"I'm beginning to see a whole new dimension to that old story," she murmured, her husky voice setting his blood to humming again.

"For better or worse?" he asked gruffly, kissing her chin.

"Definitely better."

"Now about that bath," he said, easing to a sitting position.

"Mmm." She licked her lips, and he all but groaned. Her throat was flushed, and the shadowed cleft between her breasts was dewy. His imagination had him lapping up those pearly beads of moisture one by one. A quick glance at the clock told him that that particular pleasure would have to wait.

"Much as I'd like to spend the rest of the day wrapped around you in this bed, I'm forced to confess something important."

She smiled, her eyes still dark with passion. "What's that?"

"You're about to be late for work."

Chapter Twelve

"I still think we should paint it yellow."

Sophie wiped her nose with the hand that held the paintbrush and regarded the ancient biplane with a critical eye. It was primitive by modern standards, a toy constructed of wood and fabric and held together by thin wires and Ford's determination. Even though he'd repeatedly rhapsodized over the Jenny's aerodynamic stability and reliability as a World War I training plane and barnstormer after the war, she still shuddered every time she thought about his actually flying it.

"She's a she, not an it," Ford corrected, rising from an inspection of the plane's undercarriage to drop a kiss on her nose. "All airplanes are female."

"How do you know?" she asked, secretly enjoying the masculine aroma of sweat and lacquer thinner that clung to his paint-spattered shirt.

His grin was cocky, his cocked-hip, legs-planted-wide stance pure male. Since the night they'd spent together he'd been blatantly and aggressively courting her. For a man who loudly and regularly proclaimed his inability to flirt, he was proving to be an ardent, irresistible lover. Knowing that she couldn't stay in Clover much longer made the time they spent together that much more precious to her.

"Because Jenny there's a lot like you, darlin' Sophie. One minute she's treating this old boy sweet as you please, and the next she's frustratin' him all to hell," he drawled, sidestepping the punch she aimed at his flat belly.

"Watch it, buster," she threatened, working at a menacing look that only won her another of those slow-forming, beguilingly off-center grins.

"Watch what, sugar? The way your skin turns pink when I kiss your breasts, or the way your eyes get all dreamy after sex."

"Shh, someone might hear you."

Experiencing equal parts of acute embarrassment and extreme sensual pleasure, she cast a quick look around the cavernous hangar. Ugly as sin, the place smelled like machinery in various stages of repair and stale smoke from the cigar the owner, Bud Staley, puffed on incessantly.

"No one's here but us," Ford said, moving closer. "Bud's busy givin' a lesson up there," he said, pointing a greasy spanner toward the high arching ceiling. "And I haven't seen another soul since we got here."

It was Sunday, her day off. For the third week in a row, Ford had wheedled her into spending it with him. For the third week in a row she'd tried to use spending time with Jessie as an excuse to give her some breathing room from his determined pursuit. And for the third week in a row, he'd simply included Jessie in his plans.

At the moment she was asleep in a portable playpen a safe distance from the paint fumes. Sophie had resisted when Ford had suggested buying the folding contraption that also served as a bed in a pinch. He'd simply ignored her protests and bought it, anyway. At the same time he'd bought the best car seat he could find and installed it in the back seat of the Camaro.

So far, they'd used both a half-dozen times, mostly when she'd visited him at his house. She knew it wasn't smart or even safe to continue a relationship with him that she knew had to end, but every time she brought up the subject of breaking it off, he simply kissed her into a bemused silence.

"When are you going to stop stalling and take me for a ride in this crate?" she demanding, loving the indignant look that came over his rugged features whenever she maligned his beloved Jenny.

"Watch your tongue, woman," he drawled, moving closer.

The weather was warmer than normal for late January and even warmer under the hangar's metal roof. Wrestling with a stubborn lug bolt on one of the Jenny's wheels had put him into a sweat, staining his shirt in a triangle stretching in a narrowing line from his strong throat to his navel.

"You're wasting your breath threatening me, Sheriff Maguire. I know what a softie you are under that macho crust."

Scowling, he hooked his clean hand around her waist and lifted her to her toes. "Only with you," he declared gruffly before subjecting her to a long, draining kiss that had them both wanting more.

"Have dinner with me tonight," he ordered as she drew a shaky breath. "We'll drive to the shore and have lobster."

"I can't. Katie and I are taking Jessie to the petting zoo at the mall in Magnolia."

He dropped the spanner into its proper drawer in the outsize tool chest and wiped his greasy hand on one of the rags he kept handy.

"Sounds like fun," he said as he tossed the rag on top of the chest. "I'll be honored to escort three such lovely ladies."

Sophie returned the brush to the can of lacquer thinner with the others and wiped her hands on the bandanna she'd tucked into the back pocket of her jeans.

"Ford, be serious. People are beginning to think of us as a couple."

"Now that's downright silly," he declared firmly. Before her stomach sank all the way to the floor, he shot a look at the baby, his expression softening. "You and me and Jess, we're a threesome. Some might even call that a family."

"But we know we're not."

He glanced down at his grease-stained running shoes for a moment before directing his attention her way again.

"Maybe we ought to give some thought to changin' that." His voice was so calm, his tone so matter-of-fact, that for an instant she didn't realize exactly what he'd said. When she did, she felt as though she'd just been offered the greatest gift in the world, only to be told that she would die an agonizing death if she accepted it.

"Careful what you say," she teased, feeling sick inside, and yet determined not to let him see how shaken she really was. "Jenny's liable to get jealous and refuse to start the next time you want to take her for a joyride."

Ford watched her eyes turn haunted again and cursed his lack of finesse. "Not to worry, honey," he said with a wink. "By the time a lady gets Jenny's age, she's most generally hard of hearing."

She took up her paintbrush again and dipped it into the dark red lacquer before slanting him a wry look. "Good thing for you, too, considering the language I heard coming from beneath her this afternoon."

Ford grinned because he knew that would please her, but his gut was slowly twisting into a familiar knot.

"Guess I'm too used to workin' out here alone," he told her with his best good-old-boy manner. "Best watch it from now on, I'm thinkin.'"

"Best do that," she teased before directing her attention to the underside of the lower of the two wings.

Ford watched her for a long moment, admiring the ripely feminine contours of her bottom as she concentrated on her task. It was the first time he'd seen her in tight jeans, and those were definitely world-class, worn soft enough by countless turns in the washing machine to cling provocatively to her hips and thighs in just the right fashion to rile a man's blood but good.

The tug between his legs told him that he was treading on dangerous turf. Even if she would let him make love to her here, he wouldn't. The only privacy was provided by the office, and he hadn't set foot in that twenty-by-twenty cubical since he was eighteen. He never would.

Still, a man's mind and his body sometimes ended up in a no-holds-barred brawl, something he'd only recently come to understand. His mind told him to walk away. His body wouldn't let him. For better or worse, he wanted her, and in a town as small and inbred as Clover that meant marriage. Anything less would only serve to dishonor her, and he'd as soon as chew barbed wire before he'd do that to her or her daughter.

But a man who'd spent the whole of his adult life running from commitment wasn't inclined to make sudden moves where marriage was concerned. He figured to ease into it, letting himself get used to the idea while he worked at convincing her he'd be a good husband to her and a devoted daddy to Jessie.

But son of a gun, every time he tried to get past that velvet-lined wall of hers, she hid behind a quip or a laugh, or sometimes a moody silence. Something was eating at her from the inside out.

Someday she would trust him enough to let him help, he vowed as he skirted the propeller to take another whack at changing the worn-out tire. Until then, he would bide his time, if not patiently, at least silently.

Someday, somehow, as sure as God made sunshine and little green apples, she was going to have his ring on her finger and his baby in her belly.

Sophie decided to leave Clover for good after Emma and Mike's wedding, which was set for the last Saturday in January. Everyone would be exhausted from the festivities and less likely to notice her absence in the fabric of their lives.

By the night of Mike Flint's bachelor party, she was running mostly on nerves, so distracted she'd had to make three trips by taxi to Ford's place before the food and drink and decorations were as perfect as she could make them.

The party had been set for the night before the wedding and was to begin at eight o'clock. Ford had left work early, showing up around four with more on his mind than finger food and chili. He'd come to help, he'd told her, and then proceeded to shanghai her into bed for a wild half hour she could ill afford to spare. Consequently, she'd been harried and rushed when she'd left at seven forty-five, promising to return at midnight to help him clean up. Privately, she doubted that the party would be over by then, but Ford had gotten that leave-it-to-me look on his face and all but promised to come looking for her if she wasn't stepping over his threshold at the stroke of twelve.

By eight-thirty she'd given Jessie her bath and played with her for a while before getting out the maps she'd checked out of the library earlier. By nine she had them spread out on the bed, along with the bus and train schedules.

"Looks like upper New York state might be our best bet," Sophie mused aloud while Jessie toddled her way around the perimeter of the bed, holding on to the spread for support. "Hmm, here's a place called Phoenix near Syracuse, or better yet, Fair Haven. I like that, don't you?"

With a sigh, Sophie put down the atlas and picked up the bus schedule. "There's a bus that leaves at 11:00 p.m. every night. Looks like it has—" she paused to count "—nine stops between Charleston and Syracuse. Takes almost twelve hours."

Jessie jabbered a happy response, then slanted her mother a look as if waiting for a response. "Yes, I know, sweets," Sophie told her with a smile. "That means we'll have to spend the night in a hotel until we can find something permanent, but if we're careful it shouldn't cost too much."

Jessie looked at her with big eyes, her expression thoughtful as though she'd caught her mother's subdued mood.

"I think another rooming house at first, don't you, Jessie Bear? Some place cozy and friendly. Oh, I know we'd be lucky to find a place as perfect as Katie's, but I'm sure we'll find something clean and roomy in our limited price range."

Jessie cocked her head at the mention of Katie's name.

"No, sweets, you and I are going bye-bye on Sunday night. Katie can't come with us. No one can." And no one would know where she was going. Her conscience already stung at the lies she would have to tell and the deceit she intended to practice on her friends.

"I know it will be hard on you to leave, Jessie," she murmured, her voice subdued. "And I'm so terribly sorry about that. About a lot of things." Like walking out on Peg without notice, and leaving her Sunday school class without a teacher and Katie without a boarder during the slow winter months.

She had it all worked out, her story already set in her mind. Sunday morning she would feign a headache as an excuse to stay home from church and Sunday school. When the others returned, she would claim to have received a phone call from an aunt in Montana. Her favorite uncle had had a heart attack, you see. And she was desperately needed to help out on the ranch while he was recovering. There would be an outpouring of sympathy and offers of help, all of which she would reluctantly decline.

Saying goodbye to Ford would be close to unbearable. Telling him yet one more lie would be like slicing herself into small pieces. And yet what choice did she have? The longer she stayed, the more he would become an unwitting accessory to her crime. And if the truth should come out, he would be utterly humiliated. What kind of sheriff takes a convicted felon and wanted fugitive for a lover?

"He'd be destroyed, Jess," she whispered, drawing Jessie into her lap and hugging her tightly. "People would blame him and laugh at him."

She shivered, the pain crushing. "I didn't want to love him, I swear. I tried so hard not to. You know, you were there when I told him to leave me alone. But he wouldn't listen. He never listens."

Jessie struggled to free herself, and Sophie eased back, stifling a sob. "Sorry, sweetie, I didn't mean to squeeze you so hard. Mama's not herself tonight."

"Mama?" Jessie twisted in her arms in order to direct an inquisitive look her way. Sophie's hand shook as she smoothed the baby-fine hair away from Jessie's dumpling cheeks. It was getting longer, and thicker, like hers. Unlike hers, however, Jessie's hair was developing a tendency to curl. Wells had had curly hair, inherited from his mother along with her acerbic wit and elegant style.

"Before we were married, your daddy used to recite poetry to me by candlelight and send me fresh roses every other day," she murmured. "I thought he was the most romantic man I'd ever met."

Ford was anything but. Instead of reciting pretty words by candlelight, he was far more likely to drag her out to a dusty, dirty airport and hand her a paintbrush instead of long-stemmed roses.

"He reads Louis L'Amour instead of Proust," she murmured, her throat aching. "And sometimes he even says 'ain't.' He's stubborn and he refuses to share his feelings and he's much too set in his ways. And if the light's wrong, he looks more rugged and tough than good-looking."

She drew a weary breath. Her chest felt tight, making it difficult to breathe properly. "It's no use trying to talk myself out of it. I love him, and I'll always love him."

She dropped her gaze to her lap and stared at her bare ring finger. "Fifty years from now I'll be just like Miss Fanny, still longing for his kiss, his touch." Her voice splintered, and she inhaled deeply. "Except that I'll have to live with knowing he's been just a phone call away all those years." A phone call she knew she would never make.

Ford stood to one side of the fireplace, watching one of the young guys who worked for Mike Flint on his salvage rig helping himself to another shot of rye. If the kid wasn't drunk, he was only a couple of drinks from it, and he made a mental note to take the boy's keys before he shoveled everyone out.

"Hell of party, Ford, old son."

Frankie Fall was an all-right guy, a maverick, to be sure, but the kind of straight-arrow politician Ford respected. Big as a barn, he nevertheless had a remarkable intellect and a passion for restoring old automobiles that matched Ford's passion for antique airplanes.

Years ago, Ford had played high school football against Frankie, two hick quarterbacks with strong arms and thick heads. In spite of scholarship offers from area colleges, both had skipped college and gone directly into law enforcement—Frankie with the county, Ford with the town of Clover. Neither had had a choice. Frankie had needed a good job to take care of the baby his high school sweetheart had been expecting, and Ford had had Lucy to support.

Frankie had been married to that same woman for eighteen years now and, at last count, had four boys. Ford had coached the two youngest in Little League a few years back, taking them all the way to the statewide World Series.

Ten years ago, when Frankie had been badly injured on the job, he'd had to retire from the county mounties and had run for the school board. After that, it had been a fast, straight climb to the mayor's office.

"How're you doin', Frankie?" Ford swirled the ice cubes in his ginger ale and figured it was close to time to organize rides for the guys who'd had too much party to drive.

Frankie took a swig of beer, then belched. "Can't complain. Loretta talked me into this island-cruise package for our anniversary, and I gotta tell you, son, that was one hot vacation. I'm still walkin' crooked."

Ford offered the obligatory grin. "You always were short on stamina, which, as I recall, made it real easy to whip your butt on the football field."

"Heck's fire, Ford, you never can get it straight in that stubborn head of yours who whipped who."

The guest of honor ambled up in the midst of the debate, his weathered hand wrapped around a tall one. Mike was a few years younger than Ford and Frankie, but he'd grown up listening to them bicker.

"Don't tell me you two are still arguin' about who's toughest?" he asked, quirking a shaggy blond eyebrow.

"No argument to it," Frankie declared on another deeply satisfying belch. "It's in the record book in black and white. Ford blew the championship game big time." He took another swig, then wiped his mouth with the back of his hand. "Threw him two interceptions in the last quarter, big as you please. Hell of it was, he had him a perfect season until then, didn't you, old son?"

Ford shrugged. He'd played that game with his chest strapped up like a mummy after he'd cracked three ribs in practice the day before.

"Like you said, Frankie, the final score's all that counts."

"Bet your ass," Frankie boomed before slapping Ford on the back again. "If y'all will 'scuse me, I got a dead soldier here I need to trade in." With a farewell belch, he ambled off.

Watching with a sailor's sharp eyes, Mike shook his head. "Tell you true, Ford. Old Frankie'll still be tellin' that same story when you two are danglin' great-grandbabies on your knees on the porch of some old-folks' home."

"Like hell," Ford muttered, and Mike laughed.

"Maybe it's all this wedding business that's been happenin' recently, but I keep hearin' rumors that the mighty Ford Maguire is about to fall the same as Ben and Matt and me."

"Since when do you go around listenin' to rumors?" Ford grated.

"Since Emma's been askin' me what I know about the sweet little Yankee lady waitin' tables over to Peg's."

Ford eyed his friend impassively. "Just what *do* you know, son?"

Mike cocked his head and let a grin spread slowly over his weathered face. "I know I'd better be real careful what I say next or I might find myself standin' at that altar on tomorrow afternoon with a sore jaw and no best man."

"You got that right!"

Mike's grin faded. "Just in case I forget to mention it, thanks for all this," he said, gesturing toward the crowded room with his drink. "Emma was in a pet, thinking you were goin' to bring in a stripper from Charleston or, at the very least, show some of those stag films they run at the Sons of the Confederacy meetings on special occasions."

Ford snorted. "My granddaddy took me to see one of those films when Mama was in the hospital havin' Lucy. Believe me, they're borin' as hell." Not to mention demeaning to women. He wasn't a prude, but he didn't like to see anyone victimized, even if they got paid for allowing it.

"Figured as much." Mike finished his drink, then glanced at his watch. "You wouldn't take it wrong if I hauled ass out of here pretty quick, would you?"

Ford hid his relief behind a curious look. "Got a heavy date later, do you?"

"I'm not too proud to admit that I do. Emma's offered to make me coffee if I just happened to stop by."

"Do me a favor and take your boy Jack there with you. Last thing this town needs is the sheriff brought up on charges of aidin' and abettin' public drunkenness."

"Be happy to oblige." His grin slanted. " 'Sides, I hear the law around here comes down like a ton of bricks on drunk drivers."

He stuck out his hand, and Ford took it, an odd lump in his throat. "See you in front of Reverend Bendix."

"Come early," Mike drawled, raking a quick, nervous hand through his sun-streaked blond hair. "I got me a feelin' I'm goin' to be too nervous to work up a decent spit."

"You'll be fine." Ford caught a flash of light out of the corner of his eye and realized that someone was driving up the lane. Maybe Sophie decided to come back early, he thought, his pulse quickening at the thought.

"Latecomer?" Mike asked, following his gaze.

"Everybody's here who was invited," Ford said before making his way to the door.

He was halfway down the porch steps when he recognized Lucy's small car come into the circle of light from the pole lamp at the edge of his yard. Anticipation turned instantly to alarm, and he broke into a fast jog, reaching the car just as she killed the engine. He had the door open before she'd even removed the key from the ignition.

"What's the problem?" he demanded, helping her from the low bucket seat.

"No problem," she said, tossing back her long hair the way she'd done countless times as a girl. "In fact, my dearest, darling, overprotective brother, everything is gloriously right."

She started to fling her arms around him, but he caught her arms and held her away from him. She was wearing blue again, and another of those damn short dresses. He suspected both were that oily bastard Dooley's doing.

"Talk," he ordered, narrowing his gaze.

She jerked her chin at him, her mouth forming a pout that he'd seen too many times before. "Let go and I will."

He had half a mind to apply the flat of his hand to her fanny the way he'd done a few times in the past when she'd pushed him too far. Instead, he let her go and folded his arms over his chest. "Okay, talk."

"First, I want you to promise not to yell at me."

He felt his belly knot. It was a good bet he wasn't going to like whatever it was that had her coming to see him in the middle of the night.

"When was the last time I yelled at you?" he demanded.

"When I was fifteen and Punky Webb's car broke down on the way home from a football game."

"I didn't yell at you, I yelled at Punky."

"Yes, and you scared him so bad I didn't have another date for the rest of the year."

"Just as well," he muttered, glaring at her. "And for the record, I haven't yelled since."

"You haven't needed to. Once the word got around that Ford Maguire was prepared to wail the living daylights out any guy who so much as looked cross-eyed at his sister, I might as well have joined a convent for all the boyfriends I attracted."

Ford rubbed the spot at the back of his neck that always gave him trouble when he had to deal with his sister's problems.

"You had dates. Lots of 'em. I ought to know. I paced the floor enough times, waitin' for some yahoo to bring you home."

"I might have had dates, but even the guys brave enough to take me out weren't brave enough to do more than give me a nervous peck on the cheek at the door before turning tail." She drew a fast breath. "I think I'm the only twenty-seven-year-old virgin in both Carolinas and Georgia, too."

Ford felt his jaw tighten down hard. "What's wrong with that?"

She sighed. "Nothing...exactly. Except that's about to change."

Ford stiffened, feeling his anger flash white-hot before he brought it under control. "If that bastard Dooley has touched you," he said between his teeth. "I'll kill him."

"He hasn't," she said hastily, "but that's going to change, and don't look at me like that, because that's the reason I drove all the way out here tonight. To tell you that he's asked me to marry him, and I've accepted."

Ford's house was ablaze with lights when Sophie paid off Arnie and carried her sleeping daughter up the walk to the door. Balancing the baby, her purse and the diaper bag while opening the door required as much patience as dexterity.

"Oh, my," she murmured, casting a quick look over the party debris littering every table and much of the floor. She was still shaking her head when Ford came in from the vicinity of the kitchen.

"Now, honey, don't get all bent out of shape," he urged quickly. "I'm fixin' to help with the heavy jobs."

Her already morose mood took a nosedive. Tonight was the last she would spend under Ford's roof, the last time they would make love. The last time she would fall asleep in his arms. She didn't want to waste time washing dishes and polishing furniture.

Don't think about it, she warned herself sternly as she felt the tears pressing her throat. Concentrate on now, this minute. And then the next, and the next.

"I hope you know where we can rent a bulldozer, because from the looks of all those beer bottles and other stuff, that's what it's going to take," she muttered, shooting him a look that he returned with a decidedly embarrassed grin.

"I'd intended to have this mostly done by the time you got here, but Lucy showed up unexpectedly and we had one of those tussles that wear me out."

Sophie studied his face. He did look a bit frayed around the edges—and extremely virile in a red-and-black flannel shirt that added breadth to his already impressive chest.

"Let me put Jessie down, and then you can fill me in on Lucy's latest while we work," she murmured, wondering how she was going to find the strength to get on that bus in a little less than forty-eight hours.

"Here, let me," he said, slipping his hands between her and the baby. Four months ago she would have fought tooth and nail before she'd let anyone else hold her child. Now she simply smiled and let him take her. Funny how easily trust grew when you loved someone, she thought, rolling up her sleeves. And how easily it could be destroyed, sometimes with just a barbed word, or an act of cruelty.

A memory of those last strained months with Wells rose in her mind, only to be banished as ruthlessly as he'd tried to kill their baby. Ford was Jessie's father now, at least for the hours that remained to them.

By the time he returned she'd carried most of the empty glasses to the sink, and had returned to the living room to collect the empty bottles and cans for recycling.

"Looks better already," he said, looking supremely pleased as though he himself had been the one doing the work.

"I realize that washing up and disposing of the trash was included in the price I quoted you, but this place needs a good hosing," she muttered, eyeing a smear of guacamole on the coffee table, not far from an overflowing ashtray.

"You're right," he drawled, coming up behind her. "You definitely deserve a bonus."

He stroked her hair, then drew down the neck of her sweatshirt with a caressing fingertip before dropping a kiss on the skin he'd uncovered. His mouth was warm and clever, sending a ripple of sensation down her spine.

"I will never, *ever* agree to cater another bachelor party," she murmured on a gasp as he suddenly swirled his tongue over the skin he'd just kissed. "Ah, don't do that," she managed to rasp out between delicious little shivers.

"You don't like to be kissed?" His mouth made a seductive foray along the neckline of her shirt, pausing to trace the folds of her ear before he nipped the sensitive earlobe with his teeth.

"I, um, what did you say?" she asked, her mind suddenly attending to more immediate matters, like the invasive warmth stealing up from the cleft between her breasts.

"I said, don't you like to be kissed?" The low, throaty timbre to his voice seemed to shiver through her, leaving her feeling itchy inside.

"I . . . yes, when I'm not trying to, ah, work."

"All work and no play makes Ford a very horny boy." The low throb of need in his voice sent pleasure spilling into her midsection.

"Everything makes you horny," she murmured, and then felt herself grow hot when his laughter rumbled close to her ear.

"Just everything connected with you," he corrected, nipping her ear with his teeth while his arms stole around her waist to pull her back against him. "Like the smell of soap you use. And the way your hair feels against my mouth and the little snoring sounds you make when you sleep."

"I don't snore," she managed to expel along with a small gasp.

He pressed his lips to her neck, touching her with the tip of his tongue. "Well, maybe it's more like a cute little purring sound," he murmured before concentrating on her ear.

"Purring is not nearly as, ah, bad as hogging the covers."

"A traditional male prerogative." She smiled to hear that his voice had become nearly as husky as hers. Whatever else he might be feeling about her—or not feeling—he seemed to be as vulnerable to her sexually as she was to him. It seemed a miracle that he could want her so much—the same plain, boring woman Wells had called frigid.

"Ford?" she whispered, aching to give him something in return.

"Hmm?"

She turned in his arms until they were face-to-face, his hands still linked loosely at the small of her back. "You look very tired."

He narrowed his gaze suspiciously. "I do?"

Nodding, she ran her fingertip along the taut line of his lower lip. "Tense, too."

"Yeah?" His eyes were definitely darker and definitely wary.

"I think you're right about working too hard," she murmured, threading both hands into the thick silk of his sin-black hair.

His nostrils flared, and a flame took hold in his eyes. "Maybe I should take some time off."

"Definitely," she murmured, absorbed in a study of his mouth. His lips were supple, his teeth white and not quite perfectly aligned, and he had a small white scar curving downward toward his hard jaw.

Enchanted, she arched upward until she could reach his mouth with hers. Instead of kissing him, however, she touched her tongue very lightly to the right corner, the one that never really relaxed, even when he smiled. His breath hissed between his suddenly parted lips, signaling a rare loss of control.

"I read somewhere that kissing is a great exercise for reducing stress," she whispered as she drew back far enough to watch his expression.

"Is that an invitation or a challenge?"

"Definitely an invitation."

Something wild flashed in his eyes, making the centers widen and darken. Her sudden aggressiveness was as arousing as it was unexpected. Even as he bent his head to kiss her, her fingers were busy with the buttons of his shirt.

"Whoa, honey," he said, half in protest and half in anticipation.

Ignoring him, she skimmed her hands across his belly, then tugged the shirt free. Simply the friction of shirt against skin had him half-aroused. When her fingers slipped beneath the waistband of his jeans to free the button, he felt his body surge to full readiness.

Everything happened fast after that. Between hot, drugging kisses, they undressed each other, careless of buttons and snaps and zippers until they were both wild with need. But it was Sophie who led, Sophie who took him on a breathless, sensual ride that had him mindless and wanting.

It was she who drew him to the soft cushions of the sofa, she who pushed him to his back so that she could rain soft, open-mouthed kisses over his face, his shoulders, his chest. Yielding control was as foreign to him as tears, but somehow it was easy to give when she asked, a joy to receive what he had meant to give.

When at last she straddled him, he was helpless to do more than sink desperate fingers into the cushions beneath him and try to keep from bringing down the roof with the groans each shift of her body wrung from him.

The last thing he knew before the world erupted in a savage convulsion was the sound of her voice, telling him that she loved him.

Sophie put the last of the serving bowls in the dishwasher and arched her tired back before attacking the counter full of glasses and dishes.

The smell of stale booze assaulted her nose, making her terribly sad. What had seemed so festive only a few hours earlier now seemed to mock her. All the prewedding parties were done. Tomorrow Emma and Mike would marry, and begin their life together. Sunday night, she would leave as she'd come, with only a few belongings and her daughter. Her eyes stung, and her throat ached, but Sophie refused to cry. The hours were going to tick away, no matter how she spent them. Besides, she didn't dare let Ford see that she was upset.

A quick glance over her shoulder told her that he was still sound asleep on the couch where she'd left him nearly a half hour before, drowsy and spent after their lovemaking. As soon as she was done in the kitchen, she would wake him with a kiss, and together they would check on Jessie, taking turns kissing her as she slept. And then they would go to bed. More than making love she wanted to sleep in his arms, so close her heartbeat would synchronize with his. And then in the morning, they would make love one last, lingering time.

Biting her lip, she reached for the last glass, only to find it sticky with the residue of a Bloody Mary. She froze, her gaze riveted on the red liquid. In her mind she heard voices—hers, begging Wells not to hurt the baby; his, an ugly snarl of sound, spewing invective. And then a last terrible scream as he lost his footing and plunged headfirst toward the floor below.

Suddenly it wasn't juice but blood she was seeing, its coppery scent filling her nostrils until she gagged. It was Wells's blood staining her hands, Wells's last terrible cry imprinted on her brain.

"Sophie?"

Dimly she was aware that Ford had come into the kitchen and was calling her name. She tried to reassure him only to discover that her teeth were chattering so violently she couldn't speak.

Ford closed his arms protectively around her and tried to make sense of the wild emotion in her eyes. "Baby, what's wrong?" he asked, his voice as soothing as he could make it. "Are you hurt?"

"He was trying to k-kill me," she stammered, her teeth still chattering. "He was so s-strong, he c-came at me—" She broke off, remembering the terror that had given her the strength she'd needed to break away just as he'd been poised to throw her down the steps.

"*Who* tried to kill you?"

"Wells. My husband." She gulped air, chilled to the bone. She couldn't seem to stop shivering. "We argued, and he l-lost his temper. I'd never seen him like that. He was vicious, like an a-animal.'' Closing her eyes, she buried her face against his shoulder and tried to wash the hideous memories from her mind.

"It's okay now,'' he said, stroking her back slowly and gently. "It's over. It's all over.''

She put her arms around his waist and hung on, needing to absorb his strength. "It'll never be over,'' she whispered. "Not as long as his parents blame me.''

"Shh,'' he whispered, feeling her arms tighten around him. He'd never felt so helpless, so damned useless. It was a man's job to protect his woman, not dump his problems on her. It was also his job to take on her problems and do his best to solve them for her. What he couldn't solve, he carried without complaint, knowing that at least he was sparing her more pain. But this was beyond him.

"I didn't intend for the evening to end like this,'' she whispered brokenly. "I'm sorry. I'm so sorry.''

"Shh.'' Ford brushed the disheveled hair from her face and was dismayed to find his hand wet with tears. The need to see laughter in her eyes instead of sadness ran through him with a strength more powerful than the fiercest rage. Whatever she wanted, he would do his best to give her.

"He ordered me to have an abortion,'' she said in a numbed monotone. "He always used s-something, he s-said, so it couldn't be his.''

Oh, God, he thought, wanting to strangle the man with his bare hands. "He was wrong.''

Sophie heard the quiet steel of conviction in his voice and gave her heart to him forever. "You believe me,'' she whispered, tears she didn't want to shed now streaming down her face.

"Yes, I believe you,'' he murmured, his voice thick.

"But your m-mother—''

"You're nothing like my mother, Sophie. It took me a while to let myself believe that, but, subconsciously, I think I knew that the first minute I laid eyes on you.''

He took her face in his hands and kissed her trembling mouth. "Oh, Ford, I love you, more than you'll ever know, but—''

"No buts. We've done enough talkin' for one night. What you need right now is sleep, and this old boy is goin' see that you get it.''

Before she could utter a protest, he'd swept her into his arms and was marching through the living room, one very dear, very tough, very naked man.

Chapter 13

Sophie had arranged with Peg to get off early on Saturday, but she hadn't felt comfortable leaving the diner until the morning rush had eased. By the time she got back to Katie's, Miss Fanny had given Jessie her bath and settled her in her crib to play while she'd attended to her own toilette.

As soon as the bathroom had been free, Sophie had taken a quick shower, washed the smell of frying bacon from her hair and blown it dry. While Jessie chattered to the fluffy white bunny Ford had given her for her ten-month birthday, Sophie carefully applied her makeup, then slipped into her only pair of panty hose and the same cotton bra Ford had asked her to remove for him. Remembering, she felt her skin warm as the familiar heaviness settled low in her body. She suspected that it would take a very long time before she stopped missing him.

"Mama?"

"Yes, sweetie, Mama's here," she murmured, taking her new dress from the hanger. "We're going to a wedding today. Aunt Katie's going to be the bridesmaid and Ford is going to be the best man."

He was coming to pick them up in less than thirty minutes. She and Jessie were to be his guests, though Emma had made it very clear just yesterday when she'd been visiting Katie that she was happy Sophie had agreed to attend. She'd even extended an invitation to the housewarming she and Mike were planning shortly after their return from their honeymoon, an invitation Sophie had accepted, even though she knew she'd be long gone by then.

"Mama!" Jessie rattled the bars of her crib, her patience finally reaching its limit.

"Just let Mama put on her dress, and then we'll get Jessie dressed, too," she said, opening the closet door. The dress was a simple shirtwaist of crinkled periwinkle cotton. She'd bought it because she liked the way the skirt swirled whenever she walked. And because a wedding was supposed to be festive and gay, she'd replaced the simple stretchy belt with brightly colored scarves twisted into a flowing sash.

"Okay, Jessie Bear, first we'll change this soggy old diaper, and then we'll get you dressed."

Five minutes later she was buckling Jessie's fat, restless foot into one of her new white satin slippers when Katie came in, looking like a fairy-tale princess in yellow satin and lace.

"What do you think?" Katie asked, her voice a little breathy and her color heightened.

"Turn around," Sophie ordered, tilting her head for a better view. Frowning, Katie spun in a slow circle, careful to keep her hands from mussing the full skirt.

"You are utterly and truly gorgeous," Sophie told her with absolute sincerely. "Yellow is definitely your color."

"You don't think my hair's too fussy?" Expelling a nervous breath, Katie patted the cascade of light brown curls that Jeannie at the Beauty Boutique had spent a good hour creating.

"Not a bit. In fact, it makes the hat look even prettier tilted to one side."

Katie crossed to the mirror and eyed her image critically. "Considerin' that this is the third time I've been asked to stand up with one of my friends, you'd think I wouldn't be as nervous as a long-tailed cat in a room of rockin' chairs."

Keeping one hand on Jessie's shoulder to keep her still, Sophie rummaged in the drawer for the mate to the shoe the baby was presently trying to remove.

"Trust me," she said, coming up with the other shoe. "You look beautiful, and you'll make a superb bridesmaid."

"I think that's becoming my callin' in life. 'Always a brides-maid, never a bride.' " Katie drew another long, nervous breath before turning to face Sophie again. "You look pretty spectacular yourself. I love that dress, by the way. Where did you find it?"

"Just between us, I found it at the resale shop over on Cyprus Street," she said, lifting Jessie, now coiffed, adorably dressed and fashionably shod, into her arms for a quick cuddle. "I spent more than I should, but I couldn't resist."

Her dress hadn't cost nearly as much as Jessie's, and yet she'd had to wrestle with her conscience before she'd bought herself anything at all. Every cent was precious now.

After four months of making every penny do the work of two, she'd managed to put aside a small nest egg, enough to buy a bus ticket to Syracuse and tide them over for the week or so it would take for her to find work and bring home her first paycheck.

Before the bank closed on Friday she'd drawn all but a few dollars from her checking account. She hadn't dared to pack yet, but she'd made sure all of Jessie's things were clean, and that she had an adequate supply of disposable diapers, baby food and canned formula.

Sunday morning, after the sham phone call, she would get out the battered suitcase she'd bought at a garage sale in Portland and fill it up with Jessie's things first, then with her own. Whatever was left, Katie could give to the Salvation Army.

"Katie? Oh, there you are, dear." Miss Fanny came bustling into the room with Rose Ruth at her heels. Both ladies were turned out in their finest—her signature rose-colored silk for Rose Ruth and flowered crepe for Miss Fanny. Both were wearing what Rose Ruth called their best "Sunday go-to-meeting" hats.

"Birdie," Jessie squealed as soon as she spied the fluttering feather trailing from Miss Fanny's hat.

"No, sugar, that's only a birdie's *feather*," Miss Fanny trilled, squeezing the fat little hand Jessie reached toward the tempting feather.

"Birdie," Jessie insisted, drawing her eyebrows together stub-bornly.

Sophie captured Jessie's hand in hers and returned her to her crib and the toys there in hopes of distracting her. "Doesn't Katie look marvelous?" she said to the ladies while handing Jessie the bunny, which the baby promptly threw at her.

"Absolutely," Miss Fanny agreed emphatically, adjusting Katie's hat veil to hang just so. "I do believe this dress is even prettier than the last one."

"It is charming," Rose Ruth mused, "but I believe I favor the one she wore at Hannah's weddin'."

"That's because you favor lilac over yellow, Rose Ruth. You always have, from the time you were a girl. I remember very clearly that I wore a lilac frock to your sixth birthday party and you spilled chocolate ice cream all over the front simply because it was prettier than yours and you were pea green with jealousy."

"Now that is the most outrageous lie I have had the displeasure to hear you utter, Frances Ann. I do believe you are approachin' senility faster than I previously thought."

"Well, I never," Fanny exclaimed, brown eyes snapping.

Sophie caught the gaze Katie aimed her way, and they both glanced away hurriedly before each gave way to giggles.

"What time is it?" Katie asked anxiously, checking the alarm clock pointedly. The two ladies broke off glaring at each other to simultaneously check their watches.

"Almost one," Miss Fanny said quickly, her expression smug at having beaten the enemy.

"More precisely, seven minutes till," Miss Rose Ruth corrected, before turning on Fanny again. "You did tell Arnie one-thirty on the dot, did you not? The last thing I said to you last night was to remember to tell him one-thirty, and not to be late."

"I told him," Fanny declared peevishly. "One-thirty on the dot."

The faint chiming of the doorbell had the elderly ladies exchanging startled looks. "That must be Ford," Sophie said hastily. "He's promised Mike he'd be there early to help him tie his tie or hold his hand or maybe lock the door so he can't change his mind."

"Not much chance of that," Katie said, checking her hairdo in the mirror one more time. "I've never seen Mike so docile."

"Poor Ford," Miss Fanny said, expelling a weighty sigh. "I'm sure he's going to have mixed feelings when he gives Lucy away next month."

"And to a man none of us really know all that well," Rose Ruth added, handing Sophie the diaper bag she'd packed and had ready on the bed.

"Mr. Dooley seems nice enough," Katie said as the ladies trailed out. "And he is one good-looking gentleman."

"Lucy's certainly smitten," Sophie said, following Katie over the threshold. "It was all anyone was talking about at the diner this morning."

"I'll bet," Katie exclaimed as Sophie closed the door. "And I'll bet Ford will have a lot to say to his sister in the next few weeks."

"We'll see you girls at the church," Miss Fanny said as she opened the door to her room.

"If Arnie shows up when he's supposed to," Rose Ruth amended archly.

Katie bit her lip and Sophie held her breath as they walked side by side down the wide staircase. When the click of the latch told her that the ladies were safely behind a closed door, she expelled the trapped air and laughed out loud.

"Those two," she murmured. "They never agree on anything, and yet one would be lost without the other."

Sophie expected Ford to be wearing a suit. When she started down the last flight of stairs and saw him standing at the bottom dressed in a midnight blue tux she felt as though her stomach had suddenly filled with warm honey.

Resting one forearm on the newel post, he had the other stuck in the pocket of his trousers while he listened intently to something Roy Dean was telling him. Instead of muting the aura of toughness about him, the formal clothing only added to it, she realized. Like a razor-honed sword sheathed in wear-softened leather.

He glanced up, his gaze locking on hers, and she felt a jolt of heat. For him. From him.

"Fo'!" Jessie shouted happily, extending her arms toward him well before Sophie had reached the bottom step.

"There's my girl," he said, giving her a kiss as he took her into his arms. Giggling, she bestowed a sloppy kiss on his cheek that had him grinning.

"My, my, Roy Dean, look at these two lovely flowers of the South," he murmured, his drawl thicker than usual. "Yes, sir, I do believe you and I are the two luckiest men in this town to be privileged to escort these beautiful ladies."

"My sentiments exactly," Roy Dean said, smiling paternally at Sophie first and then at Katie. "You look very like your mother, my dear. She, too, was a rare beauty."

Katie's cheeks turned pink. "Now I know why I asked you to be my escort," she said, her eyes suspiciously shiny.

Ford shifted Jessie to his other arm and extended the one he'd freed to Sophie. "Ready, Ms. Reynolds?"

She managed to smile without her lips trembling too noticeably. "Ready, Sheriff Maguire."

Roy Dean opened the door, then winked at Sophie as Ford escorted her over the threshold.

Though it wasn't spring on the calendar, the air felt wonderfully warm and soft, and hazy sunshine streamed through the still-bare oak tree like a benediction on the bridal couple.

"It's a perfect day for a wedding," she murmured, feeling almost dizzy as Ford cast a heated glance in her direction.

"Beautiful," he said, his dark, intense gaze roaming over her face like a caress. "I like the dress," he added, his voice deepening, "and I can't wait to see it layin' on the floor next to my bed later." His sudden grin was part thoughtful lover, part arrogant devil, and she had to struggle to keep her lips in a straight line.

"I haven't agreed to spend the night with you," she reminded him firmly as he pulled open the car door and tossed the diaper bag onto the floor behind the seat.

"You will," he said as he fitted Jessie deftly into her car seat and tested the belt latch to make sure it was secure.

"Oh, yeah? And just what makes you say that?" she demanded as she slipped into the bucket seat.

"I saw the way you looked at me when you were comin' down the stairs."

"What way?" she asked before she realized he'd set her up.

"Like you couldn't wait for me to do this," he said, bending suddenly to cover her lips with his. His mouth was hot, his tongue hotter as it slipped between lips she parted instinctively, eagerly. She felt sizzling pleasure, tasted desperation. His hand was warm against her neck, his strength gentled by his own choice, even as he uttered a groan so primal it verged on violent.

When his mouth left hers, she wanted to whimper at the sense of terrible loss. "Later," he murmured hoarsely, his mouth still close, his eyes glittering with need and promise.

"I'll think about it," she managed to say before drawing in a desperately needed breath of air.

"You do that, sugar," he said, his grin flashing almost as white as his dazzling shirt. "And while you're at it, think about this, too. As soon as you get off work on Monday, you and I are drivin' to Charleston to buy you a birthday present." He closed the door on her startled protest.

"How did you know I have a birthday coming up?" she demanded when he climbed behind the wheel and slanted her a cocky look that all but melted the buttons on her dress.

"Us lawmen have our ways, honey," he said, twisting the key in the ignition.

The roar of the engine drowned out speech for a moment, and she found herself fighting down panic. "You sneaked a peak at the application I filled out for Peg, didn't you?"

He turned to look through the rear window as he backed the car to the street before letting his gaze rest on hers for an instant. "Now, honey, you know I can't divulge my sources," he drawled before shifting into first and applying the gas. "But I will say I figured you for being a mite taller than five-two-and-a-half. Must be those sexy legs I keep thinkin' about at the most inappropriate moments."

Sophie drew a relieved breath. She was right. Somehow he'd charmed Peg into a look at her application. Not that she was surprised, she admitted, folding her hands around her purse. When he set his mind to it, Ford could charm the leaves from the trees. Hadn't she sworn to stay as far away from him as possible, only to end up in his bed only a few months after making that vow?

"Have you given any thought to what you might want for this birthday of yours?" he asked, driving with one hand and capturing hers with the other.

"A card will do just fine," she said, her heart aching. She didn't know exactly where she would be in six days, but she knew she wouldn't be with him.

"I figured on a card," he said, flattening her hand against his thigh and covering it with his. "The question is, what should go with it?"

Your love, she thought sadly. Only your love. "Nothing," she said firmly. "I'm too old for presents."

He slanted her an amused look. "Lucy was always partial to silver jewelry for special occasions. But I figure you'd like gold better. Something delicate and feminine, something along the lines of a ring."

She stared at him, seeing only him. "Ford—"

"Guess this is a dumb time for a man to be askin' a woman to marry him, huh?"

"I . . ." She blinked, then realized that he was pulling into the church parking lot.

"Never mind answerin' now, sugar. You'll have plenty of time to accept tonight, when we're alone."

Sophie was still numb as he escorted Jessie and her into the church.

It was a beautiful wedding. Everyone said so, and Sophie agreed whole-heartedly. But it had been the best man she'd watched while the bride and groom repeated their vows.

The reception was held immediately after the ceremony in the church basement. It was a happy party, with balloons and flowers and a three-piece band setting the mood. Standing with the others from Katie's, with Jessie chattering in her arms, Sophie had had to fight back tears as the handsome groom swept his bride into his arms for the first dance.

The floor had been jammed ever since. As tradition demanded, Ford, as best man, had danced first with Emma's matron of honor, a plainspoken feisty widow in her seventies named Martha Balanski, and then with Katie.

Obligations fulfilled, he'd asked Sophie for the next dance, leading her onto the floor with a look of pride so fierce she'd gone weak inside. Though he'd held her at a decorous distance, the suggestions he'd whispered in her ear had had her blushing and deliciously aroused well before the dance ended. While she'd taken Jessie to the ladies' room to change her diaper, he'd danced with Miss Fanny and Miss Rose Ruth in turn, and then with his sister.

By the time Jessie had started fussing, her two honorary grandmamas had been more than ready to leave and had volunteered to take her home with them in Maxwell's taxi. Sophie smiled at the thought of the three of them tucked into their beds for a long afternoon nap.

The party was still in full swing when Ford looked at his watch, and then at her. "Wish I hadn't promised Eli I'd take the last half of his shift for him," Ford groused, glancing down at her with raw frustration seething in his eyes.

"When do you have to leave?" she asked, wishing the same thing.

"I've got a few minutes yet," he hedged.

She smiled. "I guess that's why Ellie's been looking at her watch every few minutes." She directed his attention to a group of young matrons seated near the beribboned gift table, chirping and chattering like brightly colored birds. Already a week overdue, Ellie was sitting with her hands folded over her enormous stomach, visibly uncomfortable and obviously impatient for her husband to join her.

"Poor thing, I know just how she feels," Sophie murmured, remembering the last few weeks of her own pregnancy. It had been a bittersweet time for her. Even though she'd been eagerly awaiting the baby's birth, she'd also known that she wouldn't see her child again until her release. At the time, she'd had no inkling that the Manwarings had planned to rob her of her own child.

"She does look downright miserable," Ford muttered close to her ear.

"I imagine she is miserable, physically that is. Every day after your due date seems like a week."

Ford heard the strain in her voice and consigned the man who'd put such hurt in her to the hottest fires in hell. "Were you late?" he asked, thinking about the faint white lines on her now-flat belly.

She touched her stomach, as though remembering. "Four days."

"Was the delivery painful?" The question came hard, yet he had to know. His mother had described his own birth in graphic terms, then sworn she'd never have another child. Lucy had been an accident, one Susannah Maguire hadn't accepted happily or silently.

"It hurts to have a baby," Sophie admitted, lifting her gaze to his. The concern she saw there touched her deeply. "But it's bearable because you know when it's over you'll have brought another special soul into the world."

"Not that I'm prejudiced, you understand, but I'd bet money Jessie was a beauty right from the start," he declared gruffly.

"Absolutely!" she exclaimed softly. "Not that I'm prejudiced, either, of course." Somehow she managed the smile of maternal pride she knew he expected. Each minute that passed brought her closer to the moment when she and Jessie would board the bus taking them away from him.

"I wish I could have seen her." His eyes were suddenly very dark. "And you."

"I looked like a blimp." Especially in the shapeless prison garb. Somehow she managed to keep from cringing at the thought of Ford seeing her then. Lack of sunshine had given her a sickly pallor and the shock of finding herself caged had taken the life from her eyes.

"Hey, you two, wasn't it a lovely wedding?" Lucy exclaimed as she sidestepped one of Mike's crew who gave her an approving once-over. Radiant with happiness, Lucy was wearing a blue silk suit and a matching hat. Sophie had already told her how flattering both were to her slender shape and coloring.

"Beautiful," Sophie agreed, answering her smile with one of her own. "I understand best wishes are in order for you, too. I hope you and Joe will be very happy."

"Might as well wish for the moon," Ford said, his face taking on a hard, intimidating line that didn't seem to faze Lucy in the least.

"Thank you, Sophie," Lucy said, pointedly ignoring her brother whose scowl deepened.

"Don't think we've talked this through, because we haven't," he told her sternly before slipping an arm around Sophie's waist to pull her toward him.

"I'll be off duty at seven sharp. Be thinkin' about where you want to have dinner."

Sophie drew a breath, conscious that Lucy was watching them with bemused satisfaction. "Don't work too hard," Sophie ordered softly, loving him with her eyes.

"Not much chance of that when I'll be mostly thinkin' about tonight." He bent to kiss her, oblivious of the stares coming their way. "Be ready at 7:05. I'll pick you up." His mouth found hers one more time, and then he was on his way, striding through the assemblage with that rolling, cowboy walk that never failed to fire her blood.

"Now that was something I never thought I'd see, straight-arrow Ford Maguire kissing a woman in public," Lucy mused, watching Ford until he left the hall.

Sophie forced a smile. "Don't blame me," she said lightly. "I've done everything I could think of to discourage him."

Lucy reached out a hand to squeeze Sophie's. "I know, sugar. Just like I know what Ford's like when he gets his mind set on something. Not even God and all His heavenly angels can keep my brother from getting something that's really important to him."

Sophie nodded, but her thoughts were with Ford and the choices he'd made. Agonizing choices to make, and painful consequences to bear as a result of those choices. To her knowledge he'd never complained.

Lucy waved to someone across the room before turning to Sophie again. "I know it isn't mannerly to talk business when we're having such a good time, but I hope you'll agree to cater my reception."

Sophie felt a pang of sadness. "I didn't realize you'd set the date?"

"Oh, yes. March the tenth. Joe hates long engagements." She glanced around, her expression turning wistful. "I just wish he could have been here today."

"How long will he be gone?" Sophie watched Emma beaming at something Mike was whispering in her ear and felt a leaden sadness settle inside her.

"A few weeks," Lucy said morosely. "He's up north on business."

"What kind of work does he do?"

"Investments, mostly. It's too complicated for my poor brain to comprehend."

Sophie told herself that Lucy's choices were hers to make, just as Ford's had been his, just as her own choices had been hers to make and live with. She'd just about convinced herself to make an excuse and walk away when she heard herself asking Lucy if she was absolutely certain Joe was the right man for her.

Lucy looked startled before a coolness came over her. "I love him, if that's what you mean."

"Please don't misunderstand," Sophie said quickly, already regretting the impulse to offer advice that Lucy clearly didn't want. "It's just that I know what can happen when you're swept off your feet by an older man. I...it happened to me once. Wells and I were married three months to the day after we met, and I'll spend the rest of my life wishing I'd insisted on a longer engagement. If I had, I'm certain I never would have married him."

A reluctant sympathy softened Lucy's resentment. "It's not like that with Joe and me," she murmured. "And in spite of what my brother thinks, I can take care of myself."

"I thought that once, too, but Wells was a master at manipulation. He'd nearly turned me into jelly, before I realized what was happening." In one of life's cruel ironies, she'd made up her mind to leave him one week before she'd discovered she was pregnant.

"It's really sweet of you to worry about me, Sophie, but honestly, everything's going to work out fine. You'll see."

"I hope so," Sophie told her. "But Ford's right, Lucy. You haven't known Joe long enough to really understand what he's like."

"I've known him as long as you've known Ford," Lucy shot back, her eyes turning distant again.

Sophie drew a breath. "There is one major difference, however," she said softly, far too close to tears. "I'm not going to marry Ford."

The boarding house residents were on their own on Saturday nights. Katie provided access to the kitchen and the larder, but most of her boarders preferred to eat out.

The house was quiet as Sophie came down the stairs a few minutes before seven. The parlor was empty, and there wasn't a sound from the kitchen. Upstairs, Miss Fanny was in her room with a book, her door and Sophie's ajar so that she could hear Jessie if she cried. Katie hadn't yet returned home, and Miss Rose Ruth had gone to dinner with Doc Gossely.

Expecting Ford to arrive at any minute, Sophie drew on her jacket and went out to the front porch to wait. The night air had a flavor of frost, though the temperature was still far above freezing.

Trailing her fingertips along the porch railing, she walked slowly past the parlor windows, expecting with each step to see Ford's Camaro pulling into the driveway. When she reached the swing in the far corner, she glanced at her watch and saw that he was five minutes late. She hesitated, then sat down and put the swing in motion, trying without much success to ignore the worry niggling at her. It wasn't like Ford to be late without a reason.

By 7:20 worry had her biting her lip, her gaze riveted on the street, her mind all but conjuring up the sight of a midnight blue Camaro.

By seven-thirty, she was worried enough to start walking toward downtown. Ten minutes later she was in the stark basement foyer of the town hall, pressing the buzzer by the door to the sheriff's department.

The deputy who admitted her was about Eli's age, and as blond as Eli was dark. "May I help you, ma'am?" he asked politely, his gaze taking a fast inventory of her appearance and, she suspected, potential for trouble.

"Is Sheriff Maguire still here?" she asked, glancing past his shoulder toward Ford's office. The door was closed, telling her nothing. As far as she could see, there was nothing pressing going on. Certainly the young deputy didn't seem to be in the least hassled or overly worried.

"Last time I saw the sheriff, he was headin' back to his office," he told her, casting a fast look over his shoulder. "Do you know where that is?"

"Yes, thank you," she said, moving past him.

She knocked once, then opened the door at his command. He was sitting behind the desk, his expression controlled, his eyes bleak. Something was terribly wrong.

"Hi," she said when his gaze locked on hers. "I thought maybe you were tied up, so I walked on over." She curved her lips in what she hoped was a casual smile.

"Sit down," he said, glancing at the other chair in the windowless cubicle. It wasn't a request, and Sophie felt a stir of anger.

"Thank you, but I prefer to stand," she said, allowing her smile to fade.

He shifted, his back pressed hard against the back of the chair. "Suit yourself."

It took her a moment to realize that he had become a different man from the one who'd dragged her into his arms in a blatant show of masculine possessiveness just a few short hours ago. Even a cursory glance at that hard jaw told her that this man was capable of deep, abiding rage when provoked, perhaps to the point of violence. Like his father, she thought on a flare of very real fear. And then she remembered the gentleness she'd sensed in him earlier and knew that he would never hurt her—not in the physical sense at any rate.

She took a step forward. "Ford—"

"I had a visitor this evening," he said, his tone running close to cruel. "A private detective. He left me this." He took a single sheet of cheap paper from beneath the blotter and flipped it closer. It was a duplicate to the poster she'd destroyed.

"I . . . see," she managed to force past the taste of bile in her throat.

"Then you're one up on me, Mrs. Manwaring." The steel in his voice was layered with ice, and the low sensual drawl had been replaced by the clipped cadence of cruelest sarcasm. It was a voice she'd never heard before, one she hoped never to hear again.

"There's nothing I can say, except that I didn't want this to happen."

He lifted one black eyebrow, the only sign of movement in that deathly still face. His hair was disheveled, as though he ripped his hand through more than once, and his mouth had a controlled look.

"Meaning you figured you were safe in a hick town with a hick sheriff too besotted to question the pack of lies you fed him, isn't that about the size of it, Mrs. Manwaring?"

"Don't call me that!" she cried through a mix of fear and anger and guilt.

He flicked a glance at the poster, his mouth twisting in disgust. "Exactly which of your various names would you prefer, then?"

Sophie knew then that any attempt to make him understand would be futile. Worse, it would only demean them both.

"I assume I'm under arrest," she said with as much dignity as she could summon from the chaotic tangle of emotions threatening to send her to her knees.

His gaze flickered, and for an instant she saw anguish glittering in his eyes before they became hard as quartz once more.

"I sent the guy on his way with a head full of lies, but likely, he'll be back. You have thirty-six hours. If I see you after that time, I'll arrest you."

Hope trembled like a wounded bird in her breast. "And if you don't see me, what then?"

"Either way, I'll be on the phone to the Portland PD."

Sophie closed her eyes on a spasm of relief. He was letting her go! "Thank you," she said when she could speak again.

The hand resting on the arm of his chair closed into a fist, but his expression remained icily controlled. "Don't thank me yet. There are conditions to my...generosity."

A hole opened in her stomach, but she managed to keep her composure. "I assume you're going to tell me what those might be."

His mouth moved. "Number one, I never want to see you or hear from you again, nor do I want to know where you're going. Number two, you aren't to contact anyone else in Clover."

"Is that all?"

"And number three, I want to settle some money on Jessie."

"We don't need your money." Her voice was calm, but her heart was breaking.

"You'll take it, anyway. Jessie doesn't deserve to suffer for her mother's sins."

The hurt went to the bone, stripping away the last of her already-battered defenses. "Don't you think I want that, too?" she flung at him, her voice splintering. "She's all I care about, all I thought about while I was locked up in a place even smaller than this for the first six months of her life. Knowing that I would see her again was all that kept me sane when the walls started closing in. Remembering how it felt to hold her in my arms kept me *alive.*"

"Damn it, Sophie, you broke the law." He slammed his fist on the arm of the chair before standing so quickly the chair went flying backward to hit the wall. "What do you expect me to do, pretend I don't care about that?"

"No, I want you to understand *why* I broke those laws," she cried, wanting desperately to go to him, yet knowing that he would only shove her away if she did.

"I'm listening."

"No, you're not. Look at you." She gestured impatiently at his stance.

"What the hell are you talkin' about?"

"Look at yourself," she repeated, drawing a hasty breath. Frowning, he glanced down. At the big hands fisted on his lean hips. At the legs spread wide for balance. What he couldn't see was the set of his jaw and the pride-stiffened shoulders.

"You're standing there like a gunslinger ready to draw your gun and shoot me down, no matter what I say."

A flush the color of sun-hardened brick ran along the rise of his cheekbones, and his eyes flashed. "Convince me, Sophie. Give me a reason to trust you again."

She swallowed the words of anger and pain and tried for calm. "After Jessie was born, the law required a custody hearing before they could take her away from me. It lasted ten minutes." She smiled, but felt no amusement, only a sharp, cutting frustration. "Wells, Sr., is a retired judge, you see, and my mother-in-law's family has been involved with local politics since Oregon Trail days. So it was just naturally assumed by everyone but me and my attorney that they would make far more suitable parents for my child that I could ever hope to be. After all, they'd raised an exemplary son. So *exemplary* that he was prepared to kill his own child so that he wouldn't have his perfect life disrupted."

Her lips trembled, and she paused to bring her emotions under control again. "Silly me, I thought if I could just convince the judge how warped Wells had been by those 'wonderful' parents of his, he would understand why I was terrified they would do the same to Jessie. Instead, he came close to citing me for contempt. For defaming the name of a *good* and *decent* man who couldn't defend himself."

Some of the anger bled from his eyes. "Why didn't you appeal?"

"I did appeal. It was denied."

"So you decided to take the law into your own hands."

"*Yes!*" she shouted, sobbing in frustration. "And if you just get past that hurt pride you're standing on to judge me you'd realize that I didn't have a choice."

"Don't try to feed me any intellectual crap about choices, Sophie. You're talkin' to a man who's had it up to here with choices." His hand made a sharp cutting motion at the level of his throat. "I might not always like the ones I made, but at least I can sleep nights."

Sophie's patience snapped. "Bully for you," she shouted, her own hands fisted now as she advanced on him. "I'm glad your choices worked out. I'm glad you never had to choose between breaking the law or losing the only thing in life you love. But I did, and I'd do it again."

She waited until she felt the heat from his body before she stopped. Though she trembled, she managed to stand tall as she looked him in the eyes.

"I tried every way I knew how not to involve you in this, but you kept telling me the past didn't matter." His mouth flattened, but he remained silent, unyielding. She wanted to shake him. She wanted to beg him to hold her. She did neither.

"God help me, I loved you so much I let myself believe that."

He flinched then, and some of the ice left his eyes. "You could have told me—"

"And then what? Make you an accessory to a felony?" She drew a harsh breath. "At least this way one of us can sleep at night."

She turned and walked out, hoping with every step she took to hear him calling her back. Instead, she heard only the sound of his door slamming shut behind her.

Chapter 14

Sophie heard footsteps on the stairs and glanced up to find Lucy standing by her half-opened door, her hand poised to knock. "Hi," she said when she realized Sophie had seen her approaching.

"Hi." Sophie finished folding the blouse she'd just taken from its hanger and added it to the already overflowing suitcase on the bed.

"Katie says you're leaving."

"Yes, our bus leaves at eleven," she said, straightening.

Lucy stepped into the room as though unsure of her welcome. Though the two of them had crossed paths often in the past four months, Lucy had never been to Sophie's room. Nor had Sophie been to Lucy's house, the one that Ford had signed over to her on her twenty-first birthday. Sophie found herself regretting that bitterly. She wanted to take as many memories of Ford with her as she could gather to her. Seeing the place where he'd grown up, actually walking through the rooms and feeling the energy there, might have helped her understand him better.

"I hope it's not because I was, well, a bit testy with you at the reception yesterday," Lucy said after a moment of tense silence.

Sophie shook her head. "I'd already forgotten all about that, Lucy. Truly."

She checked the time, then took one last look around. The closet door stood open with only a few forlorn hangers dangling from the rod to show that she'd even been here.

Other than the few things necessary for the trip, Jessie's clothes and toys were already in the suitcase. Sophie had already decided to take the stroller and, of course, Bun. These days Jess never went anywhere without Bun clutched under one arm. The poor rabbit was becoming dreadfully bedraggled, as only a much-loved toy could get. Drawing a ragged breath, she realized that she'd forgotten for a moment that she wasn't alone.

"I'm sorry," she told Lucy on an intake of air. "I didn't mean to ignore you. I guess I'm just a little . . . distracted."

Lucy came toward her, looking perplexed. "Forgive me for being tacky enough to ask pushy questions, but does your leaving have anything to do with my brother?"

"No, my uncle is ill," she said, repeating the lie she'd already told Katie and the others. As she'd expected, everyone had rallied around, offering hugs and travel advice, and even money, though none of them really had all that much to spare. Roy Dean had even gone so far as to offer to drive her to Montana, so that she and Jessie wouldn't feel so alone.

She'd cried then and, pleading a need to pack, fled to her room, leaving Jessie with the rest of her "family" for as long as possible. They were downstairs in the parlor, taking pictures with Katie's camera, pictures that Sophie knew she would never see. Jessie was too young to remember the wonderful people at Clover Rooming House, but Sophie knew she'd never forget them.

Satisfied that she had everything she closed the closet door, leaving the hangers for the next occupant.

"Does Ford know you're leaving?" Lucy persisted.

"Yes, of course," Sophie hedged, unable suddenly to meet Lucy's anxious gaze. The hazel color of Lucy's eyes tended more toward green than the gray predominating in Ford's, but the resemblance between brother and sister was too much to handle in her distracted state.

"Oh, then Ford's going with you to Montana. Katie must have forgotten to mention that when she called to tell me you were leaving."

Surprise had Sophie turning back to look at her. "Why would he do that?"

Lucy narrowed her gaze, emphasizing the similarities between brother and sister even more strongly. "Sophie, I know my brother better than he thinks I do, and I'm telling you this right to your face. Either I misread the look I saw in his eyes earlier, or you didn't tell him the truth, because if he thought someone he loved was in trouble he'd find a way to get you out of it or he'd glue himself to your side to make sure you didn't have to suffer alone."

Sophie nodded. "Yes, that's exactly what he would do," she said in an achingly quiet voice. "If he loved someone."

"But he does love you, Sophie," she cried softly. "And you love him. I saw that yesterday when you were dancing together."

Averting her gaze so that Lucy wouldn't see the tears drenching her eyes, Sophie concentrated on zipping up the bulging case. When she was finished, she dragged it from the bed and straightened the quilt until it was as neat as it had been when she'd arrived.

No doubt Katie would sell the crib, though it might be better to have Roy Dean carry it up to the attic in case another nearly destitute mama arrived with a baby in her arms and little more than the clothes on her back. Perhaps, if she left a note... No, she couldn't risk it. Not with the Manwarings' detective already so close.

"I guess that's it," she said, taking a deep breath that turned jagged. She turned to offer her hand to Lucy, only to be struck by the look on her friend's face.

"Lucy?" she murmured urgently, worrying about her sudden paleness.

"When I was nine, Grandma Maguire died and left me this ring," Lucy said tonelessly, extending her hand. The ring was slightly larger than a woman would wear, with a strange milky stone in an exotic setting. Just looking at it gave Sophie a chill.

"Very pretty," she murmuring, staring into Lucy's slightly unfocused eyes. It was as though she hadn't spoken.

"Sometimes, when I looked at it," Lucy continued in that same singsong voice that Sophie found intensely disturbing, "I...saw things before they happened. I knew Mama and Daddy were dead that morning when I went to fetch Ford from his room. He used to get really mad and insist that what I saw was just a dream so I stopped trying to convince him. I didn't see things after that, but just now..." She took a deep breath, her gaze suddenly taking on a keen look that pierced Sophie's composure.

"You're in terrible trouble, aren't you?"

Intending to do just the opposite, Sophie found herself nodding, tears flowing unchecked now down her cheeks. "I wish I'd stayed on the bus all the way to Florida the way I'd originally planned," she whispered, sinking to the bed and burying her face in her hands. Conscious that Lucy was hovering, she managed to put together a good imitation of a confident smile.

"Sorry to unload on you," she murmured. "I'm fine now."

"What about Ford?" Lucy asked softly. "Is he fine, too?"

"He will be."

Lucy walked to the door and pushed it shut before turning to face Sophie again. She looked shaken, but determined to make her point. Like Ford, Sophie thought.

"I'm not sure why I feel compelled to tell you about something that happened more than twenty years ago, but I do." She asked Sophie's permission with a glance. Suspecting that she was making a terrible mistake, Sophie nodded.

Lucy remained where she was, standing with her back to the heavy door, her hands clasped in front of her like a dutiful child. "I was about six, and Ford was fifteen when he brought home this baby rabbit he'd found in the woods. It was just a little bitty thing, still trying to nurse on its dead mama when he spotted it. We named it Flower. Well, actually I did. He favored Bugs as I recall." Her smile was wispy and short-lived.

"He fed Flower with an eye dropper until she was old enough to be weaned, and she got so she'd follow him around like a puppy. He never said so out loud, but everyone knew he was crazy about that little rabbit."

Sophie bit her lip. Was that why he'd taken Jessie to see Mr. Shepherd's rabbits? Because he'd had such fond memories of his own childhood pet?

"I was playing in this fort I'd made in the azalea bushes one day when Daddy came around the house in a right temper, yelling for Ford to get his...behind out of the house. Ford used to study night and day, and he was always up in his room staring at a book. Anyway, out he came, and right behind him came Flower."

Lucy paused, as though to organize her thoughts, and Sophie sat without moving, her heart thudding so loud she was certain Lucy could hear it where she was standing. In her mind she had a vivid image of Ford as a gangly boy of fifteen with his eyes fixed on the sky and his heart set on reaching the stars someday.

"At first I didn't understand what Daddy was yelling about, and then it came to me that he was saying that he knew all about Mama running around with other men behind his back, and Ford needn't pretend he didn't know, too. I guess you know all about that, though?"

Sophie nodded. "I'm sorry to say I do."

Lucy's smile came and went, but her eyes remained haunted with those long-ago images. "Somehow Daddy had heard that Mama used to take Ford with her sometimes when she went to meet those . . . men and he wanted Ford to tell him who they were. Ford refused, and Daddy threatened to whip him good if he didn't change his mind. Ford just stood there, staring Daddy down."

Sophie drew in a sharp breath, feeling her eyes opening wider out of shock. "Your father beat him?"

Lucy shook her head. "It would have been better if he had. Instead, he grabbed Flower by her ears and held her over this old rain barrel that used to sit under the drainpipe. Mama always swore rainwater made her hair silky and sweet."

"Oh, no!" Sophie exclaimed softly. "He didn't drown her?"

Lucy nodded. "Ford fought Daddy with everything he had, but Daddy was bigger than Ford then and stronger. In the struggle Ford's shoulder was terribly dislocated, but he kept fighting. But it was too late. Flower was dead."

"It must have been horrible for both of you," Sophie exclaimed softly, hurting for the sensitive, caring boy who had become the hardened man.

"I've never forgotten the look on my big brother's face when he lifted Flower out of that barrel and hugged her against his chest. Tears were running down his face, and he was in terrible pain from a bunch of torn ligaments in his shoulder, but he wouldn't let me touch him, and he wouldn't let me call Mama or Doc. He just sat there until he didn't have any more tears, then he got up and carried Flower into the woods to bury her. I waited until he came back, and then I asked him why he didn't tell Daddy what he wanted to know."

"What did he say?"

Lucy smiled. "He said that Mama had made him promise never to tell anyone where she went or what she did. You see, promises are sacred to Ford. Mama always said he was a throwback to antebellum times when Southern men were willing to die to preserve their honor, or the honor of someone close to them."

Sophie felt raw inside. "So he was faced with breaking his promise and losing his honor or keeping his promise and losing the pet he loved."

Lucy nodded slowly. "I've never seen him cry since that afternoon, not even when we buried Mama and Daddy. Maybe he can't, the way he could never bring himself to trust a woman enough to fall in love. Until now."

Sophie closed her eyes, her throat scratchy from unshed tears, and her heart aching for the pain she must have caused him.

Lucy came closer. "I don't know if that helps you or hurts you more, but I know I feel better for having told you."

"Thank you."

"He does love you," Lucy said with audible urgency. "Maybe he can't tell you yet, but I feel it here, inside." She pressed the hand wearing the ring against her heart, and Sophie fought back a sob.

"Maybe he was beginning to," Sophie admitted, feeling the brutal truth rip through her. "Now I'll never know for sure."

"Does that mean you still plan to leave?" Lucy asked, her tone disbelieving.

"Yes, just as soon as I give Jessie a quick bath." Sophie stood, willing strength into her suddenly watery knees. "Please don't look at me like that, Lucy," she cried, crying openly now. "I'd stay if I could, but believe me when I tell you I just don't have a choice."

Katie drove them to the bus station. The ladies insisted upon coming along. There was a certain ritual involved in saying goodbye, Sophie soon discovered. First came the usual cautionary advice and comments on the weather forecast and time changes. And then, as the luggage was being stowed in the underbelly of the big bus and the soon-to-be departing passengers were assembling in the shelter of a garishly lit, metal carport outside, the advice turned more specific.

"Now remember, sugar, don't eat fish in any form at roadside restaurants," Miss Rose Ruth cautioned, her white eyebrows bunching at the thought of possible consequences.

"And be sure to carry that can of disinfectant I gave you when you go into the lavatories," Miss Fanny added, her eyes red-rimmed and shiny.

"Don't be silly, Fanny," Rose Ruth protested. "Those folks at the bus company wouldn't let their passengers use unsanitary facilities."

"Now who's being totally ridiculous," Fanny proclaimed, pursing her lips.

"You have our number, right?" Katie asked after she and Sophie exchanged hugs. "And you'll call when you get settled in at your aunt's?"

Sophie nodded, unable to voice another blatant lie. While her three friends took turns hugging and kissing the baby goodbye, Sophie took her ticket from her purse. The bus she and Jessie were about to board would take them by a circuitous route to Richmond, Virginia, where the ladies expected her to transfer to a bus heading west. Instead, she was booked all the way through to Syracuse.

"Five minutes, ladies," the bus driver cautioned as he passed.

"Oh, dear," Fanny said, fumbling in her bag for her ever-present hanky. "I promised myself I wouldn't make a fuss."

"Go ahead and fuss," Rose Ruth said, plucking her hanky from her bag, as well.

Sophie was about to take Jessie from Katie's arms when she saw Ford's Camaro pull into the lot. Out of uniform again, he was wearing the worn jeans and a faded work shirt like the one that had irked his sister so much on Christmas Day.

He looked devastatingly male—and very tired. He didn't smile as he joined them. Instead, he greeted the others with a nod, then directed a cool look at Sophie.

"Can I have a private minute?" he asked, his voice wiped clean of all emotion, even disgust.

"Of course."

He glanced around, then drew her to a corner of the outdoor boarding area. "I wanted to give you this," he said, drawing a white envelope from his back pocket. Ignoring her frown, he tucked the envelope in a corner of the diaper bag she'd forgotten she'd had slung over one shoulder. "I figured cash would be best. Small bills."

The irony of a man like Ford forced into deciding the best way to help her escape the law was searing. "I'm so terribly sorry," she said, her voice breaking.

He accepted that without comment. "I'd like your permission to kiss Jessie goodbye." The formality hurt her terribly. The lack of warmth in his eyes hurt more. It was as though they'd never been welded together by the sweat of passion. As though he hadn't shuddered in her arms, and she in his.

"Please don't hate me," she whispered, needing to touch him so badly her arms ached for him as they'd once ached for Jessie.

His mouth twisted. "If only I could," he said. The bitterness in his tone ripped at her, but he was already striding back to the others.

She returned more slowly, unable to draw her gaze from the sight of Jessie cuddled against his big chest while he whispered something in her ear. Ignoring the questions in Katie's eyes, and the tears in her own, she stood a few feet apart from the rest of them, struggling to find the strength to climb those few short steps that would take her from Clover forever.

Spying the driver approaching again, she stepped forward to take Jessie from Ford's arms. "No, no," Jessie protested, clinging to his shirt with surprising strength.

Ford's face twisted. "Go with your mama, slugger," he ordered, his voice thickening.

"No, no." Jessie buried her face against his shoulder, her trust complete, her love unconditional.

"Looks like that young 'un don't want to leave her daddy," the driver joked as he took his position next to the door.

Sophie was conscious of the sympathetic looks her friends sent her way, but her attention was focused entirely on Ford.

"Her daddy could come with us," she said softly, pleading with her eyes and her heart.

His eyes went black with pain, but his movements were rigidly controlled as he freed himself from Jessie's tiny grasping hands and settled her into Sophie's arms.

"Goodbye, Sophie. Have a safe trip."

She nearly lost it then, but the discipline she'd learned in prison saved her. "Goodbye, Ford," she murmured, her voice trembling only a little. "Take care of yourself."

He nodded, the ice back in his eyes.

She was the last one to board. The driver was checking his roster as she turned to climb the steps, a last flurry of farewells and good wishes still ringing in her ears. Blinded by tears, she cried out when a strong hand gripped her arm and spun her around. His mouth came down hard on hers, his kiss searing her with his pain and love.

"God bless you both," Ford whispered, his voice ragged with an agony he could no longer hide.

"And you," she whispered as he released her. And walked away.

The thirty-six hours he'd given her were almost up. Ford had spent the day sitting alone in the house that seemed cold and empty now, drinking steadily.

His goal was to be so stinking drunk by the time he made the call to Portland he'd be too numb to feel the pain. So far he'd only succeeded in making himself so dizzy he'd damn near knocked himself out bumping into furniture whenever he got up to fetch another bottle from the supply Sophie had left with him after Mike's party.

He knew he wasn't drunk, because he still hurt. No matter how much poison he threw down his gullet, he still felt Jessie's tiny fingers clutching at his shirt. No matter how viciously his stomach might protest, he still tasted the pain in Sophie's kiss.

"Nope, not nearly enough," he muttered, bringing the bottle to his mouth for a long, searing swallow. He'd lost the ability to taste the stuff a good hour or so back. Right about the time he figured Sophie's bus would be getting into wherever it was she was going.

In a few minutes, he would pick up the phone and call the number given to him by that sleazy PI. What the hell was his name? Hangman? No, Hegelman.

"How's that for a Freudian slip?" he muttered, slugging back another two fingers or so. Liquor was supposed to be numbing, damn it. So why the hell did he still feel as though he'd been skinned alive and left to die a slow death under a blazing sun?

Because you love her, you jackass. And you're going to spend the rest of your life trying to forget how she feels and tastes and smells. With his luck he'd live to be a hundred, he thought, staring at his reflection in the window.

"Damn if you don't look almost that old now," he muttered. His hair looked as though he'd combed it with an eggbeater. He hadn't shaved since Saturday morning, and the only reason he didn't smell worse than he did was because he'd gotten caught in a downpour at about 6:00 a.m. when he'd found himself walking in the woods, trying to argue himself out of turning her in.

"Here's to Ford Maguire, keeper of the faith," he muttered, lifting his glass to the sorry-looking excuse for a man glaring back at him.

He saw her then, wearing the same shirt and jeans she'd been wearing when she'd boarded the bus. The booze, his mood, the churning in his gut—he figured they were enough to bring on a hallucination this real. Weren't they? His only answer was the sound of his labored breathing and the roar of the blood moving through his head.

Though he knew she was only a figment of his booze-soaked imagination, he watched her hungrily, the hole in his belly yawning wider until it was as deep and as black as the pit of his own personal hell where he knew he'd spend the rest of his days.

"You're in my blood, Sophie Reynolds," he muttered, need and grief pounding in his head so fiercely he could scarcely hear the words he uttered. "Damn it, you're in my soul and heart, every place but my house where you belong."

"Don't be so sure about that, my darling."

Ford turned at the sound, adrenaline whipping his already ravaged system into overload. The bottle dropped from his hand, exploding into jagged bits when it hit, but he ignored the mess at his feet as she moved toward him.

"Why is it I'm always cleaning up after you, Ford Maguire?" she murmured, her eyes very dark and intense. He could smell her, damn it. That light, airy, powdery scent that combined the drawing room propriety of a lady with the untamed spirit of a sensual tigress.

"What the hell are you doing here?" He was shouting before he thought to temper his anger as was his custom of long-standing.

"I came back to keep you from doing something stupid, like resigning," she shot back, twin roses blooming pink in her cheeks.

His jaw dropped, then snapped shut, but not before Sophie had seen his gaze flicker to the single sheet of stationery on the table. The telephone was there, too, along with a small white business card.

"I assume that private detective who spoke to you left the number of the person in Portland handling my case," she said, advancing quietly, her knees not quite steady.

"Where's Jessie?" he demanded, raking his hand through his already wrecked hair, a hand that trembled visibly, she noticed. Just as she noticed the marks of suffering on his face, and the ravages of too much Scotch and, she suspected, nothing else in his belly.

"Our daughter is with Miss Fanny," she said softly. "They were absolutely ecstatic at seeing each other."

"You should be a thousand miles away from here by now." His voice was harsh, his drawl more slurred than usual. Apparently the bottle on the floor wasn't the first he'd killed. Compassion and remorse fought a pitched battle inside her, just as she'd been battling with herself for the past twenty-four hours. Twelve hours north, twelve hours back south. All the while wondering if she was doing the wrong thing.

Perhaps Ford wasn't going to resign. Perhaps she hadn't felt a shudder of despair run through him when he'd kissed her goodbye. By the time she'd seen the lights of Clover in the distance she'd been a quivering wreck.

"Why don't I make a pot of coffee first, and then we'll talk."

"No coffee," he grated. "Just answers. Now."

She drew a breath. "I thought losing my child was the worst thing that could ever happen to me. I was wrong. Losing the man I love is worse. But worst of all would be trying to live the rest of my life knowing I'd destroyed him. So I came back."

He ran his tongue over his mouth. His lips were numb. "I have to turn you in," he said, each word a bloody wound inside him.

"Actually I've given that some thought, and I think it would be better if I turned myself in." Still watching him, she pulled the card closer, glancing at the number handwritten beneath the printed name.

"Don't," he cried when she reached for the phone. "I'd have to be the one to arrest you."

"I know that, just as I know it will be awful for us both when you do, but we've both gone through some bad times before, and survived. This time..." She was forced to stop and refill her lungs. "This time we'll face the pain together." Drawing back her hand, she moved closer. "Or didn't you mean it when you asked me to marry you?"

"Hell, yes, I meant it!" he shouted, reaching for her. His mouth was hot on hers, the taste of Scotch as strong as the wild surge of joy running through her. He framed her face with hands that shook, his need alive and savage.

"You're mine, damn it," he whispered between kisses.

"Only yours, always yours." Her mouth molded his. His tongue found hers.

"We'll fight," he vowed hoarsely when at last, starved for oxygen, they drew back.

"Whatever happens, I love you," she murmured, running her hands over him possessively, goaded by passion and relief.

"Then for God's sake woman, say you'll marry me before I lose what's left of my sanity," he growled, his eyes so suspiciously shiny her breath caught.

"They might put me back in prison, at the very least for breaking parole," she whispered, trying not to flinch at the thought. "In fact, they probably will."

His jaw bunched, giving him that fierce, dangerous look she'd loved and feared from the first moment she'd seen it. "Then I'll marry you there," he said with quiet, implacable force. "I'll find a job in Portland, wherever the hell that is, and I'll wait for you to get out."

"No, I won't let you ruin your life."

A smile found his eyes, and lingered. "You and Jessie *are* my life."

"Oh, Ford," she whispered. "I love you so much. Can you forgive me for lying to you?"

"Already done."

"Just like that?"

"Just like that." He offered her a lopsided grin. "'Course if you ever do it again, I'll be forced to put you under house arrest. Might have to keep you in that bedroom yonder for days until you learn the error of your ways."

"I have to tell you, Sheriff," she murmured through her tears. "I'm a slow learner."

"That's okay, sugar," he said, drawing her into his arms again. "I'm a very patient man."

Epilogue

"I can't do this. I really can't." Sophie touched the single pearl at her throat and tried to stop the roaring in her head.

"Of course you can, dear," Miss Fanny said firmly, skewering her flowered hat to her hair with a lethal-looking hat pin.

"No one gets married in a dress like this," she said, staring at her reflection in Miss Fanny's mirror. The champagne silk looked like burnished skin beneath a froth of shimmering glass bubbles.

"You do when your fiancé insists," Katie murmured, concentrating on getting the orchid corsage pinned to the dress's bodice just so.

"You look more like a bride than I do." Sophie eyed Katie's simple ivory sheath with envy.

"I'd rather be wearing beads and marryin' the man I love and who loves me."

"But that's just it, Katie, this dress is too sexy for a wedding dress," Sophie wailed, biting her pale lip.

"After six weeks of celibacy, my brother would think anything you wore was sexy," Lucy said, her green eyes shining with excitement. Her own wedding was only days away, though Ford kept muttering about locking her in her house and throwing away the key.

"There you go, all set," Katie said, stepping back to admire her handiwork. "I know it had to be terrible for you to be back in prison for a month, but you really are blooming,"

Sophie smiled her thanks, still self-conscious about discussing the time she'd served for violating her parole or the events that had led to her imprisonment the first time. As it was, every time she thought about the masterful way Ford had defended her to the parole board she wanted to laugh and cry and thank God for creating such a man in the first place.

"Katie's right," Lucy pronounced firmly, her eyes bright. "I believe you've even managed to gain a little weight on prison food."

"I still can't believe those nasty folks at the prison wouldn't let us send you some fresh fruit at the very least," Miss Fanny muttered, drawing her eyebrows together in a very unladylike frown.

"Like Ford said, rules are rules," Lucy reminded her before glancing at her watch.

"Is it time?" Sophie asked, her mouth suddenly dry.

"Almost."

"Reverend Bendix finally made it," Miss Rose Ruth said as she joined them. As the self-appointed coordinator of the wedding, she'd been downstairs waiting for the minister. "No thanks to you, Frances Ann Bedford."

"What *are* you goin' on about now?" Miss Fanny demanded peevishly.

"I specifically asked you to request the reverend's presence by one-thirty, did I not?"

"Perhaps that is what you *meant* to say, Rose Ruth, but you *said* two o'clock, and that is exactly what I passed on to Reverend Bendix."

Miss Rose Ruth drew a huffing breath. "That is the most blatant untruth you have ever uttered in all your seventy-nine years," she exclaimed.

"Seventy-six," Fanny corrected with a haughty lifting of her head that set the feather in her hat to bobbing. "You're seventy-nine."

"Perhaps you have also forgotten that you and I have always been the same age."

"Now that is not true—"

"Ladies, please!" Katie said, clapping her hands. "Sophie's already as nervous as all get-out. Why don't we all go on downstairs and give her a minute to compose herself."

"Good idea," Lucy said quickly, giving Sophie a hug. "Welcome to the family, big sister," she murmured, her eyes filling with happy tears.

"I've always wanted a sister," Sophie told her, her voice breaking. "I'm so happy it's you." They hugged again, before Katie claimed Sophie for a sisterly hug of her own.

"As your official bridesmaid, I want to say that I am so very happy for you. And Ford. You both deserve all the happiness in the world."

"Exactly my sentiments, my dear," Miss Fanny murmured, kissing Sophie's cheek. "And I am so proud you are to be married in Mama's dress. I just know she and my Johnny Ray are up there right now, smilin' down on us."

"Oh, Miss Fanny," Sophie cried, wiping away a tear. "I hope so."

"Now see what you've done, Fanny," Rose Ruth chided impatiently. "You've make the child cry on her weddin' day."

"Don't blame Miss Fanny," Sophie said, kissing her elderly defender's papery cheek gently. "I feel as though I've been in tears for most of the six weeks I've been away from y'all."

"Why sugar, did you hear that?" Miss Rose Ruth exclaimed. "Won't be long and no one will ever know you weren't born and raised here just like the rest of us."

It took more urging from Katie and some diplomacy from Lucy, but finally Sophie found herself alone in Miss Fanny's room, staring at the door to the hall. Once she went through that door and walked down those steps she was committed.

"Oh, Ford, I hope I can make you happy," she murmured, closing her eyes for a long moment.

Opening them again, she found herself staring at the woman framed by that same door. "Darlene?" she whispered. "Is it really you?"

"Yep, it's really me," Darlene said, laughing. "Or what's left of her after two flights and a bumpy bus ride."

"This is a wonderful surprise," Sophie said when they'd exchanged exuberant hugs. "How on earth did you manage it?" Still on parole, Darlene had been denied permission to leave the state, and Sophie had been crushingly disappointed not to have Darlene at her wedding.

"I didn't. That stubborn man you're about to marry bullied the board into it at the last minute. How he did it I don't know, and I don't want to. All I know is I have to be back in the state in seventy-two hours."

"I can't wait to introduce you to my friends. You'll love them, and they'll love you."

Darlene looked around gingerly, her heart-shaped face reflecting cautious approval. No one looking at her now would take her for the drug-addicted call girl she'd been three years ago. Not only had she kicked her drug habit, but she'd earned a nursing degree in prison and was now working at a free clinic in the city's worst district.

"I've already met one of your friends," she said when her inspection was completed. "Cute guy by the name of Roy something or other."

"Roy Dean," Sophie said softly. "One of Jessie's honorary grandpas."

Darlene smiled. "I saw Ford, by the way. He looks about as nervous as a man can look and still be standing on two feet."

Sophie felt love well in her heart. "I'm so very lucky, Dar," she murmured. "I have so much—Ford, Jessie, my friends. You."

"After what you went through, you deserve it all. And more." She touched a porcelain figurine of a rebel soldier on Miss Fanny's dresser. "Guess they're still fighting the Civil War down here, huh?"

"War of the Rebellion," Sophie corrected, her nerves spiking again.

Darlene shrugged. "Whatever they call it, they sure do raise fighters down here in Dixie. Lord, I never saw a man more hellbent on beating the Manwarings at their own nasty game than that slow-talkin', slow-walkin' sheriff of yours. He must have talked to a hundred people, trying to find something on Wells to refute their story of the perfect husband and would-be father."

"He might have held the gun, but you provided the ammunition," Sophie said, allowing her gratitude to flavor her voice. "Finding that call girl who knew all about Wells's sexual perversions was a stroke of pure genius."

"I'll accept that," Darlene said with an impish grin. "But Ford was the one who got her to agree to testify at the custody hearing."

Sophie still quaked inside when she remembered the venomous look Anita Manwaring had given her in the judge's chambers that morning. Once the Manwarings had been told about the prostitute and the things she'd been prepared to divulge publicly about their "perfect" son, their righteous insistence that Sophie was an unfit mother deflated like a balloon filled with so much hot air. It seemed that they cared more about protecting the Manwaring name than raising another Manwaring child.

"I almost feel sorry for Anita and Wells," she murmured. "Until I remember what they tried to do."

"Forget them!" Darlene ordered, linking her arm with Sophie's. "Let's get this wedding over with so we can get on to the serious partying."

"Let's."

Sophie was fine until she turned the corner and saw Ford waiting for her at the bottom of the steps, holding Jessie who was dressed in pink to match the healthy glow in her chubby cheeks. He was wearing his midnight blue tux, looking as handsome as she'd ever seen him. He also looked ferociously impatient.

"Treat her right, or you'll answer to me," Darlene said, punching him softly in the arm cradling Jessie against his shoulder.

"Yes, ma'am," he said, bending to kiss her cheek.

Darlene tossed Sophie a good-luck smile before heading for the parlor, her heels clicking impatiently on the foyer floor. Sophie heard music and the buzz of conversation. She saw flowers on every available surface and smelled their perfume. It was her wedding day, the only one she wanted to remember.

"About time your mama showed her face," he growled to Jessie, who giggled.

"It's a bride's prerogative to be late on her wedding day," Sophie murmured, her stomach jumping, and her voice shaky.

"Guess it is at that." He cleared his throat. "You look beautiful."

"So do you."

His mouth quirked. "I feel like a sissy piano player."

Sophie giggled, then pressed her trembling fingers to her lips. "I guess you'd be annoyed if this baby I'm carrying turned out to be a son with a passion for Chopin."

His face went still. Only his eyes moved as he glanced down at her belly, then sought her face again. "You're pregnant?" His voice was scratchy and thin.

"Six weeks along. I figured it happened the night of Mike's bachelor party. We got so involved we forgot to use anything, remember?"

"Are you all right? Healthy, I mean?"

"Blooming, according to Katie."

His eyes turned very dark, and a muscle jerked along his jaw. "A man would be a fool to doubt a lady's word."

Sophie wished she hadn't let Katie take her flowers with her. She needed something to hold on to. "You don't seem very happy," she murmured, trying to keep her disappointment from showing.

"Honey, happy doesn't even begin to describe how I feel." He swallowed hard, then slanted her a look of pure male frustration. "Guess you want me to put it in words, huh?"

"That would help."

He took a deep breath. "Sophie Reynolds, I love you with all my heart, and I love this little hellion almost as much." He kissed Jessie's cheek, then placed a gentle hand on Sophie's belly. "And I love baby, too."

"Even if he turns out to be a girl?"

"Even if he turns out to be a sissy piano player, though I have to warn you, honey, I plan to do my level best to turn him into a macho dude like his daddy."

Sophie laughed, and then she cried. And then she took his arm and walked into the parlor to join the rest of their family.

* * * * *

Don't miss the next book in Silhouette's
exciting *ALWAYS A BRIDESMAID!* series.

Here's a sneak preview of

THE ABANDONED BRIDE

By Jane Toombs

available in September from Silhouette Shadows

Chapter 1

Lucy Maguire sprang up from the bed. Enough mooning over the past. She'd never been a person who collapsed in a crisis, and she damn well wouldn't begin now. Her brother hadn't scared off Joe Dooley, but someone else had, and she meant to find out who and why.

Moping about in her underwear definitely wasn't the way to begin, so she shed all her wedding finery and pulled on jeans and a T-shirt. Noticing the moonstone necklace—the stone of love—coiled on the nightstand next to her bridal bouquet, she picked it up and worked the clasp, finding nothing wrong. Maybe Katie hadn't hooked it together quite right. She returned the necklace to her jewelry box and eyed the bouquet with distaste.

She really didn't wish to look at it ever again. Hurrying out her back door, she shredded the roses into her compost heap, barely aware that the rain had stopped. Her next-door neighbor's cat sauntered over to see if Lucy was discarding anything edible and she glowered at the female tabby. "If Polly would get your tubes tied or whatever it is they do to cats, you wouldn't attract every tom in the neighborhood, and I'd get some sleep."

Crumpling the unrecyclable parts of the bouquet, Lucy sat on the damp grass near the compost heap and began to pet the cat.

"You shouldn't have anything to do with those toms," she told the tabby. "Males can't be trusted."

She should have listened to her brother. Ford's vague suspicions of Joe certainly seemed to have some foundation. Why otherwise would Joe have fled at the sight of that man in black? Lucy shook her head. Where was her sense of loyalty? Maybe she was too quick to condemn Joe. There might be a logical explanation for his disappearance.

Ford had gone after the two men, and if she knew her brother, he wouldn't be satisfied until he found out exactly what was going on. It could be the man in black was the one in the wrong, couldn't it? Before she condemned Joe, she would wait and hear what Ford had to say.

And there was always the chance that Joe would contact her and explain. She must keep an open mind. He'd told her over and over again how much he loved her and how he wanted nothing else in this world except to make her his wife. She'd believed him.

And she loved him in return. Didn't she? Frowning, Lucy looked down at the cat. "Do I love Joe Dooley or not?" she asked the tabby.

"I hope to hell and back the answer is no."

Ford's voice jolted Lucy, and she glanced up to see her brother standing framed in her open back door. Putting the cat aside, she rose and hurried to the house.

Moments later, brother and sister faced each other in her kitchen. "Where's Joe?" she demanded.

He shrugged. "Who knows? Not me and Max Ryder."

"Is Max Ryder the man in black?"

"The what? You mean the guy in the church? Yeah, Ryder's his name. He's a P.I."

Lucy, familiar with police jargon, knew that meant private investigator. "Why did he chase Joe from the church?"

"You know that wasn't the way it happened. Joe saw him and took off. Naturally Ryder went after him. He's been trying to nail Joe for months. And for good reason."

Lucy put her hands on her hips. "What reason?"

"I can't tell you. It's confidential. You'll have to trust me until I look into the situation and get down to the nitty-gritty."

Ignoring her belligerent stance, he reached out and put an arm around her, drawing her close. "Look, sis, I know you're upset and

I don't blame you. You have every right to be. But don't take it out on me. As soon as I can, I'll tell you everything. Right now, believe me when I say you were damn lucky that Ryder showed up before you said 'I do.'"

Always a Bridesmaid!

Join five unforgettable couples for all the festivities as they say "I Do"...with a little help from their friends!

AABLIST

MILLION DOLLAR SWEEPSTAKES (III)

No purchase necessary. To enter, follow the directions published. Method of entry may vary. For eligibility, entries must be received no later than March 31, 1996. No liability is assumed for printing errors, lost, late or misdirected entries. Odds of winning are determined by the number of eligible entries distributed and received. Prizewinners will be determined no later than June 30, 1996.

Sweepstakes open to residents of the U.S. (except Puerto Rico), Canada, Europe and Taiwan who are 18 years of age or older. All applicable laws and regulations apply. Sweepstakes offer void wherever prohibited by law. Values of all prizes are in U.S. currency. This sweepstakes is presented by Torstar Corp., its subsidiaries and affiliates, in conjunction with book, merchandise and/or product offerings. For a copy of the Official Rules send a self-addressed, stamped envelope (WA residents need not affix return postage) to: MILLION DOLLAR SWEEPSTAKES (III) Rules, P.O. Box 4573, Blair, NE 68009, USA.

EXTRA BONUS PRIZE DRAWING

No purchase necessary. The Extra Bonus Prize will be awarded in a random drawing to be conducted no later than 5/30/96 from among all entries received. To qualify, entries must be received by 3/31/96 and comply with published directions. Drawing open to residents of the U.S. (except Puerto Rico), Canada, Europe and Taiwan who are 18 years of age or older. All applicable laws and regulations apply; offer void wherever prohibited by law. Odds of winning are dependent upon number of eligibile entries received. Prize is valued in U.S. currency. The offer is presented by Torstar Corp., its subsidiaries and affiliates in conjunction with book, merchandise and/or product offering. For a copy of the Official Rules governing this sweepstakes, send a self-addressed, stamped envelope (WA residents need not affix return postage) to: Extra Bonus Prize Drawing Rules, P.O. Box 4590, Blair, NE 68009, USA.

SWP-S895

Can an invitation to a bachelor auction, a personal ad or a kiss-off bouquet be the beginning of true love?

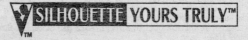

Find out in Silhouette's sexy, sassy new series beginning in August

WANTED: PERFECT PARTNER
by Debbie Macomber

LISTEN UP, LOVER
by Lori Herter

Because we know just how busy you really are, we're offering you a FREE personal organizer (retail value $19.99). With the purchase of WANTED: PERFECT PARTNER or LISTEN UP, LOVER, you can send in for a FREE personal organizer! Perfect for your hustle-'n-bustle life-style. Look in the back pages of the August *Yours Truly™* titles for more details.

And in September and October, *Yours Truly™* offers you not one but TWO proofs of purchase toward your Pages & Privileges gifts and benefits.

So act now to receive your FREE personal organizer and pencil in a visit to your favorite retail outlet and pick up your copies of *Yours Truly™*.

Love—when you least expect it!

YTT2

As a _Privileged Woman,_ you'll be entitled to all these _Free Benefits._ And _Free Gifts,_ too.

To thank you for buying our books, we've designed an exclusive FREE program called _PAGES & PRIVILEGES™._ You can enroll with just one Proof of Purchase, and get the kind of luxuries that, until now, you could only read about.

_B_IG HOTEL DISCOUNTS

A privileged woman stays in the finest hotels. And so can you—at up to 60% off! Imagine standing in a hotel check-in line and watching as the guest in front of you pays $150 for the same room that's only costing you $60. Your _Pages & Privileges_ discounts are good at Sheraton, Marriott, Best Western, Hyatt and thousands of other fine hotels all over the U.S., Canada and Europe.

_F_REE DISCOUNT TRAVEL SERVICE

A privileged woman is always jetting to romantic places. When _you_ fly, just make one phone call for the lowest published airfare at time of booking—or double the difference back! PLUS— you'll get a $25 voucher to use the first time you book a flight AND 5% cash back on every ticket you buy thereafter through the travel service!

SIM-PP4A

FREE GIFTS!

A privileged woman is always getting wonderful gifts. Luxuriate in rich fragrances that will stir your senses (and his). This gift-boxed assortment of fine perfumes includes three popular scents, each in a beautiful designer bottle. <u>Truly Lace</u>...This luxurious fragrance unveils your sensuous side. <u>L'Effleur</u>...discover the romance of the Victorian era with this soft floral. <u>Muguet des bois</u>...a single note floral of singular beauty.

FREE INSIDER TIPS LETTER

A privileged woman is always informed. And you'll be, too, with our free letter full of fascinating information and sneak previews of upcoming books.

MORE GREAT GIFTS & BENEFITS TO COME

A privileged woman always has a lot to look forward to. And so will you. You get all these wonderful FREE gifts and benefits now with only one purchase...and there are no additional purchases required. However, each additional retail purchase of Harlequin and Silhouette books brings you a step closer to even more great FREE benefits like half-price movie tickets... and even more FREE gifts.

L'Effleur...This basketful of romance lets you discover L'Effleur from head to toe, heart to home.

Truly Lace... A basket spun with the sensuous luxuries of Truly Lace, including Dusting Powder in a reusable satin and lace covered box.

Complete the Enrollment Form in the front of this book and mail it with this Proof of Purchase.

PROOF OF PURCHASE

Offer expires October 31, 1996

SIM-PP4